DRAGONKIN

BOOK THREE: UNDERSKY

iBooks

Habent Sua Fata Libelli

iBooks
Manhanset House
Dering Harbor, New York 11965
bricktower@aol.com • www.ibooksinc.com

Library of Congress Cataloging-in-Publication Data

Bailey, Robin Wayne
Dragonkin; Undersky
p. cm.

      1. Fiction. 2. Fantasy—Dragons. 3 Fantasy—Epic Fiction, I. Title.

978-1-59687-528-8, Hardcover
978-1-59687-841-9, Trade Paper

Copyright © 2006 by iBooks
Cover art copyright © 2006 by iBooks

Dragonkin is a trademark of iBooks
An original publication of iBooks
An ibooks, inc. Book

Edited by John R. Douglas

Cover art by Troy Howell

Original interior design by Gilda Hannah

February 2019

DRAGONKIN

BOOK THREE: UNDERSKY

ROBIN WAYNE BAILEY

For Diana Bailey, Ron Davis, and Tonya Howell—
They know why.

For Samantha Myers—
She knows why, too.

And for Richard Curtis—
Thank you

Visit Robin Wayne Bailey's website:
http://home.earthlink.net/~robinwaynebailey

Through an age of fire and light
We rode the winds in agile flight
From morning til the dark of night.
Our compass points and guides
Were sun and star and shining moon;
The mountains and the deep lagoons,
Far forests, canyons, sandy dunes
Our kindred graced and occupied,
And many thought of us as kings
Of earth and air. Our thunderous wings
And fire caused fear and awe and whisperings,
And we were deified.

—A song from
The Great Book of Stormfire

Table of Contents

Prologue

RONO, THE FIRST STAR OF EVENING, shone with special luster in the deepening eastern twilight. Its silvery light shimmered on
the tender green leaves of Wyvernwood as the gentle breeze murmured through the trees. The warm smells of Spring wafted in the
air—the rich scents of fresh earth, the perfumes of daffodils and crocus
and sweet grass.

Sweeping the last broomful of dust out the open door of her cave,
the Dragon Marina paused from her labors and smiled to herself.
Another winter gone, and the new season and the awakening forest
lifted her spirits. The fireflies winking in her yard and at the forest
edge made silent music with their flickering. Setting aside her broom
and stepping past her threshold, she reached out with gentle care and
allowed one of the tiny creatures to land on the back of her left paw.
Its soft rhythmic glow glimmered on her argent scales.

"*Twinkle, twinkle, little friend,*" Marina chanted in a quiet voice.
"*Spread your wings and swift ascend.*" With an easy gesture she shook
the little bug free and watched as it spiraled upward and away to join
a group of its companions.

A pair of pale, yellow-winged sulfurs darted past the tip of her nose
as they chased each other on the evening breeze. *Silly butterflies!* she
thought. The creatures circled her head and flitted off. She blinked
her large eyes and watched them until they disappeared among a thick
patch of nasturtiums. *Silly, yet beautiful!*

Marina couldn't quite remember when she had felt so good, so
full of life. Something about the new spring made her tingle all
over; some sense of expectation and surprise stole upon her and
filled her Dragon heart. She looked up toward the sky where, one
by one, more stars broke through the deepening gloom to bejewel

the cloudless heavens—red Burbur in the south and in the west the pale constellation called the Piper.

She fixed her gaze again on bright Rono, which was always the first and brightest star.

"I spy! I spy!
Way up in the velvet sky
The first star of night I see!
Now my wish will come to be!"

With secret embarrassment, her voice little more than a whisper, she sang the words of the old nursery rhyme. For an instant the breeze became still as if it paused to listen, and the fireflies and the butterflies ceased their play. Putting a paw to her Dragon lips, feeling almost like a child again, Marina gave a self-conscious laugh.

The breeze resumed, and another voice issued suddenly from the forest. "This is the way the world ends," it said in rich, unfamiliar tones. "Not with a bang, but with a chuckle."

Marina gave a start, but calmed herself as she stared with curiosity toward the trees. "That's true," she agreed. "Nature has a sense of humor, or else I would not be." With her sharp gaze she spied an old owl that had settled on the thick branch of an oak. "Nor would you, silly bird, with your saucer-shaped eyes and hooky beak. Was there ever a funnier looking creature than you?"

The owl fluttered from its hiding place and perched on a new limb closer by. It gave a shrug and fluffed its feathers. "Well," it answered. "There are the satyrs."

Marina tilted her head and thought for a moment, then nodded agreement. "Point to you, old owl," she acknowledged. "But you're still the funniest looking bird." She flexed the tip of her tail and waved it in a dismissive manner. "Now fly away, mouse-breath."

The owl blinked its big, round eyes in indignation. "You...! You...! You...!"

Marina reached back and drew closed the door to her cave. She loved the fireflies and butterflies, but she didn't want bugs flying in and cluttering up her nice home, nor birds either, of any kind. "Stutter, stutter, mumble, mutter," she said over her shoulder to the owl. "Shiver, quiver, fumble, flutter." She waved her tail again. "Fly away, I say. On such a perfect evening I'm going for a stroll."

The owl spread broad gray wings and rose upward. "I see a plump mouse now," it announced with enthusiasm. Dipping one wingtip, it plunged back into the forest.

Marina hoped the mouse was sharp-eyed and alert.

The breeze gusted again, and the forest branches rustled. With her silver wings folded upon her back, Marina began to walk up the side of the hill. The sulfurs rose up from the nasturtiums to accompany her, and a small swarm of fireflies lit her way, although she really didn't need their light. Dragons saw very well in the darkness, and it wasn't even quite dark.

Before she reached the summit, the wind shifted, and a whiff of wood-smoke tickled her nose. Then a small cacophony of excited shouting came over the hilltop. For a moment, Marina stopped and frowned at the noise. It jarred the evening's tranquillity and disturbed her peaceful frame of mind. Yet it also piqued her interest for as she listened she recognized the sound of children's voices.

Her frown fading, she increased her pace and arrived at the summit. The pair of sulfurs perched on the top of her head and fanned their wings while the fireflies hovered close around like a diminutive advance guard. "Children of the night," she whispered to the fireflies, "at ease, you little dazzlers!"

As if they understood, the twinkling insects drifted off a little way or settled into the rich grass, but they didn't wander far, and the butterflies stubbornly maintained their lookout.

Marina gave an amused sigh as she gazed down into the valley below the hill where a sprawling village of farmhouses and barns nestled. Lamps and lanterns burned in the windows, but like her, many of the citizens had been drawn outside by the beauty of the evening. Fat minotaur farmers walked hand-in-hand with their bovine-faced wives. Satyr couples strolled in the dusty roadways. A lone old human male with a wavy white beard leaned on a fence rail and blew random notes on a reed flute.

A narrow stream ambled along the near side of the village, and on the closer bank, someone had built a bonfire. An old minotaur, his hide grown gray and shaggy, leaned on a staff near the fire, watching while the village children danced and leaped around it. As if sensing suddenly that Marina was also watching, the minotaur gazed up at her. Stiffly, he lifted a hand and waved.

Raising a paw, Marina returned the wave, and a brief soft sadness—or perhaps it was only melancholy—brushed across her mood. Chergo, the minotaur, had lived in the valley all his life, as had most of his family before him. Marina could remember when the farmhouse built by Chergo's great-grandfather had been the only homestead down there. It pained her to see Chergo so old, so near the end of his time with no heir to call his own. He was the last of his line.

Near the fire a couple of satyr boys began to scuffle, and one of them punched the other. Chergo shouted a stern warning and thumped his staff on the ground, but the other children clustered around the boys in a tight circle, wide-eyed and excited as they chose sides and cheered for one or the other and screamed encouragements. On the fringes of the circle a small black and white dog began to bark and scamper around the children, seeking a better view of the match.

Far up the roadside, the satyr couple saw the altercation and, becoming alarmed, hurried toward it. Hobbling into the fray, Chergo tried to break up the fight, but only got knocked down for his efforts. A pair of minotaur children separated themselves from the others to try to help him up, but the fight continued. Concerned for Chergo, Marina spread her wings and prepared to fly down and stop the battle, herself.

Then, a blast of red-orange fire shot across the sky from the direction of the forest on the village's edge, and an instant later, the Dragon Puck raced over the treetops. He clutched loads of kindling in his claws, and it was suddenly plain that it was he who had built the bonfire for the children.

He gave an angry roar that stopped the fight instantly, and dropping his load, folded his wings and landed on the edge of the stream. The children fell back as he strode into their midst and their shouting ceased. The bonfire's flames glimmered on his golden scales as he loomed over them and glowered.

"Well?" he said after a tense moment. "I'm waiting."

With sheepish expressions, the two young satyrs reached out and shook hands. "We were just having fun," one of them said as he wiped the back of a hand over his swollen nose.

The satyr couple from the roadside, parents of one of the fighters, finally reached the gathering. While the mother made sure that Chergo was all right and offered profuse apologies, the father grabbed his son by a budding horn. "I'm going to make sure you have fun all week!" he scolded. "In your room!"

"I've got a better idea," Puck said to the father. He swept his gaze over all the children, and then with a sudden smile that suggested wisdom beyond his Dragon years he looked to his mother still on the hillside and beckoned. "It would be a shame to waste such a good bonfire. I think we need a story." He beckoned to his mother again.

Spreading her wings, Marina glided with gentle grace down the slope and settled beside her son near the fire. She smiled at Puck and touched his shoulder affectionately with the tip of one silver wing. He was nearly as tall as she was now, and she didn't see as much of him since he'd made his own cave on the far side of the valley.

Chergo shuffled forward. "Welcome, Marina!" he called. "I see you've brought your entourage, too!"

The pair of sulfurs fluttered in a circle around her head and perched on the tip of her nose to fan their wings. The swarm of fireflies chased after her as well and filled the air with merry lightning.

"We need a story, Mother," Puck said with a soft grin, "and who better to tell it than you."

Marina gazed around at the children. One by one they drifted closer to her and seated themselves in the grass near her feet. The light from the bonfire lit their upturned faces with a ruddy glow, shimmered on the satyr-children's ivory horns, and filled the large eyes of the minotaur-children.

In the village, others took note of Marina's presence, and word quickly spread from house to house. The adults left their evening chores and their suppers and their comfortable easy chairs and walked across the meadow to join their offspring.

"You keep to yourself too much these days, Marina," Chergo said as he leaned on his staff. "Everyone is coming to see you."

Marina blinked her eyes and wrapped her wings around herself. It was true that she seldom came to the village anymore. She had her flowers and her gardens and her cave to occupy her time and all her forest friends to keep her company. All her books, too. Maybe she did feel a little lonely since Puck had moved out on his own, but she didn't dwell on it. She felt nothing but pride for her son.

"We always need stories," she said to Puck, but she spoke loudly enough for all to hear. Then she directed her gaze toward the two young fighters. "Stories remind us of who we are and, just as importantly, of who we can be. They're our history and also our hope for a better world to come." She looked at all the children now gathered with their parents around her feet. "Whether we tell them in books or songs or in paintings, we are the sum total of all our stories."

Puck nodded his Dragon head. "That's a good beginning," he said.

Marina looked at her son as she squeezed one eye shut. "Oh, no," she answered. "I've told all my stories." Folding her wings tightly against her back, she sat on her haunches and looked up at Puck. "Tonight, in this deepening darkness with the stars over our heads and this nice fire to warm our bodies and good friends all around to warm our hearts—you become the storyteller."

Puck protested. "But I don't know any stories!"

Marina squeezed her other eye shut. "Nonsense," she said. "You know them all. I taught them to you just as they were taught to me. Now it falls to you to teach so that our stories are never lost." She opened her eyes again and regarded her son. With the bonfire's flames dancing on his golden scales he looked like a pillar of fire.

This is how great Stormfire must have looked, Marina thought wistfully, and for a moment she forgot where she was and her mind wandered back to younger days. She had never known the legendary leader of the Dragonkin, but she remembered all his stories.

Puck cleared his throat, looking somewhat disconcerted. All the children waited in expectation as they nestled into their parents' arms or stretched out on the grass. "Well, then," he said at last, turning up his paws in a gesture that was both an acceptance of his task and an invitation to his audience.

Marina smiled to herself. He was a natural showman.

"We begin as all good stories begin. With a poem." Pausing, he tilted his head back and stared straight upward at bright Rono. Marina looked up, too, and all gazes followed. Puck's whisper rose like a soft invocation.

"*It's light brings inspiration,
Unlocks imagination.*"

Wrapped in her wings, warmed by the fire and the company, Marina began gently to rock herself as she listened and let her thoughts get lost in the words.

The sulfurs flew from Marina to Puck and settled on his head between his ears. The fireflies, though—their tiny hearts were loyal.

One

ALONE IN THE CAVE that once had belonged to his father, the Dragon Chan sat on his red-scaled haunches and contemplated the small crystal figurine that set on a writing desk in a corner by the dark fireplace. The Glass Dragon seemed to stare back, studying him as he studied it, patiently challenging him, testing him.

Chan felt the subtle throb of power emanating from the talisman like he felt his own heartbeat. On some strange level it was linked with him now, a part of him. Even in his sleep it hovered on the edges of his dreams, never disturbing him, only watching and waiting and sometimes, he thought, trying to instruct.

"I don't understand," Chan murmured to the talisman. A cool shiver rippled up his spine and tingled in the tips of his wings. He closed his eyes and gave a low chuckle. The thing had him talking to himself.

Of course he didn't understand. The Glass Dragon was beyond his understanding, beyond anything in his experience. The small bit of crystal contained one of the last three drops of magic left in the world, a drop preserved by his father, the great Dragonkin leader, Stormfire. Yet that was long before Chan's birth. What did he know of magic?

What did he know of his father, for that matter? He thought he had known Stormfire, but he was no longer sure. His search for the Glass Dragon had left him questioning everything—his father most of all— and answers eluded him.

A winged silhouette appeared at the mouth of the cave, eclipsing the red sunset beyond as its claws locked on to the stony lip. After a moment's hesitation, the Dragon Harrow folded his black-scaled wings, bent his head and entered.

"I feel it too, you know," he said in a low, rumbling voice as he dragged the claws on one paw across his broad chest. "It's like some bothersome itch that I can't scratch enough."

Without answering, Chan turned his gaze back to the Glass Dragon on the writing desk. It didn't surprise him that his brother also sensed the talisman's presence. According to all the stories and prophecies, any one of Stormfire's three children might have found it. *Three dragon triplets; three talismans; three drops of the last magic in the world.*

"Your journey to the Haunted Lands has marked you, Brother," Harrow said with a rare note of concern as he stretched out his sinuous neck to peer more closely at the talisman. "How long do you plan to play the recluse, hiding down here in our father's cave from the rest of Stronghold? Everyone's asking why you've sequestered yourself when our sister is missing. Aren't you worried?"

Turning one golden eye on his brother, Chan gave a soft sigh. "Aren't you?" he answered. "You have wings to fly, Brother. You could be out looking for her, instead of prowling about down here aggravating your itches."

Harrow pretended to ignore the sarcasm as he leaned still closer to the talisman. Extending the tip of one claw he seemed about to touch it, but then drew back. "We should be looking for the other two," he said with sudden sharpness. "Can't we ask this one where they are?"

"I don't think it works that way," Chan answered with a shake of his head.

Harrow sneered. "You don't know how it works!"

Chan blinked his eyes, and the tip of his tail made a soft, impatient thump on the cave floor. "True enough," he admitted. "Why don't you try it? Ask it a question. Then shake it up and turn it over. Maybe the answer will appear on the bottom."

Harrow spun around and brought his huge head close to Chan's. "You shouldn't mock me," he said in a hurt voice. "I could have gone in search of this talisman had I not been wounded in battle at Redclaw, but I went after Gaunt and the griffins that murdered our father."

Chan rose and stretched. Stormfire's cave was large and deep enough to allow that luxury. "If you want the Glass Dragon," he said in a weary tone, "then take it. If you can figure out what it does, then do so. It doesn't belong to me, Harrow, or to you. It's a legacy for all of the Dragonkin."

Harrow frowned and scratched his chin. "Why don't you ask Ramoses to examine it?"

Chan shrugged. "He's already done so, and he's as much at a loss as we." Flexing his wings and giving a yawn, he stepped past his brother and moved toward the cave entrance. "You're right about one thing, though. I've hidden down here long enough."

An exhilarating rush of wind brushed his face as he spread his wings and glided outward. It buoyed his spirit. The canyon walls loomed full of shadow and color and striation, and the dark mouths of other caves gaped wide in the stone, yet it held a beauty that thrilled him.

Below, the Echo Rush swept along between shores of rock and sand. Deep in shadow at the bottom of the canyon, the water looked black, swift, and dangerous. A pair of silver-haired wolves wandering idly along its banks looked up with thirsty expressions as Chan passed overhead. With the Blackwater River poisoned and polluted, more and more of the creatures of Wyvernwood were venturing to the Rush for drink.

One of the wolves lifted a shaggy head and howled.

Dipping his right wingtip, Chan banked on an updraft and gyred upward to climb above the great rift. On the southern rim, lush forest grew right up to the stony edge, but on the northern rim lay the sprawling village called Stronghold.

Throngs of Stronghold's citizens stood assembled along the rim to watch the sunset. It was a nightly ritual, a celebration to bid the sun goodnight and to wake the moon. Minotaurs beat artfully fashioned log-drums in complex and stimulating rhythms while satyrs played music on pipes and flutes and families of foxes and bears danced. A group of Fomorian females kept time with tambourines and zills as their mates shook tinkling chipolis and chimes. A couple of human children entertained watchers with acrobatic tricks and tumbling routines.

The crowds waved as they saw Chan, and the music reached a new crescendo that soared over the canyon and filled the reddening sky. It gladdened Chan's Dragon-heart to see so many of his friends. He felt their excitement and even shared it. Yet at the same time their adulation in their welcome made him uncomfortable.

It wasn't just the sunset they celebrated. Word had spread among them that one of the legendary talismans had been found and that Chan had brought it back to Wyvernwood.

In their eyes Chan was a hero.

Higher in the sky, the Dragons of Stronghold flew graceful circles over the canyon and the village. Cobalt-blue Ramoses, the oldest of all the Dragons, sailed wingtip to wingtip with his blue daughter, the Dragon Diana. Their wings glittered in the fading sunlight.

Nearby, he spied his mother, ebon-scaled Sabu. Behind her, flying in casual escort, came the twins, Kaos and Sakima, and then emerald Fleer with scarlet-winged Tiamat. Snowsong, Paraclion, Maximor, Starfinder—they were all there winging through the sky. With Harrow below in Stormfire's cave with the talisman, only one among all their number remained absent.

His triplet sister—the Dragon Luna.

"Still no sign of Luna," Diana said to Chan, seeming almost to read his mind as he flew up beside her. Diana was Luna's best friend.

"She's strong," Chan answered, wishing that he felt as confident as he sounded, "and fast. Faster than all of us. And smarter. Wherever she is, she'll be all right."

Diana's Dragon lips drew into a taut line as she shook her head. "Luna's been gone too long, Chan. Wyvernwood is big—but not that big. No creature in the entire forest has seen her since she drove the griffins from the Redclaw fortress. Harrow was with her, but she slipped away from him. Why? We've searched everywhere for her, and for the human girl, Ariel, too." Diana squeezed one golden eye shut. "They've both disappeared. I think they've left Wyvernwood just as you did."

The same thought had crossed Chan's mind. Privately he wondered if his headstrong sister had taken off on her own quest for the talismans. He gazed toward Luna's mate, Tiamat, and resolved to speak with the red Dragon before the night was done.

His mother, Sabu, appeared at his side, and she brushed his wing with her own as a sign of greeting and affection. "So you've returned to the sunlight side of the world," she said.

Chan glanced westward and grinned. "Not much sunlight to return to."

Sabu stuck out her Dragon tongue. "Don't get smart with me, youngster," she said. "You may be a hero to them, but don't forget that I hatched your speckled little egg, and if you've finished playing with your father's silly trinket, we can use your help."

His father's trinket—the Glass Dragon. He smiled to himself as Sabu managed the almost impossible, speaking in a loving tone to her son even as her voice dripped with disdain for her husband, Stormfire.

Not for the first time of late, he wondered what had transpired to drive such a wedge between Sabu and Stormfire. Only lately had he realized that the wedge had even existed, and he chided himself for his blindness.

He'd been blind about many things.

A chilly breeze blew across his neck, bringing with it the faint smell of distant rain. He craned his neck as he flew and stared toward the north where dark clouds full of pale lightning were gathering on the far horizon. They promised another storm.

"More rain," Sabu said with sullen bitterness as she followed his gaze. "Enough to fill our rain barrels if we're lucky, but not enough to wash Degarm's poison from our rivers."

He glanced downward as their circling took them once more over the Echo Rush. The two wolves were gone. Now a pair of brown bears prowled the northern shoreline while a family of deer soft-footed through the rocky sand on the south bank.

Because of the direction of its flow, the Echo Rush remained safe from the lethal poisons Degarm had dumped into the Blackwater River, which was the main artery of Wyvernwood. Nothing could drink there and live. Some of its branches were almost as bad.

So much had happened in Wyvernwood during his absence. His heart swelled with anger, and for the first time he considered revenge, a fiery revenge on the cities of his enemies. The inhabitants of Wyvernwood desired only peace and to be left alone, but the age-old war between Angmar in the north and Degarm in the south had shattered their hopes time and again as the two sides made the forest a battleground.

He frowned as he thought of the talisman—the Glass Dragon—on the writing table in Stormfire's cave. Then he considered the two others—the *Diamond Dragon* and the Heart of All Dragons. Once united, the legends claimed, all three talismans would point the way to a new homeland for the Dragonkin.

But what if the Dragonkin didn't want to go?

"Alert! Alert! On guard!"

Every Dragon looked to sharp-eyed Fleer, who flew a wider arc on their western flank. On the ground, the Minotaurs with their keen hearing also heard the emerald Dragon's warning and ceased their drumming. The satyrs in turn stopped piping, and throughout Stronghold all eyes scanned the sky.

"Crows!" Someone shouted. "They're back!"

Panicked screaming rose up from the village. The crowd broke away from the rim and ran. Some raced for the protection of their homes, slamming doors and shutters tight. Others grabbed for clubs and rakes and axes, anything with which to defend themselves.

The leaves of the trees shivered and shook as a great rush of birds shot upward, and the air filled with screeching and cawing. Smaller birds—sparrows, finches, doves, and quail—fled their roosts and nests to get out of the way, while larger birds—hawks, owls, and aggressive woodpeckers—shot forth to intercept the swift-flying force of crows.

Out of the trees the crows raced on a flurry of wings. Half-hidden by the shadows and deepening dusk, they kept silent until they were almost upon Stronghold. The hawks and owls met them first. Feathers exploded and blood showered the leaves and the ground. Talons and beaks flashed. Still the crows surged forward, too numerous and with surprise on their side.

In Stormfire's cave, Harrow lay flat on the floor with his tail curled around his body and over his Dragon nose. On the other side of the cave, the glass talisman shimmered with a faint and unimpressive light. In Chan's absence, the small figurine's glow seemed to have dimmed, as if it were at rest or waiting. Still, Harrow couldn't tear his gaze away. The crystal sang to him, but with a quiet and distant voice he couldn't understand.

He felt sure that Chan heard it more clearly, and he chided himself for the jealousy he harbored in his heart. He loved his brother, but lately every word that passed between them seemed to be an opening for an argument. It dismayed him, because he knew the fault was his.

He blinked as he looked at the tiny Dragon on the writing table. "Sing to me," he whispered. "Teach me to understand." But the talisman paid no attention, and the song it sang remained distant and weak and incomprehensible. After a moment, Harrow closed his eyes. For some reason he couldn't explain he felt like weeping, but tears wouldn't come. *So much to do*, he thought. *So many questions to answer.*

The talisman's song, so soft and easy, was almost a lullaby, and he welcomed the drowsiness that stole upon him.

Yet, on the brink of sleep, all his senses snapped alert. Maybe it was the sudden silence of the drums and the music on Stronghold's rim, or maybe it was the first sounds of chaos and fighting that woke him. Before he could lift his ebon-scaled head, the cave entrance filled with winged shapes. Straight for the talisman they flew, their tiny round eyes gleaming with malice in its glow.

Then, as one of the birds locked claws on the small Glass Dragon, its song changed, became a vibrating scream that filled the cave. The bird immediately dropped the talisman again. The figurine fell on the table with a clatter, and the would-be thief slammed into the wall as it veered away.

Almost invisible in the cave's blackness, Harrow chose that same moment to spring up from his hidden corner and let out a roar. "My father's treasure!" he shouted. "Black cousins—let me show you real wings!" Spreading one huge leather pinion protectively over the talisman and the writing table, he smashed at the crows with his other.

Over the rooftops the invaders flew and down the streets into Stronghold's square. There, the villagers met them with their clubs and tools, and they swung at the immense black birds with a determined fury. Still, a dog-faced fomorian went to his knees screaming with three crows on his back. A minotaur clutched his face and fell across his drum with a pain-filled roar.

Then, a human boy charged into the center of the square. A crow dived straight for his face, but the boy drew back an arm, and with confident strength he dealt the bird a swift blow and sent it crashing to the ground.

Chan recognized the boy at once and cried a warning. "Jake!"

If Jake heard, he paid no attention. He drew a sling from the pocket of his trousers with one hand and with the other hand he drew a stone from a pouch at his belt. In one smoothly practiced motion, he fitted the stone in place, whipped the sling once around his head, and let it fly.

With a sharp screech a large crow plummeted earthward. Jake fitted another stone to his sling.

Cursing, Chan swooped low over the village with Diana and Ramoses close behind. With broad leathery wings they batted scores of crows from the sky.

Sabu followed them down, and landing on the edge of the square she spread her wings wide to protect and shelter some of the villagers.

Suddenly a blast of fire brightened the sky over the village heralding another entrant to the battle. Harrow gave a mighty roar as he rose over the canyon rim. Chan's heart lurched as a wave of heat brushed his back, but then he breathed a sigh of relief. Sometimes he didn't give his brother enough credit. Harrow had aimed his fire skyward away from the village and away from the summer-dry forest.

Still, the fiery threat had an effect. Some of the crows, losing heart, veered away with a desperate cawing and turned southward to race across the canyon. Tiamat, Kaos, and Sakima gave chase, toasting a few tail feathers with their own searing blasts.

The fight was far from over, though. The remaining crows pressed their attack, slashing at Stronghold's citizens with talons, ripping flesh and fur with snapping beaks. Their small eyes gleamed with vicious light as, with sheer numbers, they brought down creatures far larger than themselves.

As if to highlight the strange battle, a bolt of lightning shot across the sky, and thunder rolled. In the west, only a blood-red stain marked the spot where the sun had fallen. Shadows danced and flickered at the edge of the forest, making it appear that all of Wyvernwood had somehow come alive.

This is madness! Chan thought as he slapped his wings together on a pair of crows. He shot a look around for Jake. The boy's arms were bloody with scratches, but he fought on with grim courage, holding the center of the square almost single-handedly as he sought to rally the rest of the villagers.

Then, without cause or warning, almost all fighting stopped. A strange electricity vibrated through the intensifying gloom, and a pale white light rose shimmering on the northern horizon.

Another bolt of lightning, Chan thought at first, but he knew at once that it was not. The new light shone with a steady glow, growing brighter as it approached at a rapid speed.

Fearing some new threat, Chan rose higher into the sky to join his brother, Harrow. "They came to steal the talisman," Harrow said, his voice a tense whisper as he opened his clawed fist to reveal the Glass Dragon. Then, twisting his head, he stared toward the strange glow. "What in all of Wyvernwood is that?"

"What in all of Undersky," Chan answered uneasily. His golden eyes turned silver with the increasing brightness as he stared toward the glow, and his scales tingled with an almost familiar sensation. It was an itching, but it was also a sound, music beyond hearing, and a taste beyond expression. It puzzled his ears as it dazzled his eyes

His eyes shot wide with sudden realization, and he flew still higher into the air for a better view of the approaching light. The sensation it gave off—it was the same sensation he felt from the Glass Dragon!

Only this sensation felt stronger, far more intense, like a song far too loud in his ears!

Even the crows felt it. They darted about in sudden confusion, knocking into each other, slamming into the walls of houses. Some tumbled to earth, directionless and disoriented. None of the villagers cared or paid the crows any attention. With rapt gazes, they watched the sky.

High above the treetops, the pale light shot toward the canyon and sailed far out over Stronghold. For an instant it seemed to hover over the tall pinnacle of stone called Stormfire's Point. Then it settled there to shift and coalesce, to take shape and display a pair of shimmering wings within its brilliant halo.

"That's Luna!" Chan shouted. On the ground, others took up the shout, and the Dragon Diana rose upward with hope in her eyes.

But if it was truly Luna, his sister had changed.

Abandoning the perch that had once been her father's funeral pyre, Luna sailed into the sky again and approached Stronghold. For a brief moment, she hovered like a mysterious new moon over the square.

On the edges of the square, the villagers stared upward, and then began to shrink away. Awed by the beautiful new strangeness of Stormfire's daughter, they still sensed an *otherness* they couldn't understand, and it frightened them. Slowly they retreated into the shadows of doorways and alleys where her light didn't reach.

Only Jake stood his ground in the center of the square. Unafraid, he gazed upward with wide eyes and called her name.

With wings outspread, Luna stared downward at the boy. "Luna!" he called again. "Luna, where is Ariel?"

Luna looked down upon Jake, and then swept her gaze over the entire village as if she had never seen it before. Lastly, she gazed toward her brothers. "Harrow...?" she said, her voice distant and uncertain. "Chan...?"

Her light dimmed to a scintillant sparkling that danced over her ivory scales. At the same time she closed her eyes, and her head drooped. All her strength seemed to leave her wings.

Chan cried out. Sabu screamed a terrified Dragon scream as a collective gasp went up from Stronghold.

Home at last from some unknown journey, Luna crashed earthward.

Two

THE GRIFFIN MINHEP WAITED at tense attention on his hind legs and tried to look his tallest and most menacing. Every golden hair on his leonine body bristled, and every feather on his eagle's head stood on end. His tail twitched back and forth, and his great wings itched. His gaze roamed surreptitiously over the immense stone walls with their elaborate tapestries and gaudy banners, over the vaulted ceiling and the pebbled mosaic floor.

He knew in his heart that he'd made a mistake coming here.

"So you Griffinkin have failed me again!"

A cold anger filled Minhep as he turned his gaze with slow deliberation toward the one place he'd been trying not to look—the high dais where Angmar's fat King Kilrain sat upon his throne with a circle of silent advisors around him. The Griffinkin leader raised his paws and flexed his claws to show their razor sharpness.

"Have a care, human." He clacked his beak as he answered. "You made your arrangement with Gaunt, not with me. I am not your lackey."

Kilrain's heavy-lidded eyes blazed. Leaning forward, he slammed a meaty fist on the arm of his throne. "I made my arrangement with all the Griffinkin, you louse-brained fool! When Gaunt accepted my deal and signed his name in blood he bound every griffin in Wyvernwood to me! You are all bought and paid for!"

Ignoring the archers around the room, Minhep threw back his head and howled. "No one owns me!" he roared. "Especially no pink-skinned man!"

Kilrain shot to his feet. "I kept my part of the bargain!" he shouted, his face darkening with rage. "I rebuilt Redclaw Fortress and gave it to the griffins!"

"You didn't build it strong enough!" Minhep shook one lion paw as he answered Kilrain. Then with a sudden weariness he moderated his tone, and his huge shoulders slumped. "Stormfire's damnable children have driven us out," he admitted. "Redclaw is no sanctuary for us anymore."

Kilrain glared at Minhep and openly sneered. "How can this be?" he said with a shake of his head. "Griffins are the strongest of all creatures!"

Minhep wrapped his feathered wings around himself as he looked away. Shame warmed his face, and a sense of bitter frustration filled him. Yet he said nothing and kept his thoughts to himself. *Sometimes strength alone wasn't enough.* It was a heretical thought for a griffin, and still he knew it was true.

Little by little, he'd discovered that there were things in Wyvern-wood older than the Dragons and the griffins—things from darker times when the world had been different, things from before even the Age of Dragons, which now was passing.

Some of those things, he suspected, lived beneath Redclaw's ancient foundations. No one lived who remembered what that place had originally been built for or what purpose it had served. But in the final moments as he gathered his griffins and fled Redclaw, he had glimpsed something in the shadows of its towers—a woman who was not a woman at all—and his heart had turned to stone with fear.

Minhep could think of no reason, though, to share this information with the King of Angmar. Gaunt might once have trusted Kilrain—but Gaunt was moldering in his grave.

He lifted his head again, finding a measure of pride as he looked Kilrain in the eye and remembered that, king or no king, and archers be damned, once he could have ripped the man's head off with a casual swipe of his paw and licked the blood from his claws as if it was candy. He smiled to himself, reassured to realize he still had that capacity for violence, that raw impulse. For now, though, he kept his impulses under control.

"I came only to inform you," he said to Angmar's king, "that the Griffinkin are leaving. There's no place for us anymore in Wyvern-wood, but somewhere in vast Undersky, perhaps even on the far side of the world, we had a home once. Maybe we can find it again."

Kilrain stared at Minhep, and then barked a harsh laugh as he sat back on his throne and adjusted his silken robes about his chubby legs. "You're worse than a louse-brained fool, Minhep," he said, turning sideways on his seat and folding his arms across his chest. "You're a dreamer!" He wagged a be-ringed finger. "That's very un-griffinlike!"

Minhep's black eagle-eyes narrowed to slits. "There's a fool here," he answered in a low voice, "but it's you, Kilrain. You're a fool to insult me, and you're doubly a fool if you think your little soldiers with their pointy little sticks can stop me from tearing the beating heart from your flaccid chest." He turned his gaze away from Kilrain and slowly swept it over the assembly of archers, coldly grinning as he noted their nervous shuffling and the beads of sweat appearing on their brows. He could smell their sudden fear like week-old chicken entrails.

"I came here only as a courtesy," he continued. "But there isn't a drop of courtesy in all of Angmar. So I'll gather my griffins and go before someone makes a mess on your fine mosaic floor." He turned another gaze over the archers, adding, "It can be so hard to clean."

Kilrain answered in a sharp voice. "Did you say *your griffins?*" He thrust a hand into the air. Around the room every archer responded, swiftly fitting shafts to bowstrings, drawing their arrows with trembling hands. "I told you!" Kilrain shouted, leaning forward again. "I own the Griffinkin! Your brothers know the meaning of a deal even if you don't!" His advisors drew into a tighter, more protective circle around their king, but Kilrain ignored them.

For the first time, Minhep noticed the dark gleam of madness in the eyes of Angmar's monarch. He knew he wouldn't leave this chamber without a fight. The humans knew it, too. The smell of fear in the chamber intensified.

Kilrain clutched at the front of his robes with one hand until his knuckles turned white and the rich fabric threatened to rip. "You're quite alone, Minhep!" he railed. "I've already replaced you as the Griffinkin's leader!"

Minhep shook his head and laughed. "No griffin would dare...!"

Kilrain turned pale and stone-faced. He wasn't used to being laughed at by anyone. "Goronis is the new leader! He's already accepted the role—and a new mission!"

Minhep's shout echoed from the walls, causing one of the advisors to throw up his hands and faint behind the throne. A frightened archer's hand slipped, and an arrow zipped through the air. Minhep swatted it aside as if it was a bothersome insect. "What mission?" he demanded, swelling out his chest. "What have you done, you pathetic flesh-sack?"

The remaining advisors closed ranks around Kilrain and tried to hustle him to safety, but he batted away their grasping hands. With surprising agility for a man of such rotundity he leaped onto the seat of his throne to shout over their heads. "I've sent them to Thursis!" he cried. "Every single one of them under Goronis's command! To kill a Dragon there! The Dragon that killed Shepar—my son!"

"You're a maggot-mouthed liar!" Minhep answered. "There are no Dragons on Thursis!"

"There's one!" Kilrain shouted. "The Dragon Rage!"

Minhep stared at Kilrain uncertainly. He knew the Dragons of Wyvernwood by name, and there was no such creature! And yet, the madness on Kilrain's face mingled with such despair and pain, that Minhep hesitated and wondered.

"Kill him!" Kilrain cried to his archers as his advisors dragged him away. "Kill him now! Bring the beast down, and make me a carpet from his carcass!"

Arrows flew through the chamber. Minhep snapped his wings wide with tremendous force, sweeping many of the shafts away even as he lunged toward the dais. Still, he felt a deep sting in his rump, followed by another, and cried out in anger and pain.

A soldier sprang suddenly in front of him, waving a sword as he attempted to block the way up the stone steps that led to the top of Kilrain's dais. Minhep batted the sword away with one paw and closed his beak on the soldier's arm. With a powerful toss of his head, he flung the man across the room.

Kilrain was gone. Only a few of his advisors remained around the throne watching in wide-eyed fear while their monarch made his escape. Bowstrings twanged, and more arrows flashed toward the Griffinkin leader. Two struck him in the shoulder, but such was the thickness of muscle there that they didn't penetrate deeply.

Spreading his wings, Minhep rose toward the ceiling. The chamber, though large, didn't allow a lot of room to fly, but he didn't need a lot of room. He scattered the archers like ten-pins, knocking them down with his wings as he swooped low, seizing them with his claws and using his great griffin strength to fling them around like ragdolls. Some he carried high toward the vaulted ceiling and dropped. His beak ripped flesh. His claws showered the walls with blood. Dropping their bows and their swords, the archers and soldiers followed the example of their king. Those that could, fled. The rest crawled back into the shadowy corners, trembling and clutching their wounds.

Minhep glanced around once more for Kilrain, but there was no sign of the Angmar's king. No matter; a more important matter occupied his mind—Goronis, his Griffinkin, and this unknown Dragon called Rage.

Landing on the floor once again and ignoring his own wounds, Minhep strode toward the pair of great doors at the rear of the chamber. For a moment, he hesitated. Then, muscles bulging beneath golden fur, he raised his paws and struck with both clawed fists. Wood shattered; broken beams and splinters exploded outward, and Minhep stepped through the ruin.

The halls were empty. The sounds of screaming and fighting from the throne room had efficiently served to clear his path. Snatching the shafts from his shoulder and rump and casting them aside, Minhep made his way toward daylight with a grim determination.

In the square outside, the citizens of Angmar stopped in their tracks and stared as the griffin leader suddenly appeared. Minhep paid them no attention. The stench of Mankind filled his nostrils; it would take him hours to wash the cursed smell out of his hide. Yet he lingered. With his keen eyesight, he searched the parapets and tall towers for any of his Griffinkin; he scanned the sky, the balconies and rooftops, the nearby streets.

He really was alone. His Griffinkin had abandoned him and left him behind.

Minhep clenched his beak tight and curled his paws into fists. So be it, then. Let Goronis be the leader. Minhep had never asked for the responsibility, and he didn't want it any longer. He had the sky, and no griffin needed more!

Spreading his wings again, he glided over the heads of the humans in the square, feeling cold pleasure as they shrieked and scurried out of his path, threw down their baskets, and hurled themselves under wagons or into the shadows of fountains. They were frightened mice to him, and the panic and fear on their pallid faces gladdened his heart.

Soaring upwards, he spied the highest tower in Angmar City and circled it once, twice. It would be an easy matter with his strength to shatter the structure and topple it to the ground. Yet at the last moment, even as he flew toward it with an upraised paw, he turned aside. Though built of stone blocks, there was a grace and beauty to the tower that even he could appreciate, and that made it worth sparing. He looked around for another target, instead, but before he could decide the urge to commit violence melted away.

Minhep shook himself, convinced that he was taking ill with something. What else could explain his unnatural pacifism? He put a paw to his feathered forehead to check for a fever. Nothing. His heart wasn't even beating fast.

Forgetting the city and its soft-skinned human occupants, Minhep gyred higher and higher in ever-widening circles toward the sun. An exhilarating wind blew against his face as he stretched his wings. For a moment, he glanced eastward. That way lay the Windy Sea and the island of Thursis, and that was the way his brother griffins were going.

For an instant, Minhep's heart became heavy, and sadness clouded his far-seeing eyes as he considered his options. He'd spent his entire life in Wyvernwood, serving first the great Gorganar and then his son, Gaunt, always a soldier and an order-taker, and then briefly the Griffinkin leader, himself.

As if seeing it with newly opened eyes, he stared into the vastness of the bright blue sky. It seemed to stretch on forever and ever, and the few wisps of clouds on the distant horizon called his name. Dipping his right wing, he made a graceful turn and flew alone northward and westward deeper into the cold reaches of Angmar and toward unknown lands.

Minhep smiled to himself. More than ever before in his life, he felt free. The Griffinkin didn't want him, and he no longer needed the Griffinkin.

Three

RONALDO LAY STRETCHED full-length on his gray belly on the lush grass amid blossoms of bluebells, sweet williams, and wild rose moss that grew on the banks of the long river that cut through the heart of Thursis Island. The sun-dappled water purled and gurgled pleasantly, and he soaked the tip of his tail in its delicious warmth as he studied the incredible apple-sized jewel sheltered on the earth between his paws.

With the point of one claw he turned it in the grass. The sunlight danced on its diamond facets, exploded into countless shards and dazzling sparks that strained even his Dragon eyes, and yet he didn't blink, couldn't look away. Instead, ignoring the tears that sometimes misted his vision, he locked his gaze on the jewel with a determination, hoping for yet another glimpse of the shape that sometimes moved within it.

It was little more than a flicker, a fleeting image that played hide-and-seek among the facets, appearing first in one and then another or briefly at the heart of a cluster of facets, impossible to catch with the eye for long. The harder he looked, the harder it became to see. If he turned his head ever so slightly, almost as if he were fooling it into thinking he was looking away, it appeared for an instant in the corner of his eye.

"Little Dragon," he whispered to the image, for so the tiny figure inside seemed to be when he could see it, with wings of scintillant color and scales of indescribable brilliance. "I think you're teasing me." He folded his front paws under his chin, lay his gray head down, and stared directly into the diamond's fiery heart.

"If you keep that up," said a diminutive, drunken voice in his left ear, "you'll go blind. You shouldn't play with your jewels."

17

Ronaldo didn't turn his head to answer. He heard the buzz of minuscule wings and felt a soft familiar tickle of feathers against the side of his head. A moment later, delicate clawed feet locked hold on the end of his nose.

Ronaldo's eyes crossed as he focused on the little hummingbird perched so unceremoniously on his proud snout. The impudent creature faced him with an unabashed grin, crossing his own eyes in mockery as he swayed from one tiny leg to the other. Then, without warning, the hummingbird hiccoughed.

"You've been in the lousewort again, haven't you, Bumble," Ronaldo chided.

Bumble fluttered into the air and then resumed his perch. "You betcha!" he admitted with exuberance. "One hundred percent pure nectar—and *smooooth!*" Sensing the Dragon's disapproval, he narrowed his tiny brows and glared. "Don't be such a stiff, Ronaldo! This island isn't exactly bustling with thrill rides and action attractions, you know!"

Ronaldo frowned. "You're the one who's stiff, Bumble-bird," he answered. "I'm sorry if you're bored." He turned his gaze back to the huge diamond between his paws. "But I've got to figure out what this is!"

"I've told you what it is, you stubborn overgrown firefly!" The Last Unicorn in the World shook her head as she strode through the grass along the bank downriver and came his way. She batted her eyes twice, and they changed color in the sunlight, shifting from gold to blue, then to green, then violet as she fixed him with her gaze. "It's magic! It's one of Stormfire's three lost talismans, and instead of lying there on the ground playing patty-ball with it, you should be taking it to Stronghold as fast as you can!"

Ronaldo wasn't convinced. He knew the stories of the three talismans—the Glass Dragon, the Diamond Dragon, and the Heart of All Dragons—as well as any Dragon or creature of Wyvernwood. The ornament before him shimmered with a rare beauty and mesmerized with its luster. Truly there was something special about it.

But was it magical? Was it one of the talismans? He'd spent days asking himself that question, days and nights since Bumble had found it and since he'd dug it out of a mountain fissure.

"Humans have such beady little eyes!" Bumble muttered for no apparent reason. Springing into the air, he flew a dizzying series of circles and landed on the tip of Marian's horn.

"You should talk!" the unicorn scoffed as she stopped before Ronaldo.

"Should talk?" Bumble fanned the air with his wings in indignation. "I do talk! I have an extensive and educated vocabulary! This Bumble-bird talks all the time!"

"Endlessly," Ronaldo agreed with a quiet sigh.

Bumble lifted his head and puffed out his chest. "Someday I'm going to write a book," he proclaimed. "I'll call it, *Your Eyes Are Speaking, but I Can't Hear What They Say*." He looked from Marian to Ronaldo and back to Marian as he grinned. "Catchy, don't you think?"

Marian blinked, and her eyes changed back to blue. "I think you're not really a hummingbird at all," she answered curtly. "You're a loon."

Bumble rose into the air, flew a circle around Marian's horn, buzzed both her ears, and tickled her nose with his swift wings. "And you're a grouch!" he answered, hovering right between her eyes. Then he flew to the talisman and perched on that. "I'll never remember a title that long, anyway," he said, suddenly glum. "I nearly forgot to tell you that the humans are on the mountainside watching us again."

Ronaldo gave a low growl, lifted his head, and stared toward the nearby slopes. A ragtag band of Angmaran sailors, no more than ten in number, crouched behind trees and huddled in the bushes with wide and wary eyes. Weaponless, though, they offered no threat to Ronaldo or his friends, and the Gray Dragon relaxed.

Bumble sailed upward again for a better look at the clutch of castaways. "Everyday they come a little bit closer," he noted. "I think you've developed a fan following!"

Ronaldo squeezed one eye shut as he glared at the hummingbird. "Smart thinking, Bumble-bird," he replied. "I destroyed their ships, stranded them here, and now they're my groupies?"

Marian paced back and forth, her gaze also directed toward the half-hidden band. "Stranger things have happened," she said. "Especially with humans. They've heard about Dragons all their lives, but you may be the first one they've ever seen, and they've certainly never been so close to one."

"Nor to a unicorn," Ronaldo reminded her. "Maybe we should put on a show for them. You sing, and I'll dance."

Marian turned to him, then abruptly grinned. "That would set the arts back several hundred years, wouldn't it?"

"Break a leg!" Bumble cried with a small hiccough. "I think we'd be a hit! Bright lights, music, dancing, and a full orchestra of satyrs and minotaurs! Think of it as a good-will tour to the Nations of Man!"

Ronaldo and Marian exchanged glances and rolled their eyes, but on the mountain slopes, the brush rustled softly as the Angmaran sailors stole just a little bit closer. Marian chewed her unicorn lip thoughtfully. "The scary thing is," she said after a moment, "that it's probably not a bad idea."

The Gray Dragon lifted his head once again to watch the humans. "They're afraid of us," he said, "because they don't really know us?"

Marian nodded. "It's an almost revolutionary insight, isn't it?" But then she shook her tangled mane and pranced to the river's edge. "Still, I've lived a long time, Ronaldo. Longer than you. I knew the races of Man well once, and I remember the days before the Dragon Wars." Turning, she stared toward the slopes again, and her voice dropped. "They are not to be trusted."

"And yet, when I was half-mad with rage," Ronaldo reminded her, "you prevented me from killing them."

She looked at him again, and her eyes sparkled. "I never said I was consistent. Or even logical. Indeed, I'm quite capable of holding many conflicting opinions and points of view at the same time!"

Ronaldo bowed his head as a Dragon smile flickered over his scaled face. "You're a natural politician."

Marian turned and swished her tail at her Dragon friend. "If you're going to insult me, I'm heading to the other side of the island. Maybe Finback will appreciate my company. He knows how to treat a lady."

Ronaldo glanced at the oversized diamond jewel between his forepaws, then briefly closed his eyes as he thought of their sea serpent ally. He hadn't seen hide or hair or green-gold scale of Finback for days. Maybe he had been too preoccupied with his strange treasure. He'd forgotten his manners and his friends.

"Let's all go," he said, clutching the jewel tightly as he rose onto his hind legs and stretched. He hadn't realized how cramped his muscles had become lying on the ground. It felt good to flex his wings, and he fanned them several times, putting on a show for the Angmarans watching on the slope. He almost felt sorry for them, ragged and so far from home.

I think I'm a little homesick, myself. The thought startled him, but he couldn't deny that it was true. Suddenly he missed the comforts of his cave and the peaceful contentment of the Whispering Hills. And his paints. He couldn't remember the last time he'd touched a brush to canvass.

"Lookie, lookie, Marian!" Bumble shouted in his tiny voice. "Ronaldo's glassy eyes—all sad and blank!" He dived downward, folded his translucent wings, and landed on the unicorn's horn. "Remind me again—what's it mean, that look?"

"That wistful, kind of stupid *poor-me* look?" Marian answered, making sure her voice was loud enough for the Dragon to hear. "Oh, that can mean several things. If it's just in his right eye, it means he's about to turn into the Dragon Rage again and lay waste to the whole island."

Alarmed, the little hummingbird shot into the air. "Not Bumble!"

With the tip of her tail, Marian flicked water from the river at Bumble, and continued. "If it's just in his left eye, then that means he's been in your lousewort and it's having the same effect on him as it does on you."

Bumble darted toward the Gray Dragon, flew circles around his head, then returned to Marian. "The greedy blackguard! My lousewort? Do you know how much of my precious lousewort he'd have to consume to get as silly as me?"

Marian rolled her eyes again. "Bumble-bird, there isn't enough lousewort in the world to make Ronaldo as silly as you."

Bumble started to say something, then hesitated. He tilted his small head, and scratched himself with one clawed foot as he thought that over. "Well," he said at last, "then good. I think." He twisted his head around to regard the Dragon again. "But what's it mean when both eyes go sad and glassy and kind of stupid?"

It was Marian's turn to hesitate, but finally she answered, and there was an unmistakable satisfaction in her tone. "It means he's thinking of home."

"Home!" Bumble repeated with a soft sigh. He became completely still, which was a rare thing for a hummingbird. Then he beat his wings furiously and hopped the length of the unicorn's horn and perched in the strands of her forelock. "But this is home!" he declared. "We've got forest and flowers! You're here! Ronaldo's here!"

Ronaldo blinked as he snapped out of his reverie. "Calm down, Bumble," he said quietly. "You've just forgotten, and that's my fault for not reminding you." Like all hummingbirds, Bumble had trouble remembering things. Unless he was constantly stimulated with stories and tales or ensconced in his familiar surroundings, memories and details just slipped through his pea-sized brain.

The Gray Dragon felt a surge of guilt. He looked at the large diamond in his paw and then closed his clawed fist around it. "I've been selfish and thoughtless," he said to Marian. "I promised to take care of him, but I've made a mess of things."

Marian moved to Ronaldo's side. "You didn't make a mess of things," she answered. "War makes a mess of things. It takes on a life of its own, a horrible life. And it confuses us, and it changes us all." She bobbed her head up and down, crossing her eyes as she looked at Bumble still perched on her forelock. "We can remind him again. Sometimes we all need to be reminded."

Ronaldo pursed his Dragon lips and nodded. "I guess that's what stories are for."

"Finback!" Bumble cried as if he hadn't been listening to their conversation. "I remember Finback. *Serpens Aqua*—the Scourge of the Deep! The Ancient One—He of the incredibly potent fish-breath!"

The Last Unicorn in the World laughed out loud. "Well, that's one memory he's still got nailed down!" She laughed again and directed her gaze toward the mountain slopes. "I'll race you!" she said. "Right through the humans! It'll be fun to watch them scatter!"

Without another word Marian took off. Her mane and tail flashed in the wind as her hooves pounded the earth, and the sunlight danced on her horn with brilliant fire. For an instant, Ronaldo felt the artist in him stir. He knew there were mysteries about Marian that he still didn't grasp, but when she turned wild and carefree like that, he knew there could never be a more beautiful sight.

"Mount up, Bumble!" he called to the dazed little hummingbird, who hovered in the place where Marian had just stood. "If we let her win, we won't hear the end of it for days!"

"Please don't let her win! Please don't let her win! Please don't let her win!" Bumble begged as he darted into the cup of the Dragon's left ear and nestled there. He pressed his wings to his head and rocked back and forth. "Oh my head! Too much lousewort!"

Spreading his wings and clutching his diamond treasure tightly, Ronaldo sprang into the sky. Marian hadn't yet reached the foot of the mountains, but the humans leaped from their hiding places and ran with panicky determination back up the slopes, slipping and sliding on loose rock and skree, on thick patches of grass, scrambling on their feet and hands and knees.

Climbing high and fast, Ronaldo flew after Marian with Bumble safely in his ear. In no time, he overtook the unicorn. Marian was swift and with her amazing stamina she could run endlessly without tiring. But she couldn't fly!

Ronaldo rejoiced to feel the wind on his wings. With grace and power, he glided in a sharp circle around Marian and laughed as he swept up the slope. "That's how it's done!" he cried to Bumble.

"I know!" the hummingbird shouted into the Dragon's ear. "Bumble flies circles around Marian all the time. It pisses her off!"

Ronaldo clucked his tongue. "Such language from one so small!" he chided. "Remind me to tell you about the Whispering Hills and our real home!"

It was Bumble's turn to laugh, and his voice was high and sweet as he answered. "I didn't really forget!" he said. "But you and Marian can get so serious, and a hummingbird has to have some fun!"

Ronaldo growled low in his throat as he flew. "Remind me to make a paintbrush of your tail feathers, you little faker."

Bumble fluttered his wings, tickling his Dragon friend. "If you're actually going to take up painting again, I'll let you."

On the ground below, the humans suddenly stopped running. Ronaldo stared downward, puzzled at the way they shielded their eyes with their hands and gazed back at him. They didn't scream and shout anymore the way they used to; they didn't even pick up rocks to defend themselves. *They're still afraid*, he noted, *but not as afraid as they used to be.*

Then he reached the top of the mountain. It wasn't the highest peak in the chain that ran the width of the island, but it still afforded a nice view. Landing, he looked for Marian. She was halfway up the slope, right in the midst of the humans, and charging hard. Her hooves tore chunks from the ground, struck sparks from the stone. Sure-footed, she never slipped or slowed.

Bumble poked his head out of Ronaldo's ear and gazed down at the unicorn. "Nyah, nyah, nyah!" he said with a flutter.

Ronaldo took to the sky again and banked westward. A rich green forest stretched below and beyond that a broad beach of glittering white sand. But it was the sea beyond that made his heart sing. He loved the way the foam-capped breakers rolled on the blue water, the way the afternoon sunlight shattered into stars and diamonds on the rippling surface. Reminded of the diamond in his fist, he opened his paw and gazed at the fantastic jewel, and found it hard suddenly to judge which sight thrilled him more.

Flying at his utmost speed, he swept downward over the forest and the beach, out over the sparkling water of the Windy Sea, out over the bay of Thursis Island, and again his heart sang at the beauty of it all. Dipping low, he dragged his tail across the surface and threw a spray of water into the air. A rainbow shimmered in the veil of droplets.

Then, his good mood plummeted as the water seemed to grow still for a moment and the waves settled. At the center of the bay, the tip of a single tall mast jutted up from the waves, a stark reminder of a tragic battle. *Of a horrible mistake*, he thought grimly. Circling the mast, he hung his head in shame.

He'd come to Thursis to rescue the Merfolk, who called the island their home, from their Angmaran conquerors. But he'd found them all dead, every Mer-man, Mer-woman, and child, and the rivers and streams all blackly poisoned. Blaming Angmar, he'd attacked and burned their navy, sinking every single ship and killing many sailors.

But his vengeance had been misdirected. Angmar had conquered the island to use as a base against their enemy Degarm. But they hadn't killed the Mers, nor poisoned the waterways. Degarm had done that to make the island useless to Angmar.

A dark and terrible part of him—the part called Rage—still hungered to strike a blow at Degarm to make them pay. But pay for what? For the slaughter of the Mers? Or for his mistake? For the lives he'd taken in his reasonless anger?

He shook his head as he turned back towards the beach. Marian was waiting there, prancing and flipping her mane, watching him with her keen eyes, reading him like an open book.

He'd made a mess of things; not all her consolate words could change that fact. *You're an artist, Ronaldo, or you once were*, he told himself. *Better to leave war to the warriors, or at least to those who understand such things.*

But he couldn't help wondering—did anyone really understand it?

Back on the beach, Marian raced back and forth. At first, Ronaldo thought she was merely playing, kicking up sand and tossing her mane and tail, splashing in the surf. But as he approached the shore, he heard her frantic cries and increased his speed again.

"From the west!" she shouted, and it was the first time Ronaldo ever heard fear in her voice. "Griffins! A score of them!"

His claws dug into the sand as he landed. Automatically, he stretched a protective wing over Marian as she grew still and stared across the sea. He followed her gaze with a growing sense of dread.

The griffins were a small dark cloud that grew rapidly nearer. Ronaldo locked his jaws and flexed his claws as he felt his heart hammering. Where was that part of him now called the Dragon Rage, the avenger and the destroyer, who had so ruthlessly shattered the ships of Angmar?

"Run," he said to Marian. "Find shelter in the woods. Protect the humans if you can."

A tiny voice chirped inside his ear. "Have no fear! Bumble is here! Let them come by day or night—I never flee when I can fight!" He shot out of Ronaldo's ear to hover in the air. "Did you say griffins?" He gulped.

"I've done my running for the day," Marian said in a surprisingly cold voice.

Ronaldo knew better than to argue with her. Side by side, they waited on the sand with Bumble darting between them from one brow to the next. "Give a blast of fire," Marian said calmly. "The only way to protect the humans is to draw the griffins' attention to us and give them the fight they're looking for."

Ronaldo glanced at her from the corner of his eye. She never failed to surprise him, and through his own nervous fear he drew strength from her resolve. "It's funny," he confessed. "I just forswore war, and here we are again."

"Whatever happens," she said without looking at him, her gaze fixed on the approaching griffins, "don't drop the talisman."

Ronaldo had almost forgotten the diamond in his fist. Uncurling his claws for just a moment, he gave it a quick glance. Something sparkled at the center of it, a tiny Dragon shape that seemed to watch and study him through the facets.

His hammering heart calmed as he closed his fist again, and all his fear dissolved. Without any further hesitation, he blasted red fire skyward. It was a warning and a challenge, and he followed its bright explosive force, spreading his gray wings wide and soaring upward through the center of his own blast.

Across the bay the griffins came, skimming low over the blue water. Eagle eyes glittered, fixed on Marian and Ronaldo, and leonine claws flexed to rend and rip.

"Hi ho! I go! Bumble strikes the first blow!"

Before Ronaldo could stop him, Bumble flashed upward, almost invisible but for a faint greenish blur. The first griffin to reach the beach cut a swath through the air with a massive paw as he swatted at Bumble—and missed. The little hummingbird hit the larger griffin deep inside the ear, striking with beak and claw. The griffin roared, then screamed a shrill bird-like cry of agony as it clapped a paw to its head. Half maddened, it swerved, colliding with the nearest griffin. Feathers exploded, and both beasts plummeted into the bay.

Ronaldo watched in horror. "Bumble!" he cried.

The rest of the griffins drew back in uncertainty and confusion as they watched two of their comrades thrash in the sea and sink. Ronaldo doubted if they had even seen Bumble, and their natural cowardice caused them to hesitate.

"Hit them now," Marian commanded, "before they regroup."

"Aye, Captain!" he answered, charging forward. For a brief instant, he gazed across the waves seeking the mast he'd seen before and not finding it. He wondered now if he'd really seen it at all.

Before he could decide, something else parted the waves. A massive and monstrous head shot upward on a sinuous scaled neck. Lidless black eyes glittered with anger, and a spined dorsal fin arched sharply to display an arsenal of deadly spikes. A wall of seawater rose with it, launching high with stunning force, washing over the eagle-winged attackers.

Finback struck one of the griffins with a bony, pointed snout as he rose to an impressive height in the griffin's very midst. Then, without pause, he twisted his head and opened his mouth to blow a powerful jet of water that knocked another attacker into the sea.

Finding courage in numbers, a trio of griffins dived at Finback's head, but with a speed that belied his immense size, the wily sea serpent slipped back beneath the waves only to rocket upward again and spray another jet of water into the faces of the trio. With the merest twitch of his neck, he batted yet another griffin across the sky.

That was enough. Gathering up their wounded, the griffins turned tail and raced back toward the mainland. Northwestward—toward the coast of Angmar, Ronaldo noted with a curious frown. He followed them for a short distance to make sure they didn't circle around the island.

When he returned to the beach, he found Bumble preening on the tip of Marian's horn and Finback's head resting on the warm sand. The sea serpent wore a self-satisfied grin and looked up as Ronaldo landed.

"Well, if it isn't my old friend, Rage," Finback chuckled.

"Ronaldo," the Gray Dragon corrected with an embarrassed look. "Thanks for the help—again."

Finback displayed rows of yellowed teeth as he opened his jaws wide and smiled. "Think nothing of it, youngster," he said. "Since I met you, I've been having the best time I've had in ages. The best time! Why, living on the bottom of the sea all these centuries, I'd completely forgotten what a crazy party the upper world can be!"

Marian paced forward and nuzzled Finback. The two were old friends. *Old, indeed*, Ronaldo reminded himself. They were both creatures of an earlier time when the Age of Dragons was young. "Finback has a proposal for us," the unicorn said.

Bumble flew to the point of Finback's nose. "Hey, did Ronaldo see the Bumble-bird in action? There's a story to tell! You'll never let me forget that one, will you, huh?"

"No, Bumble," Ronaldo answered with a grin. "And I'm sure you won't let us forget it, either."

Finback shook his dorsal fin, churning the water around his long neck. "It's always the small guys you have to watch out for," he said with a sage nod. Then he looked to Ronaldo again. "I figure it's past time the three of you got back to Wyvernwood. Marian says you have something important in your possession that you need to deliver."

Shooting a look of annoyance at the unicorn, Ronaldo started to speak, but Finback continued. "Let me guard Thursis," he offered.

"I'll keep it safe just in case there are any Mers left anywhere with thoughts of returning. And the only ship I'll allow in these waters is the one that comes to pick up the castaways—if one ever does come for them."

"That will free us to return home," Marian added with a note of urgency.

Ronaldo really didn't need that much convincing. He liked Finback, and he knew the sea serpent would keep his word. It was unlikely that any Mers survived to return, but it satisfied him on some level to know that the island would be preserved and kept safe.

"I would like to ask one favor," Finback added. He looked from Ronaldo to Marian and back again, strangely hesitant. "Let me see it."

Ronaldo thought for a moment and then opened his fist. The over-sized diamond shimmered on his gray-scaled paw.

Finback stared until his black eyes began to mist with tears. "Go now," he said with a sniffle. "There's still hope in this world. Leave me here to savor that for a while."

"What is it?" Ronaldo pressed, startled by Finback's reaction. "Tell me what it is?"

But the sea serpent said no more, and after another moment he slipped back into the water and vanished.

"You'll have to carry me," Marian said unenthusiastically. "But fly low, and if you drop me I swear I'll shove my horn up your...."

"Such language!" Bumble interrupted as he nestled into Ronaldo's ear again.

Ronaldo agreed. "And from an old lady!"

Four

PERCHED WATCHFULLY on the rim of Stronghold Canyon, Chan stared southward and tried to calm the anger in his heart. He scanned the empty blue sky, studied the still branches of the thick forest on the canyon's far side, noting the lack of motion. It was as if Wyvernwood was holding its breath. As if it was waiting in dread for the next blow to fall.

His gaze flickered to the Echo Rush below. A family of deer was gathering on the sandy shore for an early morning drink from the pure, clean waters. They looked thin, even more skittish than usual. Even in the shadow of Stronghold where all creatures were welcome, they seemed genuinely afraid. Chan wondered if he could say anything at all to ease their fears. He wondered if they would listen even to a Son of Stormfire.

"*Sumapai*, have you slept at all?"

Chan glanced down at Jake as the human boy approached. *Sumapai—teacher, guide, guardian, more than brother and more than friend.* He smiled gently at the boy's flattery. Jake seldom called Chan by his name anymore. They were *Sumapai* and *Chokahai—student, acolyte, more than friend and more than son.*

"You know the answer to that," Chan said. "You've stayed up all night watching me from the shadows, and you thought I wasn't aware of it." He twisted his long neck and looked back over his shoulder toward the village square. An immense patchwork tent had quickly been sewn together from blankets and sheets and curtains and erected over his sister, Luna, on the spot where she had fallen.

"How's the shoulder?" Chan added. Luna had nearly fallen on Jake, and only a desperate dive on the boy's part had saved his life. Still, the tip of her ivory wing had clipped him and knocked him down.

"Gregor says I'm part Dragon, part lightning, and part rabbit's foot," Jake answered with a shrug. "Fast as a streak and hard to kill and luckier than I have a right to be." He touched the tightly wrapped white bandage on his upper arm. "Carola clucked and fussed like an old hen until I finally let her put this little patch on me."

Chan squeezed one eye shut and grinned as he looked at the boy. "An old hen, eh? Considering that she's half cat and all claws, you'd better not let her hear you say that. And for that matter, I wouldn't be too quick to tell the rabbits what Gregor said, either."

Jake turned away and scuffed the ground with the toe of his boot. He looked suddenly like he was supporting the weight of the world on his young, muscled shoulders. Like the deer below, he seemed nervous and worried.

"You've got something on your mind, *Chokahai*," Chan said.

Jake drew a deep, sharp breath and exhaled. "The same thing you've got on yours," he shot back. "You've been thinking about it all night. Just make the decision, *Sumapai*! I'm ready to go!"

Chan bent low and brought his scaled face close to Jake's. "Come closer," he said to the boy, and Jake leaned closer. Without warning, Chan flicked the tip of his tongue over Jake, licking him from his bare belly to the top of his head. Startled, Jake sprang away, tripped over his own feet, and fell on his backside.

Chan chuckled at his prank. "The Glass Dragon is safe, and we have time to consider our best course of action." His grin broadened as he extended a careful claw and tickled his young friend. "Or would you have us all trip over our feet and fall on our rumps?"

But Jake wasn't in the mood for fun and games. Slapping at Chan's tickling paw, he rolled away, got to his feet, and wiped a hand over his wet face. "The crows are enslaved to Degarm," he pressed. "If they came to steal the talisman, that means Degarm knows about it!"

A new voice spoke from behind them. "You should listen to the boy. Human he may be—fault of birth not to be held against him—for as humans go he's almost Dragonkin."

Chan turned his head as old Ramoses, blue wings folded tightly over his back, crept toward them. In the morning twilight, Ramoses looked tired as if he hadn't slept either. His scales possessed little of their old shine, and his claws were yellowed with age. Only his voice, so deep and vibrant, hinted at his former power.

Jake bristled. "I *am* Dragonkin!" he said, thrusting out his chest.

Ramoses inclined his head apologetically. "Of course," he said. Then he continued to Chan. "The talismans contain the last magic in the world, Son of Stormfire," he said. "Knowledge of their discovery is already spreading, first throughout Wyvernwood, and now into the nations of Man. It was inevitable that this would happen."

Knowing that the old blue Dragon spoke the truth, Chan gazed southward across the canyon again. Major news traveled fast in Wyvernwood. A bear told a satyr, who told an owl, who told a deer, who told a crow. Among the Dragonkin there was an old saying: *news has wings.*

Jake stepped closer to Chan again and stared in the same direction. "I was born in that country, and I know those people," he said fiercely. "I've seen all their cruelties and ambitions. They'll come for the Glass Dragon, *Sumapai*. They'll bend their entire will toward obtaining it."

"When did you get so wise?" Chan whispered as he drew the boy still closer with his tail.

Jake leaned against Chan and gave a small wink. "I think Carola puts something in her cookies."

"That's not wisdom," Ramoses laughed. "That's catnip. But sometimes the effect is similar."

Chan remained quiet, but he was grateful for Ramoses' laughter. If only for a brief moment, the sound of it lifted his spirits. He glanced toward the tent where his sister, Luna, lay unmoving, and he remembered the bright sound of her laughter. There was too little laughter in the world. Surreptitiously, he moved the tip of a claw toward Jake and prepared to tickle his young friend, his *Chokahai*.

"Don't even think about it," Jake warned without looking, as if he had eyes where he shouldn't have. "I'm still pouting. You licked me like a lollipop."

It was Chan's turn to shrug. "What can I say? I'm a Dragon with a sweet-tooth," he said. "But listen closely now, because you're about to hear the three most important words in the world—*you are right.*"

Jake looked up. "I'm right?"

Chan shot out his tongue and licked the boy again with enough force to send him rolling. "Go dress for a journey," he said as Jake sputtered. "Be quick, and look your best as befits an ambassador to Degarm."

Eyes widening, Jake hesitated for just a moment, and then exe-cuted a sharp backflip and ran into the village at his best speed. Chan watched the boy go with mixed emotions, always proud and always nervous about taking him into danger. Yet Jake had proven his worth more than once, and Chan had sworn never to leave him behind.

"You think you can negotiate with Degarm's leaders," Ramoses observed.

Chan chewed his lower lip and lashed his tail in controlled agitation. "You don't know me as well as you think you do, Old One," he said in a grim voice. "I have a warning to deliver, not a negotiation. I'm Stormfire's son—but I'm not Stormfire."

Ramoses closed his eyes. "There's more of your father in you than you realize," he answered.

Chan let that go, unwilling to argue the point. "Summon the Dragonkin," he said, rising to his full height and stretching out his wings. "Tell all who will come to gather on the square. But do it quietly. I don't want Luna disturbed."

Ramoses frowned. "The way she returned to us," he said. "Is it some effect of the talisman?"

Chan raised one Dragon brow as he regarded the blue Dragon. It hadn't occurred to him that Ramoses, always so smart and knowledge-able, didn't understand. He closed his eyes for just a moment, feeling for the steady pulse of the Glass Dragon once again in Stormfire's cave under Harrow's watchful eye. Yet along with it he felt another, stronger vibration. They were like two songs, flirting and interweaving in harmony, always weaving strange music in the back of his brain. In some unknown language they sang to him, and sometimes he thought he could almost understand.

"No effect of the Glass Dragon, old friend," he said at last. "And it's not one talisman we have to defend now. It's two."

With speed that belied his age, Ramoses twisted about. "You think Luna has brought back another talisman!"

"You still don't see," Chan said with a shake of his head. "You don't feel it? I don't know how or why, but she hasn't brought back a talisman." Entwining his long neck around Ramoses, he fixed his old mentor with a direct look. "*She is a talisman*," he explained. "Somehow, Luna has become *the Heart of All Dragons*."

Ramoses swallowed. Slowly, the gleam of understanding came into his eyes, and he stared over Chan's shoulder toward the tent. Then without a word, untangling himself from Chan, he flew into the air. His years seemed to melt from him as he sailed across Stronghold. With every beat of his wings he appeared to grow younger and stronger. It might have been a trick of the morning light. Or it might have been the delight he took in the news he carried.

Or perhaps, Chan thought to himself as a deep sense of satisfaction and resolve swept over him, *it's a kind of magic.*

The rising sun shimmered on Jake's Dragon-scale shirt and new black leather trousers as he sat in the saddle behind Chan's head. Around his wrist, he wore his sling like a bracelet, and on his belt he wore a pouch filled with missiles. But these were not his only weapons. Over his shoulder hung a new ashwood bow made for him by Carola's husband, Gregor, and bound in place on each side of the saddle were two quivers full of arrows.

With his handsome young rider mounted, Chan walked into the village square. All eyes turned his way as he stopped on the perimeter on the farthest side away from Luna's shelter. He scanned the crowd, noting the nervous faces, the grim expressions, the doubts, and the anger.

But he saw more than that. These were his neighbors and friends, these creatures, and they were all beautiful to him—not just the Dragons, but the minotaurs and the satyrs, the fomorians and the Wyrms, the bears and foxes and eagles. He'd grown up with many of them, and he knew them all everyone by name, and he knew with a sudden fierce passion that surprised him that he would do almost anything to protect them.

For that reason he had consented to Jake's bow. "I can protect myself well enough with my sling and my own innate skills," Jake had argued convincingly. "But with the bow I can protect others who can't protect themselves."

Chan waited until the crowd fell quiet, until all whispering ceased. He looked first to Harrow in the center of the square. "I ask you, Brother, to be the guardian of the talismans. Keep them safe, and keep Stronghold safe." He bowed his head for just a moment. "Though we're triplets, you were the first-hatched. I have no authority to give you or anyone orders, so I only ask this—I humbly ask."

Harrow regarded his brother through slitted eyes, but he nodded his head. "Once again you get to go off adventuring, and I'm left behind to play the village nursemaid and baby-sitter." But then Harrow grinned. "You'd have hatched first, but even in the egg you spent too much time contemplating your navel. I like this new Chan better."

Chan looked past his black-scaled brother. Sabu, his mother, stood near Luna's tent. Her scales were as black and glittering as Harrow's. Perhaps for that reason, Sabu had always seemed closer to Harrow than to her other children. Yet, he didn't fault her, and he knew that in this troubled time she wouldn't leave Luna's side, and that was just as well. Nor would Diana and Tiamat, who stood with her.

He turned his attention to the sky where Sakima, Kaos, and Snowsong glided in tight circles, and stretching his long neck upward, he called out to them. "Take every Dragon that will go," he told them, "and every falcon, hawk, owl, or eagle. Scour Wyvernwood and drive the crows from our forest. They are no longer welcome among us."

Raising a paw high, Bear Byron rose up on his hind legs and stepped forward. "Hey, we don't all have wings, ye know, but we'd like to do our share, too!"

Chan nodded. Bear Byron was one of Stronghold's leading citizens, and his gruff voice always bore weight. "Our enemies can't always be seen from the air," he answered. "Everyone needs to stay alert. Organize messengers and spread word throughout Wyvernwood to Grendleton and the Whispering Hills, to the Valley of Eight Winds, and to all the other villages and settlements. Get watchers on the banks of the Blackwater River and all of our waterways. Will you organize that, Byron?"

The large brown bear gave a stern nod.

Carola, the fomorian cat-woman stood nearby with the human girl-child called Little Pear at her side. "Are we at war?" she interrupted, giving voice to a question so many others feared to ask.

Chan thought for a moment as he surveyed the faces of his neighbors. "I hope not," he answered finally. "But we're not going to be caught off-guard again. Our rivers aren't going to be poisoned again. And if we're attacked again, we're going to make someone very sorry."

No cheer went up, and that was as it should be. War was something only fools got excited about. Let the humans wave their flags and sing their anthems. None of that meant anything when the blood began to flow.

Two human boys walked forward hand in hand, Trevor and Markam, Jake's younger companions. "Are you coming back, Jake?" Trevor asked. "With Ariel gone, too, who's going to look after us?"

Jake leaned down from the saddle, and Chan bent his neck even lower so that Jake could answer his friends. "This is our home," he said. "We're Dragonkin now as much as anyone here. Everyone here is gonna look out for you. And you look out for Little Pear." Reaching out, he joined his hand to Trevor and Markam's in a three-fold grip. "And when Ariel does show up, first give her a hug and welcome her back—and then you kick her butt for me."

Markam's face clouded up with doubt, and he looked on the verge of tears. "I'm worried about her, Jake," he said. "What if she never shows up? What if something's happened to her?"

"Then you still keep an eye on Pear," Jake answered in a tight voice. "And you leave the butt-kicking to me. One way or another, I'll find her or find the one that's hurt her. You count on that."

There was nothing more to say. Chan looked to Harrow again and nodded as he felt some subtle understanding pass between them. More than ever before he felt a bond with his brother. He hoped that it was more than just the songs of the talismans, which he knew Harrow also heard.

The Glass Dragon and the Heart of All Dragons. Both were home now with the Dragonkin in Stronghold. Yet there was a third, the Diamond Dragon. He couldn't help but wonder if it was also already on its way here—home.

"Are you ready, *Chokahai?*" Chan said to his rider.

"Are you done making speeches?" came Jake's sarcastic answer. "It's only morning, and there's time for a few more before the day ends or sleep overtakes us all."

Chan spread his wings. "What did you have for breakfast?" he asked, changing the subject.

Sensing some retaliation, Jake tensed up as they rose into the sky and turned southward. "Why are you asking?" he said suspiciously.

"Call me curious," Chan answered as he launched into a steep climb above the canyon. "I'm wondering how long you'll keep it down." With that, he reversed direction, folded his wings, and plummeted earthward.

Feeling the straps around his legs strain, Jake clutched his saddle tightly with both hands and let out a long, high-pitched howl. "I can take it!" he cried through gritted teeth. "I can take it!"

Chan chuckled with mischief as he swooped upward again, drawing another shriek from the boy. They might be flying into trouble, but that didn't mean they couldn't have a little fun on the way. "If you say so," he laughed.

Five

"SHE'S GONE!"

A small gray mouse-wife darted through the flaps of Luna's makeshift tent and, rising up on her hind legs, clapped her forepaws over her mouse lips as if to stifle a scream. Her wide black eyes gleamed with hysteria, and her slender tail lashed back and forth.

"She was right there before my very eyes, as purely lovely as an evening star!" the mouse-wife continued in a shrill, squeaky voice. "And then she wasn't there! I didn't even blink, I swear it!"

Sabu shot a look at the little mouse-wife, then spun toward the tent with astonishing speed. But Tiamat was faster. With a swipe of his paw, he ripped the tent open and thrust in his head. Diana tore the rest of the fabric away. A collective gasp went up from the citizens of Stronghold.

"What did you do?" Sabu roared at the trembling mouse-wife.

The little creature cringed. "What did I do? *What did I do?*" She folded her paws over her ears, and then with a shake of her head she rose up again, finding courage. "I'm a mouse, for mouse-kin's sake! What do you think I did? Carry her off under your very Dragon noses? She disappeared, I tell you, quieter than a mouse-sneeze and twice as quick!"

Tiamat brought his ruby-scaled face close to the ground. "Nobody was supposed to enter Luna's tent! Nobody was supposed to disturb her!"

"So smoke me!" the mouse-wife answered indignantly, her hysteria turning into anger. "I sneaked under the tent for a closer look at Stormfire's daughter. Now you think I'm a thief? A kidnapper? You think there's a mouse-sized black market for sleeping Dragons?" She jumped into the air in her excitement and spun about to face Sabu. "It scared the mouse-fur off me, I tell you!" She thrust a paw at Tiamat. "And now he's yelling at me, and his breath smells like

37

a chimney! It's all bad for my lungs, and not so good for my poor heart, either!"

Harrow strode through the crowd and brought his face down close to the mouse's. "Climb up on my nose, little one," he said in a soothing tone. "You wouldn't make much of a stain between Tiamat's oversized toes, but never tempt a Dragon with a temper."

At the forefront of the crowd, Bear Byron nodded. "That there's a good rule," he agreed. "Take it to heart, Missie Mousie."

Sabu frowned at Harrow. "No one's going to hurt her," she said sternly. "We just want to know what's happened to Luna!"

The mouse-wife scampered up onto Harrow's nose and clung tightly to his scales as he straightened to meet his mother's black-eyed gaze. "I don't have an answer," he said, feeling the little mouse's racing heart through the sensitive tip of his snout and taking pity on her. "But if this small one says she just disappeared, then I believe her." Tiamat roared again, upset and afraid for his missing mate. "Dragons don't disappear! No one does! She's got to be lying?"

Diana spoke up more reasonably. "If she didn't disappear, then where did she go? She couldn't have sneaked away without someone noticing."

The little mouse-wife paced on Harrow's nose and perched between his eyes. "Hmmmph!" she snorted. "Take it from an expert—Dragons don't *sneak!*"

"I told you before," Harrow insisted. "After we drove the griffins from Redclaw, Luna and I were flying home. One moment, she was right behind me. The next moment she wasn't. I thought she'd turned away, and I searched everywhere for her without finding even a trace."

Looking only a little bit ridiculous with the mouse-wife between his eyes, he twisted his neck and leaned closer to his mother. "It's the talisman," he whispered with a measure of awe. "There's magic at work."

Sabu stared long and hard at her son, and her dark eyes glittered, not with excitement, but with fear. "But is Luna controlling this talisman?" she asked. "Or is the talisman controlling her?"

"Magic!" Tiamat snarled. With another swipe of his paw, he scattered the shreds of the tent, sending ribbons of fabric into the air. "Who needs it? We're better off without the stuff!"

Luna woke to an unusual sensation, a warm tingling like gentle fire spreading all through her from the tip of her ivory-scaled nose to the tip of her tail, from wingtip to wingtip. She stared at the motley tent roof with a small sense of panic as the sensation filled her eyes. Her thoughts churned in confusion. Where was she? Stronghold, probably. On the grassy ground, definitely. Vague memories of a homecoming stirred in her brain, of Chan and Harrow, of falling. Scratching the ground with one claw, she struggled to rise, but before she could even lift her head, the strange sensation surged.

Quicker than a heartbeat the tent roof vanished, and a bright canopy of stars took its place. The sensation weakened, ebbed like an out-bound wave, and yet an aura of its warmth and power remained, a tingle in her blood, in her heart. *It's connected to me*, she realized as she rose uncertainly to her feet.

The wind gusted on her Dragon face, and the sound of dry leaves rustling filled the air, causing her to turn. The treetops of Wyvernwood swayed under the force of the breeze, and nighthawks and owls sprang from the branches to glide through the darkness, riding the currents with their sharp gazes locked on her. She could sense their surprise.

"You think you're surprised!" she muttered half to herself.

She knew these woods and recognized the stark, clear-cut border that marked the edge of the clear space in which she stood. It was no natural clearing, but a wide range of devastation and destruction caused by griffins, who had mercilessly ripped the trees and shrubs from the land. With a low growl, she turned again and with narrowed eyes gazed on the broken walls of Redclaw.

The moonlight limned the five tall towers and the shattered rooftops of the now-abandoned fortress, lending the ancient structure a mystery and an eerie beauty that it didn't deserve. It was as old as Wyvernwood, she knew, and perhaps older. And although no one knew it but she, there were sleeping things below those towers that were best left undisturbed.

She glanced at her shadow on the ground, but it wasn't a shadow at all, because shadows were dark things. Her shadow, if it could be called that, was pale light. It lit the ground and the air all around her. She displayed her wings, spreading them to their fullest, more than a little puzzled by their strange glow, and more than a little afraid.

Something stirred in the ruins of Redclaw's shattered gate. A loose rock clattered, and a footstep followed so softly that only a Dragon's ears could have heard it. Luna stared, yet she saw nothing. "Who's there?" she called.

The night became suddenly still. The wind died, and the trees ceased their rattling. The birds circling in the sky fled. Around the ancient fortress walls the shadows turned blacker and deeper even as the moon's limnification ignited its edges and angles.

Luna stretched her long neck toward the gate, her eyes narrowing. Then gathering her courage, she moved a few steps closer. There was nothing there, she told herself. And yet there was something, and it was watching her. She took another step closer, and stopped.

The darkness at the very center of the gate parted like the edges of a curtain, and a small figure appeared with a grin on her child's face and eyes that sparkled like stars. Her long black hair stirred around nude shoulders as if in a wind that wasn't there, and in one hand she held a silver mirror.

Luna gasped and started forward with a cry of excitement. "Ariel!"

The little girl held up her empty hand in a warning as she shook her head. "I'm not ready yet," she answered in a firm voice. Then she softened a little. "But I felt you near and woke to come say hello."

"I miss you," Luna whispered, lowering her head as she remembered the brash, impetuous Ariel who had faced down night-trolls and fought invading navies and who, by her bravery and daring, had become Luna's rider. She looked up again. This Ariel was different somehow, not so brash, and more mysterious.

Ariel's grin became a smile. "We'll never be apart, Luna," she answered, sounding more wise and knowing than a child should have. "But I can't stay here now, and neither can you." She turned her mirror carefully and held it up to Luna. "I want you to see yourself, my forever-friend, and know how beautiful you've become!"

Luna gasped again as shards of radiance exploded from Ariel's mirror. An image swirled on the glass, a Dragon face that she barely recognized as her own amid all the aching light, and behind it, or maybe upon it another face, hers and yet not hers.

And then the night filled with a rush of voices, songs and choruses that might have come from the mirror or might not have. Luna reeled.

Without thinking, she flexed her wings and rose into the sky. "I don't understand!" she cried.

But Ariel didn't answer, nor could Luna find the child anywhere on the ground. The voices swelled in her ears, and the strange tingling heat she'd felt before engulfed her senses. In the blink of an eye Red-claw vanished.

Luna stifled a scream as she stared into a blood-red sunset over a mountain range whose soaring peaks looked as sharp as sharks' teeth. The land below her looked as treacherous. Twisted trees jutted up from the earth like bony clawing hands, and pools of floodwater shimmered blackly under the fading sun's weird glow. "By all the fires of the world...!" she muttered. "I'm trapped in some kind of nightmare!" In fear and frustration, she lifted her head and blasted a great plume of flame skyward.

As if in response, the mountain peaks came alive with a furious rush of movement. Immense serpents on impossibly thin wings sprang upward and undulated through the twilight toward her. The grotesque nature of their unlikely flight unnerved Luna, and she blew another blast of fire to warn the creatures away.

Still they charged forth, scores of them—*Dragons*, she realized, but no Dragons she'd ever seen before! In answer to her fire, one puffed out its whiskered cheeks and exhaled a wind so chill it nearly froze her eyes. Two more of the creatures, flashing above her, shook rain from their wings. Claws glittered like argent metal and jaws clacked and snapped. But they offered no other threat as they circled around and around her.

"Can you speak?" Luna cried. "What are you?"

The wind-Dragon passed by her right wingtip. *Cousins.* The answer came on a puff of cool air. *Qin, we call ourselves.*

Another flew close to her left wingtip. *Extinct, we thought your line! Pleased we are to learn not!*

Stay! came the wind-voice of yet another.

"I can't!" Luna shouted in fearful desperation as music filled her ears again and she felt the surging tingle. "I'm unanchored somehow. Is this even Undersky?"

Undersky! The rain-Dragons swept by on either side, repeating the word in awe as if they hadn't heard it in a long time. *Undersky!* Or maybe the word didn't come from those wonderful creatures at all, but from the voices and the songs! She couldn't tell. The sounds were blending together, and it was maddening!

In the next heartbeat everything changed again.

As far as she could see the world tossed and rolled, glittering like liquid glass under clouds of bright stars and a shimmering moon that hung in the sky like a round smile. A salt breeze filled her wings as she glided in a wide arc above the waves. A whale and its calf cut frothy wakes through the black water as they swam side by side over the gentle waves. Admiring their grace and power, Luna followed them for a while before turning away.

Gliding higher into the night, she scanned the horizons for any sign of land. Not even an island or an atoll broke the fluid surface. In ever widening circles, Luna continued to fly as a troubling sense of oppression crept over her. Little by little, the eerie beauty of the unbroken sea faded, and she saw it instead as a strange kind of wasteland as desolate and empty as any she'd ever seen.

Gazing upward, she searched the heavens for Rono or for any other familiar star by which she might navigate. She found only confusion and a growing unease.

> *I spy! I spy!*
> *Spread across the velvet sky*
> *Abundant stars wherever I roam,*
> *But none to guide me safely home.*

The old child's rhyme stole unbidden into her thoughts, and with unconscious effort she rewrote it to reflect her uncertainty. Unlike her father, Stormfire, or her brothers, or even old Ramoses she'd never been interested in poetry or story-telling. But now, as loneliness and fear took seed inside her, she drew solace from the words.

> *Where am I? Where am I*
> *In this dark and endless sky?*
> *If my wish could come to be*
> *I'd be home with my family.*

As if in answer a rushing tingle shot through her, and the pure white light that filled her wings flared with such brightness that the glow of it seemed to set the sea on fire. For the briefest moment, Luna saw her reflection on the surface as she'd seen it in Ariel's mirror, and she gasped as once again the world changed.

Bright day replaced the darkness and the night. Sunlight warmed her wings and her Dragon face, and the sharp tang of salt air gave way to familiar forest smells. Luna's fear melted, and her spirits soared as she studied the hills and the woodlands over which she now flew.

Wyvernwood! She rejoiced inside, sure that she was finally home and that her wish had come true just as she'd wished it. The Blackwater River cut its wide path through the land immediately below her, and far off to the left she spied the reassuring peaks of the Imagination Mountains.

There was no sign of Stronghold, though, so she wasn't exactly home, and she quickly determined from the mountain peaks and from the river's course that she was far south of the canyon and the village. Dipping her wing, she turned eastward and in no time found herself above Marrow Lake.

At least I know now where I am, she thought with a grateful sense of relief. *There must be a poem in that, too.*

But Luna didn't get a chance to compose it. A motion in the southern sky caught her attention, a bare red-orange dot like a drop of flame that shimmered in the sunlight as it sailed above the trees. Another Dragon, she realized with some puzzlement, seemingly headed for Degarm. Then as she focused more keenly on the shape, her heart leaped with excitement.

"Chan!"

The exuberant shout ripped from her. Of course, he was too far away to hear. Filled with sudden curiosity, Luna banked away from Marrow Lake and straining to her utmost speed, raced after her brother. What was he doing so far from Stronghold? Hoping to attract his attention, she exhaled a blast of fire and called his name again.

But it wasn't her voice she heard. Wild music flashed through her brain, and the world shifted again in a tingling instant. Chan and Wyvernwood and all that was familiar vanished. Sunlight gave way to darkness again—but no darkness she had ever known before.

Luna stared, numb at first, and then with a rapidly growing horror at the immense blue globe that dominated the black sky. The wind in her wings felt thin, *wrong*! Heart pounding, she landed on a jagged pinnacle. The air in her lungs tasted strange!

With a dreadful reluctance, she stared upward again. An intense vertigo swept over her. Unbalanced, she lost her clawed grip and fell backward. Only by reflex did she manage to spread her wings, slow her fall, and settle with rough grace on the dusty, grassless plain at the pinnacle's base.

Luna squeezed her eyes shut and tried to will herself to wake up. She flicked out her tongue to sample the air; it tasted just as strange, just as wrong. Once more she opened her eyes.

The blue globe revolved with slow majesty, filling half the sky as it turned in its ponderous pace. Luna screamed once, her mind reeling, rejecting what her eyes saw. As if hypnotized, she watched the parade of continents and islands, the gentle swirl of vast oceans and seas, the teasing white veils of clouds that danced ghostlike over it all.

"I spy! I spy!" Luna whispered in a shivery voice. She hesitated, swallowing before she could form the next word. "*Undersky*," she hesitated again, unable to finish her rhyme, her gaze locked on the blue world overhead as one thought crowded out all others.

I'm standing on the moon!

Six

RONALDO STUDIED THE VAST BLUE EXPANSE of the Windy Sea as he sailed on widespread wings high above its tossing surface. Approaching noon, the late-morning sun scattered diamonds across the water and played intricate tricks of light in the mist and spray. With an artist's appreciation for such effects, he wondered how he could capture them with his paints.

In the western distance he spied the coastline of Wyvernwood. So far away, it appeared only as a deep green darkness on the horizon, yet it filled him with an overwhelming sense of home, and a pair of tears leaked from his Dragon eyes. Not so long ago he'd thought he would never return to Wyvernwood, that he didn't really fit there anymore. He'd changed so much. Yet, as he approached the coast, his thoughts turned to his comfortable cave, his paints, and all his friends in the Whispering Hills.

A sharp sensation in his right paw interrupted his memories. Flinching, he dipped a wing and veered into an unexpected updraft. His stomach lurched for an instant as he fought to compensate and correct his flight.

Clutched securely in his claws, the Last Unicorn in the World writhed and groaned. "By the fires, I'm gonna be sick and puke all over your shiny scales!"

Ronaldo craned his neck and glared at Marian with a mixture of surprise and amusement. "You bit me!" he accused.

Her white mane streamed in the wind, and her wide eyes looked unfocused as she surveyed the rolling sea. "We're too high!" she moaned as a tremor shook her body, "and I swear my head's competing with the rest of the world to see which can spin faster." She shut her eyes as she kicked the air with her hooves. "And you're squeezing me too tightly! If only Finback had taken me home, I could have ridden safely on his back!"

"You want me to put you down?" Chuckling, Ronaldo relaxed his grip ever so slightly.

Marian gasped. "If you drop me, Ronaldo, I swear I'll shove my horn so far up your backside your screams will shatter timber from one end of Wyvernwood to the other!"

Ronaldo's chuckle became a deep-throated laugh. "That assumes I drop you over Wyvernwood, doesn't it?" He relaxed his grip again, drawing another gasp from Marian before he wrapped her securely in both of his front paws. "Why are you so nervous?" he asked, turning serious. "I've carried you before."

"Over land, yes," she acknowledged, "but not over sea. The water just won't hold still, and my breakfast..." She stopped abruptly, and her eyes unfocused again.

"Maybe you shouldn't think about breakfast," Ronaldo advised.

A tiny voice spoke in the Gray Dragon's left ear. "At least she had breakfast," Bumble muttered unhappily as he shifted his position near Ronaldo's eardrum. "The bravest hummingbird in the world is starving to death, but does anybody care? I'm weak with hunger, and my head is reeling. I can barely remember what petunias look like. Or begonias, or ocotillo." With a despairing moan, he shifted position again, turning first on one side and then on the other with a soft, ticklish flutter of his wings.

"What I wouldn't give right now," he continued with a dramatic sigh, "for some delicious bottle brush nectar to wet my parched and sun-swollen tongue! Or if just once more before I die in this foulsmelling wax factory I could savor the smallest drop of honeysuckle!"

Ronaldo's eyes narrowed. "Wax factory?" he shouted. "Are you talking about my ears?"

The tiny hummingbird shifted again. "Well, they really could stand a washing," he answered in a lower voice. "I'm not sure I'll ever get the stains out of my feathers."

Marian gave another nervous gasp as Ronaldo shook his head to dislodge Bumble. "All right, you little hitch-hiking freeloader," he answered sharply, his vanity wounded. "Out you go! We're close enough that you can make your own way to Wyvernwood!"

Thrown from his perch, Bumble tumbled through the air. Then, snapping his wings wide, he looked at the tossing sea, gave a short hummingbird scream, and flashed back to Ronaldo's ear again. "Nice ear! Safe ear!" he proclaimed, shivering. "Best ear in the whole wide world!"

"That's better," Ronaldo said with some smugness. "I'm going to have to start calling you *Grumble*."

"Call him anything you want," Marian suggested with a weakly sarcastic grimace, "so long as you call when you see the first flower bed."

For a few precious moments everyone became quiet again and Ronaldo flew as gently as he could to avoid upsetting Marian. The shoreline of Wyvernwood loomed ever closer. Its white sand beaches made a fine, glittering line between the blue of the sea and the deep green of the forest, and the highest treetops waved in the breeze as if beckoning them home.

Home.

There was that word again.

He squeezed his right hindmost paw around the hard, faceted shape of the Diamond Dragon, which he carried there. He wondered if Marian was right, if it really was one of Stormfire's talismans. As he gazed ahead at Wyvernwood, he almost hoped that it wasn't for he knew the legend of the talismans as well as any Dragon.

If the beautiful stone that he carried was indeed one of those magical objects, then Wyvernwood might not be *home* much longer. He wasn't sure how he felt about that. Again his thoughts turned to his comfortable cave and his beloved Whispering Hills.

Then, telling himself that he was worrying too much, he shrugged. The Diamond Dragon was only one of three talismans, and only when all three were found and united would they point the way to a new homeland for the Dragonkin. He'd be old and gray before that happened.

Well certainly old, he was sure. He was already gray.

Ronaldo felt Bumble shifting around again, then felt diminutive talons lock hold on the outer edge of his ear. The sensation was mildly annoying, and he was about to complain, but with a soft, frantic buzz of wings, Bumble retreated inward again to nestle near Ronaldo's eardrum.

"You know about the short memories of Bumble-kin," the hummingbird whispered uneasily.

Ronaldo caught the edge in Bumble's voice. "Your memory is getting better," came his cautious answer. "Why, you remember things for days at a time now without constant reminding. And why are you whispering?"

Bumble shivered, and Ronaldo felt it like an itch in his ear.

"Poor sick Marian!" the hummingbird answered, jumping up. "With her upset innards, Bumble fears to upset her more!"

"More?" Ronaldo said, his voice rising in irritation. He wished that Bumble would keep still. "Bumble-bird, what are you flapping your bill about?"

Bumble fluttered his wings, causing Ronaldo to wince and veer sideways. Marian groaned and hung her head. "I'm not gonna be sick!" she muttered, slurring her words. "I'm not gonna be sick!" And then, with more conviction, "I *am* gonna be sick! All over your pretty scales and your pretty golden claws!"

"Do it, and I'll drop you horn-first on your head the moment we reach land and leave you sticking in the ground like a road sign," Ronaldo promised.

"Warning: unicorn crossing," Bumble whispered in a low secretive voice, sounding a little more like himself. Then suddenly the little bird stiffened and became motionless as if frozen. A moment later he resumed his whispering, but it was a quieter, thoughtful whispering. "Hmmm," he said. "There's something in that. Something important." He began to tap one tiny foot. "Drat my tiny Bumble-brain and double-drat my memory. What was it? Something important." He tapped his foot faster.

"Stop that!" Ronaldo snapped.

Bumble stood still for a moment, but just as Ronaldo began to relax, the little hummingbird became excited. "I remember! I remember!" he cried. In the tight confines of Ronaldo's middle ear, he started jumping up and down and bouncing like a small feathered ball. "Warning! Warning! Warning!" he shouted.

Half maddened by the sensations in his ear, Ronaldo roared and rolled into another updraft. Marian groaned loudly as the strong warm current rushed suddenly around them and swept them higher into the sky. "Two words to remember, Ronaldo!" With her eyes squeezed tightly shut, Marian choked out the words. "Hummingbird jelly!"

"When Bumble screamed," the hummingbird said, ignoring the unicorn's remark. "Did anyone ask why? Nooooooooo!" He shook his small head as he tapped his foot again inside the Dragon's ear. "Not fear of water! Not fear of flying home alone! Bumble is the bravest Bumble in the world!"

Marian went limp between Ronaldo's paws. She didn't look well at all as she rolled one eye toward the Gray Dragon. "His ego's getting bigger than he is," she said. "Have mercy, Ronaldo, and just drop me now."

A long, slithery tongue tickled the inside of the Dragon's ear as Bumble answered Marian with a rude noise.

Ronaldo loved his friends, but he found himself growing weary of their grousing and more than impatient with Bumble's antics. He turned his gaze toward Wyvernwood's shoreline. It wasn't far away now. "Mind your manners!" he told the hummingbird. "And tell me what you think you remembered?"

"I remembered to warn you," Bumble answered in a petulant tone, hating to be scolded.

Ronaldo frowned. He hadn't meant to hurt his little friend's feelings, but by the fires even a Dragon's patience had its limits. "Warn me?" he said. "About what?"

Bumble began to tap his foot again. "Let me see if I can remember." The tapping stopped and then resumed. "No, not that," he said. The tapping stopped and resumed again. "Not that, either."

"Hummingbird jelly," Ronaldo murmured through tight-clenched jaws.

"About the griffins," the hummingbird quickly supplied.

Ronaldo drew a deep breath. "What griffins?"

Bumble grew still and whispered directly into Ronaldo's eardrum. "The ones that are following us."

The Gray Dragon twisted his head around and glanced back over one wing, veering off course again as he strained for a view.

Marian gasped. "Where did you ever learn to fly?" she complained. "I've seen bats hold a straighter line!"

Ronaldo barely heard. His heart began to hammer as he searched the sky far behind them. The bright sun almost hurt his eyes as he searched for shadows against its light. Off to the north, a low bank of wispy clouds drifted. He studied them carefully deciding that they were too thin to hide griffins.

The Gray Dragon frowned. As crazy as Bumble could be, Ronaldo didn't doubt that the little hummingbird had seen something; he'd proven himself a reliable partner on too many occasions. Yet no matter where he looked—above, behind, or all around—the sky remained empty.

Fixing his sight on the shoreline ahead, and mindful of Marian's discomfort, he tried to relax and fly a gentle course. Once they were home with solid ground beneath them everyone would feel more at ease. Still, Bumble's odd warning continued to worry him. Craning his neck back over his wing he searched the sky once again to no avail.

Then, on an impulse, he craned his neck the other way and looked under his wing instead, past his tail, and down toward the sea. The sunlight sparkled like fire on the water, dazzling, and it took a moment for his eyes to adjust. When they did, a chill shivered through his spine.

Eight griffins flew just above the waves, pacing Ronaldo and flying so low that they cast no meaningful shadows to give themselves away. It was a marvelous tactic that even a Dragon could admire, especially for creatures that were not by nature given to stealth.

Alarmed and yet curious, Ronaldo angled southward. Careful to keep their distance, yet never losing pace, the griffins did the same. After a few moments, Ronaldo turned northward and watched as his pursuers maneuvered to follow.

"You sadistic, overgrown worm!" Marian grumbled. "You're deliberately *trying* to make me sick!"

Ronaldo ignored his unicorn companion. She remained blithely unaware of their danger, nor would it serve any purpose to tell her. Carrying her in his claws over water, he was in the worst possible situation for a fight. Licking his Dragon lips, he tilted to the right again and watched the griffins match his course.

This time, though, the griffins didn't just keep the pace. They charged forward, climbing high and fast, forsaking stealth.

They know I've spotted them, Ronaldo thought grimly. *Now they'll attack before I reach land.* Surprised by his own calmness, he gazed toward Wyvernwood again, and his eyes narrowed to slits. There was nothing to do but race for it.

"Hold on," he said.

"Hold on to what?" Marian snapped. "*You* hold on! You're carrying me!"

With a powerful beat of his wings, Ronaldo surged forward. Stretching his sleek body into the wind, he clutched Marian tightly and drew her close to his chest.

"Whoa, big boy!" she cried, suddenly alert. "I didn't know you cared that much!" As if her sickness had passed, the Last Unicorn in the World turned her head from side to side, searching the skies as she added, "We're in some trouble again?"

"It's the glue that binds us," Ronaldo answered. "If we're not chasing trouble, trouble's chasing us!"

Bumble called excitedly from inside Ronaldo's ear, his small voice barely audible over the rush of wind. "This time it's chasing us! But we kicked their furry butts once!" Leaning out of Ronaldo's ear, he raised one thin wing. "Yo! Bring it on, you ugly bunch of mother...!"

Putting on another burst of speed, Ronaldo flattened his ears, and Bumble tumbled backward with an awkward cry before he could finish his challenge.

"Damn!" Marian said. "That bird's getting an attitude!"

Ronaldo didn't argue. He glanced backward once more, and his heart began to hammer. The griffins were gaining rapidly. Drawing a deep breath, he blew a powerful blast of fire, hoping it might slow his attackers, but he knew his best bet was to reach land as swiftly as he could.

"Whatever happens," Marian shouted, "don't drop that jewel!"

The sandy beaches of Wyvernwood shimmered invitingly, and just beyond the swaying trees waved him forward. *Home!* He repeated the word over and over like a drumbeat in his head. *Home! Home! Home!* The forest sprawled before him, rising and rolling over ancient hills, descending into mist-shrouded valleys and washes. He took it all in from the air as he raced for *home*, and all the rich scents of earth and leaves, grass and flowers, all the wonderful welcoming odors that he loved so well rose up on the breeze, encouraging him to even greater speed.

"Drop me, Ronaldo!" Marian cried. Half blinded by her own lashing mane, she had twisted her neck around to mark the griffins' advance. "You won't make it carrying me! The talisman is more important!"

"You're the Last Unicorn in the World!" Ronaldo answered through tightly clenched jaws, and for him it was answer enough.

But Marian persisted. "I can swim! It's not that far!"

Ronaldo's only response was to tighten his grasp around Marian and to push himself even harder. His muscles strained, and his wings began to ache. He had no intention of dropping Marian, but fearing that his strength might give out or that the griffins might knock her from his grip, he swooped suddenly low, skimming just above the glistening surface.

The griffins, flying in close formation, were above him now and just behind. Raising his head without slowing, Ronaldo exhaled another blast of fire and was rewarded with a cacophony of griffin screams.

"Pretty flames," Marian reported, "but no scorch marks. It only scattered them!"

Bumble banged on the inside of Ronaldo's ear. "Lemme at 'em! Lemme at 'em!" he shouted but, digging in his small talons, he remained safely where he was.

A pair of griffins zoomed up on Ronaldo's left flank, their feathered wings rippling with the speed of their charge. For all their viciousness and savagery, the Gray Dragon could still admire the power and grace they displayed. Turning his head ever so slightly, he met the gaze of one of the creatures. Its eyes were filled with anger and bloodlust.

"Okay, I've admired it," he muttered to himself. With that, he banked suddenly, dipping the tip of one stiffened wing into the Windy Sea. A wall of water shot upward as he cut a trough through the waves. It caught the pair of griffins with stunning force, knocking them out of the air.

"Finback would be impressed!" Marian called.

Ronaldo allowed himself a tight grin as he changed course for Wyvernwood again. "I'm rather impressed myself."

"Don't be too impressed," Marian warned as she swept her gaze around.

"Griffins to the left of us!" Bumble sang as he fluttered his wings in excitement. "Griffins to the right! Another up above, and it's looking grim tonight! Go, team!"

Marian blew a rude noise. "It's daytime!"

"Sure, but that didn't rhyme!" Bumble shot back, blowing an equally rude noise. "Here they come! Dive! Dive!"

Desperately, Ronaldo raised his head again and blasted a stream of fire. He couldn't see the griffins, nor did he try to find them. The shoreline wasn't far now. He was almost home! Then he could release Marian, drop the talisman into her care, and turn and fight!

But as if in answer to his blast of fire, two more great blasts of red-orange flame erupted in the skies above Wyvernwood. Ronaldo's heart leaped at the sight, and a moment later two Dragons sailed over the treetops along with a veritable army of eagles, hawks, and owls.

"That's Fleer and Snowsong!" Marian cried in recognition.

Sunlight danced on Fleer's emerald scales as he charged from the forest and out over the water. Right at his side, white Snowsong blew another stream of fire that touched the sea surface and raised a roiling cloud of steam.

Disdaining greetings, Fleer, Snowsong and their army hit the Griffins. The sky filled with feathers and blood, with caws and screeches and the stench of singed griffin fur.

Bumble bounced up and down at the edge of Ronaldo's ear as the Gray Dragon landed on the white sand and turned to watch the battle. "Now that's what I call shock and awe!" the little hummingbird shouted. "Mission accomplished and an end to all hostilities! Or at least an end to the hostiles!"

Ronaldo paid little attention. Setting Marian safely down, he folded his wings tightly against his body and tried to draw a breath. Bands of pain squeezed his chest. Every part of him ached. "We made it," he murmured. Looking up, he tried to focus on the battle, but the blue sky, the sunlight, and the action all spun like a crazy kaleidoscope of color.

The last of his strength drained away, and Ronaldo fell forward. The claws of one paw sifted weakly through the sand, which sparkled before his eyes as the surf rushed almost to meet the tip of his nose. "Home," he whispered. "There's no place like home."

Exhausted, the Gray Dragon closed his eyes.

Seven

LUNA STARED IN UNBLINKING FASCINATION and terror
at the blue world floating in the heavens above her. The shimmering
swirl of clouds upon its slowly revolving surface possessed a mesmeric
quality, and the thin air set her head to spinning. Her lungs began to
ache, and her eyes filled with a chilling cold.

With an effort of will she jerked her gaze away. A despairing cry
tore from her lips as she studied the jagged mountains, the ashen seas
of dust, the awesome craters and escarpments that scarred the landscape. So much desolation and harshness!

And yet there was beauty, too, a starkly cold and lifeless beauty
that seared itself into her heart and spirit. No blade of grass, no flower,
no tree grew for as far as she could see. Nothing moved except the
smallest eddy of dust in a weak and dying zephyr.

The ache in Luna's lungs became a burning pain. She sucked another
breath, fighting panic. The thin air was barely enough for a Dragon to
breathe! The pounding of her heart filled her ears with a frantic frightened rhythm. Her senses reeled as her gaze refused to focus any longer.

Desperately, she lifted her face once more to the blue world above
and spread her wings. With a furious beating, she tried to rise toward
it, but her effort only stirred a cloud of dust that filled her mouth and
nose and choked her.

Unable to fly, she strained once more to focus her vision and
watched the brown land masses parade across the world. In vain she
searched them, hoping for one sight of Wyvernwood. Thoughts of her
mother and brothers flashed through her mind, of her friend, Diana,
and of Ariel.

"Tiamat!" she whispered as she wrapped her wings around her body.
The cold was beginning to stab and sting. It penetrated her veins,

reached for her heart, but she clung to a vision of her ruby-scaled mate. "If I die here, I'll take your memory to comfort me!"

But another sensation worked its way through the stinging cold, a tingle and an itch that brought strange warmth and a music that shattered the oppressive silence. Luna knew its significance, and she rejoiced, glad to leave such a wasted place. But at the same time an involuntary cry ripped from her. "Where?" she demanded of the force that seized her. "Where are taking me now? Why?"

Bracing herself, she tried not to blink, curious to see whatever she might see on the way to her next destination. But despite herself, she did blink, or at least a momentary blackness filled her eyes, and when she opened them again she gasped.

The stench of Man filled her nostrils and another overpowering miasma of filth and sewage. She blinked again against the intense midmorning sun as she turned her face up toward it. She welcomed the hot wind and the waves of heat that chased the moon-chill from her bones and knew that she was home again.

Well, not *home* exactly.

A rock bounced off the end of her nose. A gruff voice shouted, "Dragon!"

Turning her face away from the warming sun, Luna took note of her new surroundings. Walls of wood and stone rose around her, and beyond that rooftops and minarets of astounding height. She found herself in some kind of square or courtyard, and around a large fountain men and women with their children stood frozen in mid-step. They stared at her with looks of fear on their pink faces.

Then, as if some signal had been given, they began to run. Screaming women dropped laundry baskets, scattering clothing on the cobbled ground or upon the pool that surrounded the fountain. Men snatched up the children and tucked them under arms as they fled with their wives. A braver man threw another rock before he ran. It bounced harmlessly off Luna's side, but an empty basket flew through the air, followed by a weightier half-filled water urn. Near her left foot an armored soldier drew his sword as he backed uncertainly away.

"You call that a weapon?" Luna said, smiling to reassure the soldier. Without lifting her foot, she extended one shining ivory claw. It was almost as long as the soldier was tall, and he jumped away. She smiled again. "That's a weapon."

Turning pale, the soldier threw down his sword and joined the others in a mad dash to the courtyard gate. "Hey, wait!" Luna shouted with some amusement. "I come in peace and with good will!"

Humans never believed that line, of course. Her contact with the world of Man had been limited, but she'd had just enough experience to know that much. She gazed at the soldier's abandoned sword. What was it about humans that made them think a weapon was the answer to everything?

With a shrug, she spread her wings in the now empty courtyard and rose into the sky. It felt wonderful to fly again, and she swept over the city in a wide arc, gliding low above the narrow streets and buildings, weaving a course among the gilt-roofed minarets and the white marble towers.

As she flew, her eyes began to widen with a gentle sense of wonder, and she wheeled back among the structures, circling some of them numerous times. Never had she seen such impressive architecture! Everywhere she looked the squares and courtyards were filled with fountains or sculpture gardens. Soaring arches lined the broad roadways, seeming to serve no purpose other than ornamentation, and graceful bridges spanned the tranquil river that flowed through the city's center. Upon the river, boats and ferries floated, many carved to resemble fish or birds.

"I didn't know that Man was capable of such beauty and accomplishment!" Luna said to herself as she turned back for yet another tour of the city. And yet, despite the grandeur and beauty, she wrinkled her nose, for there was still the ever-present stench.

A flurry of motion caught her attention. Atop a high wall surrounding one of the tallest structures, lines of men scurried into position. Sunlight glinted on helmets and armor, on the tips of arrows and spear points. Bows bent in straining arms.

Luna flew closer as she studied their grim gazes and frightened faces, and her Dragon lips drew into a taut line. This was the Mankind she knew. "Put down your weapons!" she called hoping against hope as she circled the tower. "Extend a welcome hand! Just say the word, and let me land! Can we not become friends? Let us speak poetry together!"

A great cry went up from the men on the tower, and they sent their answer on a black cloud of feathered shafts. The tiny barbs shattered or bounced harmlessly off her scales, though a few embedded in the

thinner leather membranes of her wings. With a shout of frustration
she shook them loose, and circling the tower yet again she drew a deep
breath. A single blast of flame would teach them all better manners!

But Luna drew up suddenly and beat her wings with such power
that she hovered in midair before the scores of archers as they fitted
new shafts to their bowstrings, and though they raised their weapons,
she held back her fire.

Pale, terrified faces turned up toward her. Luna saw the trembling of
the archers' hands, the shaking of their arms as they took aim. Sweat
beaded on helmeted brows, and pink tongues darted over lips dry with
fear. Her anger melted, transformed itself into pity and sadness.

Would it always be so with these humans?

"How can I convince you that I mean no harm!" she shouted with
a growing sense of desperation.

Yet before the last word left her Dragon mouth, another swarm of
arrows zipped across the sky. She barely felt their tiny stings, and yet
they struck a deeper blow that shivered through her heart. "Stop!"
she urged as the archers reached into their quivers.

Luna squeezed her eyes shut. *What can I say?* she thought. *What can
I do?*

But there was nothing to say or do. A familiar sensation tingled
through her, and the very air around her surged with an explosion of
music.

The City of Man disappeared, and the landscape changed. Spreading her wings on a fresh wind, Luna gazed down upon a barren, trampled plain and an army of marching men.

The music surged again. Mountains rose up around Luna, old
mountains with weathered peaks and tree-covered slopes and shad-
owed valleys that spilled down into thick gray mist. Luna dipped a
wing and glided on a chill breeze past a low, rounded summit, and a
shrill scream greeted her.

What, in Stormfire's name, was that? Heart pounding at the unexpected sound, Luna turned back. The echo of the scream still played
among the hills and canyons, and she listened to it fade. In all her life,
she'd never heard such a sound!

Then, the scream came again, and near that summit from behind
an outcropping of creamy boulders, a creature gazed at her with lonely
and bitter eyes.

Luna's breath caught in her throat as she swept past. She'd never seen such a creature, and yet she knew it. She'd heard the tales of its lion's body and its human face and its blood-freezing scream.

A manticore! she cried in silent amazement. *But they were all long dead!*

As if in denial, the manticore screamed again and slipped once more behind the rocks. Luna swiftly turned back to the outcropping. Yet, try as she might she could find no trace of the creature.

"Come out!" she called. "I am Luna, Stormfire's daughter!" But the only sound she heard was the gentle moan of the breeze and the eerie susurrus of the mist over grass and leaves.

She thought of the manticore, perhaps the last of its kind, and remembered in particular its eyes. Such loneliness in those old eyes! A rush of questions flashed through Luna's mind. Had the creature been left behind in the Great Exodus to Wyvernwood? Had it stayed behind of its own will in these desolate mountains?

Like a whisper of an echo the mountains gave an answer. *Home,* the mountains said, and the valleys murmured, *home.*

"I'm beginning to understand." Luna cast the words onto the breeze and listened as they chased each other from peak to peak.

Opening her wings, she soared higher into the sky, her heart swelling with excitement, knowing what was to come.

Tingling, music, and darkness.

Harrow lay curled on the floor of his father's cave with all the volumes that comprised the Book of Stormfire spread around him. Even though it was summer in Wyvernwood a warm fire burned in the fireplace. The heat meant nothing to a Dragon, and the glow provided pleasant light for reading.

But he wasn't reading now. With his chin resting on one of the large open pages and his eyes closed, he dreamed of all the faraway places that he feared he would never see. His father had seen them, though, and written about them. The tales filled Harrow with a sense of excitement and wonder, but also with a sense of sadness.

So many nations, so many glittering kingdoms had already passed away. The Book contained pages of them, lists of lands that were old and gone when Stormfire had been young, and places older still that even Stormfire had only heard about.

In his dream, Harrow saw the wind-swept deserts of Aruzun-La. He splashed in the rainbow waterfalls of ancient Diamant, prowled the dark jungles of forgotten Chongo. He knew the stinging cold of the ice-capped Azgonat Mountains at the top of the world.

But even in his dream he inevitably returned to Wyvernwood.

A bit of wood popped in the fireplace, and Harrow opened one eye. The fire continued to burn merrily, and the books were safe, but with the tip of a claw he moved one volume a little further away from the hearth and then closed his eye again.

He dreamed of his father, golden-scaled Stormfire, the largest and mightiest of the Dragons. Fearsome, some said, although Harrow had never understood that. He always heard his father's voice when he read the books, and perhaps that was why lately he read them so often. The books made him feel as if his father was still close by, just over his shoulder, just out of sight in the shadows.

Without opening his eyes, he shifted a paw so that it rested on one of the volumes. "There's so much I don't understand," he whispered.

Stormfire's cryptic laugh came softly from the darkness. *And there's so much more. More for you not to understand. More than you can dream.*

Harrow drew a shallow breath. His father's smell still lingered in the book covers, for they were bound in the dark gold of Stormfire's sloughed skin. He drew comfort from the scent of his father. *I wish you were here*, he thought. *I have so many questions and so many doubts.*

In the darkness, Stormfire was silent until Harrow almost fell asleep again. Then from behind a drowsy veil he whispered, *You have the answers you need. The rest is trust.*

Harrow opened his eyes and raised his head ever so slightly. The crackling fire cast its ruddy light around the chamber, but another gleam with a different quality of light spilled over the edge of the nearby writing desk. Harrow lay back down and stared for a long moment directly into the fireplace, aware once more of a curious itching in the back of his head.

The talisman doesn't speak to me, he thought with some bitterness. Then he pursed his Dragon lips and considered. *Why should I be bitter? The talisman hasn't spoken to anyone.*

As clearly as if Stormfire was alive and in the cave beside him, Harrow heard his voice. *Trust*, his father said.

The Black Dragon shot to his feet. "Trust what?" he shouted in a flash of anger. Trembling, he gathered the volumes and stacked them on a corner of the writing desk. Then, for no good reason, he rearranged them again and piled them protectively around the Glass Dragon. The talisman's thin light rose like a beacon over the tops of the books, sparking a curious glitter on the gold-scaled bindings.

With a low roar, Harrow spun about and made his way to the cave's entrance. A fresh wind swept through the canyon, bringing all the scents of the forest. Spreading his wings, he left behind the darkness and rose into the bright day.

But he didn't fly far. A child's laugh caught his attention, and he turned toward the village. The shreds of Luna's tent had been cleared away, and the three Man-children were practicing gymnastic tricks in the center of the square. Unlike his brother, Chan, Harrow had never taken much of an interest in the children. On a whim, he settled down on the edge of the square to observe.

As he folded his wings, he watched the tiny girl perform a line of cartwheels with perfect precision. Her name, he remembered, was Little Pear. Then he looked to the boys and tried with some small embarrassment to remember their names. *Trevor and Markham.* The harder part was telling which was which, for they were twins alike in almost every feature and physical detail. The two bare chested boys nodded approval and muttered some comments. One of them performed the same series. They seemed to be teaching Little Pear.

Intrigued, and with nothing else to do, Harrow stretched out on his belly. One of the boys glanced his way and whispered to the other. All three children paused. "Do you object to my presence?" Harrow asked.

None of them spoke, but Trevor and Markham shook their heads, and Little Pear smiled. For a brief moment, they huddled together, whispering. Then, the two boys sprang away side by side, performing an exquisite sequence of backflips in perfect unison. When they stopped, one of them beckoned to Little Pear. Her short blond hair bounced around her determined face as she performed the same series. But instead of sticking the landing on her final flip, she fell backward onto her rump and slammed a fist on the dusty ground in frustration.

After an initial flash of concern, Harrow pressed his lips together to resist a chuckle.

With an encouraging whoop, Trevor and Markham whisked Little Pear to her feet. "Again," one of the boys said. "Watch your rotation," said the other. Little Pear wiped a dusty hand across her cheek and nodded.

Again both boys performed the same series of backflips in flawless unison, and the moment they stuck their final landing, Pear began her run. *Flip, flip, flip, flip...* Perfect!

Wearing big grins, Trevor and Markham rushed to Pear and rumpled her hair. Even Harrow quietly and unobtrusively thumped the tip of his tail on the ground.

"Now you know your spot," one of the boys said to Pear.

The other boy said, "This time, we'll be here waiting."

"I'm ready," Little Pear said as she paced back to her original starting point.

This time, she performed the series alone, but as she began her fifth flip, Trevor and Markham dropped to their knees and joined hands. Instead of sticking the fifth flip, Pear sprang upward again. The boys rose beneath her, their arms crossing right in the small of her back, assisting her still higher. Tucking into a tight ball, Little Pear somersaulted through the air and landed in perfect balance.

A moment of silence, then all three children erupted in cheers, Little Pear most of all. "I did it! I did it!"

"I wish Jake was here to see that!" one boy said.

"And Ariel!" the other said.

Then all three stopped laughing and looked at each other. Their faces turned grim, and their shoulders sagged. They were worried about their absent friends.

Harrow felt as if he'd been struck a blow. As he watched the three children fret about their friends, he discovered that he was worried, too, about Chan and Luna. In an unlikely instant, he suddenly shared something in common with these human younglings. *We're not so unalike*, he thought.

"Show me more," he urged.

The children brightened at his encouragement. Trevor looked at Markham, or maybe Markham looked at Trevor. "The new pass?" one boy said, and the other boy nodded.

Little Pear stepped aside. Then, moving as one, Trevor and Markham struck poses. No word passed between them, but at the same time they launched forward, diving into a series of twisting flips and acrobatic maneuvers, dynamic and yet astonishingly graceful. Their precision was eerie, almost supernatural.

When they finished, Harrow thumped his tail on the ground. "Trevor!" he called, pleased with himself when one boy looked up. "Markham!" he called, and the second boy flashed a breathless grin. "All of you come closer!"

The three children ran to Harrow. Dusty and panting they stood before him as he studied their faces. "Little Pear," he said.

The girl frowned. "Just Pear," she instructed, giving the boys a nudge in the ribs with her elbows. "They only call me 'little.'"

"Because you are," the boys answered together.

Harrow shook his head as he stared from one boy to the other. Both brown-haired and curly, the same height and weight, the same muscularity. "How does anyone ever tell you two apart?"

The two grinned and looked at each other. "That's easy," Trevor said. He pointed to Markham. "He has one blue and one brown eye."

Little Pear chuckled behind her hands. Harrow sensed the beginning of a joke. But as he stared at Markham he discovered the boy did indeed have one blue eye and one brown eye. Then he looked at Trevor again and blinked in amazement. "But so do you!" Harrow answered.

Pear laughed out loud while the two boys maintained innocent looks.

Trevor pointed at Markham again. "But his blue eye is the right one," he said.

Markham pointed back at Trevor. "His blue eye is the left one."

Harrow stopped listening and craned his neck upward. A cacophony of caws and screeches issued in the distance, and a moment later a rush of black shapes filled the sky.

"Crows!" Pear cried in alarm. She threw her arms around Trevor.

Markham put an arm over her shoulder. "It's all right," he reassured Pear. "They're not attacking."

The boy was right. The crows were racing southward as swiftly as their wings could take them, driven by the fiery breaths of the Dragon Paraclion and a host of hawks and eagles.

But a golden glint on the neck of one of the crows caught Harrow's eye. He growled low in his throat and stood up so quickly that the children jumped back in fear.

"Sorry," he apologized. He looked at Trevor and Markham. "Quickly, I need you to watch the talisman. Will you do it?"

Markham and Trevor nodded. "But it's in Stormfire's cave!" Markham said.

"That's not a problem," Harrow answered. Wrapping his claws around the two boys, he sprang into the air. Their surprised shouts and excited screams filled his ears.

"Take me! Take me!" little Pear called.

But Harrow could only carry two. Sweeping out over the canyon rim, he deposited the two boys in the mouth of the cave and turned away again.

"Wait!" Trevor called. "We don't have any weapons! What are we supposed to defend it with?"

Markham elbowed his twin. "Our lives, stupid! Don't you ever read? It's in all the books and stories. If someone tells you to guard or defend something, it's always *with your lives!*"

Trevor gave his twin a dubious look. "I'm not sure I like the sound of that."

The crows were a black cloud in the distance, but Paraclion's fire made them easy to follow. Turning away from the boys and straining to his best speed, Harrow raced across Wyvernwood, bending treetops in his wake until he climbed higher above the forest. In very little time, he overtook Paraclion and the cadre of hawks and eagles.

The Silver Dragon gave Harrow a stern look. "Youngster, shouldn't you be guarding the talisman?"

Harrow bristled at Paraclion's imperious tone, and he glared. "Were you not so old and your eyesight so weak," he countered, "you might have observed what I saw from the ground as you passed above Stronghold."

A screech sounded startlingly close to Harrow's right ear. "Watch your tongue, hatchling. I'm old, too, but my eyes are a damn sight sharper than yours."

Harrow turned his head toward the voice and met the dark-eyed gaze of Skymarin, Lord of Eagles. His white pinfeathers rippled on the wind as he easily kept pace with the Dragons, and a pair of his eagle brothers, displaying smooth grace, flew protectively close behind him.

"Point taken, Lord of Eagles," Harrow answered in a more respectful tone. "But put your sharp eyesight to use for us. One of those crows wears a chain and a gold medallion around her throat. I saw it flash in the sunlight as she flew overhead."

Skymarin directed his gaze forward. "That would be a strange ornament for a crow to wear," he agreed. "Indeed, it would be strange for a crow to wear anything at all."

Paraclion's gaze narrowed as he, too, stared ahead. "Why do you say *her?*"

Harrow concealed a smirk as the Silver Dragon's tone turned more polite. Paraclion knew he'd missed a possibly important detail. "Because she was larger than the other crows, and therefore I recognized her." He looked to Skymarin again. "Look for the necklace. Single her out from the others and bring her to me."

With his eagle brothers at his side, Skymarin shot ahead. The crows tried to scatter as the larger raptors plunged in among them, and their panicked caws and screeches reached a cacophonous new level. One crow, braving all, darted away from the rest. A bit of gold glinted around her ebon throat. Skymarin folded his wings, and stretching out his neck, dove at a steep angle. His speed was astonishing.

The crow gave a desperate screech. Skymarin reached out with powerful talons. Black feathers exploded in the air. The brief chase was over.

Harrow nodded with smug satisfaction. "Keep driving them south," he said needlessly to Paraclion. He'd never really liked the Silver Dragon, whom he considered far too vain about the bright color of his scales. "I'm about to have a conversation."

"One crow to another," Paraclion answered. Then, as he put on a burst of speed, he called back over his shoulder. "A little black humor."

Harrow ignored the remark and scanned the ground below. The summit of a hill offered a good landing place, and he descended toward it, folding his wings closely and dropping through the trees. A beehive depending from one of the branches came suddenly alive, and a furious buzzing filled the air. A golden swarm of angry insects charged forth. But then, with one look at the Dragon in their midst, they became polite and retreated home again.

Harrow chuckled, and a moment later a pair of eagles flew downward to perch on stout branches near Harrow. Skymarin followed with his crow captor clutched tightly in his talons.

The crow twisted her neck toward Harrow. Her dark eyes were wide and moist with fear, and she trembled visibly in Skymarin's relentless grip. "Bullies! Brutes! Monsters!" she screeched. "Is this how a Son of Stormfire treats a queen and a lady?"

The bees buzzed again in response to all the commotion, but they kept their distance.

"Hello, Esmeralda," Harrow answered. With a slow blink of his eyes, he inclined his head. "Your Majesty."

"That's better!" Esmeralda snapped with renewed dignity. "Now let me go, you offensive creature!"

Harrow nodded to Skymarin, and the Lord of Eagles released his grip. Instantly, Esmeralda shot upward in a crazed bid for freedom. Skymarin screeched, but anticipating such a move, Harrow reached out and snagged Esmeralda before she cleared the upper branches.

"Behave yourself," Harrow warned as she struggled and beat her wings inside his massive paw. "If you break your wings, I'll leave you for the bees. You'll make fine royal honey."

Esmeralda grew still, and after a moment, Harrow opened his fist ever so slightly. Peering out between his claws, she glared with black, round eyes. "Bully! Brute! Monster!" she said again, but with less energy.

"You're repeating yourself," Harrow answered in a tight whisper. Raising his paw, he brought her closer to his face and yawned. Her pounding heart began to race, and she trembled as she squirmed. The Black Dragon smiled. Esmeralda thought he was going to eat her, but if he did he'd never get the bitter taste out of his mouth.

She didn't know that, though. "Why have the crows become allies of Degarm?" Harrow asked in a civil tone that still managed to convey menace. "And who gave you the pretty trinket you wear around your throat?" Slowly, he opened his paw.

Esmeralda shivered and looked around desperately for any hope of escape. Then, with a sharp sigh, she lifted her head and looked Harrow straight in the eye. "What have the Dragons ever done for any crow?" she demanded. "You're overgrown worms with an over-inflated view of your place in the world! You fly through the forest like you own it! Look how you nearly destroyed that beehive! Did you even notice it?" Esmeralda hawked a wad of crow saliva and spat on Harrow's paw. "Wyvernwood! Hah! You even named the forest for yourselves! As if it wasn't here before you came!"

Taken aback by Esmeralda's anger, Harrow hesitated. "Degarm poisoned the Blackwater River with your help," he accused, recovering himself. "Then you tried to steal..." he hesitated again, choosing his words carefully. "...something of value from Stormfire's cave."

Esmeralda spat again. "The Glass Dragon!" she screeched. "As if everybody with a pair of ears and half a brain doesn't already know that you've found it. As if everybody in the world isn't going to try to take it from you! It's magic! Real magic!"

She fluttered her black wings hard enough to scatter feathers, but she made no effort to fly away. With eyes that gleamed with hatred, she gave a laugh. "And as for the poison in the Blackwater River? Hah! Ask your precious sister about that!" Folding her wings across her chest, she nodded smugly.

Harrow's gaze narrowed at mention of Luna. "What are you talking about, you crazy bird?"

Leaning forward, Esmeralda kicked at the scaled paw she stood on. "You crazy Dragon! Did you ever ask yourself *how* the river got poisoned? Well, the Queen of Crows will tell you!" She tapped her foot in an imperious display. "Degarm sent barrels of stuff—entire cargo holds full—on ships bound for Angmar. Black ships in the black of night sailing up the Blackwater under your noses. But the poison was supposed to be used there deep in that nation's heart against Degarm's old enemy!" Her tapping foot became still, and she leaned even closer toward Harrow to make her point. "Only your uppity sister and her man-child pet destroyed those ships, unwittingly spilling the stuff in the heart of Wyvernwood instead!" She dealt his paw a defiant third kick. "What do you think of that, you crazy Dragon?"

Harrow roared, and the force of it blew Esmeralda off his paw. Tumbling over and over through the air, she finally spread her wings and, recovering her balance, landed on a limb beside Skymarin. She made no effort to flee. She was enjoying herself too much.

"You Dragons are the biggest threat to Wyvernwood!" she shouted. "You bring nothing but trouble! And if you don't bring it, you attract it! You want to know why the crows are helping Degarm?" She brushed the tip of one wing over the shiny medallion she wore around her neck. "Not because they give us shiny trinkets—although they do that. But because they're holding my husband hostage! Prospero! Our king! He rots in a gilded cage beside the throne of Degarm! And the

Dragons have done nothing to save him! You aren't even aware of it!" She spat again and then shat a white load on the limb where she stood. "For Prospero's sake, we've sold our loyalty! Now get over it!"

With that, Esmeralda launched herself into the sky. Harrow started to grab for her, but Skymarin called out. "Let her go," he said. "You have the answers you wanted, and more. Now what will you do with the knowledge?"

The Son of Stormfire stood mute as he watched the Queen of Crows disappear through the branches. Then he looked at Skymarin and his eagle brothers. "I don't know," he admitted, half numb.

He looked toward the beehive and the bees, who were now quiet.

Eight

RONALDO WOKE TO A DULL POUNDING IN HIS HEAD. In the right side of his head, to be specific. Carefully, he peeled one eye open and discovered that the horizon had somehow tilted to a peculiarly vertical angle. Only when the breeze blew a grain of sand into his eye did he realize he was lying on the beach.

Did I really pass out? he thought. *How embarrassing for someone who used to call himself Rage.*

Still, he made no effort to move, and for several long moments, he closed his eyes again. His wings felt like great weights, and he ached in too many places to count. Worst of all, his head throbbed with a distant, but unrelenting pain as if someone was beating him around his temple or his ear.

The Gray Dragon let out a soft sigh that stirred the sand around his nostrils. Then his eyes snapped open. *His ear?* Could it be? Was it possible?

"Oh dear," he muttered. With considerable effort, he lifted his head ever so slightly.

Bumble shot out and collapsed on the sand nearby. Coughing and gasping for breath, the little bird staggered around and then rolled over on his back and, with wings flopping and twitching, he thrust his feet straight up. "Air!" he panted. "At last! Air!"

Ronaldo had fallen to the ground on the right side of his face, and Bumble, who had been riding in his ear, hadn't gotten out in time to avoid being trapped. "Sorry, Bumble-bird," he apologized, fixing one eye on his little friend.

The little hummingbird gave a twitch and a shiver. "Bumble thought he was going to die!" he said with wide, black eyes. "Asphyxiate! Suffocate! Smother, choke, and—and discomboobulate! Not to mention drown in softening ear effluvia!" He shook his tiny feet, which were indeed coated with a sticky-looking amber substance. "What a horrid fate for the Bravest Hummingbird in the World!"

Ronaldo blinked with his one open eye. "Discombobulate," he corrected in a weak voice.

Folding one wing against his small, feathered body, Bumble turned over on his side and glared. "When your best friend faints and falls on top of you," he insisted, "the word is definitely discom-*boob*-ulate!"

A pair of golden hooves stirred sand and stopped in front of Ronaldo. Opening both eyes, he let his gaze roam up well-formed fetlocks, strong legs, a powerful chest and a sleek neck. He stopped there, closed his eyes, and sighed again. "I'll bet that's Marian," he said.

Bumble rolled over on his back, folded his wings over his chest, and crossed his legs. "I'm afraid I don't remember her name. Hummingbird, you know. Small brain." He began to whistle.

Phooey! Something thumped on the tip of Ronaldo's nose and bounced into the sand. "You dropped something," Marian said. "Nice to see you're finally awake, *Rage*."

Ronaldo winced. He'd seen it coming, and Marian wasn't the type to let an opportunity slide by. Reluctantly, he opened his eyes once more. The oversized jewel she called *the Diamond Dragon* lay immediately in front of him. The sunlight danced upon it, and it dazzled his vision.

"And your little bird, too," she added with a casual shake of her white mane. "Now if you can lift your head a little higher than my fetlocks, do you feel like saying *thank you* to our rescuers?"

With an effort, Ronaldo shook off his fatigue and pushed himself back onto his haunches. Marian skipped away to give him room, and a suddenly energized Bumble raced upward to seek a safe perch on her golden horn. "Satisfied?" Ronaldo said to Marian. But his attention was already elsewhere.

A great winged shadow passed directly over him and rippled along the white sand beach. Another followed behind it only slightly smaller. The Dragon Fleer circled watchfully above the shoreline. His companion, Snowsong, gyred higher and higher as if on alert, her gaze sweeping the distance. Emerald Fleer, the nearer of the two Dragons, noticed Ronaldo and landed behind Marian.

A moment later, Snowsong joined him. With unabashed awe, she stared at Ronaldo, and then folded her wings around herself as she bowed her head. "We've never met, Master Ronaldo, but I've heard so much about you and your wonderful artworks."

Wrapping himself in his wings, Ronaldo inclined his head in polite response, but his gaze remained on the White Dragon. Indeed, *white* did not do her justice. She shimmered like the sun-drenched sand they stood upon, and her eyes were red as rubies. "I'm no master," Ronaldo protested gently. "Far from it."

"Oh, he's a master, all right," Marian interrupted. "A master at getting into trouble."

Fleer stretched his long neck forward. "I see you're as modest as ever, Ronaldo," he said. "It's been a long time."

"Too long, little Brother," Ronaldo answered quietly as he admired the deep rich shade of his sibling's scales. "I'm pleased that you look so well."

In sudden excitement, Bumble flew into the air and buzzed a circle around Fleer's head. "Brother, brother, brother?" he sang in his tiny voice. "What's going on?"

Ronaldo forced a tight smile as old memories stirred to the surface of his mind. "We're both hatchlings of the same parents, although not of the same nest," he explained. "Robare and Circe were our parents—two of the most splendidly beautiful Dragons ever in the world."

"But they were quite old when Ronaldo hatched," Fleer continued, taking up the tale. "And older still when I came along. Ronaldo had already sought his own cave and established himself in the Whispering Hills, so we never really grew up together."

Ronaldo's lips drew into a tighter line, and he looked away from his brother to hide the small hurt he carried inside. He lingered with his memories, toyed with them as one often did a sore tooth or a tender scab. Stern Robare, as large and powerful as Stormfire himself, had treated him well and taught him much, but in the end had not approved of his interest in art. Circe had been more supportive, but quietly so, sometimes making paint brushes for him from duck-down and slipping them to him, but only when Robare wasn't around to see.

And in their darkly emerald presence, Ronaldo had felt even more acutely his own plain grayness. From the corner of his eye, he glanced again at Fleer, who possessed the same intense coloring as their parents, and felt just a twinge, not of envy, but of regret. Somehow, in some manner that he'd never completely understood, he'd disappointed Robare. Still, he'd loved his parents, and he'd grieved when shortly after Fleer's hatching they took their last flight together beyond the Imagination Mountains.

Snowsong spoke up again. "Master Ronaldo, you don't look well. Are you sure you're recovered?"

Fleer inclined his head as he drew himself erect and grinned at his gray brother. "Your speed was most impressive." He allowed a mischievous chuckle. "Especially for one your age."

Ronaldo barely heard. Still ensnared in his memories, he craned his neck toward the forest where the trees were filled with hawks and eagles and other birds. Fleer's army, he recalled, all waiting watchful and expectant. "For what?" he whispered to himself.

"For you, silly Dragon," Marian said as if she'd read his mind. "And for that pretty bauble in the sand at your feet."

Bumble hopped up and down on the tip of Marian's horn. "Ronaldo has parents!" he repeated over and over, beating himself in the head with one wing as if he was trying to hammer the fact into his forgetful little brain. "Ronaldo has parents!"

With a snort of annoyance, Marian shook her head, flinging the hummingbird into the air. "Shut your beak, Bumble," she warned.

Fleer and Snowsong both leaned close, stretching their long necks above the Last Unicorn in the World for a look at the glittering jewel in the sand. "Marian says you've found the third talisman," Fleer said.

"*The Diamond Dragon*," Snowsong murmured at the same time.

"The third?" Ronaldo shot a curious look at Fleer. His gaze narrowed, and his tail began to thump with sudden nervousness. "You speak as if the other two have already been found!"

Fleer and Snowsong exchanged glances with each other and with Marian. Clearly, the three of them had been talking while Ronaldo lay unconscious. "We believe they have," Fleer said. "At least one of them, definitely. The other is..." he looked with a frown to Snowsong.

"Problematical," she finished.

Ronaldo rolled his eyes. "Problematical," he repeated. "Isn't everything?"

With a toss of her mane and a flip of her tail, Marian turned to Fleer and Snowsong. "It's not coincidence that Stormfire's talismans are all turning up at the same time. We need to get this one to Stronghold as quickly as possible."

Fleer nodded his head, but hesitated. "I don't understand, though, why Ronaldo..."

Marian stamped a hoof, and her violet eyes changed to a hard gold. "What you understand isn't important right now," she snapped. "The safety of the *Diamond Dragon* is paramount. The crows have already tried to steal the *Glass Dragon*, and a pack of griffins just chased us halfway across the Windy Sea. So shake a scale, young Dragon! You're our escort!"

"I don't think the griffins were after the jewel," Ronaldo said. He was still unwilling quite to accept that the trinket at his feet was the legendary talisman.

Marian spun about again and lifted her head high. Her eyes flashed with a storm of rapidly changing colors as the anger in her voice grew. "Well if they weren't," she hissed, "they soon will be! Mark my words!"

The Gray Dragon stared gape-jawed, taken aback by the Unicorn's intensity and the change he suddenly saw within her. The light-hearted, sometimes comical Marian that he knew no longer stood before him, and he wondered where she had gone. This new unicorn seemed like some other creature, an older and more ruthless representative of her kind.

"She's right, Brother," Fleer agreed. "The sooner we get the talisman to Stronghold the better it will be for all."

"And many there will be glad to see you," Snowsong added. "It's been far too long since you visited us." With that, she spread her wings and climbed into the sky, circling higher and higher above the beach. Fleer followed, but then turned inward to take a point above the forest.

"Well, if I must go, then you're coming, too," Ronaldo said to Marian as he plucked the *Diamond Dragon* from the sand with one hind claw. Then he snatched Marian up in his forepaws, carrying her exactly as he had before. Too late, she gave a whinny of protest, but the Gray Dragon, spread his wings and flew upward at a shallow angle, skimming the treetops and ripping leaves from the branches before he found the strength to climb higher and join his brother.

"You did that on purpose!" Marian charged as she shook twigs and leaves out of her mane.

A greenish blur darted upward from the edge of the forest and found its place in Ronaldo's left ear. The little hummingbird smelled of honeysuckle. Apparently, he'd taken time for a quick snack.

Fleer's army of eagles and hawks and owls rose up from the forest to surround them. There were other birds, too. Starlings and bluejays, woodpeckers and more. Beaks and talons flashed in the sunlight. Some of the birds flew among the Dragons while others maintained a perimeter, and they all made their way across the sky in a grim and eerie silence, and with a sharp-eyed attentiveness that hinted at danger.

With Fleer on his left side and Snowsong on his right, Ronaldo concentrated on his flying. His fatigue lifted slowly as he worked the stiffness from his wings, and his spirit began to lift as well. The wind on his face never failed to invigorate him, and he found something strangely glorious in the avian armada of which he found himself a part.

"Marian," he whispered. "Is this really the *Diamond Dragon* I carry?" He still couldn't make himself believe it. "Can it be?"

"You're a madcap Dragon," Marian answered, but her tone was softer than before, more affectionate. "It's not the talisman you doubt, Ronaldo. It's yourself. Stop doubting and let it sing to you."

Clutching his claws tighter about the brilliant, apple-sized jewel, Ronaldo thought. He imagined that he could almost feel the rainbow beams of light reflecting from its many perfect facets, that he could feel the rays tingling on his scales. And he recalled the tiny, shadowy Dragon-shape that he sometimes thought he glimpsed within it.

A soft wisp of sound brushed across his mind, the merest hint of a music like none he'd ever heard before. It startled him, but it also soothed him. *Is the Diamond Dragon singing to me*, he wondered, *as Marian said it would?*

"I don't understand." He hadn't intended to speak those words aloud, but they slipped through his Dragon lips to fall on Marian's ears.

"But you will," she assured him. "Soon enough you will." Then she, too, breathed soft words not meant for other ears as she turned her head and gazed toward the east, toward the sea that was no longer there. "*And when you do, my friend, I hope you won't hate me.*"

Ronaldo blinked, uncertain if he had actually heard what he had heard. An uneasy shiver passed through him from the tip of his nose to the tip of his tail. He tried to think, to make sense of it all. He'd had plenty of adventures with Marian and Bumble, traveled far across Wyvernwood and to places beyond. But for the first time he felt himself caught up in something beyond his control, something bigger and grander than he was himself, and something more dangerous than any danger he had ever faced.

Even with Marian in his paws and Bumble in his ear, he felt terribly alone. A glance toward the brother flying majestically at his side did nothing to allay that feeling.

Even the music was gone.

Turning inland and then southward, they passed over Grendleton, a stony village occupied mostly by Wyrms, wingless cousins of the Dragons. The creatures turned out to look up through the trees and watch in silence as Fleer's army darkened their sky.

On a hillside farther south a family of lions rose nervously from their resting place beneath a broad shade tree. They all watched in silence, and the three cubs moved closer to their mother.

Along a narrow creek a pair of beaver looked up and then dived into the water and out of sight. A black bear stood his ground as they approached, but then ran into a thicker part of the woods.

Ronaldo began to feel tired again, and Marian's weight became a burden. Snowsong noticed and insisted that they find a place to rest. When a suitable summit presented itself, the three Dragons descended. Taking great care, Ronaldo set Marian down first. The hawks and eagles and all of Fleer's army found perches in the surrounding trees along the slopes. Without a word to anyone, Bumble sped off in search of food.

For several moments, Ronaldo watched as Marian stalked around the grounds. At first he thought she was only stretching her legs, which no doubt were cramped from being carried for so long. But he knew by her expression and her posture, and by the peculiar flashing of her eyes that her thoughts were on weighty matters. When he set the talisman on the grass, she turned his way briefly, and her gaze fastened on the jewel, but then she moved farther away to be alone.

No one spoke. A throng of yellow sulfur butterflies fluttered around the talisman as if attracted to its radiance, silent, as one would expect from butterflies. But a group of bees had gathered, too, and landing in the grass to fan their wings, they became silent. Not even a breeze blew to rustle the leaves. For a crazy instant, Ronaldo wondered if he'd gone deaf. Then, on an impulse he lifted his head and began to sing.

"This land where the trees
Grow wild as they please,
Where the rivers are shining and blue,
Where the night wind sings
Of fantastical things
In a world that seems once again new . . ."

The Gray Dragon hesitated and looked around with mild embarrassment to see if anyone was listening. Nearby, Snowsong smiled politely and waited. Fleer seemed to be listening, too, and a couple of the owls had moved to closer branches. Ronaldo frowned and chewed his lip as his embarrassment deepened. Finally, he continued.

"I'll stick to my paints
Cause a poet I ain't;
I've no talent for verses or rhymes.
It's really quite sad—
I'm so tragically bad
I just fall on my face every time!"

With that, Ronaldo gave a melodramatic sigh and fell forward, curling his body as he collapsed on the ground. But when a weak and tiny voice shouted, "Let me out! Let me out! Air! I'm suffocating!" Ronaldo shot erect again, his heart pounding and his eyes wide.

"Bumble?" he called.

The little hummingbird flew a circle around his nose. "Gotcha!" he answered, shaking with laughter as he perched between Ronaldo's nostrils.

Marian paced closer, looked up, and gave them both a look as she swished her tail.

"I was just trying to lighten the mood," Ronaldo muttered.

"I think it's light enough to fly," she answered. "Now pick me up and let's get going."

At a nod from Marian, Fleer, Snowsong, and their feathered entourage took to the sky. Ronaldo closed his grip around the Last Unicorn in the World. *The mood isn't the only thing around here that could use a little lightening,* he grumbled privately as he spread his wings and followed them.

From inside his right ear Bumble asked, "Is Ronaldo hearing the music of the talisman?"

Ronaldo felt the jewel gripped in a hind foot. He hadn't forgotten to pick it up. "Not at the moment," he answered with some disappointment.

"Then listen to the music of Bumble!" The little hummingbird laughed as he settled himself closer to Ronaldo's eardrum, and then he began to whistle. After a moment, he paused. "Gotcha!" he laughed again. "That was a good one! I'm hot today!"

Ronaldo growled low in his throat, but concentrated on his flying. In the distance off to the west, he spied the Dragon Maximor, amber in color, with an army of birds similar to Fleer's. They were driving a dark cloud of crows before them. Ronaldo watched them until a range of wooded hills rose up and blocked the view.

Then, almost without warning the green forest split apart and they sailed outward over the vast expanse of Stronghold Canyon. The afternoon sun shimmered on the soaring canyon walls, and Ronaldo caught his breath at the sight of the multi-hued strata and the surging river at its bottom.

Leading the way, Fleer angled steeply downward over the rim and into the canyon itself, and all the birds that made up his army followed like a great train. They were still apparently east of the village. Fleer didn't slow as he guided them along the river. Indeed, he seemed to increase his pace, eager to be home.

"It's magnificent!" Ronaldo murmured. It had been a long time since he'd visited Stronghold, as Snowsong had said, a very long time.

"It's older than I am," Marian answered smartly.

A great pinnacle of stone rose up before them—Stormfire's Point. Fleer led a course around it, and then swooped upward and over the northern rim of the canyon again.

The village had grown since last he'd seen it, but that was to be expected. It seemed also that word of their coming had preceded them, for great throngs of minotaurs, satyrs, fomorians and other creatures filled the streets. The square at the center of the village, however, had been kept empty. Only a single Dragon waited there.

Sabu.

Snowsong veered away, taking the army of birds with her. Beckoning with one wing, Fleer led Ronaldo downward.

"Easy," Marian begged. "My legs feel like kindling."

"I'm sure," Ronaldo answered as he set her gently on the ground. "And my hind foot has a major cramp from grasping your precious talisman for so long, so we'll just have to lean on each other." They exchanged wary glances. "Front and center, Bumble-bird," Ronaldo called softly. "Whatever happens here, I know you'll want to be in the middle of it."

"Aye-aye!" the hummingbird responded as he stirred from his perch in Ronaldo's ear and shot toward Marian's horn. "Reporting for duty! Mission accomplished!" He stretched his wings and yawned. "Are we there yet?"

"We are," Ronaldo answered. Lifting a hind foot, he opened his claws and dropped the *Diamond Dragon*, letting it fall with a thump on the green grass. He'd really had quite enough of the thing, whatever it was.

From the far side of the square, Sabu stared for a long moment. Then, dropping to all fours and folding her black wings tightly against her body, she crept forward. Stronghold's citizens also began to venture closer.

"Everyone seems to be holding their breath," Ronaldo observed in a whisper.

"Did you fart?" Marian inquired, seeming more like her old self.

Sabu stopped a short distance from the talisman. A shadow passed overhead, and blue Ramoses landed next to her. He also folded his wings and bent low to study the jewel. Its rainbow light reflected in their eyes, shimmered on their scales. Sabu stretched out her neck and sniffed it.

But then she drew back and stood rigidly erect. "This can't possibly be the *Diamond Dragon*," she announced stiffly. She looked Ronaldo coldly up and down and then glared at Marian. "I don't know what trick you're playing, Unicorn," she hissed, "but The Book of Stormfire says that the hidden talismans would only be found by Stormfire's children."

Closing his old eyes, Ramoses also rose, only to bow again. "Welcome, Master Ronaldo. You're too long absent from the Home of the Dragonkin."

Frowning, Sabu slapped the old Dragon's shoulder with the back of her paw. But when Ramoses straightened again and looked directly at her, a nervous light stole into her ebon eyes. Almost against her will she turned her attention to the talisman on the ground. Then she looked at Ronaldo again, at Marian, and back to Ramoses.

"Same old Sabu," Marian said disdainfully. With a toss of her mane, she looked to Ramoses. "It's time."

"Time for what?" Ronaldo whispered, growing as nervous as Sabu seemed to be.

"The truth, my friend," she answered. She looked at Fleer and then turned to face Ronaldo squarely. "Robare and Circe were not your parents. They only raised you."

"Parents?" Bumble hopped up and down on the tip of Marian's horn, slapping a wing against his head as he muttered to himself. "Bumble must remember! This is gonna be good!"

"Shut up, Bumble," Marian said. With a shake of her head she sent the little bird into an aerial spin and faced Ronaldo again.

Ronaldo blinked furiously and began to thump the ground with his tail. His heart hammered, and a dark fear closed around him. "Sabu is right!" he insisted. "Only the Children of Stormfire can find the talismans. Harrow, Chan, and Luna! They're the ones...!"

Marian moved closer until the tip of her horn almost touched Ronaldo. *"You are a child of Stormfire!"* she said. "His first-born son! Forgive me, Ronaldo, but I've carried this secret for years!"

Sabu recoiled, her black eyes wide with anger and fear. "It's a lie!" she cried. "It's not possible!"

Opening his eyes, Ramoses turned to her. "It's true," he said quietly.

Ronaldo shivered violently. "It's not true!" he said in a tight, harsh whisper. "Please don't let it be true! I don't want it to be true!"

He gazed suddenly at the ground. The talisman still lay where he'd dropped it with the afternoon rays of the sun dancing wildly upon its gleaming facets, playing light tricks, casting beams and streamers of impossible radiance. Its beauty dazzled his artist's eye, but he didn't care. In a blind rage, he bent and scooped it up, then turned toward the canyon and prepared to throw it as far as he could.

A surge of music stopped him, a rush of sweet sound that filled his mind. In one heartbeat it filled him, changed him. The music poured into his heart, flowed through his veins, washed over him. His gray scales shimmered, faded, and transformed, took on all the colors of fire—silver, gold, red.

In one heartbeat, he had the one thing he wanted most. He saw himself with impossible eyes, as if he was standing outside his own body, appraising his new beauty.

And in one heartbeat, he rejected all that the talisman offered. "This is what I am," he said, gray again from head to foot. He looked down at Marian with tears streaming from his eyes. "I know *who* I am."

A shadow blotted out the sun, and Harrow's voice screamed, "No!" The force of his outcry shook the leaves. Sabu spun about, and the citizens of Stronghold cowered rooted where they stood

In a jealous fury, talons outreaching, the Black Dragon dived.

Nine

THE VILLAGE AT THE BOTTOM OF THE VALLEY looked much like the previous two: an unplanned conglomeration of flimsy homes constructed from the corpses of slaughtered trees, muddy streets that meandered without design, and barns and silos that seemed to lean whichever way the wind blew. Indeed a good wind would probably blow them over, and they surely leaked when it rained, and they couldn't possibly keep out the cold and damp of winter. Even the dirtiest cave or burrow would have provided better shelter.

Only the surrounding fields with their neat furrows and rows of green-growing vegetables demonstrated any sense of order. A dozen shirtless men sweated and labored in the hot afternoon sun, pounding the ground with hoes. Awkward in their work, stooped and bent over, they looked frail and weak and weathered.

A narrow river flowed through the center of the village. Along its banks women washed the pathetic coverings they called clothes while older males fished and kept watch over the younglings. A few brainless dogs sniffed at the ditches or yapped at the chickens that pecked around in the yards.

From the summit of a high hill on the east side of the valley, Minhep sharpened his claws and beak with a stone as he watched and waited. The sun warmed his broad leonine shoulders, and he fanned his feathered wings in lazy anticipation. Setting the stone aside, he studied his claws and licked them clean, then buffed them on his chest.

He counted the men in the fields again and then turned his attention to their plump wives and the whiny brats by the river. "A griffin's work is never done," he sighed as he spread his wings and rose into the sky. With the sun at his back, he began a swift and silent climb that took him directly over the village. With the humans on the ground oblivious, he circled once and then twice. "It isn't easy being mean," he muttered as he started his descent.

He fixed his gaze on a meaty housewife. Kneeling by the river as she worked, her broad rump offered an irresistible target. "Who says the sun doesn't shine there?" he chuckled to himself as he dived downward. "Here comes daddy!"

She gave a sharp yelp as his claws ripped through the thin fabric that covered her backside, and he chuckled again. She hadn't even seen him coming! Wet clothing flew up into the air, and her basket overturned. "En guarde!" he cried, striking with just enough force to propel his hapless prey headfirst into the water.

Another woman kneeling beside her looked up with a startled expression that turned to wide-eyed terror. Then, clapping a hand to her mouth, she screamed an ear-shattering note. Minhep laughed as he banked and turned back toward her. She struggled to rise and run as the other women were running, but the muddy ground betrayed her and she sprawled.

"Hello, my pretty!" Minhep said as he hovered above her. "Do you want to have a good time?" With a swipe of one large paw, he split her laundry basket, scattering sheets and underwear upon the river. Voicing a second short scream, the woman tried to scramble away on her hands and knees, and Minhep frowned. "Is it my breath?" he called. When she didn't look back, he sighed again. "Rejection is such a bitch."

With gleeful abandon he swooped toward a pair of fishermen and knocked them into the river. "There's fishfood!" he laughed, watching over his shoulder as they thrashed in the water.

Further up the bank a third fat fisherman with a bare belly and rolls of flesh that hung almost to his knees threw down his fishing pole and tried to run. Minhep extended his talons. With no effort at all he overtook the unfortunate man and lifted him by his shoulders. "Oh, my aching back!" he moaned as he flew upward with his wriggling burden. Then he called to the thrashing pair at the river's edge. "Look out below!"

The fat fisherman made a satisfying splash. Minhep chuckled. "It's raining men!"

Still chuckling, he glided across the village toward the fields. The barechested workers, alerted by the screams from the river, saw him coming and threw down their hoes. Only one brave young man stood his ground, daring to toss a cabbage.

Minhep batted it aside. "I hate vegetables!" he said, as he snatched the young man up and deposited him on the rooftop of a corn silo. "But I like spunk, and you got that, kid."

He turned back toward the village and, flying low, zoomed down its main street. Pale-eyed humans scrambled to get out of his way, throwing themselves into doorways and into the ditches. At the mouth of an alley a small brown dog growled and bent protectively over an old bone.

"Fetch!" Minhep laughed, snatching the bone away from snapping jaws. With a flick of griffin strength, he tossed it beyond the farthest edge of the village and out of sight. The dog wagged its tail, barked, then took off after it. Minhep shook his head in disgust. "That's what I hate about dogs," he grumbled. "No self-respect!"

With a flutter of his wings, he landed on the roof of a house and dug his talons into the shingles. From inside, he heard a shrill scream. It only encouraged him to scratch and dig faster, and in no time he made a nice-sized hole and poked his head through into a bedroom.

"I just love unwrapping presents," he said to the lovebirds cowering under the covers. He winked at the male. "Apparently so do you!" He winked at the female. "You lucky girl!"

The two humans gave simultaneous shrieks, and then casting modesty and blankets aside, they sprang up and ran hand-in-hand naked into broad daylight.

Flying into the street again, Minhep spied a haycart and shattered it with a backhand stroke. Hay and splinters of wood showered down around the griffin, causing him to scowl, but he turned toward the house across the street with its white picket fence and yard full of chickens. With a swipe, he shattered the pickets.

One of the chickens jumped up and down in a crazy outburst of excitement. "Free at last! Free at last!" it cackled as its companions dashed around it and fled down the road.

Minhep stared at the chicken. "Hey, feathered fowl!" he cried. "You can still talk!"

The chicken lifted its beak. "Of course I can!" it answered indignantly. "But what's the point? Nobody listens to a chicken!"

The Griffin nodded. "True enough."

"Just do me one favor before I run away like all the other chickens," the chicken asked, eliciting another nod from Minhep. "Knock this place to the ground. Smash it flat and piss on the rubble!" The bitterness in the chicken's crackly voice was palpable.

"Hate your keeper, do you?" Minhep said.

The chicken spat and scratched at the dirt with a claw. "I can't even tell you!" it answered. "Always plucking us, wringing our necks, frying us up and eating us! I've lost a lot of good friends here! So knock it down! Flatten it! This house is a monument to carnivorous excess!"

Minhep frowned and rubbed his beak with the tip of one wing. "I'm something of a carnivore, myself, you know."

The chicken blinked, and then began backing away.

"But I'm a griffin on a mission," Minhep continued in a light-hearted tone. "Minhep is my name, and radical urban renewal is my game!"

Stepping past the chicken, he ripped into the house with malevolent delight, shattering its walls, smashing its roof. The sounds of cracking boards and timbers ricocheted through the village, and a cloud of dust rose up as the structure collapsed.

When the job was done, Minhep looked around expecting a cheer or a thank-you. But the chicken was gone.

So, it seemed, were the villagers.

For a short time the griffin wandered through streets, occasionally knocking down some building or doing random damage, peering into windows and doorways, living rooms and kitchens, always looking and listening for the occupants. "Come out, come out, wherever you are!" he called in his most inviting voice. "Ally ally, oxen free!"

But he was alone. The humans had escaped into the woods or beyond the hills or down the river. Even the young man he'd left on the silo roof was gone.

"I feel so empty," he said to himself as he lingered in a kitchen to eye the half-dozen pies left unattended on its counter. He stuck a claw into one of the pies and licked it to sample the flavor before he devoured all six. With a loud burp he moved back into the street.

Just over the eastern hills, the pale ghost of a moon floated low in the blue afternoon. Minhep flicked his tongue over the tip of his beak as he paused to gaze upward, and for a moment he stood as if entranced by the silvery disc. Once, when he was little more than an ignorant youngling still testing his wings, he'd stared at the moon as he did now and wondered what was there, and determined to satisfy his curiosity he'd flown higher and higher, as high as he could.

After all this time he still remembered the stinging laughter of the other Griffinkin.

With a heavy sigh, he lowered his gaze and looked around. Nothing moved as far as he could see. Even the dogs and the chickens had fled. With no one to talk to, nobody to tease, chase, or torment, Minhep folded his paws and lay down in the dusty street. Through half-closed eyes he noted the shattered porches, the damaged rooftops, and the splintered carts that marked his passage. A shoe lay in the middle of the street and beyond that some scattered pieces of silverware, a candlestick, and an overturned sewing basket.

Any griffin would have felt proud, but Minhep only frowned. "My heart just isn't in it," he muttered. "There's no fun anymore in random destruction." Indeed, he wondered suddenly if there had ever been any real fun in it. With his head resting on his paws he rolled his eyes toward the moon again and for the first time in a long while allowed it to fill him with an old childhood sense of wonder, and cat-like he began to purr.

He wasn't sure how long he lay there. Not more than a few moments, surely, although the beginnings of a dream had begun to flicker through his brain. But suddenly the feathers on the back of his eagle's head tingled and stood on end, and Minhep knew that he was no longer alone. His eyes snapped open.

Another griffin lay in the street facing him almost nose to nose, and their gazes locked. Startled, Minhep sprang up, snapped his wings wide and raised his claws in anticipation of an attack.

The other griffin only yawned. Minhep studied the newcomer with a squinting gaze, and then blinked in recognition. "By all the Great Trees!" he whispered, half disbelieving his own eyes. "Morkir? Prince Morkir!"

The younger griffin yawned again and lazily swished his tail. "You used to call me *Mad Morkir*," he answered with a hint of amusement.

Folding his wings over his back, Minhep sat on his haunches and gaped. "Well, yes, that too," he admitted. "And lots of other names after you went to live with those snooty Dragons."

Morkir chuckled. "Hey, when your older brother murders your father and starts looking at you with knives in his eyes, it tends to make you feel unwelcome."

Minhep shrugged. He couldn't very well argue with that. "Gaunt had his flaws," he acknowledged, and he began ticking them off on his claws. "Ambition, greed, murder, insanity..." He fixed an apologetic gaze on Morkir. "But then, I was never the brightest egg in the nest, and I took my friends where I could find them."

"Gaunt." Morkir lifted his head and spat. "We shall not speak of him again."

"As you wish," Minhep answered, rising. He gave Morkir a cool and appraising look. The young prince had muscled up since Minhep had last seen him. "Then, is it time to fight?"

Morkir stretched and then rose from his reclining position into a defensive stance. The two griffins circled each other warily. Minhep gave a low growl, and Morkir answered with a half-hearted snarl. When they had completed three circles and each stood upon his original spot, Morkir paused. "Had enough?" he asked.

Minhep nodded, and both griffins lay back down in the dust. "Well," he said. "That wasn't quite the action-packed moment we'd all been waiting for, was it?"

Morkir snorted. "It's nice to see that you've developed a sense of humor since I last saw you."

The older griffin swished his tail as he studied the young prince. Ignoring Morkir's remark, he asked, "What are you doing here, Son of Gorganar?"

Morkir clacked his beak softly and inclined his head to one side. "I might ask you the same," he said. "Didn't I leave you in Redclaw on the griffin throne, a brave new commander and king of all Griffinkin?"

"I'm terribly disappointed in myself," Minhep replied unconvincingly, because he was rather glad to be rid of the burden of command. Nevertheless, he told Morkir the story of how Kilrain had betrayed him and set Goronus in his place as the new Griffinkin leader, of how the Angmaran king had then sent the griffins off to kill some silly Dragon on the island of Thursis, and of Kilrain's own foolish attempt to murder Minhep. "As you can see," Minhep concluded with a yawn to match Morkir's, "I'm still recovering from the shock."

Morkir nodded sympathetically. "I can see you're quite shaken," he said as he turned his head from side to side. "All this destruction and there's not a drop of blood on your claws, nor anywhere that I can see. You must be off your game."

Minhep looked down at his paws and then quickly hid them under his chest. His eyes narrowed dangerously. "Are you ready for round two yet?" he asked.

"You're too tough for me," Morkir answered meekly. "I'm still recovering from the last go-round. Not to mention my own shock at seeing you again."

Minhep's tail lashed back and forth, and his eyes became bare distrustful slits. Gorganar's son had changed. *Mad Morkir* was plainly gone, and Minhep couldn't quite put his paw on the creature he saw now. "You didn't tell me why you're here," he said.

The younger griffin lifted his head to gaze past Minhep and toward the horizon, and his expression softened. "The mountain couldn't come to Morkir," he said in a cryptic voice, "so Morkir went to the mountain."

Minhep frowned and swished his tail faster, raising a small cloud of dust. *What in the world is that supposed to mean?* he wondered without speaking. *Maybe he's still as mad as a flying monkey!*

"And to many other places besides," Morkir continued with the same distant look. "Places to enchant you. Places to make your feathers shrivel and curl up." He lowered his gaze to Minhep again. "Undersky is a far larger and more mysterious place than you know, my friend," he said. He paused again, and then fell into verse.

"But no matter how many roads you roam,
All roads eventually lead you home."

Minhep sat back on his haunches again. He wasn't sure which surprised him more, that Morkir had just called him *my friend*, or that the young prince had attempted poetry. Self-respecting griffins just didn't engage in such poofery!

Yet, whatever form the words took, they rang with a note of truth. He looked around and then beyond the damage he'd caused, to the horizons, and finally upward toward the moon's pale disc. A twinge of sadness and longing touched his heart—he disdained to call it home-sickness—but he didn't even know where he was.

"You were on your way back to Wyvernwood?" Minhep asked.

Morkir opened his beak wide and forced a smile. "*Home* is a word with many meanings," he replied, turning cryptic again. "When I saw you descending from the hilltop to attack this village I decided to watch and learn what was in your heart these days."

"You sound like a teacher!" Minhep sneered.

"A student," Morkir corrected as, rising to stand, he made a sweeping gesture. "Undersky itself is the teacher." He looked pointedly at Minhep. "You terrorized these people, created a little havoc, but you didn't harm anyone—not human, dog or even chicken. You didn't kill." He thrust out his beak and leaned forward. "Why?"

Minhep's frown deepened. His head hurt, and he felt suddenly nervous in Morkir's presence. "Because it was pointless!" he shouted in frustration. "It's... it's boring!"

Morkir leaned back and nodded with satisfaction, his gaze still fixed on Minhep in a way that made the older griffin squirm. "You're learning already," Morkir chuckled. "I'm ready for another round now if you think you're up to it."

The older griffin's eyes narrowed again. Dropping to all fours, he backed up a step and tensed. "I thought you said we were friends?"

The Son of Gorganar and prince of the Griffinkin laughed as he stood erect and spread his wings wide. "I didn't mean you," he said as he caught a wind and rode it upward. "I have a larger foe in mind!"

Confused and more than a little uncertain, Minhep lingered on the ground as he watched the younger griffin rise into the blue sky and wheel eastward. *Back the way I came,* he realized. And then he thought:

"*Over the hills and past the moon;*
All roads lead home—but so soon?

Realizing what he'd just done, he clapped a paw to the side of his head and groaned. Obviously Morkir was a bad influence! Spreading his own wings, he sprang into the sky with a hammering heart, determined to fly in the opposite direction as swiftly as he could.

Yet, he dipped a wing and turned. Morkir was not too far ahead, and in little time they were flying side by side.

Ten

MARIAN TOSSED HER MANE and reared as the Black Dragon plunged out of the sky toward Ronaldo. She knew Harrow and knew his reputation as an impulsive hothead, but she'd never seen him like she saw him now. His eyes burned with anger, and every muscle in his sinuous and powerful body strained as he charged downward.

The sun flashed on his scales and on his outreaching claws. "The third talisman is mine!" he screamed with an almost murderous fury.

Ronaldo stood transfixed, jaw agape as Harrow attacked. Then at the last moment some reflex took over, and he lunged away. With a sweep of one gray wing he batted the Black Dragon aside. Harrow roared in pain and surprise and swiftly turned to renew his attack.

On the grass near Ronaldo, the *Diamond Dragon* sparkled in a beam of sunlight. Marian's heart pounded. Fearing for the talisman, she reared again and lunged forward as Harrow's shadow rippled over the ground.

"Look out!" Ronaldo called.

But Marian ignored the warning. Tearing divots of grass with her golden hooves, she raced at full speed across the square to snatch the jewel up in her mouth. Nothing, not even her life, was more important than protecting it!

With a cry, fearing for her safety, Ronaldo sprang upward. But there was too little distance to spare, and the tip of his tail struck Marian, knocking her down, as he intercepted Harrow. The two Dragons collided in midair with such force that the village seemed to shake, and a shocked outcry went up from Stronghold's gathered citizens as, overhead, the combatants slashed at each other.

The Dragon Tiamat rose over the canyon rim on swift wings. "Help him!" he shouted as he charged to Harrow's aid. "Help the Son of Stormfire!"

Fearless, Snowsong shot upward to intercept the ruby Dragon. Her red eyes burned as she spread her white wings and blocked his course. "Stay back! Keep out of it," she warned as Fleer, reacting a little more slowly, joined her to flank Tiamat.

Half stunned, Marian picked herself up. Shaking away the stars that danced in her head, she cast a frantic look around. A shiver of dread passed through her. She'd dropped the talisman!

But there was no time to search for it. Loud screams drew her attention again, and the crowd surged toward her. A dark, tangled shadow fell across the square, growing larger and larger. Marian shot a glance upward. Locked in battle, pounding each other with their wings, Harrow and Ronaldo fell earthward, and Marian had no choice but to run with the others.

Without relinquishing their grips, the two Dragons crashed in a writhing mass, shattering homes and shops. On the edge of the square, a wide-eyed Sabu flew into the sky as debris rained about her. "Harrow!" she cried.

On the other side of the square, Blue Ramoses took flight. "Stop it!" he demanded. "Stop this madness!"

Neither Dragon heard. Over and over they rolled, entangled in each other, heedless of the destruction they were causing, of the danger they posed to those around them. Yet, few of the villagers ran away. Despite the risk, they stayed to watch the combatants, cheering when a blow was struck, shouting encouragements.

A familiar humming tickled Marian's ear. "What to do? What to do?" Bumble cried in his small panicked voice. "Marian, tell me! Help!" The little hummingbird flew dizzying circles around her horn and then perched on the tip. "Oh, this is bad!" he proclaimed as he turned to face the fight. "It's a left! A right! An uppercut and a jab! And there's a tail across the snoot! It's a thriller, folks! A thriller!" He darted off again, a green blur.

Keeping one eye on the fierce combat, Marian shouldered her way through the crowd. "Let me by!" she shouted as she pushed and nudged a pair of stubborn fomorians out of the way. "Move!" A minotaur scrambled out of her path, knocking a satyr over in his haste. Marian barely noticed. With a toss of her head she shoved a large brown bear aside. "Pardon me!" she muttered. Finally, she reached the square again and swept her gaze over the grass.

At the other end of the square Harrow gave a loud roar as he managed to separate himself from Ronaldo. Both Dragons regained their feet and smashed together again. Under the mighty impact, Ronaldo fell backward, but he dug his claws into Harrow's shoulders and pulled him over, too. Again they rolled, this time closer and closer to the canyon rim and then finally over it.

The crowd screamed and rushed to the edge to watch them fall. A moment later they turned again, one huge mass of desperately pumping arms and legs, running for safety as both Dragons flew upward to continue their savage confrontation above the gorge.

A lone satyr, braver than the rest or more foolish, remained on the rim. "Stay out there, you miserable worms!" he shouted angrily. "You've wrecked the very house I built with my own two hands, and my shop besides!" Waving a piece of planking, he drew back and hurled it, then cursed loudly as it fell far wide of its intended mark.

"Here now!" a minotaur shouted, running forward as the satyr bent down to seize up a rock. With a scolding look he snatched the missile away. Then he curled his fist around it and drew back. "Let me. I'm a lot stronger, and they got my house, too!" With a grunt, he flung the rock and bounced it accurately off Ronaldo's head.

Carola, the cat-faced fomorian, dashed forward and planted her hands against the minotaur's broad, hairy chest. "Not that one, you idiot!" she said, giving him a push. "The other one! Harrow started it!"

More stones and pieces of debris started flying over the canyon. "What's it matter?" someone demanded. "They're both to blame!" "Look at the damage!" still another cried. "Stronghold is ruined!" And someone else whined. "Again?"

With the citizens at the rim and no one around to interfere, Marian trotted back and forth over the trampled square, intent on finding the talisman. If she could recover it quickly she might be able to stop the fight, but first she had to know that the *Diamond Dragon* was safe. Too much depended upon it!

Over the canyon, Ronaldo suddenly gained a brief advantage and dealt Harrow a powerful blow. The force of it stunned the Black Dragon and sent him spiraling downward to splash into the Echo Rush. Harrow thrashed in the river and then with a roar, recovering himself, he shot upward again, climbing fast and high.

"You will not take away my birthright!" he shouted furiously. "Chan and Luna have theirs, and this one belongs to me! Stormfire foretold it!"

Ronaldo beat his wings with desperate energy as he hovered at a safe distance. Though he panted with fatigue and strain, it wasn't in him to retreat. "Did he foretell my fist on the end of your arrogant nose?" he answered. "Or my teeth in your hind quarters?"

Harrow spread his wings to their fullest and stretched his neck toward Ronaldo. "Impostor!" he shouted, "Don't you dare mock my father!" Drawing a deep breath, he opened his mouth. Fire bubbled in his throat and between his gaping jaws and then shot forth in a searing red stream.

Again the crowd of citizens screamed, but before the flames could reach Ronaldo, Sabu charged upward. Harrow's fire struck her and crackled around her immense black form as she intercepted the blast and hovered in its heart. For an instant her son seemed barely aware of what he was doing.

Harrow recoiled in shock. "Forgive me!" he cried to his mother.

"Stop this!" Sabu pleaded. "Both of you! Look what you've done!"

A complete hush fell over Stronghold as both combatants turned to see the rows of shattered homes and buildings, the accusing faces of distraught and angry villagers. Then an infant fomorian began to cry in its mother's arms.

"I didn't mean to!" Harrow whispered, aghast. "I wasn't thinking!"

Sabu looked at both Dragons, and her eyes were full of anger and uncertainty. "Land with me," she ordered, "before either of you does more harm."

In the square, Marian trembled as she watched Sabu turn and approach. Harrow flew obediently at her right side, black mother and black son, a beautifully matched pair. But Ronaldo hesitated, and the Last Unicorn in the World could see the pain in her friend's eyes. Wordlessly he dipped a wing and flew in the opposite direction, southward across the canyon.

Bumble appeared again and perched on Marian's head between her ears. "Ronaldo!" he called. "Ronaldo, come back! Come back, Ronaldo!"

"It's no use," Marian murmured, her heart falling as she watched the Gray Dragon sail beyond the distant treetops on the canyon's far side. "Stronghold didn't treat him very well. He's going home."

"Not without Bumble!" The little hummingbird sped off so swiftly that not even she could track his flight.

Alone, Marian hung her head and squeezed her eyes shut. It had all gone so horribly wrong so quickly! She knew the fault was hers, but there was another to blame as well.

Damn you, Stormfire, and your devious schemes! she thought bitterly, *And damn me for the part I've played in them!* She lifted her head again and looked to the horizon for any sight of Ronaldo, hoping against all hope that he could someday forgive her.

Sabu landed in the middle of the square with Harrow close at her side. "Where is the talisman?" Stormfire's son demanded before his feet had even touched the ground. "Give it to me!"

Without even looking, Sabu struck him across the nose with one wing. "Shut up, Harrow," she ordered. "Your impulsiveness and jealousy has caused enough trouble." Harrow tensed and glared angrily, but then he hung his head.

The citizens of Stronghold, quiet once more, began to draw nearer. Their faces were flushed and frightened, their nervousness plain to see as they spread out slowly in a ring. Some of the minotaurs and satyrs still carried boards or rocks, and Bear Byron's lips were curled back in a soundless snarl that showed his teeth. A pair of silver wolves paced at his side with their ears flattened.

Sabu's hard gaze locked on Marian, but before the Dragon mother could speak, another shadow glided across the grass and Ramoses carefully landed. "I call a council," he said in a clear, deep voice. "In the traditional place on the shore of the Echo Rush where there is room for all."

Sabu rose on her hind legs and drew herself up to her full height. "There will be no council!" she hissed. "I will have my answers now, right here, from the unicorn!"

"It's my right," Ramoses answered unintimidated. Then he also stood, stretching to his full impressive height. Older and taller than any surviving Dragon, he looked down upon Sabu. "You were Stormfire's mate," he continued. "But you are not queen of the Dragonkin."

Fleer swooped down and hovered. "I also want a council!" he shouted, adding his voice to Ramoses. "I'm not unaffected by these revelations!"

Sabu glared. Without further word or argument she spread her wings and rose into the sky, brushing past Fleer. For a moment she hovered above Stronghold, seeming to hesitate, a vast silhouette against the sun. Then she sailed downward toward the sharp pinnacle of stone called Stormfire's Point and, folding her wings, she perched there to wait.

Harrow bent low to the ground, bringing his great face close to Marian. "I still want the talisman," he whispered. "It's mine! Where is it?"

It was Marian's turn to glare. "It's gone," she answered harshly.

Harrow leaned even closer, letting her feel the heat of his breath as he spoke. "You're lying!"

Marian lowered her horn until it pointed straight up one of Harrow's nostrils. The air tingled suddenly around her, and her eyes began to flash in a rapid cascade of color. For an instant she seemed larger, more powerful. "Don't challenge me, youngster," she warned in a cold hiss. "You aren't Dragon enough."

"Get away from her, Harrow," Ramoses ordered. "Haven't you made enemies enough today? Look around at those you once called friends and neighbors."

Bear Byron stepped forward and shook a paw. "You were supposed to protect us!" he roared. "But who'll protect us from you, Son of Stormfire?"

A general assent went up from the villagers, and Harrow looked stung. "I—I'm sorry!" he managed.

Ramoses shook his head sadly. "Save it for the river," he suggested, and with a stern gaze he watched as Harrow flew upward and toward the canyon. Then, he turned to Marian and bowed his blue head. "There hasn't been time for a proper hello, but it's good to see an old friend even in these unpleasant circumstances."

Bending one knee, Marian returned his bow. "Harrow's not alone in his apologies," she said. "I'm sorry, too, Ramoses."

"You have nothing to apologize for," the blue Dragon answered. Closing his paws ever so gently around Marian, he lifted her and rose into the sky. Over Stronghold's rim they glided on warm winds and down toward the river below. Fleer and Tiamat already waited on the sandy shore with a sullen Harrow while Snowsong and the Dragon

Diana circled overhead with a host of birds. A long line of minotaurs, satyrs and fomorians filed down the narrow stone stairs carved into the canyon wall, and two small human figures leaned out of the mouth of Stormfire's cave to see what was happening.

The shadows had begun to deepen by the time the council was gathered, and on one shore someone set fire to an assembled pile of logs. As the first flames began to flicker and grow, Sabu flew down from her high perch.

"Now speak again your hurtful lie!" she said, glaring at Marian as she landed. "If you dare, Unicorn!"

Ramoses spoke before Marian could. "She told no lie," he answered for all to hear. "Ronaldo is your son." Turning away from Sabu, he directed a hard gaze at Harrow. "And your brother."

"The hatchling from your first egg," Marian explained.

Forgetting the others near her, Sabu snapped her wings open. A rain of sand pelted the nearest, but she barely seemed to notice. Her voice broke with emotion. "My first egg was stolen and eaten by the last of the chimeras!"

"You didn't witness it," Ramoses countered.

The council moved away from Sabu, giving her room as she began to tremble and lash her tail. Despite her own sometime-temper, a trait she shared with her son, she was respected and well-loved by Stronghold's citizens.

"But the prophecy!" Harrow interrupted as he leaned toward his mother. "Three children—three talismans!"

"I don't care about the prophecies!" his mother shouted. She turned back toward Ramoses and Marian, who stood side by side at the water's edge. "Stormfire witnessed it! He chased the chimeras, hunted them down and killed them! He told me!"

With a shake of her mane, Marian took a step forward, and when she spoke her voice was filled with sadness. "With all my heart, Sabu," she said, "I ask you to forgive me, but I swear what I'm telling you is true." Hesitating, she looked around at the crowd, studying the faces, the rapt expressions of the listeners. *I'm about to destroy a legend*, she thought to herself as she summoned the strength and will to continue, and when she spoke again her voice was firmer. "Stormfire, himself, stole your egg."

A gasp went up from the assembly. "No!" someone shouted. And from someone else, "It's a lie!" But most remained silent, attentive, withholding judgment. Sabu looked too stunned to protest.

Marian looked toward Fleer, who was listening intently at the edge of the gathering. "He gave the egg to your parents, Robare and Circe. They had no children of their own at the time, and they'd established their caves, not in Stronghold with the other Dragons, but in the iso-lated southern forests. No one was ever to know the egg wasn't Circe's. No one ever did."

"Circe cared for it as if it were her own," Ramoses added.

"And Stormfire charged me to watch over the hatchling," Marian continued. The story came rushing out of her, for she had carried her secrets too long. "For that reason I stayed in the Whispering Hills and lived in those same southern woods, never venturing far from Ronal-do, never taking my eye off him for long."

Sabu roared in anger, and bitterness filled her eyes. "You were ever his general and his right hand!" she accused. "Through all the Dragon Wars he took your counsel over mine!" Then she roared again as bitterness changed to pain. "But why? Why would he take my child from me?"

Ramoses hung his head, unable to meet Sabu's teary gaze. "Because there could be only three," he answered. "Three children to wield the power contained in the three talismans. Three children to establish a new home for all the Dragonkin." He looked up again and spoke to all the gathering. "This he foresaw, and this he recorded in the Great Book of Stormfire!"

Marian kept silent. She hung her head until her mane dragged in the sand, and she backed up several steps until she could back no more. The cold water of the Echo Rush chilled her hooves, snatched at the flaxen strands of her tail. Looking away, she noted how the shadows had deepened. The evening seemed much too dark.

"No!" Sabu screamed. "It's too cruel!" She looked wildly around, then craned her neck to stare toward the southern rim. "My son?" she whispered hoarsely. "And I drove him away?"

Harrow stretched out his wings. "Mother..."

Sabu recoiled and stared at Harrow as if she didn't recognize him. "Some part of me knew!" she continued, speaking mostly to herself as if her mind were unhinging. "Some part of me must have known!" She looked sharply at Ramoses. "I never flew again after the chimeras stole my egg! My grief was too great!" Her madness deepening, she turned again to Harrow and reached out to touch the star-shaped scars that marked his wings. "Not until you nearly died at Redclaw! Then I came for you! I flew again—for you!"

"I know, Mother!" Harrow answered, suddenly softening, genuinely frightened by Sabu's despair.

Yet Sabu couldn't be consoled. "But you tell me the chimeras didn't steal it? They weren't to blame?" With stark abruptness, her trembling ceased, and she lowered her voice. "You were!" she said to Ramoses. Then she turned her gaze on Marian. "And you. His right hand and his left!" Her voice dropped still lower until the sound was all fire and ice at the same time. "No one knew about my egg. But you two knew. Apparently you knew even more than I did!"

Sabu said no more. Without warning, she snapped her wings wide, scattering the logs of the fire and throwing up a curtain of sand and water. The citizens fell back with a collective gasp, but Sabu didn't notice or didn't care. With swift purpose she flew toward Stormfire's Point and began battering it with all her Dragon might, cracking and shattering the stone, her fury relentless while everyone watched in horror.

Unnoticed, Marian slipped sadly away and headed westward up the canyon. In time she would reach the Blackwater River, and then she would go south back to the Whispering Hills and back to watching Ronaldo, because his story was not yet over.

She had made a promise long ago to Stormfire, and whatever she thought of the great Dragon leader now, the Last Unicorn in the World kept her promises.

But the *Diamond Dragon*, what of that? She had searched the place where she had dropped it and searched the entire square without finding the jewel. Either it had disappeared—a possibility not beyond reason given the nature of the thing—or someone had picked it up.

But who?

For the moment, Marian didn't care. With the sounds of Stronghold fading behind her, she trudged through the sand and mud, grateful for the setting sun and shadows in which to hide. She had never felt the weight of her years as she felt them now.

She had never felt such bleak loneliness.

Eleven

JAKE LEANED DOWN from his saddle. His legs ached from the long flight southward, and some other parts ached even worse than his legs. He didn't complain. The wind on his face and in his hair and the beauty of the darkening, star-speckled sky as he flew high above Wyvernwood were all the balm he needed, so he made no complaint. He stretched his muscles as much as the straps around his thighs and calves would allow, which wasn't much, and turned his attention to the smoke from the chimneys of the small village over which they were passing. He didn't know who lived down there, but he could smell their suppers, and it set his stomach to rumbling.

"I heard that," Chan said with a chuckle. "I'll have to start calling you *Thunder-belly*."

Jake didn't answer. He twisted around, watching the village disappear in the gloomy distance. Too quickly the delicious cooking odors faded as well. "Call me anything you like," he muttered, sighing. "Just call me for dinner."

Chan climbed higher, rising into the milky glow of the eastern moon. Off to the west, his shadow kept pace, skimming the silver-tinged treetops like a dark companion. Off to the east, flying lower than they, a curious owl also kept pace, its round bright eyes occasionally turning a questioning look their way.

Jake took it all in, looking left and right, watching the rippling wind-swept leaves below and the brightening stars overhead. His cramped fingers uncurled from the saddle horn, and closing his eyes, he lifted his arms straight out from his sides as if he had wings of his own.

This is a perfect moment, he told himself as he opened his eyes again and drew a deep breath. He thought he had never known such contentment and such peace. If only he could fly with Chan just as they

99

were now, to the ends of the world, to the end of time, never touching down again, never letting problems and worries touch them.

But that was a boy's wish. His fingers brushed over the bowstring that crossed his chest, and his gaze fell on the leather sling wrapped like a bracelet around his wrist, and he knew with an inexplicable sadness that his boyhood was gone. He didn't know yet what was taking its place. Not yet a man either, he felt caught in some limbo between what he was and what he might become.

"*Sumapai*," Jake called as he leaned forward and placed his palm against Chan's warm scales. He marveled at the working of the great muscles beneath, at the sheer physical power of his Dragon mentor. "What's it like to live as long and know as much as you do?"

Chan was quiet for a moment. "I don't know so much, *Chokahai*," he answered, "and of what I do know I understand less than half."

Jake fell silent again while he let that sink in. The owl, he noticed, was no longer with them. Perhaps it had turned away to chase a mouse or some other lively morsel. *Still thinking about food*, he realized, scolding himself as he put a hand over his stomach. He wished the owl good hunting.

"But you're more than two hundred years old," Jake finally said.

"Almost three hundred," Chan corrected. "Ramoses would know for sure. He makes records of such things. But in Dragon terms, I'm still a youngster like yourself."

Jake scoffed. "I'm barely sixteen," he said.

"And already a world traveler," Chan pointed out. "You've been from one end of Degarm to the other and all places between with your carnival. You've sailed on a ship up the Windy Sea. You've seen Valindar and Throom Odin and Asgalun..."

"And Wyvernwood," Jake reminded.

"Of course," Chan agreed. "All that, and only sixteen." Extending his wings to their utmost, Chan glided through the darkness, dropping gradually closer to the treetops again. "How much more you've seen and done than I! Until recently, *Chokahai*, Wyvernwood has been the world to me. In almost three hundred years, I never ventured beyond its forested borders. Nor did my siblings or many of the other Dragonkin."

Jake frowned. "Why not?"

"Because we're not like humans, *Chokahai*," he explained. "We're not compelled to wander as humans are. Our curiosity doesn't drive us to new places. Yes, we're curious and we do learn. But we learn about our homes, our environments, and each other. We learn every single little fact and detail, because that's what Dragon curiosity is."

"And men?" Jake prodded.

A tremor passed through Chan into Jake's palm. Not a tremor in the usual sense, not fear or dread. A sigh, perhaps, or maybe the barest hint of a chuckle. "Men are like guests at a great banquet," he said. "They have to stick their fingers into every cake and pie, taste every wine, sample every dish, seldom pausing to savor or appreciate one before they move on to the next one. They can barely tell you the ingredients, may not even know the name of the dish, because those are details. They know only what they like and what they want."

"You think that's really how we see the world?" Jake interrupted, his frown deepening. But then he thought about the things he'd seen and learned in Wyvernwood. To a Dragon, a butterfly was never just a butterfly; it was a swallowtail or a yellow sulfur or a painted lady. A flower was never just a flower, but ocotillo or lantana or lemon bottlebrush. These were the details Chan spoke of, the deep *knowing* of the immediate world.

And now that he thought about it, men did stick their fingers into every cake and pie, usually without stopping to wash their hands or caring if they ruined the dish for everyone else. Chan called it curiosity. Rudeness was closer to the truth.

Yet none of it explained the aggression he'd seen in his own people, nor their cruelty. Especially their cruelty. Of that he had intimate and deep knowledge.

"You may be right," he conceded bitterly. "The Dragon way is better."

"Who can say which is better?" Chan asked. "The Age of Dragons is passing, Jake. Some say it's already passed, and the Age of Man is ascendant. Good and bad, they have qualities that we lack or have lost."

"You haven't lost anything, *Sumapai*!" Jake insisted with sudden forcefulness. "Whether you realize it or not, you do know so many things. And you have wisdom, too! I've listened to Ramoses and the others. I know the kindness in Carola and Gregor and the generous spirit in Bear Byron. Even in Morkir!" He hesitated, thought for a moment and then shrugged. "Okay, Morkir was a tougher nut to crack. But he learned, and he changed! And... and, well, maybe you should think about that and consider what you could teach the rest of the world if you stopped hiding from it!"

For a long moment the only sound was the rushing of the wind past Jake's ears and the steady, powerful beat of Chan's wings. When the Dragon made no response, Jake began to worry that he had crossed some line, that his words had hurt his friend, and suddenly he felt very small and very young. "I'm sorry, Chan," he said in a dejected tone. "I didn't mean that the way it sounded. I'm just a boy—what do I know?"

"More than you give yourself credit for," Chan answered. "In your heart you're Dragonkin. We learn from each other, you and I."

"And I really have a lot to learn," Jake added with a weak grin.

The Son of Stormfire gave a subtle nod as he flew. "And a lot to teach," he answered. "You're both *Chokahai* and *Sumapai*. Teacher and student, master and pupil, and I'm lucky to have you as my friend."

Jake's lips drew into a taut line and then he smiled to himself. "Well, in that case would it be all right if I asked a favor?" He hesitated and, leaning forward, put his palm on Chan's neck again. The bare touch always seemed to intensify the bond he felt with the Dragon. It made his heart beat faster to sense such power and warmth and it filled him with wonder. But at the moment, he felt full of something else. "Could we please land?" he continued. "We've been flying all day, and I desperately need to find a tree!"

Chan laughed. "Do you think you can make it to the border?" he asked. "It's not far now, and I was sort of looking forward to pissing on Degarm."

Jake gave a soft groan, and Chan laughed again, but he dipped a wing and angled downward toward a nearby hilltop where the woods were not too thick.

Once they were down, Jake swiftly unfastened the straps that held him in the saddle and, leaping down, he ran deep into a thicket. The sudden darkness briefly disconcerted him. In the sky, even as night had deepened, he'd had the moon and the stars at his shoulder, but on the ground the leaves and branches and shadows shut out the light. Cautiously he ventured a little farther, then paused again to rub feeling back into his cramped and aching legs.

A gravelly whisper came from a bush close by. "Looks like we both had the same idea."

Jake jumped and stared toward the voice, and from the blackness to his left, just barely visible, a tall grinning figure stared back. His first thought was to turn and run, but before he could move a strong arm encircled his waist and a hand clamped over his mouth and nose.

Another voice whispered harshly at his ear. "Not a sound, boy. Not a peep or a pop."

Jake's moment of panic passed and he forced himself to relax. As a reward, his captor moved a finger and let him draw a breath through his nose. "Aren't you finished over there yet?" the voice close to his ear hissed.

The first figure looked furtively around. "Some things just can't be rushed!" he whispered, sounding defensive. "What've you got there, anyway, Mikey?"

The one called Mikey gave him a shake and a squeeze. "Looks like a boy," came the answer, "but in these cursed woods you can't be too sure."

Jake rolled his eyes. Chan had spoken of luck, but what kind of luck was it when you couldn't even stop for a pee without landing in some kind of trouble?

"You're right about that," the first one agreed as he shook himself and adjusted his clothing. "Better kill him."

"Damn near put my eye out when I grabbed him," Mikey grumbled. "He's got a bow across his back."

As much as he could, Jake sighed. In the darkness, he still couldn't get a good look at either man, but he felt sure they were Degarmian soldiers, and if there were two there were probably more close by.

"Well if it's a good one," said the first, "then it belongs to me, because I saw him first."

Mikey spat. "In this darkness," he sneered, "you couldn't even see the end of your..."

Jake figured he'd lingered long enough with this pair. Mikey was strong, but he didn't know that he was holding a carnival acrobat and that was rather like holding a tiger by the tail. Before Mikey could finish his sentence, Jake stomped on the unsuspecting man's foot and at almost the same time threw all his weight backward.

Mikey's yell was only slightly muffled as Jake did a backward roll over his face. "Sorry about that," Jake offered as he sprang to his feet, free, and rubbed his bruised lips. "But not much!" He waved to the first man, who seemed to be having trouble buckling his belt. "Can't stay to play," he said.

Mikey groaned as he tried to get to his feet. "Don't just stand there!" he shouted as he fumbled for the sword he wore sheathed at his hip. "Get him!"

"Catch me if you can!" Jake laughed as he turned and ran. His eyes had finally adjusted to the darkness, and he could see the branches and bushes that might have tripped him up. Small and fleet, he dodged the obstacles in his path, and when a convenient limb presented itself, he caught, swung up, and climbed to the next one.

A moment later, Mikey and his companion came crashing through the underbrush. "I tell you, he came this way!" the companion complained. "I saw him!"

Mikey grabbed the other man's shoulder and jerked him to a rough stop at the base of the tree. "You saw! You saw! In this darkness you couldn't see..."

That reminded Jake that he hadn't yet taken care of the business that had brought him into these woods. He grinned to himself. Why not? Now was as good a time as any.

"What the...?" Mikey exclaimed suddenly.

"Hey, is it raining?" he companion asked, looking up.

"Rain, my eye!" Mikey looked up, too, which wasn't the brightest thing to do. "It's him!" he cried, pointing with his sword. "Get him! I want his filthy hide!"

"I want a towel!" the companion cried in dismay, finally realizing that it wasn't raining. "Oh, yuck!"

Jake laughed. Those buffoons would never reach him up here. "Catch me if you can!" he challenged as he moved around the boll to another branch. But Mikey sheathed his sword and, wiping his face, gave a determined roar, jumped up and caught the lowest limb. When he had one leg over it, Jake jumped to the ground on the opposite side of the tree.

"Not a sound now, boys," he teased. "Not a peep or a pop!"

Mikey, with his greater weight, had both legs and both arms wrapped around the lowest branch and was trying to muscle himself on top of it when it gave a loud warning crack. "Oh no!" he groaned.

Jake didn't wait around to see the result, but he made sure Mikey's companion saw which way he went.

Chan's going to kill me for wandering off so far, he thought to himself. But when he got back to the small clearing, the Dragon lay with his great head on folded paws and his tail curled around almost to his nose as if he was resting entirely at peace.

One eye opened as Jake ran up. "Did you stretch your legs?" Chan asked.

"New playmates," Jake whispered, putting a finger to his lips to urge silence. Then, folding his arms over his chest and crossing one leg over the other, he leaned casually against Chan's shoulder.

A moment later, with a good deal of huffing and puffing, the two soldiers emerged from between the trees. Their eyes gleamed with angry fixation on Jake. Mikey drew his sword again.

Then they both saw Chan and stopped in their tracks.

"Hello, sailors," Chan said with a blink of his eyes. "Come here often?"

Mikey dropped his sword. His companion dropped his jaw. Jake curled the fingers of his right hand and waved bye-bye to the backs of the pair as they crashed back into the forest as fast as they could go.

"Well, that was fun," Jake said.

"No, that was troubling," Chan answered. "Soldiers are like ants. Where there's one there's two, and where there's two there's four."

"And where there's four there's more," Jake finished, recalling that he'd had a similar thought.

With a sudden great lurch, Chan rose to all fours and sniffed the air. The moon, rising just over the edge of the small clearing, set his scales to shimmering, and his huge eyes burned as they caught its light. His ears twitched.

Jake gasped with sudden pain and fell back against one of Chan's legs. A shattered arrow lay on the ground at his feet, and he gingerly touched his chest where the shaft had struck him. He ran his palm over the ivory Dragon-scale shirt that had saved his life. He had Luna to thank for that. "That felt like a battering ram!" he exclaimed. "But where...?"

"Look out!" Chan snapped one wing open to shelter Jake as a barrage of arrows zipped out of the woods. Though most of the shafts deflected away or shattered, a few stuck in the leathery membranes.

"Your playmates have playmates!" the Dragon said as he shook them off.

Jake unslung his own bow, but his quivers were out of reach on the saddle around Chan's neck. "My arrows!" he called to Chan.

But the Dragon stood tall. "Not yet, young warrior," he answered Jake. "We're in no danger here."

Jake rubbed the sore spot where the arrow had struck him. He'd have a bruise there tomorrow. "You didn't just take one in the chest!"

Chan chuckled. "Open your eyes, *Chokahai*," he advised.

Calming himself, Jake swept a quick gaze around, noting the scores of arrows littering the ground around Chan. "Sorry," he muttered with some embarrassment.

"We teach each other," he reminded sternly, "so remember this: don't be so quick to reach for your weapons. It's one of mankind's gravest faults."

Peeking out from under Chan's wing, Jake directed his attention toward the forest. Among the nearer trees he could see shadowy figures stirring. Lots of them. And judging from the number of arrows in that last flight, there had to be far more than he could see. Darkness was no obstacle to a Dragon's eyes, though.

"We're surrounded, aren't we?" Jake said as Chan looked from side to side.

"More or less," Chan answered calmly. "I don't think they've managed to get above us yet."

Jake stuck out his tongue. "Very funny. Remind me to laugh in a day or two. And then remind me to get a Dragon-scale overcoat that covers my entire body."

Chan clucked his tongue. "Sounds very unfashionable." He shifted his wing to cover Jake again. "Persistent creatures."

Jake gritted his teeth as he listened to the sounds of the shafts pelting Chan, the dull thumps as they struck his wings, the more solid cracks as they broke against his scaled body. Not for the first time, he felt ashamed of his humanity, and he felt angry at his own helplessness. But he had to do something! Sooner or later, one of those arrows might find Chan's eyes. "*Sumapai*," he begged, "Fly away! Just leave me here!"

Chan didn't dignify that with a response.

"All right then!" Jake said, thinking fast. He rubbed his hands together and chewed a thumbnail. "Bluff!" he said at last.

Chan twisted his neck around to bring his face close to Jake's. "What?"

"Bluff!" Jake repeated. Then, realizing that Chan didn't understand the concept, he said, "Lie!"

The blank look in Chan's eyes suggested he didn't understand that concept, either. Or if he did, he didn't approve of it. Jake put his hands on his hips and frowned. "I thought you were an expert on our gravest faults?"

Chan blinked. "And I also told you I had a lot to learn."

Jake chewed his lip thoughtfully for a moment. "Then pay attention, because class is about to begin." Peeking out from under the Dragon's wing again, he cupped his hands around his mouth. For a moment, his anger threatened to overwhelm him again. Chan was only pinned down because he couldn't get his rider safely into the saddle.

"Hello, the commander!" he shouted, pitching his voice as deep as he could. "Who speaks for the invaders of Wyvernwood?"

From the edge of the woods a little bit downslope, a figure stepped forth. The moonlight hinted of armor beneath the cloak he wore. When he held up a hand all the shadowy figures among the trees grew still. "Who calls us invaders?" he demanded.

"No one you need to know," Jake answered roughly. "But invaders you are! Go home while you can!"

The commander barked a short laugh. "We are home, Monster! These woods are part of Degarm!"

Idiot, Jake thought with a grimace. There was the age-old story behind the war between Degarm and Angmar in the north: both nations claimed Wyvernwood as theirs. Even before the coming of the Dragonkin they had fought over it.

Jake lowered his voice and said to Chan, "I know you won't risk burning the forest, but can you blow a small stream of fire skyward?"

Chan lifted his head and a streamer of flame fountained upward. Jake called out to the commander again as loudly as he could so that all the soldiers might hear. "Then we'll scatter your ashes over it! Our patience is mighty, but not without its limits!"

The commander laughed again, more boldly this time. "You're that boy, aren't you? Some of my men saw you!" A scattering of laughter sounded from the trees.

Jake thought fast and recalled something Mikey had said. "In these cursed woods?" he responded, doing his best to sound ominous. "Can you be sure of what they saw?"

The laughter ceased, and the commander grew quiet as he considered.

"Jake," Chan said softly.

But Jake held up a hand. "Go home!" he called again. "Before the wrath of Wyvernwood descends upon you all! Other Dragons are coming! The forest itself will rise up against you! You are surrounded, and you don't even know it!"

"Jake," Chan said, interrupting again. His voice sounded strange and uncertain. "Something's wrong!"

The commander answered. "No, Dragon, or whoever you are! It's you who are surrounded, and Degarm who triumphs here this night!" He lifted his hand again as he called to his soldiers. "Fire! And keep firing! Make his blood burn!"

Another rain of arrows hissed through the air, and again Chan shifted to protect Jake. The shafts pounded down, most shattering, but some sticking briefly in Chan's wings. Wave after merciless wave rained down, more arrows than Jake ever dreamed of.

A deep shudder passed through Chan.

"*Sumapai!*" Jake cried out. A bolt of fear stabbed his heart.

From deep in the woods a new sound rose, a howling that chilled the moon and rose to a keening pitch.

Wolves!

Then with it came other sounds: the deep, guttural growls of bears and lions, and the savage whining cries of leopards.

A soldier screamed. And then screaming spread across the night. Among the trees the shadowy figures of soldiers danced in macabre silhouette with other more deadly shapes, shapes with teeth and fangs and claws, and Jake watched in awful horror as men scattered and ran.

Wyvernwood itself had risen up against the invaders!

Chan stretched his neck out close to the ground. "Jake, get on!" the Dragon urged. "We have to leave now!"

Even if the rain of arrows had not ceased, nothing would have prevented Jake from obeying that command. White with fear, he leaped into the saddle. He'd never heard such a tremor in Chan's voice!

With a powerful beat of his wings, Chan rose into the sky, and Jake clung with desperate strength to the saddle horn with one hand as he worked to fasten at least a few of the straps around his thighs. The clearing and the carnage disappeared behind them as they climbed into the bright light of the moon and stars.

But Chan didn't fly south. With a terrible cry of pain, he turned northward toward home, carving an uncertain path through the night as if blinded or maddened or both.

Tears streamed down Jake's face to be blown away by the wind. Only half-secured in the saddle, he leaned forward as he so often did and placed his palm against Chan's neck. Even through the scales he could feel a change, an unnatural heat.

"*Sumapai!*" It was Jake's turn to scream. "What is it? What's happening?"

"My wings!" Chan cried. "They burn, Jake! They burn!"

Twelve

THE KING OF ANGMAR SCOWLED as he marched up the dais steps to take his throne. It was bad enough that he was surrounded by an entourage of sycophantic advisors whose advice never amounted to much. Now he had to look over the heads of three scores of archers and a line of armored pikemen when he looked down from his high seat.

All for your protection, your Majesty, his generals had informed him. *All for your security, Sire*, his advisors had assured him with a nodding and bobbing of their shaved heads.

"All for a good show," he grumbled to himself as he climbed up on the footstool and settled himself as comfortably as he could on his throne. One of his bald advisors hurriedly arranged a thin blanket of royal purple across his lap. Kilrain waved a hand toward the doors at the far end of the Great Hall. "All right, let him in," he ordered. He glanced at the backs of the soldiers arrayed before him, noting how they trembled and shook even with their weapons in their hands. "With such a fearless bunch of pig-stickers on duty," he continued without hiding his sarcasm, "I'm sure the royal jewels are as safe as they can be."

One of his advisors leaned closer. "But your Majesty isn't wearing any. . . ."

Kilrain gave the man, some distant cousin whose name he couldn't quite recall, a withering look. "Oh, shut up!" Crooking a finger, he beckoned to one of his generals and whispered, "Take that imbecile out later and remove his toenails."

The general smiled and then bowed. "I'll bring them to you on a string."

Kilrain winced and shifted his gaze from the general to the backs of the soldiers again. *So many men*, he thought unpleasantly to himself, *and all the morons turn up in my service.*

At the opposite end of the hall the great wooden doors creaked slowly inward. Goronus, the newly appointed leader of the Griffinkin, waited on the threshold with his powerful wings folded over his back and his golden-furred chest thrust forward. Sitting back on his haunches, he extended his right front paw in salute.

"Hail, Kilrain! Master of the Northern Realm! Hail, from the king of the griffins!"

Kilrain sighed as he looked down at Goronus. *Another lackey,* he thought dismissively, *and this one with delusions of grandeur.* Was it some flaw inside his royal self that he just couldn't find good help anymore? That couldn't possibly be right. As King of Angmar he was naturally flawless.

He lifted his right hand and studied his carefully manicured fingernails. "Please tell me that you've avenged my son," he said without otherwise acknowledging the griffin. "Tell me that the Dragon called Rage is dead."

Goronus cast a wary eye over the host of archers and pikemen as he stepped into the hall and advanced toward the throne. The soldiers tensed, and the pikemen lowered their weapons with unsubtle warning.

The griffin stopped and looked around, assessing the situation. "I take it that Minhep escaped," he said with a sneer and a low chuckle. "And these pikers are supposed to stop me if I get out of line?"

Kilrain still didn't look up. "No, these pikers as you so aptly call them are supposed to *protect* me." He gestured past Goronus toward the great doors with his left hand. "Should you get out of line, *those* pikers will stop you."

Another squad of archers and pikemen filed into the hall behind Goronus.

"But I'm impolite," Kirain continued with another sigh as he pressed his palms together and rested his chin on his fingertips. "I've failed to bid you proper welcome. So welcome, Goronus, and all that." He leaned forward in his seat and clutched at the blanket. "Now about the Dragon."

Another adviser bent close. "The flagon with the dragon has the pellet with the poison," he warned.

Kilrain glared at the advisor. What nonsense was this? What poison? He beckoned to his general. "Him, too," he whispered. "Toenails."

The general executed another bow. "On a string, Sire."

"And find out about the poison."

The general bowed again looking for just a moment all too happy in his job.

Goronus cleared his throat loudly and then proclaimed, "I should like to report that a very large lizard now lies dead and rotting in the sun on the sandy shore of Thursis with its tongue wrapped around its throat and its blood staining the very waters that claimed your son, Prince Shepar!" He puffed out his chest and lifted his eagle's head high to look his most fierce while the room waited in eager silence.

After a brief pause he continued, nodding to himself as he glanced toward the upper reaches of the hall. "That would be a really grand story. Colorful, too, with all the action and gore that excites my kind and yours." Then giving a sigh of his own, Goronus let his shoulders slump and he hung his head until his beak scraped the tiled floor. "Unfortunately it wouldn't be true."

Kilrain pounded a fist on the arm of his throne. "You failed!" he shouted. "The Dragon still lives? Incompetent!" He pounded the throne again and thrust the same hand out toward one of the advisors, who instantly knelt with a nail file and a buffing cloth.

The griffin shrugged. "Now don't take it like that!" he said. "We almost had him until he beat the stuffing out of us. But he had help! Good quality help, too, not like these morons you surround yourself with!" Goronus instantly clapped a paw over his beak, knowing that he'd said too much.

Kilrain snatched his hand away from the advisor and leaned forward again. "What kind of help?" he demanded with controlled menace.

Goronus looked up, and his eyes were wide with excitement. "A unicorn!" he answered. "A real unicorn, and we thought they were extinct! A sea serpent, too—the biggest I've ever seen! Not that I've ever seen one, because they're supposed to be extinct, as well!" He swallowed and drew a breath. "But the worst of all was the invisible imp! I swear it took out two of my roughest and toughest griffins before they could even blink!"

"Maybe I should have hired the imp to kill the Dragon!" Kilrain shouted.

Goronus turned defensive. "Well, it's not like we just gave up!" he insisted. "We did our share! We got in our licks! And we chased 'em right off of Thursis, so that's yours again. Chased 'em all the way across the Windy Sea, we did, and back to Wyvernwood!"

Kilrain's eyes narrowed dangerously. "And you killed the Dragon there?"

The griffin frowned and tilted his head to one side. "Not exactly," he answered, almost whining. "He had friends waiting there. Two more Dragons, the biggest I've ever seen! They took us by surprise!"

The King of Angmar cast his blanket aside and leaped to his feet. "Unicorns, sea serpents, imps, and Dragons!" In an uncontrollable temper, he fixated on the four archers directly in front of him and dealt sharp kicks to their rumps as he spoke each word.

"Their toenails, too?" the general suggested from a safe distance.

Kilrain ignored him. "I'm sick of these creatures!" he cried, shaking his fists. "These monsters!"

Goronus curled the tips of his feathered wings. "Present company excluded I hope," he said.

"Oh, definitely," Kilrain answered, seemingly calm again, but his look was all sarcasm and insincerity. "You griffins aren't monsters!" His face purpled suddenly and he resumed his shouting. "You're idiots! You're stuffed toys! You're...!"

"We're able to fly," Goronus interrupted in an icy voice. "If you hate the Dragons so much, you prickly little fool, why not do something about it?"

The King of Angmar looked stunned. Then in a half-faint, he sank back onto his throne and locked his fingers around its arms, completely oblivious when an advisor snatched up the purple blanket and spread it over his lap again.

"Prickly little fool?" he stammered when he was finally able to focus his gaze again. "I—I rather like the sound of that!"

Behind the throne, the advisors looked horrified as they huddled together and began whispering among themselves.

The general leaned close to his king's side. "Let the archers make a pin cushion of the shaggy beast," he muttered.

"Toenails," Kilrain answered without looking at his general. "Yours. In one hour. On a string, of course." He dismissed the man with a wave. Smoothing the purple blanket with his palms, and licking his suddenly dry lips, he forced a smile and looked toward Goronus again.

"Did you have anything specific in mind?" he asked quietly.

Deep in the ancient forgotten caverns beneath the ruins of Redclaw things slept that were older even than the Dragons, things remembered only as stories or legends if they were remembered at all. Ariel moved among them soundlessly, watching over them, seeing that their dreams were undisturbed and that they rested peacefully. She was the Guardian now, and this was her task.

In those measureless depths Ariel had but one companion, and as she moved among the tunnels, turning slow backflips and cartwheels from chamber to chamber on her rounds, her companion followed, talked to her, taught her things. The companion's voice was old and cracked, sometimes little more than a whisper, sometimes little more than a draft or a breeze. Agriope was her name. A creature from another age, she lived in the dark places and seldom showed her face. It didn't matter; Ariel had come to love her.

"You have the smell of mischief on you," Agriope said, her voice gently scolding.

Ariel gave a soft laugh and stood on her hands. She didn't see as much of Agriope lately. The old one was weary and needed her sleep. "It's nothing for you to worry about," Ariel answered. Upside down on her hands, it was harder for Agriope to see her smile. "I had a conversation with some lions and tigers and bears."

"Oh my," Agriope continued, her voice dropping to a whisper of dismay. "You have the smell of daylight on you!"

Ariel righted herself and stood up. Even in the darkness she could see Agriope cringe and wave a gnarly hand before the hood that covered her face. "It's nothing for you to worry about," Ariel answered. She chuckled again and did another backflip. "I took a walk while you slept to check up on some old friends."

Agriope shuffled closer. Reaching out, she caught Ariel by the shoulders. "Hold still!" she demanded with a chuckle of her own. "You make an old woman dizzy with your tumbling and acrobatics!" She bent down and began sniffing noisily around Ariel's head and shoulders, down her arms, and turning her slowly, along her neck and back. "You have the smell of meddling," Agriope pronounced at last.

Ariel thought for a moment as she turned to face her teacher. Then she shrugged. "All right, maybe you should worry a little," she admitted. "I know you will anyway." She reached out and touched the rough woven fabric of Agriope's sleeve and felt the thin brittle bone beneath. "But I'm the Guardian now. You chose me, and you have to trust me."

Agriope withdrew and melted into the darkness. When she spoke again, her voice was as a wind against Ariel's ear. "The forest is your responsibility," she warned. "Not the creatures who live in it. Not their affairs!"

"You're wrong, beloved Mother," Ariel answered, for so she thought of Agriope. But Agriope had slept for a long time in these black caves, time enough for the world to change and change again, and although Ariel was young, there were things she thought she understood better. "We're all connected to the forest, and the forest is connected to us. The guardian of one must be the guardian of all."

"Have I chosen wrongly?" Agriope said almost to herself. "You're naïve, Ariel!"

Ariel performed a series of slow, graceful walk-overs that brought her directly before Agriope. The old one couldn't hide from her anymore, not even in such blackness. "Do we now stand at the classic divide between youth and age?" she asked with all the loving affection she could muster. "Do you tell me I'm too young to understand, and do I answer that you're too old?"

Agriope appeared to think about that. Then after a moment, she sniffed the air. "You have the smell of mischief about you," she repeated as she laid a gentle hand on Ariel's head and rumpled her hair.

Ariel raised one eyebrow and grinned. "You should worry."

Thirteen

AT FIRST LUNA thought she was back on the moon. Her heart lurched, and she braced herself for sudden cold, for thinner air. Spreading her wings wide, she swooped low to land, and her claws carved deep furrows in the gray dust as she slid to a stop.

Half-afraid, she drew a deep breath and filled her lungs. At the same time, craning her head back, she stared toward the velvet sky and the round silver disk that floated there among familiar stars. She almost laughed with relief.

Not the moon then, she thought to herself. *So where am I this time? And for how long?*

The Daughter of Stormfire blinked her eyes as she stirred the dust with her tail. It had a strange texture like soft ash or the finest pounce. The gentlest breeze raised veils and ribbons of the stuff. Wisps of it blew from the dark hilltops. Tenuous streamers trailed across the moon.

Luna swept her gaze over the barren landscape. Off to her right the black husk of a dead tree clawed its way up out of the earth like a skeletal hand. To her left, a jagged escarpment rose like a wall out of deep shadow. Under the moon's glow, the ashen plains looked almost white, seemed to glimmer like weird snow.

Cautiously, Luna spread her wings and rose into the sky once more. Once above the hills she turned westward toward a range of mountains with tortured peaks as sharp and jagged as any she'd seen on the moon. The stars and the moonglow ignited those black crags and tors with a soft halo of unnatural light that drew Luna as if she were a moth.

Yet she resisted. Held back by an unsettling fear, she flew in a wide circle and studied the landscape as far as she could see. The ground looked scorched and blasted. Here and there a little twisted vegetation

117

pushed up through the soil, but it all looked bleak and brittle, almost wintry.

A chill touched Luna's heart. At last she knew where she was.

Asgalun.

The Haunted Lands. She knew it from Ramoses' poems and from her readings in the Great Book of Stormfire. The descriptions were vivid in her memory, and yet those old stories paled against the reality, the utter lifelessness that confronted her now.

Luna choked back a whimper as she cast her gaze across the waste, sensing that it was more than just the mere panorama that rattled her. Something in the land itself sucked at her spirit, rose up with an inexorable smothering power to draw her down again and claim her. Like a creature desperate to escape a trap she climbed higher and higher.

Then her gaze touched the lambent mountain peaks again with their coronas of cold fire, and she knew that she was caught. The wind filled her wings, lifting her higher into the night. Wide-eyed and breathless, Luna began a slow glide into the west.

Over the moonlit landscape she flew with only her shadow for company. Veils of dust eddied like lazy mist over the lonely hills and barren plains, and the few dead trees and bits of scrub brush only increased the sense of desolation. Black striations began to mark the ground, deep cracks and crevices and old arroyos, as if some powerful blow had shattered the land. Luna shivered as she let her gaze follow the patterns.

A wisp of dust trailed across the moon, briefly dimming its effulgent glow. Glad for the distraction, Luna tore her attention from blasted ground and glanced upward. The moon's silvery face regarded her with placid inscrutability.

When she looked down again she blinked and frowned in puzzlement. Her shadow skimmed up the slope of a hill, but two shadows slid down the far side and over the plain. Startled, she jerked her head to the left and then to the right, but she was alone in the sky. She shot another look downward. Only one shadow now.

A trick of moonlight, Luna decided uneasily, or some strange quality of the stars reacting to the dust that drifted in the air. She breathed a wary sigh of relief.

A moment later the second shadow returned, a great winged blackness that paced side by side with her own. Luna's heart skipped a beat.

Again she looked from side to side. Nothing flew beside her; she owned the sky.

When a third shadow appeared she gave an audible gasp. Straining her wings, she climbed steeply and then bent her head back, arched her body and plunged downward in a sharp, looping dive. As she executed the maneuver she scrutinized the sky, the terrain, searched for anything that might explain such phenomena.

A chill crept through her bones as she resumed level flight no wiser than before. Studying the ground again, she beat her wings faster. Her own shadow mimicked her effort, but the other shadows moved at their own tempo, each keeping different time from the others, sometimes surging ahead, sometimes falling behind. She counted them: four shadows, and then five, six, seven.

Ghosts! Luna almost screamed the word. These were the Haunted Lands where nothing lived. It was the only explanation for the shapes that accompanied her.

But they weren't just accompanying her, she realized suddenly. They were guiding her. Without quite realizing it, she'd subtly changed her course to follow where they led. Now as she stared straight ahead her eyes widened in amazement.

In the vast mountain chain, three peaks stood out among all the rest. They loomed over the others like a single immense Dragon, two peaks forming upraised wings and the third stretching higher still and shaped like a Dragon's head. An astounding optical illusion!

A voice whispered with unexpected clarity in Luna's ear. *The Drake*, it said. *Only the wind*, Luna told herself. But she didn't believe it. She gazed at the shadows below, now a score or more, and then at the unlikely mountain formation. In her ear the voice whispered again as if to identify it. *The Drake.*

Luna's fear slowly turned to anger. Deliberately, she changed course, refusing to be led. The shadows pursued, flowing over the landscape with liquid grace, beating great wings, and lashing tails in a display that suggested impatience.

Whisperings and murmurings filled her ears, indistinct and maddening.

"What do you want?" she demanded. An ash-covered hill rose up on her right. Dipping a wing into the wind, she aimed for its summit and landed. Clouds of dust swirled as she touched down, and squeezing her eyes shut, she sneezed.

When Luna opened her eyes again the shadows were gone. Only her own black silhouette stretched down the gray hillside.

Thumping her tail nervously in the soft pounce, she turned toward the mountains and looked for the strange formation. *The Drake*, she thought automatically. But from ground-level she couldn't find it among the mountain peaks. Indeed, she wondered if she'd really seen it at all.

She waited, resting her wings, to see if the shadows would return. As she looked around a deep fatigue settled upon her. Her muscles ached. A faint weariness vibrated through her wings. As she glanced toward the moon again she put one paw to her heart and thought of the magic that had brought her here.

She'd seen sunrises and sunsets, dusks and dawns in a dizzying kaleidoscopic journey across the lands of Undersky. *And far beyond*, the moon seemed to remind her. But she couldn't guess how long she'd been gone from Stronghold. Did all those sunrises and sunsets mark the actual passing of days? Or were they just an effect of location as she popped from one side of the world to another in no particular order?

Time had lost all meaning. Whether she'd been gone for hours or days, her mind swam with sights and wonders, with new knowledge, but also with mysteries. She had more questions than she had answers. And the dearest question was when would it end?

On ivory wings Luna rose into the sky again and turned toward the mountains. As she climbed she glanced at the ground. The shadows were back, racing along with her. *Dragon shadows*, she whispered, unafraid. *Ghosts*

"I am Luna, Daughter of Stormfire!" she called, announcing herself, "and you have no power over me!" To make her point she exhaled a blast of fire. The landscape lit up like red day, expelling the shadows. When her flame flickered and faded only her own shadow remained to keep her company.

But then bright moonlight reasserted itself upon the land, and one black shape after another, the shadows of Asgalun reappeared.

"So be it," she said, accepting her persistent companions. "Show me what you want me to see."

Sullen, confused and grieving, Sabu sat alone in the dark recesses of Stormfire's cave. Although her mate had been dead for months, his scent still lingered in the corners. Her ears twitched. Sometimes she thought she heard his voice still echoing from the walls, and it was too easy to imagine his shadow looming clear up to the ceiling in the slight glow from the fireplace's coals.

On a table near the hearth, sparkling in that faint ruddy light, sat the Glass Dragon. Only by closing her eyes could she be free of its spell. It watched her in silence. If she opened one eye just the barest slit and looked quickly, she thought she saw some tiny shape peeking out from the facets.

A scowl turned up the corners of her Dragon lips even as tears rolled down her scaled face. The talisman reeked of Stormfire as surely as the cave. She squeezed her eyes shut tight and shook her head. It didn't matter; she wanted nothing to do with it. She hadn't come here for the talisman.

In this cave on this very spot where she sat she had born an egg, and from this cave that egg—her child!—had been stolen.

Avoiding the talisman, Sabu opened her eyes and stared around the cave. She had never come here again after that pain, yet she remembered every intimate feature and detail. This place had been her first home in the Great Refuge. Her nest. Only the scars of Stormfire's talons on the floor from years of pacing were new to her.

Another smell permeated the cave—the smell of lies!

A wave of emotion struck Sabu. Her heart hammered and her throat constricted until she couldn't breathe. Even then she struggled to control herself, to hold it all inside—all the pain and all the secrets!

But it was all too much, too festered.

Sabu gave a choked sob. Her mind churned with memories and images long rejected, long repressed. Churned—and overturned. A scream ripped from her, a long soul-wrenching cry of despair that spilled beyond the cave and echoed over and over again on the canyon walls.

Wrapping herself in her wings, Sabu rocked back and forth and banged her head against the wall until bits of stone began to cascade. The table shivered; the Glass Dragon vibrated toward the edge and teetered. She barely noticed as she raised her paws to hide her face.

From behind her claws she screamed again.

Then, as the pulse pounded in her temples and her heart threatened to break, she felt some gaze upon her. Gasping, she fought to calm herself, and slowly she opened her eyes.

The Glass Dragon watched her dispassionately.

"You know, don't you." Sabu strained to whisper. "I killed them all. I hunted them, stalked and murdered them secretly at night until not a single one remained." She stared at the talisman, awaiting its judgment. When it remained silent she pronounced it herself. "The chimeras are extinct." She held up her claws. The red light from the fireplace coals painted them red. "Because I made them extinct."

She hung her head and felt her throat constrict again. "They killed my child—or a few did—and I thought they all had to pay. Every chimera." Barely able to speak, she turned her gaze to the talisman again. "But they didn't! It was a lie!"

Once more Sabu hid her face. "I acted on a lie!"

Silence filled the cave as Sabu leaned back against the wall. After a while she laughed softly at herself for confessing to an inanimate object. Then just as softly she wept herself to sleep.

When she woke, the Glass Dragon sat centered on the table again, no longer balanced on the precarious edge. How it had gotten there Sabu didn't know. Nor did she really care. Wiping her eyes she gazed toward the mouth of the cave and blinked at the bright daylight.

How long had she slept? Indeed, how long had she been down here in this dreadful darkness? Her ears twitched. She could still hear Stormfire's voice in the stones if she listened carefully. His scent still lingered in the corners. She touched the scars on the floor.

Why? she wondered. *Tell me there's a reason?*

Despair threatened to overwhelm her again, but she forced it down and locked it up tight. Still, she listened to the stone for the half-imagined voice of her mate, hoping for an answer that didn't come.

She thought suddenly of Ronaldo. *My child,* she said to herself, trying the words out. *My Dragon-child!* She knew it was true, and not because Ramoses and Marian said it was. She knew in her heart the way only a mother could know. It had only taken her some time to realize it.

This hole should be filled with salt and sealed up forever, she thought as she stood up and moved toward the entrance. But that wouldn't happen. At the threshold, she lingered to glance back once more at the table where the Glass Dragon rested.

If there was any purpose at all to be found, any sense to be made from so much pain, it resided in the talismans.

Stormfire's legacy.

The last three drops of magic in the world.

Spreading ebon wings, she leaped into the warm sunlight and flew southward across Stronghold canyon. A chorus of shouts and cheers rose from the rim behind her, but she paid no attention. Nor did she glance eastward at Stormfire's Point.

She only had one thing on her mind.

As she reached the far side of Stronghold, she noted her shadow and the smooth way it rippled over the green forest, the way that birds shot up and scattered when it touched their nests and hiding places, and how they settled down again, reassured when they recognized her.

When had such fear and tension come to Wyvernwood? Why hadn't she noticed?

A second shadow appeared suddenly on the trees below, and Sabu glanced to her right.

"It's a long flight to the Whispering Hills," Harrow called to her.

When Harrow showed no sign of turning back, Sabu directed her gaze southward again and kept silent. She couldn't be angry with Harrow, but neither could she forget his fight with Ronaldo. On this trip she wasn't sure she wanted his company.

"Aren't you supposed to be guarding the village?" she reminded her black-scaled son.

"There are other Dragons," he answered curtly. "Some with cooler heads than mine and better suited for that task."

Harrow's tone surprised Sabu. There was something sad in it, regretful, almost self-deprecating. None of that was in Harrow's nature. She moved closer to her son. "What about the missing talisman?" she said. "Did you find it?"

Even as he flew, Harrow managed to shrug. "Mostly I waited for you, Mother," he answered. "I knew you'd go looking for him. Once I came to my senses I realized that finding a brother is at least as important as finding the talisman." He fell quiet for a moment and then fixed his mother with a dark-eyed gaze. "Isn't there some magic in that, too?"

"I hope so, Son," she answered. "I really hope so." *And maybe just a drop of redemption*, she added privately.

Though her wings were tired and aching, Luna followed the shadows across the moonlit wasteland, content to let them guide her. With all her fear gone, she looked on the land with new eyes, finding in it a stark and awesome beauty.

In the west, the mountains made a border for the world. They seemed to thrust up out of the land, to pierce and perforate it with a cruel majesty, domineering and powerful. They were new mountains in an old land, unblemished by time or weather.

Like some strange advance guard, a few of the shadows skimmed the ground ahead of the others. Luna had not paid them much attention for a while, but now they began to circle in a wide, sweeping arc, and as the other shadows caught up, they joined the circle. Luna fell in with them, and as she gazed downward, her jaw gaped.

Half-buried in the gray ash lay the ruins of an ancient city. The stone, the wood, every element had taken on the same lifeless, blasted color. Dust had drifted against the buildings, obscuring doorways and windows, piling over rooftops. No single structure remained intact, not even a wall.

And yet it was a city—or had been.

More, it was a city of Man.

Then the long, shallow channel cut into the land beside it must once have been a river. Luna closed her eyes and tried to imagine blue water in Asgalun. The image didn't fit, but as she lingered over it a smile curled the corners of her Dragon lips.

The shadows moved on, and so did she. The mountains loomed larger as they approached, and the formation called the Drake stood out plainly like some great Dragon-god.

Over the first foothills they glided and down through valleys where the dust wafted like mist. Soon the plains disappeared behind them. The peaks rose like jagged teeth, like broken spear points that impaled the starry sky.

With a start, Luna noticed something else. She no longer owned the sky. Each shadow on the ground belonged to its own Dragon. Silver Dragons, golden Dragons, emerald Dragons, cobalt Dragons. Dragons filled the sky above the peaks and passes, and they all raced with increasing speed toward the Drake on wings that made no sound at all.

Who are you?" Luna called, her heart pounding with excitement. "Where did you come from?"

But the Dragons didn't answer. She shot a look around, trying to read some intent in their actions, some purpose, and her gaze fell on a sleek, ruby-colored Dragon. "Tiamat!" she cried, but she knew at once that it wasn't her mate. Tiamat was home in Wyvernwood, safe she hoped.

When they had almost reached the Drake, her guides began a long sloping glide into a deep valley. The wind didn't seem to reach here, and the dust lay still and glimmering like winter snow in the moonlight. Luna gave a small gasp. She thought she'd never seen a more beautiful view.

The Dragons began to circle lower and lower, and Luna followed. When they folded their wings and made to land, Luna did the same and reached for the ground with her talons. But as the other Dragons touched the ground they melted into their shadows, and then even the shadows faded away.

Luna found herself alone. Confused, she stared around for some sign of her guides, and then she frowned. *Tricky ghosts!* Had they brought her here just to abandon her? Was there something she was supposed to see?

Slowly she turned her gaze upward, and her breath caught in her throat as she stared at the raw face of the Drake. It was some trick of the moonlight, she knew. Some inexplicable trick.

The mountain had eyes that burned—silver eyes with silver fire. They looked down upon her, locked on her.

Recognized her!

Luna couldn't move beneath their power. Her heart trembled. Her blood ran hot and cold at the same time, and her head pounded. For an instant she felt dizzy, and she clutched her stomach.

Then the sensation passed. Drawing a nervous breath, Luna looked up again. The mountain was just a mountain, and its eyes or whatever they were, had returned to stone.

But as one marvel ended another took its place. As Luna shifted position to observe the mountain her shadow also shifted, and from the shadow's dark heart, from the ashen lifeless soil, a red rose blossomed.

Luna gasped again in amazement, and then began to laugh. The happy sound echoed in the valley, among the peaks, and that was yet another miracle—laughter in the Haunted Lands.

Luna bent low to smell the new rose, but as she inhaled its sweet fragrance a pang struck her in the stomach. Again she felt a wave of dizziness and then the same hot and cold sensations. Flapping her wings desperately for balance, she started to fall.

But music surged in her ears, and darkness swallowed her. She clutched at the ground, dug in her claws to no avail. The power of the talisman swept her up.

Where to this time? she wondered.

Fourteen

JAKE WOKE WITH A GASP and bolted upright in his bed. With the back of one hand he wiped away the drops of sweat on his face and struggled to calm his ragged breathing. The sheets were damp and tangled around his legs from his thrashing, and his pillow had fallen to the floor.

The dream. Falling from the sky. Screaming until his throat went raw. Stars spinning and air rushing past his ears with a sound like ripping fabric. Calling Chan's name over and over. Chan limp, silent, plunging downward, ever downward. Then the trees, the pain. The harsh, hard earth!

Only it wasn't just a dream, and the sweat on his face wasn't just sweat, but also tears. He'd been crying in his sleep. And tossing, too. Throwing off the tangled sheets, he looked at the dark bruises on his legs where he'd struggled against the saddle straps. His entire body was a mass of bruises and cuts and scrapes, but those livid bands around his thighs were darker than all the rest.

A wave of dizziness struck him as he sat up, and he squeezed his eyes shut. Pieces of the dream still lingered in his head, flashes and images, some that he remembered clearly, others that confused and frightened him still. Gripping the side of the bed, he forced his eyes open and looked around.

The room was dark and warm. Thick quilts hung across the shuttered windows, and only the faintest light penetrated. The hand-stitched patterns were filled with a soft, homey glow. Dimly visible on a table at his bedside sat a pitcher of water and a cup. He fumbled for the cup, which still contained a few swallows, and wet his bruised mouth.

For a long moment afterward he just sat there clutching at the bed with one hand, trembling and trying to remember where he was. He set the cup down again. His clothes were spread over a wooden chair at the foot of the bed, the Dragon-scale shirt placed with particular care. He reached for his trousers. His fingertips noted the mends and repair work.

Beatrice. He smiled as he recalled the name of his hostess and his trembling stopped. He knew where he was, and he was safe. An image flashed across his brain. A young minotaur face close to his, frantically mouthing his name, shaking him. *Chernovog, Beatrice's son.*

He remembered in bits and pieces. Chernovog had found him first and brought Ranock, his father. There were more flashes. Sliding in and out of consciousness. Being carried. The strong scent of minotaur.

A weak smile crossed Jake's split lip. He winced and put a finger to it. His shoulder ached as he raised his arm. So did his ribs. *Jealous bones*, he thought to himself. *If one wants attention, they all do.* Despite the pain, he smiled again.

Chan had made it to the Whispering Hills. Or almost anyway. Jake ran his palm over the bed, touched the table. He was in the home of Beatrice and Ranock. On their farm. Chernovog was their son. Their baby was named Conniff.

His head hurt—but he remembered.

Cautiously, he bent to pick up the pillow from the floor and return it to its proper place. Another wave of dizziness accompanied the effort, but it was weaker this time, and after a moment he felt confident to stand. When he felt sure he could trust his legs, he pulled on his trousers and took a wobbly step.

The fabric, though soft, irritated the cuts on his knees, but that was minor pain compared to some of his other aches and injuries. More images flashed suddenly through his head—of falling, falling, tree limbs slashing like whips, snapping, crashing.

Jake pressed a hand to his head to force the images away and to fight back the nausea they caused. Staring wide-eyed around the room, he quickly cataloged the few pieces of furniture, studied the quilt patterns, and wiggled his toes on the bare boards of the floor. *Focus on here and now*, he reminded himself sternly. *Focus on how lucky you are.*

He drew a deep breath, let it out, and then nodded to himself. With greater purpose he reached for the door handle and pulled it open. With one hand on the wall to steady himself, he took tentative steps down a narrow hallway.

The living room was as neat as he remembered it. Beatrice kept a tidy house. He paused for a moment, gaining strength as he listened for any sound or hint that someone else was home, but he seemed to be alone.

Frowning, he scratched his head. Then he sniffed. He needed a bath badly.

Where was everyone?

He thought of Chan and frowned again. That Dragon was tough! Nevertheless, a slow worry began to build inside Jake. Ignoring his aches and pains, he made his way back to his room and felt around until he found his boots beneath the bed. One ankle protested as he pulled them on. "You're not sore," he grumbled to the ankle. "My back—now that's sore, but do you hear it complaining?" With his boots on, he straightened. Too quickly "Okay, yes you do. But never mind."

Leaving the Dragon-scale shirt hanging on the chair, he moved back through the hallway and into the living area, then to the house's front door. Pulling it open, he flinched and raised an arm to block the bright noonday sun.

While he waited for his eyes to adjust, he noticed his wrist and muttered a small curse. His sling was gone.

A warm wind brushed across his bare chest. In the front yard a pair of tall oaks shook their branches and rustled their leaves, making soft music. An old swing that hung from one of the limbs creaked gently, and someone called his name.

Uncertain where the voice had come from, Jake stepped off the small porch and looked around. Off to his right at the edge of the woods, Beatrice trudged toward the house with a large basket over one arm. Her blue dress and once-white apron flapped around her plump legs as she leaned into the wind and called his name again.

"Fair lady!" he answered, waving as he started forward to meet her, knowing how that would please and tickle her. "The prettiest sight in the Whispering Hills!"

"*Fair* is it?" she answered as she increased her pace and swung her basket. "And *pretty*, too?" She put one hand to her brown, bovine nose and twitched her large ears. Her brown eyes sparkled. "You'll have me blushing! Not that you could tell under this hairy old face! Sounds like they've taught you some pretty speech up at Stronghold!"

"They've taught me a lot of things," he answered in a more serious tone. "Most of all how to appreciate beauty in all its forms." He reached out to embrace her.

But Beatrice caught his arms, held him back, and looked at him with concern. "You should be in bed," she said. Setting her basket down, she reached out and touched the side of his head. He winced as she studied a wound at his hairline that he hadn't realized was there. "You took a severe blow."

"More than one, I think," Jake admitted as she continued to examine him. "But I'll live. Right now I need to find Chan. My saddle strap broke in the last moments, and we got separated...!" The words rushed out of him as images began to flash once more through his head.

Beatrice put a hand to his lips to hush and calm him. Yet while she tried to reassure him the troubled expression that settled upon her face did anything but that. "If you think you're strong enough," she said quietly, "I'll take you to him, but it's a bit of a hike through rough woods."

"I can make it," Jake quickly answered. He could read in Beatrice's demeanor that Chan was in trouble.

"Then go get a shirt," she told him. "Take one of Chernovog's soft tunics. You've got enough cuts and scrapes and welts already. Your back looks like a map."

He knew better than to argue with Beatrice. Planting a quick kiss on her bovine nose, he turned and ran as swiftly as he could manage on his sore ankle. He knew from his previous visit which room belonged to Chernovog, and he took the first brown garment he saw from an old trunk, slipped it over his head and hurried back outside.

"Exactly how much of a hike?" he asked with a weak grin as he rejoined Beatrice. His right ankle throbbed. So did his right knee. And he was pretty sure from Beatrice's frown that she had noticed his limp.

She studied him for a long moment before stooping to retrieve her basket. "You see the top of that hill?" she said, turning. She pointed with a thick finger to a summit that rose above the rest of the trees. "When we reach that you'll be warmed up for the rest of the trip."

Jake swallowed. Then with exaggerated bravado he took Beatrice's elbow. "Don't worry," he said, "if the going gets rough I'll help you along."

Beatrice pushed his hand away and gave him a smartly cool look. "You'll help me?" She raised a hand as if she was going to smack him.

"Impudent calf! I've made the journey twice today already, and it's only noon. I was only coming home to check on a certain soft slug-a-bed!"

"Then it can't really be that far!" Jake replied, teasing Beatrice. He started off with a jaunty step, but looked away so she wouldn't see how he gritted his teeth.

Without further word, Beatrice overtook him and led the way, steering him along in a different direction. She had emerged from the forest on one well-trod path, but she re-entered it on another. Either one seemed to lead to the hilltop, and he wasn't sure what difference it made, but Beatrice knew best, and he followed.

"Better take this," the minotaur-wife said when they'd gone a short distance into the woods. She picked up a stout branch from the ground and offered it to him as a walking stick. "I know you don't need it, but maybe you can beat off some of the flies."

He answered with a grin as he accepted the stick and leaned on it. The stick did take some of the pressure off his ankle. But to keep up his pretense, he waved a hand at the insects buzzing around his sweaty face. The summer woods were aswarm with the black pests.

But Beatrice didn't move on right away. Bending down again, she took a small paring knife from her apron pocket and dug in the ground beneath some leafy bushes. A moment later she pulled up a plant with tiny spike-like yellow flowers, shook the dirt from its roots, and lifting the basket's lid, dropped it inside.

"Vervain," she answered in response to his questioning look.

They hurried onward again. With the walking stick to aid him they made better time. Although the path was well trod it was sometimes overhung with limbs and branches or with the boughs of spreading bushes. Beatrice beat them all aside and held the stouter limbs safely back until Jake had passed.

With her round-eyed gaze always on the ground, she swiveled her head from side to side, and when she spied a plant or flower of interest out came her paring knife. "There's purslane," she announced, dropping another yellow-flowered plant into her basket. "There's chamomile," she said to herself as she collected the white-flowered herb. "Oh, and comfrey! That's good!" She sniffed the blue flowers that grew along its thick stalk, and then gathered pieces of it—leaves,

flowers, and stalk—and wrapped them all together in a large handkerchief from her apron pocket. Into the basket it went.

By the time they reached the summit of the hill, Beatrice's basket
was full. Jake didn't ask her about it; he was grateful for the frequent
pauses and chances to rest as she dug and chopped her way along the
path. He even found a certain calm comfort in the way she pronounced
the names of the herbs and in the small compliments she paid herself
for finding them. He loved her distracting, singsong murmurings.

Once, she stopped suddenly and stared off the path deeper into the
woods. Plunging through a thicket of evergreen, she bent and
snatched at the ground. When she straightened again, he held a small
white flower. "Yarrow," she said. "Didn't expect to find that!" Pulling
Jake closer, she squeezed juice from the flower directly onto his head-
wound and then pressed the flower itself to it. "Just wear it a while,"
she instructed as she patted his cheek and smiled. "It'll help the pain
and reduce scarring. And don't worry—it looks sweet."

Jake returned her smile but rolled his eyes when she turned her
back and started forward again. He could hear Chan teasing him
already.

If Chan was in any condition to tease, he reminded himself. Pressing the yarrow-flower to his head with a fingertip, he hurried after
Beatrice.

From the summit the path was less well worn, and though the view
was spectacular, neither of them lingered to appreciate it. Beatrice
knew her way as only one who'd lived in the Whispering Hills all her
life could know it.

And the Whispering Hills knew her. Undisturbed, the birds
watched calmly as she passed, and flurries of butterflies parted only
long enough for her to collect a flower or a specimen. When a large,
brightly colored snake lay sunning itself on the path, it slithered gracefully aside, and when a large brown bear rose up in the nearby brush
it only waved and went about its business.

Beatrice knew them all.

"Hello, Erskine!" she called to the bear.

"Good day to you, Lord Shiva!" she said to the snake.

And to the butterflies, "Ole', your snooty highnesses!"

The way down the hill was even more difficult than the journey up
because Jake's sore joints and muscles had to fight against the insistent

tug of gravity. Once, losing himself to momentum, he tripped on a vine and fell with a loud curse.

Beatrice waited for him to pick himself up. "We don't appreciate that kind of language in these parts," she informed him with one hand on her round hip. "It upsets Shiva, and it upsets me."

"Sorry," Jake apologized with a downcast look. "I'll bet you've got something in that basket to wash my mouth out with."

Beatrice pursed her cow's lips thoughtfully, and then gave a wink and a grin. "It's not much farther," she said gently.

Jake steadied himself with his walking stick and tried to look confident. It didn't matter how far he had to go, he'd find the strength. His scrapes and bruises meant nothing. With a flick he brushed away the yarrow flower from his brow.

At the bottom of the hill Beatrice paused on the bank of a narrow stream. When Jake knelt and cupped his hands to drink, Beatrice stopped him. "It branches from the Blackwater," she said with a shake of her head. "If it doesn't kill you it'll make you so sick you'll wish it had. Suck this if you're thirsty." She handed him a sprig of spearmint.

He'd forgotten about the Blackwater River and its poisoned waters. Jake chewed the spearmint, but a black rage swelled up inside him. With all his strength he swung his walking stick, shattering it against the bole of a tree. Filthy poisoners! First the river. Now Chan. He burned with shame to ever have been a part of Degarm! His people! His people no more and never again!

He'd make them pay for what they'd done. He'd find a way to make them pay!

Beatrice clucked her tongue. "Now that poor tree never did nothing to you"

Jake clenched his fists, and all his aches melted away. "Take me to Chan," he said grimly. Then, unable to control himself when Beatrice stared at him, he shouted. "Take me to him!"

The minotaur-wife's eyes widened in surprise, and then she shook a finger. "You mind your manners, young Dragonrider," she said, quietly stern. "I can see you're distraught, but I'm not the cause."

She stared with iron patience until Jake looked away and his shoulders slumped. He liked Beatrice and all her family, and she'd shown him only kindness. He ran a hand through his hair and looked up again. "I'm..."

"Don't," she interrupted. "The minotaurs have a saying: never apologize more than once a day, and you've had your once." Beatrice adjusted the basket on her arm and lifted her head with dignity. "Now if you're done hobbling and limping and molly-coddling yourself, and you think you can keep up with an old bovine four times your age we can go on."

"I'll never be able to keep up with you, Lady," Jake muttered as he fell in behind her.

"Flattery will get you nowhere," she answered over her shoulder. Then with a small chuckle she added, "But don't quit trying."

They pushed on through the forest, and through a grove like none Jake had seen yet in Wyvernwood. The leaves and branches grew so closely together they intertwined, forming a dense canopy that shut out the sunlight and the blue sky. The little light that did penetrate stabbed downward like narrow shafts that sparkled with dust motes and pollen.

Everywhere he looked huge spiderwebs stretched between the trees or between the branches and the ground, and in every web great wolf spiders waited, plump and satisfied and watchful. Sometimes the webs even stretched across the path. In the deep gloom Jake ducked and dodged, cringing each time he passed too close to one of the silken traps, and when a strand brushed his cheek he gasped.

Beatrice clucked her tongue again and laughed. "When you're riding on Chan's back so high up there with nothing but a few straps to hold you secure do you duck and dodge the clouds?" She laughed again.

"The clouds won't bite me," he answered, his skin crawling as he glanced nervously from side to side.

Beatrice ducked beneath a web without slowing her pace. "Spinsilver says that's because you're too stringy."

Jake stopped. "Who's Spinsilver?" he asked suspiciously.

Beatrice turned and pointed to the fat arachnid in the web across the path, and Jake took an involuntary step backward. Spinsilver was the largest spider he'd seen yet. And did he imagine it, or was it actually winking at him? With so many eyes he found it hard to tell.

"And he'll thank you to duck low and not damage his home," Beatrice continued.

Jake stared at Spinsilver, swallowed, and then ducked as low as he could while keeping his gaze on the web. "It talks, too?"

"Only to those that know how to listen," Beatrice assured him. "Now come on. We're disturbing their naptime. At dusk they really get playful."

That doesn't sound good, Jake thought with a shudder as he hurried to catch up with Beatrice. He just hoped he wasn't carrying any eight-legged hitchhikers!

The same narrow stream cut across their path again, and this time Beatrice changed direction to follow it. The underbrush grew thicker, making for hard going, but in a short time they emerged from the dark grove and into brighter territory. They climbed a low hill, and a soft breeze cooled Jake's face. He sniffed

"Lavender!" he remarked curiously.

Beatrice nodded as she started down the hill. "Granny Scylla's work," she said.

Guided by his nose, Jake quickened his step and took the lead. Down to the stream they went again, and into a shallow gully with rotted logs and wild gooseberries and purple sweet williams blooming along the muddy banks. The breeze followed them, and the smell of lavender grew stronger.

Then through the trees Jake heard voices. Someone moved up ahead. A large, barrel-chested figure clad only in boots and britches bent over a fire. Jake stepped carelessly on a twig, snapping it, and the figure turned its great bull's head to look up sharply.

"Ranock!" Beatrice called over Jake's shoulder.

With a ripple of incredible muscles, Ranock stood up. His arms were as thick as small trees, and his hands were twice the size of a man's. At seven feet tall, *imposing* hardly described him.

And yet Jake knew him as a gentle creature and a doting father who loved his children, his wife, and the Whispering Hills. "Beatrice," he called with a wave. Then his eyes fell on Jake. "And the Dragonrider, too!" Picking up a stout ax, he started forward.

A harshly brittle voice stopped him. "Stay by that fire!" it snapped. "Keep your eyes on that pot and tell me the moment it begins to simmer!"

Jake rushed forward with Beatrice close behind. But the sight he saw as he reached Ranock's side stopped him in his tracks. His breath caught in his throat, and when he tried to cry out no sound came. Ranock put a sympathetic hand on his shoulder, and Beatrice squeezed his hand.

"You should have told me," he whispered.

"It wouldn't have prepared you," Beatrice answered. "And I think you knew already, because you didn't ask."

Slowly, Jake nodded his head. He did know, or at least he'd suspected how bad it would be. Images flashed in his head again, and Chan's voice screamed in his ears. *My wings! My wings are burning!* But not with flame. With poison. A wild ride as Chan tried to reach safety. The angry howl of wind. Spiraling. Ground spinning, rushing up.

Crashing.

Chan twisting to absorb the impact.

To save him.

By the side of the stream, Granny Scylla looked up and wrinkled her ancient cow's face. "Oh, don't just stand there spouting snot and tears all over yourself! Get over here and be useful!" On stiff legs, she stood up with a wadded dripping bedsheet in her gnarled hands. Her gaze locked on Beatrice. "Did you bring me the goodies I asked for?"

"All but the hyssop," Beatrice answered. Holding up the basket of herbs, she moved past Ranock to the fire and the black pot on the rocks that ringed it. "I couldn't find a sprig or sprout of it."

Granny Scylla scowled as she wrung the heavy sheet. "Well, I've got Chernovog out looking, too. But if you've got the rest we can make do!" She glared at Jake. "Didn't I tell you to get over here and help me? If you're strong enough to get out of bed, you're strong enough to help!"

With a hesitant nod, Jake went to Granny Scylla's side. The old gray minotaur woman was the closest thing to a witch he'd ever met. *Witch in the good sense,* he reminded himself. She knew more about herbs and healing and things that grew in the forest than anyone he'd ever met, including Beatrice. Yet, she half-frightened him.

"What can I do?" he asked, trying not to sound nervous.

Granny Scylla grinned a toothless grin and thrust one end of the sheet into his hands. "Help me wring this out!" she said. "I'm not as strong as I used to be, youngin."

With the sheet stretched between them, Jake began to twist water out of the heavy cloth. He glanced at the stream where she'd apparently just rinsed the sheet. "Isn't it poisoned?"

Granny Scylla crinkled her nose and squinted at him. "We're not gonna drink it, boy!" Her laugh was a harsh cackle. "It's a cool compress for your Dragon's head. He requires something just a little bit larger than your handkerchief!"

Jake made a choking sound and then looked embarrassed. *Your Dragon.* Chan would love that.

If he lived to hear it.

With Beatrice to watch the fire, Ranock took Granny's end of the sheet and with a nod to Jake they carried it over and draped it as neatly as they could upon Chan's brow.

The Dragon lay still as death. Only the staggered rise and fall of his ribs gave any indication that he lived. His paws were curled up limp against his body, and his tail hung draped over a high limb. His right wing was pinched between a pair of trees, and the other stretched into the stream. He was covered with mud and grass, and the deep impression in which he lay told of his impact.

Fighting back tears, Jake stroked Chan's snout and ran his palm along one broken ear as he stared around at the shattered branches. "How did you ever find us out here?" he whispered.

But a cascade of images shot through his mind before anyone could answer, and he remembered.

Fire! Blast after desperate blast of fire just before they crashed! Beacons of distress! Flaming cries for help!

Then pain and blackness.

Jake sank to one knee, and Ranock caught him. "You should have stayed in bed," the Minotaur scolded.

Granny Scylla waved a dismissive hand at Ranock. "Just give him some chamomile. There's another pot in my bag over there! Make him some tea! He's young and strong!"

At least the old witch believed in him, Jake thought as he stood up on his own. He laid his palm on Chan's cool scales again and once more studied the extent of his injuries. Particularly he noted the deep red mottlings on the wings—harsh circular wounds with radiating veins of scarlet and purple. They marked where the arrows had penetrated, where the poison had entered Chan's system.

A question slipped from his lips. "How long?"

"Four days," Ranock answered as he knelt down beside Beatrice and began to sort the herbs from her basket.

Jake sighed and touched the wound on his head. For a moment the weight of all his injuries and sprains and scrapes pressed down upon him, but he shrugged them off. They didn't matter. All that mattered was the Dragon on the ground before him.

He glanced at the ruins of his saddle on the grass nearby. Ranock must have removed it. "What can I do?" he said.

Granny Scylla came up behind him, squeezed his shoulder with surprisingly strong fingers, and turned him until she could look him straight in the eyes. "Talk to him," she directed. "Get right up in his ear and tell him your life story, and then tell him his. And after that make up any old lie you like." Releasing her grip, she waddled over to join Ranock and Beatrice. "Jokes are always good."

"Right," Jake agreed. "Make him laugh."

Ranock tore a cluster of yellow flowers and dropped them into the pot. "The jokes are to make us laugh," he corrected. "We're doing the hard work here."

"Poems are good, too!" Beatrice added.

"Right again," Jake answered. He thought for a moment, and then grinned. "A lusty young Dragon of old had moves so incredibly bold. . . ."

Beatrice gasped.

Ranock gave a low chuckle.

Granny Scylla interrupted with a wagging finger and a stern look.

"He left all the girls dazed; they were simply amazed..." Jake dared to continue.

Without stirring or opening his eyes, Chan sneezed a thin stream of smoke.

"Oh, I know a better one!" cried a tiny voice from the trees. "There once was a hummingbird strong whose beak was deliciously long...!"

Everyone looked up in surprise.

Fifteen

"BUMBLE IS TOTALLY GLAD TO FIND YOU!" The little hummingbird dived down from the trees and made a green blur straight for the tip of Ranock's left horn where he took a perch. "And you!" he added, darting to the top of Beatrice's head. "And you, too!" he cried as he flew a swift circle around Granny Scylla. "And most especially you!" With that, he flew past Jake and plunged beak-first into the basket of herbs and flowers.

Granny Scylla kicked the basket with her toe just hard enough to send Bumble flying. "What are you doing, you little feather-brain?" she snapped. "We didn't set out a banquet for you! Get your own! The woods are full!"

Looking hurt, Bumble flew to the nearest branch. "I thought you were glad to see Bumble! Bumble's totally glad to see you!"

Beatrice put one arm around Granny Scylla to calm the old Minotaur. "We are glad to see you, Bumble," she answered in a soothing voice. "You've been gone a long time, and we were all worried. But we're also worried about Chan, who's very sick. Those herbs are for him."

Bumble swiveled his head in several directions before settling his gaze on Chan. "Oh, dear, dear, dear!" he said. "The aromas of such choice, fresh-picked sweets went to my head! I didn't even notice him! I feel so bad! I feel so sad!" His tiny black eyes turned to Beatrice. "I feel so hungry—be right back!"

Jake frowned as Bumble flashed away into the trees. "He didn't even see Chan?" He put a hand on his friend's head. "A Dragon this size?"

"You mean, a Dragon that colorful?" Ranock arched one bovine eyebrow and smiled at Jake. "Admit it, boy," he said with good humor when Jake's frown deepened. "Chan is hard to miss."

Granny Scylla knelt down beside the basket of herbs and the steaming pot on the fire. "Unless you're an empty-headed hummingbird with an even emptier belly," she grumbled.

Beatrice knelt down beside Granny Scylla and selected a thick sprig of comfrey. "You be nice to that hummingbird," she told Granny Scylla tartly. "If it wasn't for him Ranock and Chernovog might still be prisoners in that horrible circus in Degarm." Then she shot a look over her shoulder at Jake and Ranock as she began to work. "And you two change that compress. We have to keep Chan as cool as possible while the poison works its way through his system."

"You think he's going to live?" Jake said hopefully.

Ranock grabbed a corner of the wet bedsheet and whipped it off Chan's brow. "Granny Scylla hasn't lost a patient yet," he answered as he wadded the sheet and carried it to the stream. "And neither has Beatrice." He winked at his wife, and then added. "Although she's talked a few to death."

Jake helped Ranock wet the bedsheet in the stream and spread it over Chan's head again while Beatrice and Granny Scylla stirred the black pot and added an assortment of herbs. As the pot began to simmer, a rich and invigorating aroma rose into the air. Leaning close, Jake drew a deep breath and then blinked as his eyes began to water.

"Gravy!" Bumble shouted from a branch above Jake's head. The hummingbird had returned from his own repast. His beady eyes fastened on the pot.

Granny Scylla looked up long enough to shake a long wooden spoon at him. "Four and twenty hummingbirds baked in a pie," she muttered.

Beatrice hushed Granny Scylla. "Clean his wings as carefully as you can," she instructed, all business now as she worked. "There are more sheets and cloths in the bag over there."

Ranock went to a large gunnysack that lay half-hidden in the grass and brush not far from the fire. As he rummaged in it a variety of items tumbled out, but he grabbed a sheet for himself and tossed another one to Jake. "Looks like we're a team," he said quietly. "I don't need to tell you to be gentle. But be thorough. Those wounds are full of poison and puss."

Bumble locked his claws around the limb where he was perched, fell forward and hung upside down with his wings wrapped over his stomach. "There's an image I could do without," he protested. "I just ate!"

As if in response Jake's stomach gave a loud growl. He couldn't recall the last time he'd eaten.

"You hungry?" Ranock asked, glancing at Jake as he bent down to dip his bedsheet in the stream.

"Maybe later," Jake answered as he knelt down. He looked at his reflection in the water and barely recognized himself. The cut at his hairline made a purple circle around a crusty slash. Another dark bruise ringed his right eye. Again he realized how lucky he'd been. "Isn't this water poisoned?" he said suddenly as he immersed his cloth. "Beatrice said I shouldn't drink it."

"I wouldn't drink it, either," Ranock answered as he gathered up his wet sheet and began to wring it. "It'll still make you sick, but the Blackwater River is some distance away. This is diluted and nowhere near as dangerous as the stuff Chan already has in him. It's safe enough to wash him down."

Ranock rose and went to Chan's right wing, leaving the left one to Jake. Hesitant at first, Jake stared at the ugly red wounds until tears began to leak from his eyes. Then, drawing a deep breath, and afraid the Ranock would see him cry, he wiped his eyes with the back of one hand and got to work.

Carefully, he squeezed a piece of the sheet until a trickle of water fell on one of the mottlings. As the droplet ran over the wound it took on a sickly greenish color. Jake winced at the faintly detectable odor of infection, then as lightly as he could dabbed at the wound.

"Work faster, boy!" Granny Scylla called from the fire. "We're almost ready here!"

"Not that I'm sensitive about it," he answered through clenched teeth as he applied his cloth to the next wound, "but my name isn't *Boy*."

"Watch out below!" Bumble chirped, still hanging in his upside-down position. "He's sensitive about it!"

Returning to the stream, Ranock bent down again. His once-white bedsheet was stained with spots of red and green and also with smears of mud. The muscles of his bare, sun-bronzed back bulged as he rinsed the cloth clean again and wrung it out. "Not meaning to seem unneighborly, Bumble," he said as he stood up. "But what's a hum-mingbird like you doing in a place like this?"

"Resting," Bumble answered quickly. "Basking in the warm companionship of delightful friends. Taking a break from the Great and Noble Hunt!"

"Hunt?" Granny Scylla snorted. "I thought you looked like you'd lost your best friend."

Bumble fluttered into an upright position on his limb and extended his wings for a careful examination. "No, the Bravest Hummingbird in the World looks the same," he answered. He fluttered his wings again, displaying his bright feathers as he puffed out his chest. "Maybe I've put on some muscle." Diving from his perch, he circled the fire and the simmering pot and then settled on Chan's shoulder. He seemed to deflate and looked suddenly as if he'd remembered something. "Have any of you seen Ronaldo? He's not in his cave."

Beatrice wiped her hands on her apron as she stood up, and her wide brown eyes glimmered with concern. "Little one, we haven't seen him since the last time we saw you!"

The little hummingbird pouted and began to pace back and forth. His tiny talons tapped gently on Chan's scales as he walked, as if he was sampling the texture of them. "Bumble can smell a marigold from the far side of Wyvernwood," he said. "And I tracked Ronaldo's scent all the way from Stronghold. He came here last night, but now I've lost his scent." His small shoulders slumped. "Bumble is alone! Bumble must find Ronaldo!"

Jake moved closer to Bumble and offered his finger as a perch. He didn't know the little hummingbird well. They'd only met once before. But he knew exactly how Bumble felt. "My friend's in danger, too," he said, stroking Chan with his palm.

Bumble stepped onto Jake's finger. "Danger! Danger!" he cried excitedly.

Ranock returned yet again to the stream and dropped his cloth on the bank. "You and your friends helped save Chernovog," he said to Bumble. "So as soon as Chan is all right I'd be proud to help you with your Great and Noble Hunt."

"Can't wait! Can't wait!" Bumble darted into the air again and flew to another limb. His bead-like eyes turned upward toward the sky and he turned his head from side to side. "Trouble to the north of us! Trouble to the south! Trouble brewing everywhere! Hush my mouth!"

"What kind of trouble?" Jake turned to Ranock, and his heart began to pound. "What's he talking about?"

Bumble hopped from one leg to the other. "Look to the sun for a warning! Look to the sun for a warning!" Flying one swift circle around the fire, he called over his shoulder. "So long! Farewell! The Great and Noble Hunt waits for no one!" With that, he raced away into the forest.

"Crazy bird!" Granny Scylla muttered as she shook her wooden spoon. "I swear I can't understand half of what he says!"

"Oh hush, Granny," Ranock said with a kindly pat on her shoulder. "Everyone knows you've lost hearing in the upper ranges." He stared into the forest for a long moment with a restrained frown on his bull's lips, and then he glanced up at the sun. "Let's get back to Chan," he suggested.

When Chan's wings were bathed to Beatrice's satisfaction, Granny Scylla wrapped a corner of her skirts around her hands and seized the black pot's bail. Straining her old muscles, she lifted the pot and its sloshing contents and carried it between her legs to Chan's left wing. "Rinse those sheets again and tear one of them into smaller strips," she ordered.

Ranock tore the strips. Granny and Beatrice each took one and folded the cloth into a square. Then, dipping the cloths into the steamy medicine, they began to apply it liberally to each of Chan's many wounds. Ranock helped, reaching places that Beatrice and Granny couldn't.

"I'll start on his other wing," Jake offered, tearing off a strip of cloth.

Granny Scylla dipped her cloth in the pot again as she looked at Jake. "I suppose I did tell you to help out," she said. "But as you apply the ointment, you have to say a little chant."

Jake nodded. "What is it?"

"Say, *nasty poison stay no longer! Granny Scylla's cure is stronger!*" She looked Jake right in the eye, and her cow's face crinkled up with a serious expression. "You have to say it every time. Every time, hear? Or the medicine won't work!"

Again Jake nodded. He dipped his cloth into the pot. The concoction was hot and burned his fingers, and the fumes stung his eyes, but he gathered as much medicine as the cloth would absorb.

Chan's right wing lay wedged between two trees. Jake muttered a curse as he examined it, but mindful of Beatrice he kept his voice low.

He pressed his cloth to the worst of the wounds. "Nasty poison stay no longer!" he chanted. "Granny Scylla's cure is stronger!"

A sharp cackle came from behind him. Peering around Chan's snout, Granny Scylla threw back her head and laughed. "He fell for it! They're so cute when they're gullible!" She slapped her knee. *"Granny Scylla's cure is stronger!* That's a good one! I've got to remember it!" She laughed again as she went back to work.

When Granny's back was turned, Jake stuck out his tongue and returned to his task. His cheeks burned red with embarrassment, but as he daubed the medicine his blush turned into a grin. "Nasty poison stay no longer!" At the top of his voice he sang the simple rhyme. "Granny Scylla's cure is stronger!" As he applied the medicine to the next wound, he sang the chant again.

A few moments later, he heard Ranock's deep voice. "Nasty poison stay no longer!" Beatrice chuckled and finished the chant for him. Then both Ranock and Beatrice sang it together.

"Granny Scylla's cure is stronger!" Jake shouted as he treated another infected wound. His cloth needed to be dipped again, and he walked around to the other side where the pot sat with the others. Ranock gave him a sly wink. "Nasty poison stay no longer!" he cried.

With a serious scowl on her face, Granny worked in silence. "Yes, that's a good one, Granny!" Ranock laughed. He dealt a light slap to Granny's backside, causing the old minotaur to jump and clutch her skirts in indignation. "I'm going to remember it for a long time!" He winked at Jake again as he touched his cloth to another wound. "Nasty poison...!"

"Oh, shut up!" Granny snapped without looking around. "I'd just as soon spit on your feet as blink! Now you're warned!"

Ranock laughed as he dipped his cloth into the ointment. "I'd better come help you," he declared to Jake. "Granny's spit could knock the eye out of an owl at fifty paces in the dark of night. And that's while she's sleeping!"

They finished their treatments with the pot still half full. Every red mottle-mark and wound glimmered with a coating of the herbal remedy. "Take off your shirt," Beatrice ordered as she turned to Jake. "There's more than enough left for your cuts and scratches."

Jake wrinkled his nose, but grateful to Beatrice for her hard work and caring, he obeyed. The ointment stung as she daubed it over his back, and he yelped when she treated the cut on his head.

She gave him an appraising look as she stepped back. "Now drop those pants and let me see your knees."

With a shocked look, Jake clutched his shirt to his bare chest and backed up a step. "I think not!"

Ranock laughed again. He laughed easily and almost anything seemed to amuse him, but he came to Jake's rescue, pressing his cloth into the ointment and offering it. "Go behind some trees and treat yourself. But watch out—Beatrice likes to peek."

Jake slipped into the woods with the offered cloth and, when he was sure no one could see him, he undressed and treated his knees and all the other scratches and marks on his legs and buttocks. The medicine tingled and left a sticky coating wherever it touched, but it quickly dried, leaving a soothing coolness that surprised him.

Then, as he dressed, a different coolness brushed over him. A soft wind swept through the forest, scattering leaves and rustling branches, and a brief darkness followed as the sun unexpectedly dimmed. *That was no cloud,* Jake thought. Then Bumble's parting words echoed in his head. *Look to the sun for a warning!*

Adjusting his clothes, he shot another look up through the branches, catching just a glimpse of the sky—and of something else. "Oh, no!" he muttered. Sensing trouble, he called out to Ranock and Beatrice and began to run.

But another, far louder voice drowned out his cry.

"What have you done to my son?"

Jake emerged from the trees into the clearing of the small camp. Granny Scylla lay flat on her back, her old eyes wide with terror, while Beatrice stood protectively over her with a stout branch for a club and Ranock frantically swung the wet sheets to beat out small sparks from the campfire that had spread into the grass.

Black Sabu, immense and angry, hovered directly above them, her pulsing wings stirring dust and leaves and rippling the stream as she hovered. Her eyes shone with a dangerous light as she flexed her huge claws and stretched her long neck downward. "I said what have you done to my son!"

Jake felt his own anger surge. Running forward, he snatched the club from Beatrice and cast it aside. Then bracing his hands on his hips he threw back his head and glared at Sabu. "If I had a rock I'd bounce it off your nose right now!" He shook his fist as he shouted at

Sabu. "These are friends who are trying to help, and if you've hurt them I swear I'll kick your scaly Dragon butt!"

Sabu's eyes flashed. As she brought her great head closer to Jake he could feel the heat of her breath, but he stood his ground and refused to be intimidated. "Why, you impudent...!"

Another voice spoke from above Sabu. "Be careful, Mother. He can probably do it." Harrow chuckled as he glided over the treetops. "Do you think the little warrior would be standing there defending those creatures if they'd harmed Chan?"

Sabu hesitated, and her hard gaze softened as it turned to Chan. "Maybe I over-reacted," she said, although some doubt seemed to linger in her voice. "We came looking for Ronaldo, but on the way we encountered a hawk who told us of this!"

With the small fires out, Ranock tossed down the sheets and wiped his brow. "Everybody's looking for Ronaldo," he grumbled roughly. "Have the Whispering Hills become a crossroads? Did somebody put up a sign?"

"News has wings," Jake said to Sabu. "But apparently the facts don't." He threw up an arm to ward off a torrent of pelting leaves. Sabu's wings were generating enough power to strip the treetops. He turned his face from the worst of it, looking around as he did so. In such a dense part of the forest there was no place for the Dragons to land.

"Ranock's farmhouse is just back over those hills," he said, pointing. "Wait there, and I'll meet you as quickly as I can. There are things you need to know."

Still kneeling over Granny Scylla, Beatrice called out. "But mind you don't trample my garden, or I'll bounce a rock off your nose myself!"

Sabu still hesitated. Again she looked toward Chan, and the last of her anger seemed to dissolve. When she spoke, worry filled her voice. "Will he be all right? Is he going to live?"

Granny Scylla clutched at Beatrice's outstretched arm and sat up. "Of course he'll live, you fool Dragon!" she snapped. "Why, he's had Granny Scylla's cure, and there's nothing stronger! Ask anyone here!" With a smug grin, she looked at Jake and nodded.

"That's right!" Jake agreed. "Now go away before you bury us in debris!"

Harrow glided past again and turned in the direction of the farm-house. "Better do as he says," he called to Sabu, "before he kicks your scaly butt!"

Angling her wings, Sabu rose and turned to follow. "My butt's not scaly," she answered defensively. "It's just that time of year, and I'm molting."

Jake watched as mother and son flew away and then hurried to help Granny Scylla to her feet. Ranock had already beaten him to that task, though, and Beatrice made a show of brushing off the old mino-taur's skirts and picking leaves from her gray hair. "Blew me right over she did!" Granny exclaimed indignantly. "What a rude lot!"

With a heavy sigh, Jake went to Chan and put a palm on his neck. With loving care he stroked the Dragon and wished that Chan would sneeze again or twitch a wing or an ear. He listened to the quiet hiss of Chan's breath, watched the uneven rise and fall of his great sides, and then, leaning down, he lay his head against his friend's.

"I'll be back as soon as I can, *Sumapai*," he promised. "I know I can count on you to wait here for me, right? It wouldn't be very gracious if both of us just took off after all the kindness and hospitality we've received." Despite himself, he began to sniffle and wiped a sleeve over his face. "Beatrice says you're going to be all right, and they'll stay here to keep applying medicine until you're well. Then we'll go flying again. We'll fly to all the places we've ever dreamed about." He wiped his face again, but a mere sleeve couldn't stop the sudden flood of tears. "I'm not afraid of falling again, *Sumapai*! I'm not!"

Strong, rough hands closed on Jake's shoulders, and Ranock whis-pered. "It's all right, Jake," he said. "We'll take good care of him."

Nodding, Jake stood up straight and blinked away his tears. Yet he continued to stroke Chan, reluctant to break that slight contact. "I know," he answered. "But Granny told me to talk to him, that's all, and I just couldn't think of any poems or jokes." In better control of himself, he turned to face Ranock. "I have to go back to the house now. They're waiting for me."

"I'll guide you," Ranock offered.

But Jake shook his head. "I can find the way, and if you don't mind, I'd rather you stayed here to help Beatrice and Granny." He squeezed Ranock's forearm with his own smaller hand and looked up at the minotaur. "Keep your ax close, too. Degarm is getting bold, and they're a bigger threat to us now than ever before."

With a quick word of goodbye, he plunged into the woods and headed back the way Beatrice had brought him. Alone, the forest seemed darker, more forbidding, full of uninviting shadows. He quickened his pace. The underbrush caught at his legs; unseen roots tried to trip him; branches slapped at his face. Stubbornly, he pushed on, refusing to let any obstacles slow him down.

On aching legs he made his way across the gully. His worst pains seemed to be returning. He clutched at his bruised ribs as he studied the ground. The path had seemed so clear with Beatrice, but it eluded him now. Nervously he looked around. An unnatural quiet seemed to permeate the forest. No birds sang. No insects. Certain that he was lost, he still pressed on.

Suddenly darkness closed in like a vice. A shudder passed through Jake. He stopped and stood completely still. Licking his dry lips, he turned his gaze upward to a vast, interlacing canopy of branches and leaves. But it wasn't the canopy that told him where he was.

It was the spider webs.

Everywhere he looked the silken traps waited. In every web, alien eyes turned his way. Beatrice's voice seemed to echo in his head: *dusk is when they really get playful!* He shot a glance back the way he had come, hoping for a ray of sunlight. Was it dusk now? He couldn't tell! He wasn't even sure if he was on the same path!

Then very close to his left ear another voice whispered. Jake gasped and wrenched his head toward the tiny voice. A bloated spider, fat from a recent meal, depended from a single silver strand. *This way!* it said.

Heart pounding, Jake dodged and hurried onward. Another web stretched across the path at shoulder height. He might easily have blundered into it but for the large hairy dot at its center. The occupant unfurled its legs and stood up. *This way!*

Ducking low to avoid the web, Jake crept past. Could it be that they were leading him? And if they were, could he trust them? *Spiders!* He hated spiders!

Yet Beatrice had no fear of them at all. She had even called one of them by name: *Spinsilver!* Holding that thought close, drawing courage from it, he continued on. At the next web, he paused long enough to nod a greeting. "Spinsilver?" he asked, uncertain.

A faint murmur brushed his ear. *That's right, boy*, it said. *We're all called Spinsilver. This way!*

Repressing a shiver, Jake eased by, but he arched an eyebrow curiously. "All of you? You all have the same name?"

From close to his ear came another whisper, but Jake steeled himself and kept his gaze straight ahead. *Spider has such an ugly sound, don't you agree? Scary! Frightening! We change our image! We are Spinsilver! This way, please!*

"Have you considered shaving?" Jake muttered.

A soft chuckling shook the nearest webs.

Finally, with a deep sigh of relief, he reached the far side of the grove. The sun touched his face through a gap in the trees, and he rubbed his arms briskly to chase away his goosebumps. But as he looked around he discovered he still didn't know where he was.

He muttered a short curse. "This isn't the way we came!"

The grass at his feet rustled lightly and parted. Jake jumped back as Lord Shiva coiled and raised his colorful head. "This way, Jake!" he hissed as he stretched out full-length to indicate the proper direction.

"Many thanks!" Jake answered, moving on with a quick hop and jump. He liked snakes only a little better than he liked spiders.

At the base of a steep hill he found another old limb to use for a walking stick. His cuts and scratches felt fine, but other injuries still throbbed. He wondered idly as he climbed what treatment Granny Scylla might have for sore feet and a bad ankle.

At the bottom of the hill he found a familiar stream. It was all he could do not to throw himself down and drink, but he knew better. Still, he rested for a moment and, dipping his hands into the water, washed his face.

With water still dripping from his lashes, he heard yet another voice. The gooseflesh sprang up on his arms again, and the hair on his neck stood out. Forgetting his bruises, he sprang to his feet.

"This way, silly!" the voice said.

Jake shot a wild look around. He knew that voice!

"Ariel?" he cried. "Ariel, is that you?" A flash of something on the other side of the stream. He turned toward it. Nothing. "Where are you?" he shouted. A glimmer of something deeper in the woods, and then a sharper flash like sunlight reflected on glass or in a mirror. Leaping the stream, Jake ran after it.

Sixteen

MORE THAN EVER BEFORE Luna felt the stabbing darkness, the sudden shifting and twisting of space. Time warped and bent around her; distance lost meaning. With awareness newly heightened she sensed all of Undersky in a heartbeat.

No, not in a heartbeat.

In heartbeats.

In a flash she recalled her visit to Redclaw, her encounter with Ariel, and the mirror the little girl held up. Two faces in the reflection. Her own and another like hers, but not.

She laughed. In the deep rushing unknown blackness between one heartbeat and the next, dislocated and lost, swept up by a music and a power she couldn't control or understand, she laughed with joy, and the sound blended with the music, interwove and harmonized with it until it became an integral part.

When the darkness finally parted and the music set her down, she breathed a happy sigh. "Home!" she said as a warm breeze blew over her. She turned her face up to the afternoon sun and savored all the familiar scents of Wyvernwood and Stronghold.

A tiny mouse-wife on the ground near Luna's paws jumped up and down in excitement. "Luna's back!" she cried in a high, squeaky voice. "Smoke me, she's back! Grab hold! Grab hold lest she vanish again! Grab hold!" With that, she sprang upon one of Luna's taloned toes and locked on with a tight grip.

"No fear of that, little one," Luna promised as she bent her neck down for a closer look at the mouse-wife. Stormfire's daughter wasn't sure how she knew, but her journey was over. "Still, I thank you for such a welcome!'

"I waited!" the mouse-wife said breathlessly, refusing to let go. "I waited right here on this very spot, sure that you'd return. They thought I did you in—me, a mouse! Imagine! Now you're back!"

While the mouse-wife cheered, the other citizens of Stronghold were slow to gather around. Luna raised her head again, sensing their reticence. Even Bear Byron, her old friend, seemed to hang back. "What's happened?" she whispered to herself, and turning, she discovered the destruction behind her, the shattered homes and ruined shops, and she gasped.

But from the far side of the square a pair of youths came tumbling, cartwheeling and flipping, and behind them ran the little human girl. Breathless as the mouse-wife, they stopped before Luna and turned wide, bright eyes upward.

"Don't blame them if they're afraid," Trevor said.

Markham nodded. "There was a great fight. Harrow, and a huge gray Dragon called *Maestro!*"

"His name was Ronaldo!" Little Pear insisted with a frown. "He was beautiful!"

Trevor sneered. "Harrow beat him."

Pear's face crinkled, and she kicked Trevor. "Did not!"

"Doesn't matter who won," Markham interrupted. "Stronghold lost." He turned his head to look back at the crowd of villagers still lingering at a safe distance. "And now a lot of folks are afraid of the Dragons."

The mouse-wife piped up. "Not everyone!"

Cautiously, Bear Byron paced forward. Then Gregor and Carola, holding hands, also ventured closer. Emboldened, the rest of the villagers followed, and their whispering rose in volume as nervous expressions turned to smiles.

"It's not her fault!" Bear Byron called to the others.

"Where've you been, Luna?" Carola asked in a worried voice.

Luna bent her neck and brought her face close to the ground again. She blinked at the cat-faced fomorian as she answered. "Everywhere, I think! So many wondrous places!" She lifted her head once more to gaze over the crowd as Ramoses and Diana swooped above the canyon and landed on the rim. "Diana, beloved friend!" she called. "Fly as fast as you can and find Tiamat! Hurry!"

Diana took off, diving backward into open space and catching an updraft before turning eastward. Luna watched her go and then glanced at Ramoses. The old blue Dragon looked troubled, and Luna's brow furrowed as she wondered why. *What was this about a battle between Harrow and Maestro Ronaldo?*

Craning her neck, she gazed skyward. While eagles and hawks circled in countless numbers, where were her Dragon kindred? "How long have I been gone?" she asked quietly.

"Days and nights," the mouse-wife answered seriously as she scampered up Luna's leg to her shoulder. "Through tense hours and vicious fights."

Luna looked down at all the faces of her friends, glad to be home at last, but saddened by the uncertainty she saw in their eyes. She couldn't remember a time in her life when anyone in Stronghold had been afraid of a Dragon. Full of questions, she looked to Ramoses again.

Yet before she could ask them, a sharp pain shot through Luna's body, and her eyes snapped wide as she gave an involuntary twitch. Shaken loose, the mouse-wife tumbled through the air with a squeak, but Luna reached out despite her pain, caught her in a paw and set her safely down.

Tiamat! Thoughts of her mate rushed through her head as she squeezed her eyes shut. *My love, where are you?*

As if in answer, the air filled with a great swoosh of wings. Tiamat and Diana shot over the village, banked and turned. Tiamat beat his wings, hovering while the villagers fell away to make room. "Luna!" he called with a desperation and a relief in his voice that gladdened Luna's heart.

"Get back!" he shouted at the villagers as he landed beside his mate and coiled his long neck around hers. "Get back!"

Luna rubbed her nose against his, warmed and strengthened to hold him close again. "No, let them all come close!" she told Tiamat, and she called in a loud voice. "Gather around, everyone!"

Reluctantly, Tiamat uncoiled and looked Luna in the eye. But Luna waited until Diana had also landed and moved closer with the rest of the villagers.

"Prepare a nest," she said with her softest smile, and she began to purr as only a Dragon could. "I have an egg inside me!"

The mouse-wife jumped up and down at the news. "I knew it! Smoke me, but I could tell, and I tell you I knew it!"

Her tiny voice was almost drowned out by the cheer that went up from the villagers. The fomorian, Gregor, flapped his small white owl's wings. "Get some blankets!" he shouted. "Boil some water!"

His wife smacked him in the back of the head. "It's not a baby, you idiot!" Carola scolded. "It's an egg! What do you mean, *boil some water?*"

Gregor cringed. "I got excited!"

"Are you sure?" Tiamat said to Luna as he rubbed his cheek against hers.

"Trust me," Luna assured him as another pain lanced through her body. "And soon, too."

With a roar, Tiamat leaped into the sky, spread his wings and disappeared over the forest. It was his task to prepare Luna's nest, to make it comfortable and construct it secure. A Dragon's egg was a precious rarity.

It was also a cause for celebration.

Bear Byron rose up on his hind legs to stand tall. "We need to come together again as a village!" he called, "and this is just the occasion! Set aside your worries and fears! I've a keg of honey stored away! Let's have some music!"

"I've got some good dandelion wine," someone shouted.

Carola raised her hand. "I've got fresh-baked pies in the window!"

Someone else cried, "I'll contribute a bushel of rutabagas!"

Fortunato the Minotaur made a face. "Forget the rutabagas!" he suggested. "Me and my brothers will go get our drums!"

The mouse-wife shook her head. "Those won't cook up well at all!"

Someone laughed, and then everyone joined in. All the uncertainty and fear that Luna had seen in their eyes before melted away. Fortunato's brothers rushed off and returned with their instruments. Some satyrs hurried to fetch their pipes. In no time at all, Stronghold came alive with vibrant music.

As the crowd broke apart to gather a feast, Diana crept closer to Luna. "This is good," she said, beaming as she looked around. "We're all Dragonkin once more. You've brought us together." Leaning close, she coiled her neck around Luna's in a Dragon embrace. "When do you think it will be?"

Luna purred even more loudly at Diana's touch, and the two friends rocked back and forth to the tempo of the drums. "Tonight or tomorrow," Luna whispered in Diana's ear. A Dragon's time was never long.

Diana began to purr also. "The talismans have been found, and you carry a child inside you," she said solemnly. "Stronghold was frightened and divided as I've never seen it, but you've brought us back together." Her voice dropped to a whisper that matched Luna's. "Surely, Luna, you're meant to lead us—to wear the mantel of your father!"

Startled, Luna withdrew from Diana's embrace and looked at her friend. "I don't think so," she answered with some hesitation. Abruptly she stopped purring. Although the prophecy in the Book of Stormfire spoke of *the triplets* without naming a specific successor, she'd never seriously considered the possibility. "That will fall to Harrow or Chan."

Diana drew back also and returned Luna's gaze without flinching. "You don't sound so certain."

A frown flickered across Luna's Dragon lips, but then she forced a smile. "This isn't the time to think about such things," she said, changing the subject. "My hatchling is all the responsibility I want right now."

She looked past Diana to Ramoses, who watched patiently from the rim. She could tell by the quiet look on his old scaled face how much her news had pleased him. She had so much more to tell him, so much to relate of her strange journey and the wonders she had seen. She needed his wisdom and his guidance.

But that would wait. She looked around for another. "Diana?" she asked, "Where is Sabu?"

"Flown southward," Diana answered after a reluctant pause. She turned away from Luna and shot a look at her father as if appealing to him for help, but Ramoses maintained his dignified posture and remained where he was.

"Southward?" Luna pressed, disappointed. She wanted her mother close by. How could she not be here when Luna needed her? "But why?"

Diana looked distressed. "A family matter," she answered awkwardly. "Concerning your brothers." Swallowing, Diana found her courage and met Luna's questioning gaze. "All your brothers."

It was Luna's turn to hesitate. She tilted her head in puzzlement as she tried to read Diana's meaning. "Chan and Harrow?" she said.

Diana nodded and swallowed again. "And Ronaldo."

The word hung in the air for a long moment. Then Luna's jaw gaped. Slowly she turned her head to stare across the canyon toward the pinnacle of rock called Stormfire's Point, and she dimly noted the new scars and raw scratches in its stone.

Tiamat wheeled suddenly past the pinnacle, headed eastward toward his cave. In his claws he bore loads of wood, branches and leaves. The sight of her mate brought a fleeting smile to her lips.

"There's more," Diana continued grimly. "And worse. News of Chan that's only just reached us."

A fresh pain stabbed at Luna, so intense that she raised her head and roared. A deep shudder seized her, and she snapped her wings wide. All around the village everyone stopped what they were doing to look, and the music stopped. "Fly!" Luna urged Diana. "Tell Tiamat to hurry!"

Diana sprang away quickly, as if she had welcomed the chance to escape. With a look of apology, Luna nodded reassurance to all her friends. The music resumed at once, and so did the preparations for the feast. Soon there was singing and dancing, too, and at the far end of the square the three human children began to tumble and perform.

Luna thought suddenly of Ariel and despite her happiness, for a moment she felt like crying. She could almost feel Ariel's small weight riding on her neck, almost hear her tinkling laugh and her sometimes-angry voice. Closing her eyes, she remembered too acutely the exact moment when she lost Ariel. In her mind, she could still see the arrow and Ariel's seemingly endless fall.

She remembered, also, everything that had followed.

She hadn't told the other children yet. There hadn't been time to tell anyone. Indeed, she didn't know quite what to tell.

She stared toward Stormfire's Point again. For good or bad, it seemed that everyone had news. She tried to wrap her mind around something Diana had said. "Ronaldo," she murmured. It sounded right to her, although she couldn't explain why. But there was a suggestion of music in it like music she had heard before.

Another pain struck her. Sucking in a breath, she waited for it to pass before she approached Ramoses. "Old teacher," she said with reverence to the oldest of the Dragonkin. "I have so much to tell...."

Ramoses bowed his head. "You are the Heart of All Dragons," he answered, anticipating her. "The power of the talisman resides within you."

"I don't understand it," she insisted.

Ramoses smiled with gentle reassurance. "Neither do I," he answered calmly. "It's a mystery in a puzzle, but all the pieces are coming together. Have faith."

Luna sighed. "In what?"

Old Ramoses began to purr, and a sublime expression filled his eyes. Sitting up on his haunches, he folded his paws across his chest and fanned his wings. "In the only thing that matters," he told her. "In yourself."

Leaning forward, Luna brushed her ivory face against Ramoses'. She loved the old Dragon. It seemed he had always been by her side or close at hand when she needed him. More so than Stormfire or Sabu he had taught her and answered her questions. It was his poetry that filled her private moments, and his campfire tales that still echoed in her memories. More than a father or mother—he had been a good teacher.

"When my time comes," Luna told him, "I want three things with me. One of my father's books, a handful of my mother's scales, and a page with one of your poems." She smiled at him. "Can I count on you?"

He grinned with pleasure. "The book and the scales, certainly," he answered. "But why you'd want to expose a new hatchling to my doggerel...."

Luna interrupted as she stared past his shoulder. Skymarin, the Lord of Eagles, sailed on widespread wings above the wide expanse, skipping from one updraft to another, as graceful as he was watchful. Full of pride and dignity, he gently stroked the wind with his feathers, and no creature looked more beautiful.

Skymarin had long been a friend, but the Lord of Eagles was getting old. "I'd ask for one more thing," she said to Ramoses. "Ask Skymarin to bring me a rose. A red rose. He won't have any trouble finding one. They've become very," she hesitated for a brief moment before continuing. "...very special to me."

"I'll see to everything, Daughter of Stormfire," he said. "I only wish that Sabu were here."

Luna resisted the next stab of pain, allowing only a slight grimace as she clutched her abdomen. Looking outward, she watched Tiamat race across the canyon once again with claws full of nesting stuff. *Tonight*, she thought to herself as she drew a deep breath. *Not tomorrow!*

The drums rose to a crashing thunder, and the pipes whistled. A group of fomorians shook chipolis and bells while another group blew crazy notes from water-filled bottles. Luna closed her eyes to listen. It wasn't at all like the music of the talisman—and yet it was! She heard the similarities, the patterns, the blending harmonies, the beat.

It was all music—and it was life!

"Ask them to keep playing," Luna said to Ramoses. "Hatched or born, a child should come into a world full of music."

A wind blew across the canyon, bringing with it smells of trees and flowers, rich honeysuckle and eucalyptus and earthier scents. It rustled the leaves, and that too was a kind of music. At the bottom, the Echo Rush hurried on its way to the Windy Sea, its surface glistening in the sunlight, its ripples white-capped. She drew another breath, and the air tasted like candy.

She had never felt so at peace, so glad to be home.

But a sudden thought furrowed her brow. When the talismans came together they would point the way to a new home for the Dragonkin. So it was written in the Great Book of Stormfire. So it was prophesied.

Luna stared up and down the canyon again. All its colorful striations and features were burned into her memory. She'd spread her wings and learned to fly for the first time between its grand walls. She gazed at the forest beyond, all the pines and oaks and maples, the ash and willows, the dark groves that she loved. All the hills and lakes where she had played—what of those?

Was she supposed to leave it all behind to satisfy a prophecy?

"Ramoses," she said in sudden desperation, "what if I don't want to go?"

But the old blue Dragon wasn't there. He'd flown away when she wasn't looking, while she was lost in old memories and new worries. As she never had in her life, Luna felt deeply alone.

Well, I'm not alone! she thought, perking up as she touched her body and felt a vibration from the egg she carried. She searched the sky and spied Tiamat swift at his urgent task, and she chuckled. He'd strip the forest bare if she didn't stop him soon. Either that, or stuff his cave so full she'd never get inside. Leaping from the rim, Luna flew after her mate.

Farther ahead, Tiamat deposited his load and turned back for more, but seeing Luna he spread his ruby wings and raced to meet her. In mid-air, high above the canyon they met. Wing brushed against wing. Luna laughed, and Tiamat banked sharply to chase her. With her mate close behind, Luna climbed higher and then playfully rolled away. The ruby Dragon shot past with a roar of frustration, and Luna laughed again.

Then, above Stormfire's Point, Luna stopped playing. Pounding the air with her wings, she hovered and waited for her mate. Tiamat charged toward her, and then swooped over her head, dived downward, rose again, circling her. Each time he passed his wings brushed hers. For a moment they actually came together. Luna coiled her long neck around Tiamat's and trembled in his embrace as they fell toward the ground together, separating only at the last instant and turning to fly side by side, wingtip to wingtip to the new nest.

Entering the cave, Luna crawled deep into the brush and branches and, guided by some ages-old instinct, she began to arrange it all, weaving sticks and limbs together, binding them with willow, scattering soft leaves and grass to make a bed. The cares and worries of the world melted away. Without conscious thought she worked at a rapid pace, barely aware of the ripples of sensation vibrating through her body or of Tiamat standing watchful guard at the cave's mouth.

When the nest was done, Luna circled and circled, examining every part of her work with minute care before she curled up and lay down. The sound of her contented purring filled the cave, and the air grew warm with the increasing heat of her body. In a state of bliss, she stared through half-closed lids.

The sky beyond the cave began to darken. As the sun went down, Tiamat flew a close pattern between the canyon walls, bellowing with pride and blasting bursts of fire. Yet he never flew far from the cave.

Her view darkened suddenly as old Ramoses glided to a landing. His claws grabbed hold of the cave's lip. Outside, Tiamat bellowed a warning and hovered, but Ramoses came in.

"A Book of Stormfire," he said, placing a volume on the edge of the nest where she could see it. Immediately she smelled her father's scent; the books were bound in pieces of his molted skin and glimmered with his golden color.

"A handful of your mother's scales," he continued in a hushed tone as he scattered them over the nest. They glittered like black diamonds, and her mother's rich scent mingled with her father's.

He placed a sheet of paper beside the book. It smelled of pounded reeds and river water, of ink and of Ramoses himself. "A poem, as you requested," he said. "It isn't good enough."

As if in a dream, Luna lifted her head. "Read it, old teacher," she asked.

Ramoses hesitated and then picked up the page again.

> "At rest in fields of flowers we heard your song
> And learned it and knew you wanted to be born.
> Singing your song in warm night among the stars
> We came together singing, your voice in our hearts;
> Singing, we made your egg and heard your song inside.
> You thanked us with your song of joy and blessed us.
> Now as you are born we sing your song,
> And as you hatch we sing your song.
> When you take your mate your song will be sung,
> And when you pass beyond the mountain
> We will sing your song in joy and sadness, and
> When we remember, your song will fill our hearts.
> This is the Dragon way, to welcome and to say goodbye."

Luna regarded Ramoses with moist eyes. "It's beautiful," she told him. "It will inspire my child, and I'll read it to her often."

"Her?" Ramoses said with a blink of his eyes.

A faint smile flickered over Luna's face. "I don't know how I know," she admitted. "But I know."

He nodded without further comment, and as he replaced the poem on the edge of the nest he laid a red rose beside it. "From Skymarin," he whispered as he turned to take his leave.

One perfect rose, she noted. As perfect as a rose that grew in Asgalun and as sweetly scented. She closed her eyes, remembering the rose and also shadows of Dragon-shapes, ghosts, dancing in the darkness.

Beyond the cave from high on the canyon rim the drums and pipes and bells played, and dozens of other homemade instruments joined in. But over that music, beside it and under it, she heard another now-familiar music. *My child's song,* she thought with deep satisfaction. *This is the song of my child!*

She opened her eyes again, and the walls were alive with shadows.

Luna cried out as she felt the egg move inside her. The night lit up with fire, and Tiamat answered with a roar. The drums on the rim went crazy, and the musicians of Stronghold poured forth their own kind of magic. Again, Luna cried out, and Tiamat answered.

Pain shot through Luna, and her breath turned ragged. She felt too hot. The Book of Stormfire slid off the edge of the nest and down inside. With a grimace, she pushed it back. The ghosts on the walls flew faster and faster until Luna's senses reeled.

Something is wrong! she thought, panicking.

A soft, reassuring voice spoke to her. *Nothing is wrong, Luna,* it said. *I'm here to help and watch over you. I promised I'd always be near.*

With an effort, Luna lifted her head. "Ariel?" she whispered. Her own voice sounded distant, a faint echo of an echo. Her heartbeat and her breathing sounded louder. "You are here, aren't you?"

Of course, silly! came the answer. Something stirred in a corner of the cave. A figure moved, stepped forward, pushed back a hood. Ariel looked up and smiled. "Do you think I'd miss this moment?" She laughed. "Now get to work! You're keeping everyone waiting!"

"I'm glad, little one," Luna answered. "I'm glad that you're here with me." She closed her eyes again as an intense shudder passed through her body. All her senses seemed to distend. The scents of her parents, of Ramoses, of the rose, swirled around her, and all the earthy smells of her nest. She saw things she should see: the feasters in the village, the dancers and musicians, flashes of places much farther.

And the music! She couldn't separate herself from it. What was real? What was imagined?

What was the talisman?

Luna gave a final cry, and then for a long moment she lay completely still, exhausted. "Is it over?" she murmured.

Ariel answered with a whisper. "It's just begun."

When she felt strong enough, Luna lifted her head. The shadows on the walls were gone. So was Ariel.

Slowly her gaze fell on the egg at the center of her nest. It looked like a round ball of fire, all red and orange and yellow with swirls of blue and white, and through the shell a hint of the precious life within.

The music on the rim continued, and Tiamat swept past again, protective and watchful. Weary and content, Luna curled up around her egg and slept.

Seventeen

IN THE PRE-DAWN DARKNESS, with the moonlight still glimmering on the tossing waters of the Windy Sea, five ships without lamps or lanterns on their decks raced in a line down the coast of Wyvernwood. Black sails billowed in a blustery breeze, and black pennants streamed from their masts. Only the foamy white wakes they made marked their passage.

From the stern of the third and centermost ship in the line a pipe blew a low, musical tone. The sound carried over the water to the fourth ship in the line, and another pipe in the stern of the fourth ship passed the signal to the last ship. Making a slight alteration in its course, the fifth ship moved closer to the wooded shore, furled its sail, and dropped anchor.

One by one, each ship dropped out of the line, turned toward the shore, and lowered anchor while the others sailed on. Almost invisible as the moon went down, each waited, silent and predatory.

Then, as the first ray of dawn broke over the tossing horizon, fireboxes ignited on the decks. Great gears and ropes creaked. Torches flared. Aboard each vessel a flurry of activity erupted. The smell of oil rose into the dawn like a perfume.

With a loud crack, the first catapult fired its load. A heavy bail of burning cloth *whooshed* through the purple twilight. For a moment, the water shimmered redly. Farther down the line, a second fireball streaked across sky, and beyond that a third.

Deep into the summer-dry forest all three missiles flew, and where they struck pillars of flame shot up.

At the rail of the center ship, the King of Angmar called out. "Load again and fire! Keep firing!" As his men scrambled to obey, he turned to gaze northward. He couldn't see the two trailing ships; they were all spaced too far apart. But he could see the fireballs as they fired their first loads.

"A wonderful idea of yours," Kilrain said to Goronus on the deck beside him. "Give the Dragons a taste of their own medicine. Fight fire with fire!" His fist crashed down on the rail as he stared inland. "I'll avenge my son and my honor by burning Wyvernwood down around all their heads!"

"King of Angmar and Ashes," Goronus muttered. "Quite a legacy."

The ship rocked on the water as the catapult fired its second load. Kilrain peered through narrowed eyes at Goronus. "You sound strangely bitter."

Goronus's eyes reflected fire as he stared shoreward. "Griffins have no love of Dragons, nor of those who follow them." His voice dropped a note. "We should have ruled Wyvernwood from the beginning."

Kilrain snorted. "Instead you help to destroy what you can't have. How human of you." He lifted his head to watch another pair of fire-balls from other ships fly across the sky, and then he gave the griffin a haughty look. "By now, my army will be striking on the northern border. It's time you got in on the fun."

Goronus gave a low growl before he crossed the deck to the firebox. Seizing a pair of pitch torches, he thrust them into the flame, igniting them. "Give the signal," he called to an archer in the bow.

The archer fitted an arrow to his bowstring and tipped it into another torch. Drawing the string back to his cheek as he raised the bow, he let fly. High into the air the arrow flew, trailing oily smoke as it arced over the water.

In response, to the north and south griffins rose up from the other ships with torches clutched in their paws.

"Fly deep," Kilrain instructed. His dark eyes glittered with madness. Grabbing a torch from one of the sailors, he waved it toward the shore. "Strike fire where my catapults can't reach. Burn everything!" Spinning about, he flung the torch with all his might, fervently wishing that he, too, could strike a blaze with his own hand.

One of the sailors loading the catapult for its next shot began to sing.

"One dark night when we were all in bed
King Kilrain got an idea in his head . . ."

Goronus drew back with one of his torches and swung it forcefully. The sailor screamed as he clutched his face. Burned and blinded, he stumbled over the rail into the sea. "Always give credit where credit's due," Goronus snarled. He cast a look at the King of Angmar, daring Kilrain to disapprove, but Kilrain only folded his arms over his chest with an impatient expression.

Flexing feathered wings, the griffin leader sprang into the sky. His followers were already far ahead of him, eager to do their work, to take their own revenge for the wrongs done them by the Dragons. With torches held carefully to avoid their flickering flame, Goronus roared and gave chase.

A crackling wall of fire loomed as he approached the shore. The catapults had done efficient work in the dry forest, and the flames were quickly spreading. Directly ahead, a tall pine tree exploded. Burning fragments showered down across the sandy beach and upon the water to sputter and smoke.

Unexpectedly, a hot wind blew smoke into Goronus' eyes, and he roared again. Climbing higher, he looked down upon the growing conflagration, and his heart hammered with excitement. Driven by the wind, the flames were already licking inland. He glanced south-ward and northward where the fireballs from the other ships contin-ued to whistle shoreward.

A scorching updraft lifted him higher still, and for an instant he panicked as his mane began to smoke and singe. A needle of flame shot suddenly up from another pine tree. He swerved desperately to avoid being caught in it and burned.

Then, with a powerful beat of his wings he sailed over the wall and into cooler air. His roar turned to an eagle's screech of triumph as he glanced downward at untouched woodland. A wave of fleeing birds dotted the sky below and ahead of him, and he laughed at the crea-tures scampering and running for their lives on the ground.

Swooping low, he touched his torch to the branches of an oak. The leaves smoked and shriveled and finally caught fire. *That's one for the griffins*, he thought to himself, cheerfully pleased with his handiwork. Flying on, he dived into a dry brush thicket. Unlike the oak, it took fire easily. He sighed with satisfaction as he watched flame shoot across the forest floor.

With a bitter gleam he thought of Gaunt and Gorganar, great griffin leaders before him, who had suffered shame and defeat by the Dragons. This day he was their vindicator. With his torches he burned away that shame. To redeem the Griffinkin's honor he would reduce the Great Refuge of the Dragonkin to ashes.

It was such a simple plan he couldn't imagine why no one had thought of it before. While Kilrain launched fire from his ships on the east coast, his armies charged over the border in the north, setting fires there. The greatest blow, however, fell to him and his griffin followers, who carried fire into the very heart of Wyvernwood.

Men with their stupid wars—he sneered at them! They were so easy to trick and use! Let Kilrain take what credit he wished, claim whatever rationale he chose. The plan was his, Goronus'.

He coughed suddenly as thick clouds of smoke churned upward through the air. No visible trace of dawn remained; the smoke obscured all, and the roiling sky glowed red as blood. Hot winds buffeted him. His eyes stung and watered. A shrill screech ripped through the crackling and popping—a griffin cry.

Goronus shot a look to his right just in time to see another pine tree erupt. Its dry nettles and bark made the perfect incendiary. Fire fountained with unexpected power, snatching one of his followers in a deadly embrace. A beautiful griffin burst into flame and screamed again as it plummeted earthward burning wings.

With a gaping beak, Goronus watched in horror. And yet there was honor in such a death, he reasoned, for from that griffin corpse more fire sprang up to burn and destroy!

With savage determination he raced onward until the eastern line of the fire was safely behind him and the smoke lessened somewhat. He glanced downward for a place to touch his torch, and his eyes danced with cruelty when he saw deer and moose racing along the ground with foxes at their heels and panicked birds around their heads.

But he saw something else, too, that puzzled and enraged him. Against all nature, some of the larger birds—the hawks and owls, particularly—were carrying rabbits and squirrels and even mice in their claws, sometimes two at once, racing them to the unlikely safety of a swift-flowing stream and releasing them on its banks before turning back for others! Was he losing his mind? There was a bear down there with a family of opossums on its back!

"It buys you only a small time!" Goronus shouted from his higher vantage as he waved his torches at them.

Without warning, a high screech sounded above Goronus and before he could react, a swift shape flashed in front of his feathered face. For a brief, curious moment Goronus felt nothing. Then the griffin leader screamed in agony!

His attacker answered with an angry challenge. "Maybe I can buy them more time!"

Fighting pain, Goronus blinked furiously. His face was full of blood and stinging fire, and he couldn't quite identify his foe. Fearing another attack before he was ready, he waved his torches in a frenetic display.

"Can't see too well, you bag of fleas?" his attacker cried. "I am Pyrtanik, sister to Skymarin, Lord of Eagles, and not only have my talons scored your ugly face—I've just taken your eye!"

Goronus shook away droplets of blood and focused his good left eye as a large golden eagle banked and flew at him again. With a desperate roar, the griffin struck out, but Pyrtanik made a sharp swerve, avoiding the blow.

With a shriek and another roar, Goronus hurled one of his torches after the eagle. "I'll burn your nest!" he shouted. "I'll fry your eggs!"

"That's a feeble threat!" Pyrtanik laughed. Turning, she folded her wings back and dived like a sleek bolt after the torch to catch it in her talons and drop it in the stream where it sizzled and hissed and died in a harmless bit of smoke.

Goronus roared again and charged after Pyrtanik. *How dare she? He was a griffin, the most feared of all creatures! But she had taunted him! Injured him!* Half-blinded, he poured on the speed and reached out to snatch her, intent on tearing out her feathers and ripping off her wings. He would take great pleasure in that!

But before he could close his grip around his prey, two more eagles shot downward out of the smoke-filled sky. Again, Goronus screeched as talons raked his scalp and shoulder. Then a third eagle snatched his remaining torch!

"This can't be!" the griffin leader shouted as Pyrtanik turned to attack again with two more eagles at her side. "It's against the natural order!" He risked swift glances to left and right in a fleeting hope that some of his own followers were close, but he saw no sign of them at all.

With a curse, he dodged Pyrtanik. Still, one of her allies swerved close and raked his flank. And worse news! To his astonishment a flight of falcons, emboldened by the eagles, charged him. Fearing for his remaining eye, he dived for the treetops and the safety of the ground, smashed through branches and slipped in mud.

Already a dense smoke rolled among the stout trunks and over the brush. The acrid stench seared his nostrils and stung his one good eye, but he padded softly through the muck with his wings folded on his back, hoping for a respite from Pyrtanik and her circling comrades. He looked around cautiously. With his throat parched from the smoke and the battle, he headed for the stream.

But Wyvernwood offered no refuge to Goronus. With the forest endangered, even the smallest of its inhabitants struck back. Before he took three steps a swarm of savage bees hummed through the branches to attack him. Though their stings were small, their numbers made them fierce. The griffin leader howled and danced as he tried to beat them away with his wings. Over and over they stung his rump, his neck, his back. He swatted at them, and they stung his paws, too.

Heart pounding, desperate to get away, Goronus ran. Smoke choked him, and wave after wave of wind-driven heat rippled over his sensitive wounds as the fire he'd planned and helped to set drew ever closer. Frantic, he paused to stare up through the branches. Overhead, the eagles and hawks and falcons seemed as countless as the bees and as angry. Any bird, anything at all that could fly seemed to be tracking him through the canopy of leaves! Safe in the higher limbs, sparrows and robins chirped noisily to give away his position!

With the annoying bees still on his tail, Goronus turned toward the stream again. If he could just get a drink of water he might find strength to fight again.

But a lion snarled as it stepped out of the trees to block his path. With a look of menace, it showed its teeth and raised one set of claws. It wasn't alone, either. On a branch above the lion's great maned head, a leopard stretched out with lazy, muscular grace.

Both beasts glared at him with savage intent.

Wounded and in pain, Goronus chose not to fight. Instead, he spun about and ran the other way into the smoke and heat. With a glance back over his shoulder to determine that the lion and leopard weren't following, he veered south. The damnable bees had retreated, too.

Then, without sound or warning, a great gray paw smashed downward at him. From the corner of his good eye and barely in time, Goronus saw a hint of a shadow and dodged too slowly. Though he took only a glancing blow, the impact sent him flying through the air to slam against a tree. Pain lanced through his right wing.

A huge gray Wyrm loomed over him clenching and unclenching its fist. A cousin to the Dragons, the Wyrm had no wings, nor did it breathe fire, and yet its size made it a beast to reckon with.

And this was an angry Wyrm. Its scales were scorched and blackened, its face smudged with ash. "Grendleton is burning! The entire town!" The creature's immense tongue flicked out between needle-sharp teeth. "Many Wyrm-kin are dead. You've done your work well, griffin! The fire rages! Stick around a while to see its glory!"

With fear-widened eyes, Goronus stumbled up and backed away from the Wyrm. Even Pyrtanik and her raptors were preferable to the monster before him! He'd take his chances in the sky! With a frightened screech, he spread his wings and prepared to leap.

But his right wing didn't respond and flexing it only brought worse pain.

Broken! His wing was broken!

With the promise of death in its eyes, the Wyrm advanced and raised its fist again. Goronus still had a griffin's strength, but already he'd lost an eye and a wing, and the fire was growing ever closer and closer!

Fortunately, Wyrms were slow and ponderous. If he was quick it would never catch him. Dragging his broken wing, Goronus ran away again.

Yet, when he turned west away from the fire, a great black bear rose up with a roar and spread its hirsute arms to block his path. He was no safer on the ground, he realized in despair, than he was in the air! Whichever way he tried to run, some creature or creatures appeared to stop him. Lions, bears, great tusked boars, wolves—and now in the branches above with the sparrows and robins, the eagles and hawks sat as if in judgment, coldly watching.

Only when he turned east did the creatures of Wyvernwood leave him alone.

East—toward the fire.

Leaning on the rail of his ship, Kilrain sighed and smiled to himself as he watched the conflagration from a safe distance. With the blessing of a strong wind, the flames had swiftly spread along the entire coastline as far as he could see. He loved the way the fire shimmered and danced like a curtain or a veil. It reminded him of the aurora borealis he sometimes saw in Angmar's night sky—only so much brighter.

There was something beautiful about fire. Something cleansing. Even so far offshore, he could hear the rushing sound of it. Although muted by distance, it carried over the water. Alone with no one at his side he listened for a long time to the lapping of the flames.

There was something calming about fire.

The catapults were silent, their ammunition expended. The smell of oil still hung in the air, but now it mingled with the tantalizing perfume of smoke when the breeze shifted enough to send an occasional wisp toward the ship.

With no orders and nothing more to do, most of the crew watched in the bow and the stern or along the rail. A few climbed into the rigging and hung like spiders. No one spoke louder than a whisper, and they kept their distance from their king.

As beautiful as he found the fire, Kilrain also marveled at the red smoke that churned above it. Like something alive in its own right, it shifted and changed and took shapes. Now it was a serpent writhing above the fire. Now it was a great horse's head. Now the moon peaked through for just an instant, and it was a nest in which some frosty jewel rested.

Now it was a Dragon.

Kilrain started and clutched at the rail. Frozen in terror, he stared, unable to move or speak until he reassured himself it was still just smoke, and that happened only when the wind blew again and the smoke changed into yet another shape.

With a ragged breath he looked slyly around to see if any of the crew had noticed his reaction.

Of course they hadn't. They were all entranced by the sight on shore. He breathed a little easier. Carefully, he pried his fingers one at a time from the rail and dabbed at a bead of sweat on his brow. Then, folding his arms across his chest, he tried to look nonchalant.

Kilrain closed his eyes for a moment to further calm himself, but when he looked toward the fire he could still see the red glow through his eyelids. His mouth drew into a taut line that was not quite a smile. Would Degarm still fight so hard for Wyvernwood when it was just a lot of ashes?

He opened his eyes again. The fire seemed larger and brighter than ever and more ferocious. A triumphant chuckle slipped from his lips, and suddenly he didn't want to be alone any longer. Sliding along the deck, he leaned on the rail again beside an unwary sailor who was staring toward the coast while chatting with a mate.

Neither man noticed Kilrain right away, but that irritated him only slightly. He reminded himself that it was good for a king to communicate sometimes with the common men, and this was after all a moment of victory for them as well. He could afford a gesture of beneficence.

Slapping the unwary sailor on the shoulder, he drew a deep breath and asked in a jovial voice. "So, mate, tell me what you see out there?"

Without looking around, the sailor spat over the rail into the sea and then gave a grim answer. "I see a frikkin' hornets' nest," he muttered, "an' if ye ask me, we jus' stuck a big stick in it."

Clenching his fists and smoldering with anger, the King of Angmar took a step back and glared. Slowly, the sailor turned his head to glance Kilrain's way, and his haggard, unshaven face was a white mask of fear.

But not with fear of his king, Kilrain realized. A chill ran down his neck as he took another step back and studied the faces of all his crew. They all wore the same white mask.

"Beggin' yer Majesty's pardon an' all," the sailor dared to press, "but what would yerself do if'n someone burned down yer' barn an' set fire to yer fine home?"

Kilrain blustered. The nerve of the man—a common sailor—questioning him as if he should be expected to explain to the fool! "Assuming any Dragon can survive such a fire they won't dare come after us now!" he shouted, commanding and sure of himself. "They see what we can do! What we're capable of doing!"

The sailor risked his life with a long, scornful look before he turned away to gaze once more at the burning coastline. "If yer Majesty says so," he answered curtly.

Kilrain's hand trembled as he touched the hilt of his sword. And yet something stayed his hand. Perhaps it was all the eyes of his men upon him. Or perhaps it was something else. The smoke above the fire shifted and stirred, took shapes, and became a Dragon again. Then it was two Dragons, a pair on vast billowing wings, flying low and breathing fire across the shore.

And their eyes turned toward Kilrain.

The same cold terror that clutched him before clutched him again. Letting go of his sword, he grabbed the rail and held on. "Weigh anchor," he whispered, and after a moment's hesitation, the sailor relayed his command. "Take us away from here," the King of Angmar said. "As fast as wind and sea allow."

Eighteen

"SO YOU'RE BACK AT LAST," Agriope said in an accusatory tone as she rubbed her face with a sleeve of her black robe. "And the smell of mischief is so strong that it tickles my nose!"

Ariel stumbled through the darkness with her mirror clutched in one hand. "Teacher!" she screamed as she leaned on the cavern wall and sank to one knee. "Help me! I burn! My skin is burning!"

Agriope spun about in the blackness, and seizing her heavy robes in her gnarled hands, she rushed to Ariel's side and dropped down beside her. With deft care she placed a hand on Ariel's forehead and recoiled in shock. "Not your skin," she gasped. "It's your soul that's burning!" "It hurts!" Ariel flung herself into Agriope's arms as she cried out. "Make it stop! I'm on fire!"

With gentle strength Agriope gripped Ariel's head and placed her thumbs over the little girl's eyes to close them shut. Ariel shivered and quaked, her slim body as taut as a bowstring as she clung to Agriope. Beneath the deep folds of her black hood, a tear leaked from an old eye and a moment of doubt flashed through her mind. *Have I chosen unwisely?* she wondered as she, too, began to tremble with fear. *Have I put too much on one so young?*

"In the east," Ariel gasped in a raspy whisper. A new jolt of pain wracked her form, and the mirror slipped from her pale hand. "Too late! Too late! But they come again from the north, Agriope! I feel them coming!"

On the stony floor of the cavern, the mirror began to glow with a dull red flickering that ignited the bits of crystal and mica in the walls and in the stalactites that depended from the ceiling. Drawn by the unexpected light, Agriope stared into the ornately framed glass, which she had given the child, and the fear she felt for Ariel turned to rage.

With an inhuman snarl, Agriope shoved the mirror into a pocket of
her robe to smother its strange glow. Then, slipping her arms beneath
Ariel, she lifted the whimpering child and rushed with her burden
through the depths of the cavern. "Forgive me, little one," she muttered
as she went. "You're too young for this responsibility! The fault is mine!"

With her eyes still closed, Ariel shook her head from side to side.
"No!" she whispered, on the edge of delirium. "No! I can...! I can...!"
A new wave of agony twisted her body with such force that Agriope
nearly dropped her. But Ariel's mouth drew into a grim line as she
found the strength to master her pain. Her hand clutched at Agriope's
breast. "Teach me!" she hissed through ragged breaths.

Agriope shook her head without answering and hurried on. There
wasn't time for a lesson.

A deep chamber opened suddenly at a fork in the cavern. Pressing
Ariel's head firmly against her shoulder, Agriope stepped inside. The
dank cold smelled of dust and antiquity, and in the very farthest recess
something rested on a slab of stone.

Agriope whispered, and the sound she made was like a soft wind
whistling not just through the tunnels but down through untold ages.
Her breath made a thin white shimmering steam. "Arise from your long
sleep, my sister!" she said. "I've failed in my task and need your help!"

Ariel tried to turn her head and look, but Agriope pressed the
child's face more firmly to her shoulder as she exited the chamber and
hurried on into the darkness. A little further along she stopped again
at yet another chamber as dank and cold as the first one. Again she
stepped briefly inside. "Arise, my sister!" she whispered. "I wouldn't
disturb your rest, but the need is great!"

Through her pain Ariel managed to ask, "Sisters?" she said, her
words muffled against Agriope's robe. "Who are they?"

Agriope turned back into the cavern again and hurried onward, but
she found a small measure of satisfaction in Ariel's question. The child
seemed slowly to be mastering her pain, and that was good. Her connection to the forest was strong.

Perhaps Agriope had not chosen wrong after all. "There are things
older than the Dragons in this forest," she explained roughly.

"Wyvernwood once belonged to us!" She entered yet another
chamber and there placed Ariel on a cold stone bed. "Now rest," she
instructed. "You're not ready for what we have to do."

Rising up on one elbow, Ariel protested. "But, I can...!"

Agriope's angry voice cracked like a whiplash. "Stay!" she ordered. "This is my work! Mine and my sisters!" Her voice softened a little. "And after we're done this time, it will all fall on you, Ariel." Hesitating in the darkness, she stared at the headstrong and willful little girl. Ariel still had much to learn. A pity there wouldn't be time to teach her. She reached into her pocket for the mirror, which for the moment was just a mirror again, and pressed it into Ariel's hand. Then, almost apologetically, Agriope repeated herself. "It will all fall to you."

Turning away, Agriope moved with purposeful speed back into the cavern where, only half awake, her sisters waited for her in robes and hoods identical to her own, but moldy and caked with the dust of time. She wasted no time in greeting, but when she spoke her voice turned harsh, and all her rage returned.

"Use that tiny drop of power we kept to ourselves," she hissed from beneath her hood. "Do what must be done! Protect the forest!" She stared at each of her sisters as they nodded in silence. Their throats were too dry and full of grime to speak. "And keep our covenant with Stormfire!"

In a line they filed through the cavern to the surface to emerge in the pre-dawn among the shattered ruins of the fortress called Redclaw. Agriope laughed grimly to herself as she looked around at the broken towers and breached walls, recalling how Angmar had tried to rebuild it and how the Griffinkin had claimed it for their home —a home that was never theirs to claim.

She felt the fire now on her skin and in her eyes, as she knew Ariel felt it, and the taste of destruction filled her mouth. Her connection to the woods was old and weak, but she heard the screaming of the trees, the shuddering of the earth, the cries of all its creatures. For an instant she recoiled, overcome by the terror.

But then she steeled herself, and for the first time in long years she straightened her spine, lifted her head, and stood tall. The weight of ages seemed to fall from her shoulders as she extended her hands to her sisters. "It comes to this, my loved ones," she whispered. "We are past our time. But though this Age is no longer ours, this moment surely is!"

Gray dust shifted and fell from ancient hoods as her sisters nodded understanding, and from one a dry voice rattled. *Farewell!* Then from the other came a sound like the rustling of leaves. *Farewell, all!*

Briefly, the three sisters joined hands, and Agriope hung her head as she chanted:

> *"One drop of dreadful power*
> *to share in danger's darkest hour;*
> *though we are three, we each are one*
> *with every river, tree and stone*
> *in Wyvernwood, our sacred womb;*
> *From cradle to the dusty tomb*
> *We are her protectors —*
> *sisters, monsters, vengeful spectres!*

Agriope let go of her sisters' hands, and in the moment that their fingers parted, her sisters vanished. A gentle wind rippled over the grass that grew between the cracked cobblestones of Redclaw's court-yard where the two had stood; it stirred the dust that had fallen from their robes.

So it ends for us, she thought to herself, but there was no room in her heart for sadness. For all the great span of time she or her sisters, each in their turn, had watched over Wyvernwood. They were bound to the forest by their natures, inseparable, as much a part of it as any leaf or flower, its guardians and protectors.

And where any tree or stone or stream of Wyvernwood might be, there they could be, also. No magic in that—it was their nature.

Agriope raised her hooded head to the dawn and then turned to gaze northward through Redclaw's shattered gate. With no more effort than that, in less than a heartbeat the old fortress ruin vanished and she stood on the wooded border in the shelter of a great tree facing into Angmar.

On either side of the tree her sisters waited. One of them gave a low moan while the other pointed with a withered finger.

Far in the east a faint red glow painted a smoke-filled sky, and Agri-ope hissed as she felt the distant fire on her brittle skin. "We're too old and slow to stop that," she whispered angrily. Then she pointed across the border to the scores of torches that suddenly flared to life on the sparse Angmaran hillsides. "But these we must stop lest further damage be done!"

With slow, crackling effort one of her sisters spoke. "When shall we three meet again?"

The other sister shook back her long sleeves and pressed bony fingertips together. "Nevermore," she answered with the barest note of regret in her old, dry rasp. "Our time is near; our end is here."

Agriope reached out to hold her sisters' hands once more. She regretted deep in her soul that she could not recall their names, but too much time had passed. She knew it was the same with them. They each were buried in the dust of years. "Only the end of us," she reassured them gently. "Wyvernwood will never end. When the rest of the world passes, Wyvernwood will wave goodbye."

On the Angmaran hillsides the scores of torches multiplied and became hundreds. A soft muttering of voices grew in volume, swelled to shouts, and became a roar. With the first rays of dawn lancing across the violet sky, the torches streamed down the hills toward the forest.

From beneath the tree, Agriope studied the men who carried those torches, soldiers all, some in armor with swords or axes and others in lighter gear. The torchlight reflected on their metal helmets, turned their faces ruddy, shone in their murderous eyes as they charged downward.

"They'll try to push as far into the forest as they can to set their fires," Agriope told her sisters.

One of her sisters answered. "Then we will make a monument to their folly."

The other sister chuckled darkly. "After so long, sister," she rasped, "you still have a way with words."

Nothing more remained to be said. The three sisters separated, each melting into shadows. The wind picked up, shivered through the leaves and shook the branches, bearing with it an easy cackle, a low keening, a hiss of warning. It all made a preternatural harmony.

Along the border and in the surrounding woods, birds heard the sound and abandoned their nests in a mad flutter. Foraging deer paused to listen before running away. Rabbits dived into their burrows and foxes into their holes. A lioness roared, seized her cub in her mouth and plunged into the brush.

The line of torches spread wide as they came nearer. From beneath her hood, Agriope scowled. It was a madman's plan to send so many!

If they set their fires half of them wouldn't escape the flames! They could have stayed safely away and shot burning arrows! But this insane rush suggested a mind bent only on the destruction of Wyvernwood!

As she steeled herself for battle, Agriope thought of Stormfire. *Old friend, we've kept our covenant with you, protected the forest, watched over the Dragonkin, and guarded the Heart of All Dragons until your children came to claim it.* Glancing skyward beneath her hood, she licked cracked lips and swallowed. *But our Age has passed, and yours is passing. It's the dawn of a new day, and the children of Undersky are weeping.*

Agriope opened her hand. On her leathery palm a drop of red light shone, no larger than a Dragon's tear, a tiny drop of magic—the price of her service to the Lord of Dragons. With little time to waste, she drew a broken fingernail across it, dividing the light into three separate rays. Then, with a thought, keeping one for herself, she sent them to her sisters.

For a brief moment she gazed into the thin red radiance that remained in her hand, and her rage abated just long enough for her to taste the sadness of her passing. For one last time she allowed herself to feel the forest. Her skin burned with the fire in the east, but there was cooling wind as well, scents of marigolds and honeysuckle, the ripple and rush of rivers on her cheeks and sweet streams on her lips.

And there was life. So much life! The blossoming of flowers, seedlings pushing up through the ground. Birth and death. An egg in Stronghold! She felt it all because she was one with it.

Pursing her lips tightly, Agriope drew her fingernail through the remaining ray of light, dividing it yet again. The forest had a new protector, and one day she, too, would need a small reserve. Raising the two halves of light close to her face, Agriope whispered, "Go to Ariel."

As half the light disappeared, Agriope put on a grim smile. Half her magic would be more than enough. "Sisters," she said quietly, putting all other concern aside, "I am with you."

Racing ahead of their comrades, a group of three torch-waving soldiers penetrated the forest first. Agriope watched them from beneath her dark hood and then glanced at an ancient oak directly in their path. In an instant she disappeared and reappeared beneath its leafy boughs.

All three soldiers saw her at the same time and stopped in their tracks. Startled expressions flashed across their rough faces. Then one of them dared to laugh, and he drew back with his torch to swing it like a club.

Agriope said nothing as she raised her hands to her hood and pushed it back. The soldier's laugh became a terrified gasp. Too late, he threw up his arm to protect himself.

But there was no protection from true magic.

The power that Agriope had carried in her palm burned within her now, and her eyes shimmered with its red glow. The soldiers tried to scream, but the sound choked off unvoiced in their throats as they met her vengeful gaze. Ruddy cheeks turned pale, then gray as hard granite. Flesh stiffened, petrified, and turned to stone. Garments, armor, weapons likewise transformed. Even the torches they carried, even the flame of those torches became stone.

It was Agriope's turn to laugh, and the snakes that hung like wild hair upon her head laughed with her. It had been a long time, generations, since she had felt the exhilaration of true power coursing through her, but it was worth the wait.

Once last time, the Gorgons walked in the world.

She took but a moment to admire the cool, perfect statues with their horrific expressions and dead eyes. Her sisters would be proud. But to left and right more invaders were entering the woods, and she had work to do.

A short distance away, a soldier extended his torch toward the dry limbs of a pine tree, but before his flame could ignite the nettles he glanced sideways to find Agriope standing at his elbow. His startled gaze met hers, and magic did its work. The snakes upon her head writhed in silent glee.

A trio of Angmarans rushed past the pine tree. So intent upon destruction were they that they noticed neither Agriope nor their ill-fated comrade as they charged deep into the woods. But before Agriope could intercept them, one of her sisters rose up in their path and pushed back her hood.

Someone thrust a torch into a patch of lantana. Agriope couldn't see the fireman, but in her head she heard the fearful shrieking of the flowers as they tried to shrink away from the heat. In less than a moment she appeared in the midst of the patch and seized the torch in a firm grip before its flames could catch. "Stone," she whispered as the crouching soldier looked up and was transformed.

A chorus of warrior shouts drew her attention as another wave of invaders crashed into the forest. With boots and heavy sandals they trampled shrubs and flowers, and Agriope hated them for the damage. The screaming of the plants, unheard by Men, brought angry tears to her eyes. But Agriope heard.

Her sisters heard, too. Simultaneously, all three appeared side by side to block the charge, and as their gazes fell upon the soldiers, the air crackled with magic unleashed.

"We'll make these woods a sculpture garden," one of the sisters swore.

"Keep to the shade and shadows," the other sister warned. "The sun is rising!"

Agriope didn't linger. She was one with the forest again, sensing every movement, every sound and every threat. For one last time she was the Guardian, the Protector. When a soldier broke a spiderweb, she knew, and she was there. When another crushed a mushroom beneath a booted heel she was there. And when another thrust his torch into a thatch of lemon bottlebrush, she appeared to make him pay and then stamped out the flames.

And then a scream reverberated through the woods—a sound not heard for eons, a sound that only a Gorgon made. *Oh, Sister!* Agriope thought, knowing one of them was gone. Grief stabbed her heart. And yet, it was inevitable for they were old, and as they spent their magic they spent their lives.

For the Gorgons, that was the price of power.

In desperation, Agriope glanced around. The sun was rising, bringing with it the smell of smoke from the east. At least in this northern part of the woods no new fire burned. She and her sisters had done their job well. And yet, she could feel more soldiers on the forest's edge and feel the shuddering of the trees beneath the onslaught.

Agriope's remaining sister appeared beside her and sank down to the ground without a word. Her slitted golden eyes said that she had no more to give, and the beautiful coral-colored snakes on her head hung limp and lifeless. Somehow in the battle, she had shed the ages and looked young and lovely once again.

Kneeling down, Agriope gathered her last sister in her arms and stroked her cheek with a gentle fingertip. "This world isn't ours anymore," she whispered as she blinked back tears. "Go and rest now with our other sister in that secret place where we are young and strong forever with magic to fill your dreams."

One tremulous hand reached up to touch Agriope's face, and then it sank back to the ground. Her sister's eyes fluttered softly and closed. Barely containing her emotion, the last Gorgon rose to continue the fight.

But the branches of a nearby willow tree parted and a small form stepped out. "Don't you ever dare to leave me behind again!" Ariel snapped angrily as Agriope snatched up her hood and turned away. "Oh, don't bother with that," Ariel continued as she strode to Agriope's side. "I'm not a little girl, anymore. I'm not a little girl at all."

Agriope protested. "You're still young..."

"I know what I am!" Ariel clenched her fists and stomped her foot. Then her voice, though still grim, softened. "You made me what I am. I need a teacher, Agriope. Not a protector!"

Slowly Agriope pushed back her hood and let Ariel look upon her uncovered face. "Old habits die hard, child," she said apologetically. "But this battle isn't over, and I'm the last of my kind."

Ariel tossed her hair back and looked up at her Gorgon teacher. "That's right, you crazy old snake-charmer," she said. "And don't think I'm going to lose you." She opened her right fist to reveal a splinter of red light that shimmered on her palm. "Take this back."

Agriope hesitated before pressing her palm to Ariel's. "Sometimes the pupil can be the teacher," she said, accepting the gift. With that, she left the child. Deep within the woods, a soldier was setting fire to a dry bramble, and the flames promised to grow. Appearing behind him, Agriope grabbed his shoulder and spun him about. His eyes snapped wide with surprise as he transformed.

Ariel appeared beside Agriope. "I'll take care of the flames," she promised. "Then I'll be right behind you." Leaning her body against the stone soldier, she toppled it directly into the small fire. Sparks swirled up, but the statue's weight smothered most of the flame, and she quickly stamped out the rest.

The last Gorgon smiled at her pupil and, sensing a pair of soldiers close by, prepared to move again. But a sudden wind whistled through the forest. The branches overhead parted, and a shaft of morning sunlight speared down. With a gasp, Agriope flung up her arm and shrank away. "The light!" she cried as she struggled to draw up her hood. "I can't abide the sun!"

Ariel stared up through the leaves into the full warmth of the day. "Then it's up to me to finish what you started," she said solemnly. Reaching into her pocket, she drew out her mirror and held it with the reflective side up. "I need it back."

From beneath dark folds, Agriope stared. Then, she pressed her palm to Ariel's mirror. A line of red light glowed on the silvery surface, then diffused into it.

"Wait here in the shadows, teacher," she said. Reaching inside the black hood, she lightly touched Agriope's cheek in a gesture of affection. "There are fewer soldiers now. They've seen your handiwork and are afraid. I'll take advantage of that."

Agriope extended a trembling hand. "Be careful!" she warned, her voice weak and weary. Yet, as Ariel turned to walk away, Agriope found strength to rise. Keeping to the shadows and the shade, she followed her young pupil, curious to see what she would do.

In a tiny clearing, a pair of soldiers stood staring at a stone soldier. Not Agriope's handiwork, but one of her sisters' she guessed. Even in the daylight their torches burned with horrid brightness, and they held swords at the ready, also. On silent feet, Ariel walked up to the clearing's edge.

"Leave," she ordered in her child's voice. "You all have to leave now before I get really mad."

The soldiers glared at her. One gave a low chuckle and raised his sword.

Unafraid, Ariel raised her mirror. A beam of sunlight struck the glass and flashed with blinding brilliance. Screaming, the soldiers dropped their torches and weapons, and clutching their faces, tried to stumble away. Ariel laughed as she stamped out the torches.

Wherever she walked, the sunlight struck her mirror, and men who saw that terrible radiance screamed, blinded. Their nerves already frayed by the Gorgons and the frightening statues that seemed to be everywhere and by the realization that not one man had yet managed to strike a meaningful blaze, the remains of the Angmaran force ran before Ariel, dragging their dazzled comrades after them as they sought the safety of their own country.

On the very edge of Wyvernwood, Ariel stopped and held her mirror as high as she could. Its shining brightness crept across the divide and up the slopes as if pursuing the soldiers with its own will before it retreated again and died.

Ariel put the mirror back in her pocket. "They will see again in a few days," she said to Agriope, who remained nearby in the shadow of an oak tree. "But they will never forget." Her solemn expression melted as she turned around, and a broad smile lit up her young face. With an easy chuckle she said, "Isn't it nice to handle a problem without those fussy Dragons?"

Agriope took Ariel's hand, but her gaze wandered up through the leaves and eastward to the thick smoke that hung there like a cloud. She could still feel the burning on her skin and behind her eyes, and knew that Ariel felt it, too.

"There are problems to go around," Agriope whispered. "If you'll pardon the expression, we're not out of the woods yet."

Nineteen

THROUGH THE LONG, WARM EVENING Jake sat on the grass in the farmhouse's front yard before Sabu and Harrow. With the moon shining down upon them, he answered their questions and told of the encounter with soldiers from Degarm in the woods farther south, of the poisoned arrows and Chan's heroic flight.

"You say that lions and bears attacked the soldiers?" Harrow pressed.

"A lot of animals," Jake answered, somewhat distracted. He kept glancing over his shoulder toward the trees and scratching his head. He couldn't get Ariel out of his mind, nor could he set aside the feeling that somehow she had led him out of the forest and set him on the path to the farmhouse. But if it really had been her, how could she have come so far south?

"It was strange, too, because I don't think they actually killed anyone," he continued. "They just frightened the soldiers out of their pants and drove them away. They were very organized about it, too." He scratched his head again and frowned. "Like someone was guiding them."

"Animals?" Sabu gave him a look of disapproval. "We don't use such a derogatory term in Wyvernwood, young man." She bent down close and gave him a hard look. "Do you have head-lice?"

"What? Oh, sorry." Jake put his hand down. "There's just a lot on my mind right now. Things I don't understand."

"Leave him alone, Mother," Harrow said in quiet sympathy as he studied the boy. "He's been through a lot. Chan will recover, and now we have further proof of Degarm's intentions." He paused to look up at the bright moon. "It's after midnight. Let him sleep."

Sabu sat back on her haunches and wrapped her wings around herself. Her tail thumped the ground in agitation. "I don't know what to

185

do," she muttered. "I came to find Ronaldo. Instead I find trouble and more trouble. We can't just leave Chan lying in the woods!"

"Well, I don't think I can carry him," Jake answered with poorly concealed sarcasm as he leaned back on his hands.

Harrow spoke again. "Jake says he's getting the best care possible, and I believe him. But if it reassures you, I'll stay here. You can continue to look for our new brother."

Jake sat up again and cocked an eyebrow. "What?"

"What?" Sabu repeated, mocking him. "You're too fond of that word. When you say it you sound like an otter." Then her tail became still, and she shrugged her wings. For a moment she was silent. "It's my turn to apologize," she said at last. "I'm tired and half-crazy with worry."

Harrow drew himself to his full height, and the moonlight touched the white star-shaped scars on his wings so that they seemed to glow as he snapped them wide. "Do as I told you, Sabu," he said in a tone that brooked no argument. "Ronaldo is your only concern. Leave the rest to me."

For a moment the air crackled with tension, and Jake realized with a jolt that some recent shock had passed between mother and son, something of which he was not yet fully aware. What was this business about the Dragon Ronaldo, whose home lay just on the other side of the hill? He'd answered all the questions tonight. Maybe it was time he asked a few.

Clearing his throat to draw their attention, Jake stretched his cramped and knotted muscles and got to his feet. Yet, before he could say anything a sharp screeching sounded high overhead, and a feathered shape dived out of the night sky to strike the ground with considerable force. With a frantic flopping of wings and tail feathers, the newcomer found its legs and righted itself.

"An eagle!" Jake cried.

Trembling and weak, the great bird gave him a dismissive look. "You don't miss a trick, do you?" he said breathlessly as he dug his talons deep into the grass to steady himself. Then, turning toward Sabu and Harrow, he gasped out his news. "Skymarin sends word! In relay teams we've searched all night for you—especially you, Mother of Luna! Your daughter is with egg!"

"Luna? An egg?" Sabu's eyes snapped wide. Lifting her black head high, she blew a blast of fire straight upward in her excitement.

"Ronaldo will have to wait," she said to Harrow. "We have to go to her now! We have to be with her!"

But Harrow shook his head. "You go, Mother," he said. "It's happy news, but I have business here."

Sabu slammed her tail on the ground, causing the eagle to squawk and Jake to jump. "No business more important than this!" she insisted. "An egg, Harrow! The first Dragon egg in...!" She paused and raised a paw to scratch her scaled head.

"Lice?" Jake asked with a sweet expression.

Sabu ignored him. "In three centuries! Since you and Chan and Luna were born!"

Harrow stood firm. "Then fly swift and straight, Mother, or you'll miss the event. And don't stop to talk to gossip with any tree frogs."

Angered by his refusal, yet excited at the same time, Sabu glared at her son and then flew upward. "Just make sure you behave yourself!" she called back to him.

"Don't I always?" he answered in a sweet tone not unlike Jake's. He watched with unblinking eyes as his mother climbed higher into the sky and spread her wings against the stars. When she was out of sight, he glanced down again with a satisfied look on his black-scaled face.

Jake regarded the Dragon with a suspicious frown and one eye squeezed shut. "Are tree frogs really such terrible gossips?" he asked.

"All night long," Harrow answered, amused. "Talk, talk, talk."

The eagle flapped its wings in indignation and pouted. "Some might have thought a polite *thank-you* was in order!" he said as he pranced a few steps. "I barely made that landing, I'm so exhausted! But then I'm only the messenger, and nobody cares! Hmmmph!" He shot a round-eyed look at Jake. "You wouldn't have a fat field rat around, would you?"

Jake held up his hands in regret. "Vegetarian," he answered.

"Me, too," Harrow added. "Sorry."

The eagle squawked again as it turned and paced the other way. "Well, crap! Then it's take-out again." Pausing suddenly, he glanced up at Harrow. "Any tip?"

The Son of Stormfire inclined his head. "Try the other side of the farmhouse. There's a beet-patch, and they always attract a few rodents."

"Thanks, chum!" The eagle snapped its beak and then flew across the roof and out of sight.

When they were alone, Harrow looked down at Jake for a long moment and folded his wings. Then with languid grace he stretched out on the grass, curled his tail around to his nose and slowly thumped its tip on the ground. All the while, his gaze remained on the boy.

Folding his arms across his chest, Jake waited. He knew Dragons well enough to know that Harrow had something on his mind. He hadn't been subtle at all in getting rid of Sabu. Patiently, he stood there under that silver-eyed gaze, shifting his weight first to one foot and then to the other.

Finally, he executed a slow back walkover and, holding out his arms, bowed in formal fashion. "Well?" he said, breaking the silence. "Do I measure up?"

Harrow didn't answer right away. He didn't move at all. He just watched Jake. "I'm trying to see what Chan sees in you," he said at last.

Jake frowned inwardly as he tried to decide how to take that. Was the Black Dragon insulting him? He shifted his weight and crossed his arms again as he stared back without flinching. "My sparkling eyes," he answered. "My expressive smile. The boyish curve of my hips."

"Your smart mouth." Harrow blinked as he raised his head a little and flicked his tongue over his scaly lips. "That would certainly appeal to my brother, because he has one of his own.

With a roll of his eyes, Jake spun about and headed for the farm-house. He was too tired and too sore to play games with Harrow, and he wanted to get up early to make the trek back through the woods to see how Chan was doing. "I'm going to bed," he announced. "You can sleep out here with the field rats."

"Would you rather come with me to Degarm?"

Jake stopped. Unsure if he'd heard right, he turned his head and looked back over his shoulder. "Did someone hit you in the head with a rock when I wasn't looking?" he muttered.

"My brother undertook a mission to your king," Harrow continued, unfazed. "He thought you'd be useful at his side. Now that you've brought news of this new poison, that mission is more important than ever."

"More dangerous, too," Jake warned in a cold voice. "And he's not my king anymore." He began to study the Dragon just as intensely as

Harrow studied him. He didn't know Harrow that well, and didn't know if he could trust him. Harrow had always seemed contemptuous of his friendship with Chan.

Yet he was Chan's brother, and there was truth in what he said. The increasing threat posed by Degarm couldn't be ignored. They'd already poisoned the Blackwater River. And they'd hurt his *Sumapai*. Jake clenched his fists as he considered.

"Now you're studying me," Harrow observed.

"Some books are harder to read than others," Jake answered sharply, "and I don't like surprise endings." Yet even as he spoke he knew he was going to agree. Whether the Dragonkin realized it or not, they were at war with Degarm, and he had already chosen sides. "I don't have a saddle anymore," he said at last. "Maybe there's some rope in the barn."

Harrow stretched out on the ground again, and as Jake turned toward the barn he wondered if he was making a wise choice. The boy had courage and admirable daring. Yet he was still a boy without teeth or claws or wings of his own. The Son of Stormfire closed his eyes and with a sigh set such doubts aside. Chan believed in the boy, and whatever his occasional disagreements with his brother, he trusted Chan.

Besides, Jake would help him find the King of Degarm.

With the wind playing over his scaled back, he thought of his sister, Luna, and he smiled inwardly. An egg! What wonderful news! Yet his smile turned to a frown. With Wyvernwood in so much peril and the future so uncertain, could this be a good time for a hatchling? Still, an egg! He would be an uncle!

Alerted by Jake's footsteps, he opened his eyes. The boy wore the Dragon-scale shirt Luna had given him, and over one shoulder he carried a coil of rope. "I've lost all my weapons," he grumbled as he looked up at Harrow.

Harrow blinked. "You've always got your sharp wit."

Without answering, Jake busied himself preparing the rope, and the Black Dragon kept still as it was slipped around his neck. Then springing up, the boy settled himself and knotted several lengths around his waist and thighs.

"Watch your heels," Harrow advised as he flexed his wings. "I'm ticklish." With no more warning, he flew upward, skimming the roof of Ranock's farmhouse as he banked southward and sailed over the forest. At first, unused to Jake's weight and concerned for the boy's safety, he flew close to the treetops, but gradually he grew more confident. Jake rode with impressive skill and balance, sure of himself and unafraid, and mindful of the threat posed by arrows the Black Dragon climbed higher.

"Are you so quiet with Chan?" he called to his rider when they'd gone some distance.

Jake's voice came back barely audible over the rush of wind. "I've got a lot on my mind," he answered. After a pause, he spoke up again. "Why are you really going to Degarm?"

Harrow considered. "I guess you could say I owe a debt of honor."

The boy braced his hands on Harrow's neck as he leaned outward and scanned the forest below. "Me too," he said and then fell silent again.

While Jake scanned the forest, Harrow searched the sky for any sign of Maximor or Paraclion, but he saw no other Dragon at all. If they were still herding crows they were far away. Or perhaps they'd already turned back for Stronghold.

He glanced at the moon as it slipped past zenith, and its ivory light filled him with a brief melancholy. How many times had he flown over the forest under that soft glow? How many times would he do so again? Everything was changing.

"That's the Blackwater River ahead," Jake said suddenly. "It changes course and flows into the sea. Degarm lies on the other side."

Flying at a shallow angle, Harrow flew higher. In the moonlight the river gleamed like a silver ribbon across the landscape, and Wyvern-wood grew right up to its edge. But among the trees on the far bank, he spied the red glow of campfires, and his heart quickened.

"Soldiers," Jake said. "Let's give 'em a good scare."

Harrow considered it, finding a certain appeal in the idea. It would be fun to swoop down out of the night and scatter the Humans, send them running like frightened mice. He didn't really fear their arrows. "No," he said finally. "I have other goals."

"It's good to have goals," Jake answered in a disappointed voice. "It's even better when you let me in on them."

Harrow pursed his Dragon lips in troubled thought as he swerved away from the river. He wasn't quite ready to cross yet, and there was something different about the boy that disturbed him. He could hear it in the way Jake spoke and in his attitude. When had he developed such a hard edge?

"I intend to have a word with your king," he explained. Then he quickly backtracked before Jake could protest. "Sorry, sorry! He's not your king. I'm still trying to juggle all your sensitivities here."

"Well you dropped a ball," Jake snapped.

Harrow let that pass. "But before we make our social call I have something else in mind. To make poisons in such vast quantities there must be a factory somewhere. Maybe more than one and, logically, close to the river."

"A sizable town or city," Jake interrupted, anticipating Harrow's question. Leaning forward on the Black Dragon's neck, he looked around. "Purbur to the west," he suggested. "It's right at the bend of the Blackwater."

Dipping a wing, Harrow turned westward into the moonlight and raced along the bank of the river. The night sky over the rippling water and the dark forest made a peaceful panorama, and yet it couldn't calm the growing sense of danger. Harrow's gaze swept both sides of the Blackwater as he flew in grim silence.

He smelled their destination before he actually saw it. The fisheries that dotted the southern shoreline on the outskirts of the city poured an unmistakable perfume into the air, as did the stench of Human waste. Men did a poor job of cleaning up their messes.

Only a few lights burned in Purbur so late at night, but along the docks a few lanterns shone in the bows of fishing boats and in the windows of warehouses. Harrow climbed high again. Against the darkness his black shape would be difficult to spot, and gliding on wide-spread wings, he circled the city.

"It smells like an armpit after a sweaty workout," Jake commented. "It makes my nose itch."

Though he didn't respond, Harrow agreed. He'd never seen a place so dirty as Purbur. It offended his senses, and he wrinkled his nose in sympathy with Jake. How could any creature live in such conditions?

Though the heart of Purbur lay behind a great wall, the city had spread beyond it. In those areas the squalor was even worse. Through muddy streets a few men stumbled drunkenly, and one old man pulled a cartload of filthy rags while an old woman pushed. Harrow almost felt sorry for them.

Then, as the wind shifted a new scent touched his nose, a faint odor of bitter herbs and other unidentifiable things. It numbed his nostrils. Curious, he turned into the wind, following the strange scent.

Jake coughed. "Harrow, don't!" The boy lurched forward clutching his face. Only his ropes kept him from falling.

Harrow felt something, too, an unexpected dizziness, a sense that the world was slowly spinning around him and that it didn't matter. Lifting his head, he gyred upward in a vague euphoria, a choice that probably saved them, for the fumes didn't reach so high into the air, and the shifting wind offered refreshment.

"I think we found your factory," Jake muttered.

Harrow scoured the ground below, searching for a specific location, a building or facility in which the poison was made. Unable to spot such a place, he told Jake, "I want a closer look."

"You're crazy," Jake answered.

Harrow smiled a Dragon smile. "Yes, but isn't it fun?" Swinging upwind from the city, he approached at a much lower height, no longer caring if he was seen, and on the south side of Purbur, far beyond the walls, he spied what he was looking for.

The structure was a stockade with a wall of its own made from huge logs. But inside the stockade was another building with smokestacks. Through huge open doors and unshuttered windows, Harrow glimpsed furnaces or ovens, huge gears for grinding, stacks of barrels, cauldrons and great ladles.

But even more startling, he glimpsed the men inside. They were sweaty and naked, pathetic creatures filthy beyond description, and they all looked rail-thin and sick. Men in chains with collars around their necks, they shuffled as they went about their tasks, their skin reddened and cracked from heat, their eyes glassy.

"Go on, destroy it!" Jake urged. "It's what you came here to do, isn't it? What are you waiting for?"

Harrow shook his head to clear it. Even in a quick fly-over he'd caught some of the fumes, and he assumed that Jake had also. But then, the boy probably hadn't seen inside. He veered away seeking cleaner air, and then circled back yet again. This time, well away from the stockade on open ground, he landed. With no other outbuildings around, he folded his wings, dropped to all fours and crept forward.

"Destroy it!" Jake urged again in a harsh whisper. "They're using this stuff against Wyvernwood!"

Harrow hissed and ground his teeth. "I can't!" he answered, angry with both Jake and himself. With a silent curse, he rose on his hind legs to look over the stockade and through one of the unshuttered windows. It was even worse than what he'd seen on a quick pass, and this time Jake saw, too.

"Prisoners!" the boy muttered. "Slave labor!"

Harrow cowered in the shadows outside the stockade and glanced around quickly. Then he sprang into the air and climbed as fast as he could toward the moon, hoping its pure light might somehow cleanse him.

"If I destroy that place," he explained as he sucked fresh air, "I risk killing those unfortunates inside. My fire or the poisons would surely claim them! And what about the city—or the river? Where would all that foulness go?"

Jake was surprisingly quiet. "We didn't think this through," he agreed. "We were too impulsive."

Impulsive, Harrow thought, cursing himself. How many times had he been accused of that? How many times would rash deeds come back to haunt him? He stared back at Purbur in the distance, stung by what he'd nearly done and what he'd seen.

His contact with Humans had been so limited, he realized as he thought of those half-starved men in their heavy chains and dead expressions. "Do Men often treat each other with such terrible cruelty?" he asked.

Jake gave a bitter laugh. "We have talents and capacities you don't even suspect."

Harrow weighed the boy's words and guessed at the deeper meaning behind them. "You were beaten in the circus?"

The answer didn't come right away. "Every day," Jake murmured. "They called it *training*."

Uncertain and lost in thought, the Son of Stormfire flew in wide circles, but each circle took them farther and farther from Purbur and deeper into Degarm. He remembered the first time he had seen Jake and the other children. They were escaping from a ship in a tiny boat, and they, too, were in chains. It was the first time Harrow had ever seen chains.

He glanced at the moon again and measured its progress through the heavens. As it sank lower in the sky its glow began to light the distant peaks of the Imagination Mountains, which bordered Wyvernwood and cut through Degarm. It would be dawn soon.

"Let's find a place to rest and think," he decided as he scoured the dark landscape for a suitable place. "You're probably hungry, too. Maybe we can find you something to eat."

"Don't worry about me," Jake replied. "Back at the farmhouse I stuffed my pockets with some of Beatrice's potatoes."

"I love potatoes," Harrow said with a chuckle. "You need to stretch your legs, then. Those ropes can't be as comfortable as your old saddle."

They were well past the thin forest that grew on Degarm's side of the river. The land below was rolling plain with grassy slopes and knolls. Only a few trees grew here and there, and nothing that offered any suggestion of shelter. Finally, the Black Dragon glided toward a gentle hill and landed.

Startled grasshoppers sprang up by the hundreds, and for a moment the night hummed with tiny wings until they settled down again. Freeing himself from the ropes, Jake slid down to the ground and rubbed feeling back into his legs. Then, reaching into his pocket, he brought out two raw potatoes and offered one to Harrow.

"Toss it high," Harrow instructed, and when Jake obeyed, he snatched it in his mouth and gulped it down. Jake nibbled his potato more slowly as he paced around the hilltop. When it was finished, he sat down, and a few moments later, stretched out and slept.

Curled up with his legs underneath him and his tail trailing down the hill, Harrow watched the moon and the stars crawl across the sky. He'd always had an affinity for stargazing. He remembered how his father had taught him the constellations and told him all the stories of their naming. He missed Stormfire so much that it hurt, but he didn't think his father would be so proud of him now.

Dawn broke, blue and cool and beautiful, over the hilltop where boy and Dragon slept. Harrow opened his eyes first. Stretching his neck upward, he watched with a squinting gaze as a family of circling vultures gave disappointed squawks and flapped away.

A few moments later, Jake awoke. Stiff and bleary-eyed, he got to his feet and looked around with an expression of bewilderment before he rubbed his fists against his eyes. "I thought I was still dreaming," he muttered. Taking another potato from his pocket, he bit into it and crunched noisily. "Bite?" he asked. Harrow declined.

When he'd completed his meager breakfast, Jake roped himself into position again on Harrow's neck. Neither of them talked much. With the sun brightening and the wind in their faces, they sailed into the morning.

The land of Degarm was a strange and different place to the Black Dragon, and it fascinated him. The gently rolling hills and shallow valleys, so green and golden, possessed a charm that surprised him. He'd always thought of Degarm as a dark place, a land of soldiers and marauders, more in keeping with Purbur.

A narrow river cut suddenly through the hills. Beside it ran a dusty road. "Follow that," Jake instructed, pointing. "If King Willom still holds the throne, he keeps a summer palace at Durent. He'll be there."

"If he still holds the throne?" Harrow questioned as he banked to follow the river and the road.

"Degarm changes its rulers like I change my socks," the boy explained.

Harrow couldn't resist. "How often is that?"

"Not as often as Carola would like," Jake admitted, "but then I hang out with Dragons mostly, and they're not so particular."

Harrow chuckled. The boy seemed in a better mood, more conversational than yesterday. A little sleep had been good for them both.

On the road below, an ox-drawn cart trundled over the crest of a hill and down a long slope. In the cart's bed were baskets of fruits, turnips and peppers and long loaves of crusty bread. Harrow sniffed, identifying each by its scent. As the cart was traveling in the same direction, the driver had yet to notice he wasn't alone. On outspread wings, Harrow swooped low and glided up behind him.

"Good morning, neighbor!" he called as he sailed over the cart, and he felt Jake turn to wave as the driver barked a startled scream. Feeling mischievous, he banked and turned back. The ox plodded on, indifferent as it dragged the cart, but the white-faced man stood up to face him with a turnip in one hand and a pepper in the other.

"Isn't it a glorious day?" Harrow shouted, laughing as he skimmed low above the road.

With eyes as wide as dinner plates, the driver drew back and flung first the turnip and then the pepper in quick succession before cowering down in his seat. Harrow snatched both items in his mouth and gulped them down.

"Show-off," Jake said. Then he called down to the driver as Harrow shot past. "Can you spare some of that bread?"

Harrow circled again as the wary driver jerked his cart to a halt and jumped down and stood trembling, looking as if he'd dive under the wheels any minute. But as Harrow shot past and turned back yet again, he reached into one of the breadbaskets for a loaf and hurled it straight up into the air. Jake leaned out as far as he could, grabbed for it with one hand and missed.

"Butter fingers!" Harrow scolded. Then, taking care not to upset the cart or its baskets, he hovered. "Once more for the boy!" he called.

Hesitant, the driver reached for another loaf and, taking careful aim, launched it right into Jake's hands. "Thanks!" the boy called out.

Licking his lips and wiping his hands on his trousers, the driver answered. "I figure if ye eat that down, then maybe ye won't eat me!" He shrugged as he gazed upward and seemed to relax a little. "Them's a penny a piece, by the way, but I'll jus' put it on yer tab."

Jake tore of a bit of bread and stuffed it in his mouth. "Is Willom still king?" he asked, spewing crumbs.

The driver sneered. "King o' earth an' air, to hear the ol' fart tell it!" He winked and tossed an apple up for Harrow. "Don't tell him I said it." Walking forward a few paces, he stroked his ox between the ears, then screwed up his face thoughtfully. "You don't seem such a bad sort for a monster," he said.

Harrow landed in the road and stretched his neck out until his face was close to the driver's. Though the man began to tremble and sweat, he stood his ground. "Want another turnip?" he asked with a gulp.

The Son of Stormfire winked. "No thanks," he answered with a hint of amusement, "and you don't seem such a bad sort for a Human. I hope we'll meet again."

"Can I think about it?" the driver answered honestly.

Harrow laughed as he stood up and spread his wings. Springing high, he turned and flew along the road again, continuing toward Durent while Jake ate his bread in silence.

Not far up the road they discovered a village on the riverbank. The smells of fish and cooking and industry polluted the air, but the stench was nothing like the city of Purbur. Harrow approached it, flying low as he studied what he saw. Unlike the cart driver, the villagers reacted as he expected, screaming with their annoyingly high-pitched voices, running like mice. A fisherman fell out of his boat with a splash; a woman grabbed her child and dashed inside. As if their flimsy dwellings were any protection. Someone waved a pitchfork.

Then someone fired an arrow.

Instantly enraged, Jake thrust a hand into his pocket, drew out a potato and flung it with all his might. But for the ropes holding him in place he would surely have fallen off. Still, the potato flew with skillful accuracy, striking the archer in the face and knocking him flat on his back as Harrow glided past. "Idiot! Pig!" Jake cried in anger. "You mud-daubing son of a mare and a manure-shoveler!"

"Nice shot," the Black Dragon complimented in a calmer tone. "You dropped your bread."

Jake muttered a long string of colorful and creative curses as Harrow left the village behind, but as with the boy, his good mood had faded. He climbed higher into the sky, and though soon he spied other carts and wagons on the road he left them alone.

The road and the river soon separated, and the road led through a low range of hills. "Durent is just beyond," Jake said glumly, the first words he'd spoken for a while.

Drawing a deep breath, Harrow descended lower. He had no intention of hiding from the Humans. Just the opposite. He wanted their attention—their full attention. Choosing the highest hilltop, he landed to observe Durent before he approached it.

What he saw surprised him. "It's beautiful," he said.

Jake spat. "From the outside," he answered.

Nestled in the valley on the side of a sparkling lake, Durent spread out like a giant circus. Huge, multi-colored tents sprouted like mushrooms across the valley floor and along the lake banks, and ornately carved boats as gaily painted as the tents floated in serene fashion on the water. Hundreds of pennants and banners rippled in the breeze, and every tent-pole or pinnacle was festooned with streaming ribbons.

At the eastern edge of it all, rising between two hills, stood a palace of white stone with delicate towers and spires that shot up into the sky. Like everything else, the towers streamed with pennants and ribbons, and from every window and balcony more banners fluttered. Only a low wall of the same white stone separated the palace from the crazy colorful structures and tents that surrounded it.

At the south end of the valley another road emerged from a patch of forest, rounded the lake, and led into the town. A steady stream of ox-drawn wagons made their way along it, some laden with goods, others with passengers.

A steady stream of soldiers also walked the road.

"Now we do what we came to do," Harrow said, quietly grim as he studied the town.

Jake nodded and answered with bitterness. "Burn it all."

But Harrow shook his great head. "That's not what I came to do. I told you—I have a debt of honor." With that, he spread his wings wide and fanned them, and the sun fairly shone on his pale star-shaped scars. "But a little fire to announce us," he continued, "that's not a bad idea."

Drawing a deep breath, he lifted his head and blasted a cloud of flame straight into the blue sky. Along the road into Durent, all the wagons stopped. People stood in their carts to stare, and the soldiers stumbled into each other. With proud grace, Harrow sailed outward from the hilltop, down the slope and over the acres of circus tents.

But in the crazy streets below, people were slow to take notice. Jugglers and magicians, focused on their tricks, continued to work the crowds. High-wire walkers spanned the roadways, too intent to look up, while clowns danced and made willing fools of themselves. Tumblers, aerialists, and trapeze artists seemed to be everywhere—for them nothing mattered but their audience, and amid all the laughter and shouting, few heard the rush of Dragon's wings.

Still, Harrow's dark shadow gliding over their heads could not long go unnoticed. If the performers were too focused, the audiences were not. They froze with eyes wide and treats half-lifted to their mouths to see a sight many had never seen before. Some panicked, a few screamed and clutched their hearts, but many, thinking it some new and amazing carnival attraction, chased after Harrow with excited shouts.

Jake leaned forward. "Beyond the wall is a large courtyard where only the best acts are invited to perform for Willom," he said.

"You've performed there," Harrow said. It wasn't a question.

"Many times," Jake answered. "All of us—Trevor and Markham, Ariel and Pear. And Keven." His voice dropped and took on the hard edge that Harrow had noticed before. "Keven died before we got to Wyvern-wood, and I don't know what's happened to Ariel. We were an act, and Willom sold us to Angmar's ambassador like we were nothing!"

Harrow already knew much of that, but he'd never heard it from Jake's own lips. At last he thought he understood the boy's pain and anger. Coming back to Degarm, coming to Durent and seeing such a man as Willom again had to be hard. "I could take you back to the hills, and you could wait there," he offered.

"Not a chance," Jake answered coldly. "I have a debt of honor, too."

Harrow licked his Dragon lips. With an unexpected new worry on his mind, he determined to keep a closer eye on Jake, and he wondered again if it had been such a good idea to bring the boy along. But Chan had thought so, and he trusted his brother's judgment.

Inside the palace walls things looked even crazier and more chaotic. There were no large tents, but side shows ringed the courtyard. To one side there was a long line of cages with lions and tigers, and on the opposite side scantily clad aerialists performed on high wires, trapezes, trampolines, and other odd apparatus. Three large rings occupied the very center of the courtyard. Six large elephants paraded around one ring while a trainer cracked his whip; a high diving act held center stage; and a squad of acrobatic clowns performed in the third.

Harrow flew low above it all, drawing attention to himself. Then, he swooped high. He knew a thing or two about performing, himself, and he knew the advantage of a good entrance. Three times around the palace he glided on outstretched wings before he descended toward the courtyard again.

All eyes watched as he fanned his wings and dropped toward the third ring. In a panic, the clowns scrambled to clear space, and the crowd fell back with gasps and applause as they threw flowers and candy and coins. The divers abandoned their platform, and the elephant tamer scowled to find himself upstaged.

But as Harrow touched the ground, the palace door flung open and a company of soldiers poured out with bows and arrows, spears and pikes. And from behind more soldiers poured through the courtyard gate. Pushing and shoving through the crowds, they quickly surrounded the ring.

Harrow glared as he looked slowly around. Then, in a controlled but very loud voice he announced, "If you fire so much as a single shaft I'll huff and puff and burn your house down. And that's no fairy tale."

A trumpet fanfare sounded. The soldiers immediately lowered their weapons. All around the courtyard the performers and the crowd fell silent and dropped to their knees with their heads bowed. Even the elephants bowed.

"No dignity!" Harrow sneered as he observed the cowering pachyderms.

A throng of half-naked children marched suddenly through the palace doors scattering flower petals from baskets they carried on their arms. Behind them came a troupe of dancing girls, turning and whirling and waving their arms with light and airy grace. Next came six tiny acrobats, little people, executing handsprings and backflips. A pair of stilt-walkers followed the acrobats. Two teams of naked wrestlers followed the stilt-walkers.

"How long does this go on?" Harrow whispered to Jake.

Jake didn't bother to lower his voice. "Willom doesn't go to the bathroom without a parade. Everything's a spectacle to him."

After the naked wrestlers came two ladies leading black panthers on diamond-studded leashes. Behind the ladies came two tall and skeletal looking fellows each bearing a golden birdcage.

The trumpet fanfare sounded a second time as the parade members spread out upon the rows of steps that descended from the palace. Well-rehearsed, they half-turned to gaze admiringly up at the doors through which they'd just come, and each raised a hand as if to welcome the next act.

Six large men, bare-chested and bronzed and rippling with muscle, bore an ornate palanquin upon their shoulders. With precisely choreographed steps, looking neither left nor right, they marched forward to the very edge of the highest step. There, bending first their right knees and then their left, they carefully lowered their burden.

The sunlight shimmered on folds of golden cloth and on piles of silver cushions. Propped amid those cushions lay a slender figure with sharp-boned features and arms like pale sticks. His eyes, expressionless and disinterested, fixed on Harrow as one of his bearers leaned down to pop a grape into the royal mouth.

Harrow whispered again. "This is the great king of Degarm we've all been afraid of?"

This time Jake answered in a whisper. "Did you ever see a coral snake? Real pretty creature. Real small, too, and deadly as they come."

Harrow nodded as he swept his gaze over the strange assembly with particular attention on the soldiers positioned around. Then he faced King Willom of Degarm. "I am Harrow, Son of Stormfire..."

Willom held up a hand, closed his eyes, and turned his face away. Cut off before he could make his introduction, Harrow blinked and fell silent.

After a brief dramatic moment, Willom opened his eyes again and looked at the Black Dragon with pure disdain. "All creatures over one mile high must leave the courtyard," he announced flatly.

Harrow bristled. "I am not one mile high, and I will not leave the courtyard. Not until we..."

Willom interrupted again with a curt wave to his soldiers. "Slay the Dragon." And without a pause he extended his other hand to another bearer. "My nails need buffing."

All around the courtyard obedient soldiers drew their bows, and a collective gasp went up from the thrill-hungry onlookers. Maybe their arrows were poisoned, and maybe they weren't, but with Jake exposed on his neck, Harrow couldn't take any chance. Lifting his great scaled head, he blew a stream of fire at the upper reaches of the palace. Atop the towers and balconies, banners and pennants burst into flame and bits of burning ribbon fluttered away on the breeze. Intense black scorches that neither rain nor weather would ever remove marked the white stone.

But fire was far from Harrow's only weapon. With a sweep of his tail, he scattered half the soldiers standing behind him, knocking them over like dolls before they could fire their arrows. At the same time, he snapped his wings down upon the heads of those close by on either side.

Still, a few brave men managed to draw their bows and fire, but the thin shafts only splintered on the Black Dragon's chest. Except for the one he caught in his mouth. With a crunch, he bit through it and let the pieces fall. He smiled to himself. Nice piece of theater, that. "I'll roast the next soldier that moves!" he promised.

Free from his ropes, Jake jumped suddenly to the ground. With an amazing series of flips and aerials, impressive as any gymnast in the city, he crossed the ring and, facing King Willom, struck a bold pose with all his muscles flexed, his body rigid and tense. Then, bending swiftly, he snatched up a bow and a single arrow from a fallen soldier, fitted it to the string and aimed.

"Jake!" Harrow cried. "Don't!"

With the string drawn back to the boy's mouth, the arrow ready to fly, Jake hesitated. But his arm didn't waver, and the arrow remained on target.

Another gasp went up from the crowd. Finally they seemed to realize that they weren't watching an act.

On the palanquin, Willom lost his placid demeanor. Fear filled his eyes, and his mouth gaped with astonishment as if he couldn't believe someone was daring to threaten him. Carefully, he leaned up from his cushions, then crawled to the edge, swung his feet over and stood up. For a long, disbelieving moment, he stared at Jake.

"You!" he exclaimed. "Jacobus!"

The soldier at Jake's foot stirred, and Jake pushed him back down again with his toe. With deliberate calm, his gaze still fixed on the man who had sold him into slavery, he eased off the bowstring and lowered the arrow's point. "Shall we try a little diplomacy?" he said with a mocking sneer to Willom.

Trembling, the King of Degarm drew a soft breath and forced a smile. With hands raised high over his head, he called to the crowd. "That's our show for today! We hope you enjoyed it!" Then from the corner of his mouth he said to his bearers. "Throw them out, everyone."

The bearers filed down the steps and some of the soldiers, recovering their senses, hurried to assist them. With noisy protests, the onlookers were ushered through the courtyard gates and into the madness of the wider circus outside.

On the palace steps, the members of Willom's parade disassembled and began to hurry inside.

In a stern voice, Harrow called out. "Leave the birdcages!"

The two tall skeleton-men froze in midstep, then turned nervously and looked to their king for approval. "My talking crows?" Willom snapped indignantly. "Next, I suppose you'll want my parrots, too!"

Without taking his gaze from the king, Jake turned his head slightly. "What are you doing?" he said over his shoulder.

"That debt of honor," Harrow murmured, answering Jake. To Willom he called out, "Those talking crows are friends of mine." He smiled a Dragon smile, which can be a terrible thing. "I'd take it kindly if you'd set them free."

Frowning with annoyance, Willom nodded to the skeleton-men, who opened the latches and eased open the cage doors. A pair of large crows bolted out with caws and squawks. Straight for Harrow they flew and settled on his shoulders.

"Prospero," Harrow said in polite greeting to the larger crow. "And Esmeralda! I see you managed to get yourself locked up, too!"

Esmeralda screeched. "Don't get too high and mighty, Son of Stormfire," she snapped. "Maybe you came all this way to rescue us today—but what are you going to do for the crows tomorrow? Answer me that?"

Prospero, the King of the Crows, squawked. "Shut up, wife! You've gotten the crow-kin in enough trouble! One more word and I'll trade you in for a finch!"

On the ground, Jake glanced up at Harrow. "That's it?" he said. "That's your big debt of honor? You came to rescue a pair of crows?"

Harrow nodded, amused by Jake's outrage. "They're part of Wyvernwood," he answered simply. "For even the smallest of us we have to stand together. Once I learned why the crows were serving Degarm and thought about it, I knew what I had to do."

"Well, it's not all I came to do!" Jake shouted. With deft skill, he raised the bow and drew the string back again. Fearing for their lives, the last of the parade members abandoned their king and rushed for the safety of the palace

Alone and afraid, Willom stumbled backward, clutched at the edge of his palanquin and sat down hard. "Brother!" he cried.

Jake spat as he held the arrow steady and on target. "It's a little late for *brother*!" he answered. "About ten years too late! Ten years since father died, you took his throne and sold me to that carnival owner!"

Willom bit his lip and shrugged. "It seemed the thing to do at the time," he answered apologetically. "And he taught you a trade! You're a star!" He patted the golden sheets upon which he sat. "Let bygones be bygones! We can negotiate something!"

"This is what we're going to work out!" Jake said through clenched teeth. Without warning, he released the bowstring. His arrow flew swift and true, imbedding itself in the wood right between Willom's legs.

On Harrow's shoulder, Esmeralda screeched. "You missed! Where'd you learn to shoot, boy, in a barn?"

Turning his head, Harrow snapped his jaws at the crow-queen to shut her up. Then he let out a sigh of relief. His Dragon heart was hammering!

Jake snatched another arrow from the ground, nocked it on the string and aimed as Willom stared with his hands cupped protectively. "You are going to leave Wyvernwood alone!" he demanded. He let the second arrow fly. It struck the palanquin just an inch above the first. Without pausing, he stooped and picked up a third. "You are going to leave the creatures in Wyvernwood alone—all of them!" He fired again, embedding his arrow deep in one of the cushions.

Picking up one more arrow, he aimed again. "And if you ever call me *brother* again and I hear about it, I'll come back." He inclined his head to indicate Harrow. "Not just with him, but with all my friends, and he's a kitty cat compared to some of them!" He fired one last time, and Willom screamed a shrill note as the shaft quivered in the wood near his foot.

Drawing a deep breath and letting it out, Jake threw the bow aside and turned to Harrow. Though his face was red with anger he wore a look of deep satisfaction. "Oh, one more thing!" he called without looking back. Looking up, his gaze locked momentarily with the Black Dragon's. "I almost forgot my own debt of honor!" His hand slipped into his pocket. Then, spinning swiftly, his arm lashed out and a potato flashed through the air, striking Willom in the eye and knocking him cold.

Jake rubbed his hands on his trousers and did a backflip. "That's for Chan," he said.

Prospero whistled. "Nice shot," he complimented. "Now that's what I call real negotiating."

"Jacobus?" Harrow said with an air of amusement as Jake grabbed the ropes and swung up into place on his neck. *"Prince Jacobus?*

Jake said nothing for a few moments as he busied himself with the proper knots. "If you tell anyone I'll kick your scaly butt," he muttered finally. "Not even Chan."

Harrow smiled to himself as he rose into the sky with Prospero and Esmeralda leading the way. *He could probably do it, too,* he thought.

He glanced back at the crazy circus still in full swing outside the palace walls. No one seemed aware of what had happened inside. Or if they knew, no one cared.

Spreading his wings, he turned for Wyvernwood.

Twenty

SPRAWLED ON THE SOFT, VELVET CUSHIONS of the Angmar king's throne, Morkir yawned and idly fanned the air with his tail. His shoulders itched, and his wings felt somewhat cramped in a seat made for Humans, but he couldn't resist the symbolism.

He gazed past a pile of armor that lay on the floor at his feet and at the fragments and pieces of shattered weaponry—spears, bows, arrows, swords—that were also scattered there. At one side of the royal chamber, Minhep addressed a group of white-faced, trembling guards who stood rigidly at attention as he positioned them like ten-pins.

"Now you're sure you understand the rules?" Minhep asked. "If you dodge, then you lose a coin to the treasury," he explained again as he watched their pasty faces. "But if you hold your position, you get to take a coin from the treasury. You profit!" Then, clacking his beak and grinning, he turned and started to walk away. But pausing, he glanced back to make sure the guards were still holding formation. "Of course, if the ball hits you," he continued with a menacing chuckle, "you're out of the game."

Arching his wings, he padded across the floor to the other side of the chamber and picked up the ball, which was actually a rock the size of a Dragon's head.

One of the guards whimpered and fainted.

Morkir made a face and tapped the side of his head with a paw. "Is that the sound of knocking knees I hear?" he called to Minhep from the throne.

With a shrug, Minhep casually tossed the heavy rock to Morkir, who caught it with a single paw and tossed it back. "They won't play the game right," he pouted.

Morkir slumped forward long enough to stretch his wings and scratch his shoulder with a hind leg. Wondering if he might be allergic to velvet, he glanced toward the doors at the far end of the chamber and then sat back and drummed his claws on the arm of the throne. "You're too rough with your toys," he said in a distracted tone.

"Well, if I could go outside," Minhep protested as he tossed his rock from one hand to the other.

With a shake of his head, Morkir cut him off. "That might ruin the surprise," he answered. "Be patient. Chase a dust ball or something—there are plenty of those. For a king's castle, this place is a dump."

Minhep looked thoughtful, and then set his rock down. "That gives me an idea," he announced. Turning to his ten-pin soldiers, he wagged a claw and warned, "It'll hurt my feelings if you're all not here when I get back." Then, dropping to all fours, he scampered past the dais and disappeared through a door at the rear of the chamber.

A soft sigh escaped Morkir's beak as he regarded the frightened, but unmoving guards. With only a token force on duty in Angmar City and the general citizenry too timid to resist, he and Minhep had captured the castle easily by themselves. Since then, for the better part of two days he'd waited for Kilrain to return from wherever he'd sailed away to. Minhep was getting bored, and Morkir had to admit that he was, also.

A noisy cacophony issued from the corridor behind the throne. Human voices made plaintive protests, and Minhep gave a sharp screech. A moment later Kilrain's entire crew of advisors filed in, red-faced and quaking, with brooms and mops and buckets in hand.

Minhep followed. "Hup! One, two, three!" He sang the words loud and clear in crisp, military fashion. "We don't have to be told twice—make the throne room clean and nice!"

Reluctantly and without enthusiasm, the advisors repeated the chant as they shuffled forward in their white robes and silver sandals. "I can't hear you!" Minhep shouted. He raked his claws over the rump of one of the slowest.

"Yow!" The unsuspecting lackey stumbled over his mop and stepped on the hem of his expensive garment, ripping it as he clutched his damaged backside with one hand.

"That's more like it!" the young griffin cheered and sang out again. "We don't grumble; we don't whine! We just make the throne room shine! Sweep the dust and scour the stains!"

The advisors responded through clenched teeth as they spread out with their cleaning tools. "Or Minhep will eat our brains! Sound off! One, two, three, four—one, two!"

Amid clattering and sloshing, half of the highest-ranking nobles in the kingdom threw themselves down on their knees with mop rags and brushes while the other half launched into a flurry of sweeping and dusting. "Scrub the corners and the cracks!" one of them chanted as he bore down with both hands on a wet brush. Another answered as he gathered up an armload of broken weapons. "Or he'll give us forty whacks!"

Minhep leaned on the side of the throne and chuckled as he winked at the guards to make sure they stayed in formation. Then he smiled a griffin smile. "I think they're really getting into it," he commented as he watched the clean-up effort. "Who says you can't teach a human new tricks?"

Morkir had to admit there was a certain justice to it. "You have an admirable flair for management," he said with gentle sarcasm. "It could take you all the way to the top."

"I've been there," Minhep reminded him with a shrug of his wings.

The two griffins exchanged looks, then laughed together. With no warning, Morkir slugged Minhep on the arm, knocking him off the dais and sending him rolling in a golden-furred ball. Still laughing, but wearing a slightly dazed look, his griffin companion regained his feet, checked his wings and rubbed the spot where he'd been struck. "That'll make a knot!"

It's good to have a friend when you're so far from home, Morkir thought as he repositioned himself on the uncomfortable throne of Angmar yet again. Not that he was all that far from home now. Wyvernwood was no more than a day's swift flight away, and his old home in the Valley of Eight Winds only a little farther.

A wistful, lonely feeling crept over him as he remembered the valley, the nest in which he'd grown up with his father, Gorganar, and his brother, Gaunt. Both were dead now. He was an orphan with no place really to call home anymore.

Still, he thought of Wyvernwood and Stronghold. The Dragons had taken him in for a little while, made him welcome and been kind to him. Especially Black Sabu.

A ruckus at the outer doors interrupted Morkir's thoughts. Around the chamber, the advisors looked up from their labors and froze with wide, nervous eyes. The guards, still at attention in their ten-pin formation, looked a little more hopeful. With a powerful spring, Minhep mounted the dais to stand beside Morkir with one paw resting on the throne. Opening his beak, he gave a very un-birdlike snarl.

The great doors burst suddenly open as Morkir sat more erect. At the head of a squad of soldiers, King Kilrain strode across the threshold and then stopped. His angry gaze swept around the chamber, and he reddened at the sight of his noble advisors on their knees at common work. Then he fixed his gaze on Morkir.

"Who are you?" he roared, waving the rest of his soldiers inside. "Just what do you think you're doing on my throne, you mangy beast?"

Before Morkir could answer, Minhep took a step forward. "He's Prince Morkir of the Griffinkin," he answered sharply. "And at the moment, the mangy beast is ruling your kingdom, having effectively seized it in your absence." With a bow, he deferred to Morkir and stepped back.

The Son of Gorganar inclined his head toward Kilrain and blinked. "I hope you don't mind," he said simply.

Kilrain sneered and beckoned to his soldiers. "Kill him," he ordered with an air of annoyance.

Minhep whispered quickly to Morkir. "It always makes me goose-pimply when they say that!" Then as the soldiers drew their weapons, he leaped. With terrified shrieks, the advisors sprang to their feet and ran. The ten-pin guards broke formation and pressed into the far corners of the room as swiftly as they could, and briefly the center of the floor was clear.

Minhep snatched up his ball. "What's our strategy?" he called over his shoulder.

Without rising, Morkir scratched his shoulder again. "Aim low," he suggested as his companion raised the great stone and prepared to throw.

Kilrain turned pale. With a high-pitched shriek he dived for the floor as Minhep's ball flew straight for him, but one of his men, not appreciating that the ball was in fact a heavy stone, tried to catch it.

Even Minhep winced. "That had to hurt," he called as the poor man flew backward and crashed into two of his fellows. Before the other soldiers could recover, he leaped into the midst of them and spun with his powerful wings outspread. With one scythe-like stroke, he swept them off their feet. "Kill, kill, kill!" he exclaimed, shaking his head in disapproval as they stumbled and tumbled over each other. "It's always the same with you boys!" Hooking his claws in the front of one fallen man's tunic, he lifted him to his feet and shook him. "Don't you think it's time we all just got along?" Flicking his wrist, he flung the hapless soldier away.

"They told me at the gate that you'd come back!" Kilrain hissed as he raised up on one elbow and glared at Minhep. "So I came prepared!"

His words must have been a signal. On a balcony that overlooked the throne room, a dozen archers sprang up from hiding with arrows nocked on their bowstrings. Taking swift aim, they bent their bows.

Morkir moved with sure speed. Leaping from the throne into the middle of the room, he snatched the King of Angmar by the collar and held him up kicking and thrashing. "You know the best defense against an arrow?" he said coolly with his beak close to Kilrain's ear. "A good shield." He looked up at the archers. "Do you think he's a good shield?"

One by one, with disgusted looks, they threw down their bows. Reaching over, Minhep took the crown from Kilrain's head and balanced it in lopsided fashion on Morkir's feathered brow. Then, stepping back, he bent one knee and bowed. Around the room, the guards and a few of the soldiers followed Minhep's example and, accepting defeat, also bowed. Most, though, just stood back in uncertain fear, awaiting a command from their king that never came.

"You're making the biggest mistake of your hairball-hacking lives!" Kilrain raged, purple-faced as he dangled helplessly from Morkir's claws. "I'm not someone you can push around, no matter how strong you griffins think you are!"

Minhep looked at Morkir and clicked his beak. "I've always loved the way he blusters!" he said. "Such style! Such menace!"

Kilrain wasn't finished. "Mock me, if you dare!" he cried, kicking with futile energy and beating the air with his small pink fists. "I'm Kilrain of Angmar—Dragonslayer! I dealt with them, and I can deal with the likes of you!"

Morkir frowned and gave the man a shake. "For a soft, small, squishy thing hanging from the points of my claws," he said suddenly grim, "you make a lot of boasts."

A mad gleam filled Kilrain's eyes. "It's no empty boast, Monster," he answered. "At this very moment Wyvernwood is burning to the ground. It'll burn for days! Weeks! And when nothing is left but ashes, I'll march my army in and claim what's rightfully mine!"

Fear stabbed at Morkir's heart as he met Kilrain's angry gaze, and a chill shivered up his spine. His thoughts flashed to his home—to the darkly beautiful forest in which he'd been born, to the valley of his ancestors, to Stronghold and his friends there. *Yes—his friends!*

He pulled Kilrain close until his beak pricked the human's nose. "What have you done?" he demanded. "Where's Goronus? Where are the griffins who were with him?"

The King of Angmar barked a short laugh. "Roast meat for all I know! None of them came back!"

Even Minhep looked stunned. "Is he telling the truth?" he whispered.

Morkir looked around the room at the faces of the other soldiers, and the mixture of expressions they wore told the tale. Shame on some for what they'd done. Gloating glee on others who were pleased with themselves.

Morkir spoke in a low cold voice, addressing every one of them. "Some say that griffins are cowards." He glared at them one by one, fighting to hold back tears of anger, resisting the urge to gut their king before their eyes. "But you Men surpass us for cowardice. Like a crazed pack of wolves you try to bring down nobler creatures for no other reason except that you fear them." With a shake of his paw he dropped Kilrain unceremoniously on the floor. "I've dirtied my claws on you," he said with disdain. "The Dragons never did you any harm!"

The King of Angmar spoke in a cold voice. "They killed my son!"

Morkir removed the crown from his brow and crushed it between his paws. "You coveted Wyvernwood long before that," he reminded. "Everything you see, you covet." He dropped the ruined hunk of metal at Kilrain's feet."

"They have the power of fire!" Kilrain continued to shout. "You griffins have the strength to uproot trees! Why shouldn't we fear you? What powers do we have to survive against you?"

Morkir closed his eyes briefly. He thought of Wyvernwood burning while he talked and all his friends in danger, and at the same time he remembered all the dealings he'd ever had with the race of Man in Wyvernwood and on all his recent journeys through Undersky.

"You have the most formidable power of all," he said at last. "You lie. Even the best of you. Even to yourselves."

Morkir's heart began to hammer, and he knew he had to go before his claws drew blood, and that was something he hadn't done for a long time, a part of him he thought he'd mastered. It hurt and disappointed him to feel the urge so strongly.

"The throne is yours if you want it," he said to Minhep as he turned toward the great doors.

Minhep shrugged. "Well, I would like to try it on for size," he said, hooking his claws into Kilrain's tunic as Morkir had done. "Just out of curiosity, you know, to see how it fits." With that, he dragged the King of Angmar across the floor before the eyes of his soldiers, and positioning himself carefully and with utmost dignity upon the royal seat, he gave a sigh of satisfaction.

Then with a swipe of his claws, he ripped away the king's trousers and bent him over one golden-haired knee.

The spanking and the screaming proved quite impressive as Morkir made his way through the castle corridors and outside. The citizens of Angmar City milled around anxiously in the courtyard and in the streets beyond, but he paid them no attention except to feel a brief pity for the faint-hearted lives they led.

Spreading his wings, he took to the sky, grateful for the rush of cleansing wind on his face. Higher and higher he climbed into the warm sun and faster he flew toward Wyvernwood.

He had his own sins to pay for. He hoped it wasn't too late.

When Minhep suddenly appeared wingtip to wingtip with him, his spirit lifted somewhat. In a short time, he'd grown fond of his griffin companion and his odd sense of humor. After all, any sense of humor at all in their kind was a rare thing.

"The throne didn't suit you?" Morkir called.

"The company didn't suit me," Minhep answered as he stared straight ahead. "And to tell the truth, the throne pinched a little. And it made me itch. All those cushions—I might be allergic to velvet."

Morkir smiled a little as he raced onward. "Me, too."

Twenty-One

RONALDO WORKED WITH FEVERISH PASSION, splashing paints on raw rock walls from the most elaborate palette he'd ever prepared. Even in the cavern gloom the flakes of crystal and mica in the stone gave the colors a vibrant, glistening quality, and the resinous luster of the minerals in the rock brought every image to three-dimensional life.

With precise care and unbridled imagination he incorporated into his murals the wild streaks of luminescent and phosphorescent minerals present in the stone as well. In the flickering light of the several small fires burning around the cavern's upper shelves those shimmering lines and patches took strange and startling form, and as the fireglow dimmed and brightened and danced, the figures and effects seemed to step out of the stone.

For days the Gray Dragon worked without rest or sleep, pausing only long enough to find and mix the ingredients for his paints, driven by a powerful need to make sense of the visions and flashes of visions he had seen in one fleeting moment in Stronghold when he'd tried to throw the *Diamond Dragon* into the canyon.

He could still feel the talisman's power tingling through him, offering itself, awakening potentials and possibilities. He could still hear Stormfire's voice speaking in his brain, trying to explain and trying to apologize. So many confusing things still swam in his head, but that was the worst of it—he knew his father's voice.

His moment of anger had passed, but the hurt still lingered, so he painted and worked because only through art could he forget the pain and disappointment that overcame him when he stopped.

Filling his brush with paint, he applied the final strokes to yet another image he didn't recognize or understand: a group of

snow-capped mountains towering above a green and verdant landscape, mountains that, viewed together, somehow resembled a Dragon
of colossal size. For a long time, with his palette cradled in one elbow
he chewed the tip of his paintbrush. As he studied his efforts his ears
twitched and his tail thumped on the cavern floor.

"It's called the Drake."

Ronaldo waited for the echo to fade before he slowly turned and
looked up. "I wondered how long it would take you to find me,"
he said.

High above the cavern floor on a shelf where the outer tunnels
emerged into the single vast chamber, Marian paused as she met
Ronaldo's even gaze. Then she began the winding descent, her small
hooves ringing softly on the stone as she picked her way down. The
numerous small fires Ronaldo had made for light glimmered in her
golden eyes and turned them red.

"When you weren't at home," she answered in a quieter voice,
"I guessed you would come here to Sinobarre's old lair. I remember
how you admired this place." Reaching Ronaldo's side, she studied
the vast scope of the uncompleted mural and shook her mane. "You've
always had a flair for cave paintings."

Ronaldo pointed his brush at the group of mountains. The wet
paint still gleamed. "You called this the Drake," he said. "Why is it
important?"

Marian hesitated before answering. "It's the birthplace of your
father," she whispered, "and the ancestral home of all the Dragonkin."
Her golden horn scraped the floor as she hung her head. "Ronaldo,
I'm sorry . . ."

"I'm not mad at you," the Gray Dragon interrupted. "You've always
been a good friend, Marian. When the talisman offered me its
power..."

"No, Ronaldo, you don't understand." It was Marian's turn to inter-
rupt. As she lifted her head her eyes flashed and they changed from
gold to peaceful blue. "The talisman didn't offer you anything. You
awakened the power within the talisman."

With a flip of her tail Marian paced before the fantastic mural. The
painting, one long and continuous work, wrapped halfway around the
vast cavern, rising in some places all the way from floor to ceiling. Fragments were even painted on stalagmites. Images spread over the floor.

Marian gave a soft gasp, and when she spoke her voice was filled with awe. "I don't know how you did it," she said. "You've captured it all, the entire story—the Dragon Wars, the gathering of creatures, the battles and conflicts, the Great Exodus to Wyvernwood! There's Stormfire!" Pacing a few steps further, she gave another gasp and stared at the figure of a Dragon pierced through by lightning in mid-flight. She turned to Ronaldo with eyes full of tears. "That's Navigator!"

Ronaldo moved past her to another section of the mural. "That's you," he said. "The Last Unicorn in the World. You were wilder, stronger and much more powerful. The air around you crackled with magic and blue fire."

"It was a long time ago," Marian whispered, trembling as she stared at the painting of herself.

Ronaldo watched her, carefully noting her reaction as he struggled for understanding. "Not for you," he answered, unable to keep the sadness from his voice. "You're more than the Last Unicorn in the World. You're the Last Immortal. You know things that even the Dragons don't know, and you've seen things we never will. That's a heavy burden to bear alone, Marian."

Turning away from the mural, Marian tossed her mane. "*Immortal* is a tricky word, Ronaldo," she said. "I prefer *long-lived*. There were others like me once."

Ronaldo laughed. The sound broke from him with unexpected force, sudden and from the heart—the best kind of laugh. It made an echo in the cavern so loud that he laid back his ears. "There may have been unicorns," he said when the echo faded, "but there was never anyone like you!"

With a toss of her head, Marian shook her tears away and stared at Ronaldo for a long moment. Her eyes changed again from blue to violet, to silver and black and back to gold. "You really aren't angry," she said in a disbelieving tone.

"I was hurt," he admitted as he set his palette aside and sat down on the floor with his face close to hers. "But now that you're here, even that seems to be passing." He took her chin carefully in one paw, and with his brush in the other, he made two quick strokes and painted a smile on her nose. "You and I are pieces of a plan that someone else made long ago. I could be angry about that—or I can see it through and hope that it's for the best."

The firelight glinted on Marian's horn as she lifted her head and crossed her eyes in an effort to see what he'd painted on her. In contrast to the dangerous creature on the wall behind her, she looked silly, and Ronaldo laughed again, although not so loudly.

"There's more to tell you," she said when she gave up the effort.

A small, familiar voice interrupted. "Tell me, tell me, tell me!" Bumble cried as he darted from the outer tunnel into the cavern. "Hail, hail! The gang's all here!" he sang with jubilant enthusiasm as he flew a circle around Ronaldo's head. Then, he flew another circle around Marian. "Mammy—how I love ya! How I love ya!"

Marian winced and flipped her tail at the hummingbird.

"Missed me by a hair!" Bumble shouted.

"Your tiny memory must be slipping," Marian declared with stern indignation. "My name's not *Mammy*."

Bumble paid no attention. Flying back to Ronaldo, he landed on the Gray Dragon's snout and kicked him with a small, clawed foot. "That's for leaving Bumble behind!" he shouted. Then he kicked Ronaldo again. "And that's for leaving Bumble behind!"

Closing one eye, Ronaldo lifted his head a little. "Hey, you kicked me twice for the same thing!" he protested, although Bumble's kicks couldn't hurt him at all. He felt genuinely glad to see the little hummingbird.

"Only twice?" Bumble inclined his head, fluttered his green wings and kicked Ronaldo a third time. "That's for leaving Bumble behind!"

"I think he missed you," Marian laughed. "Isn't that a kick in the head?"

Ronaldo blinked at her. "You're not helping," he scolded.

Bumble dashed away again and perched on Marian's horn. There, with one wing folded over his chest and one behind his back, he struck a dramatic pose.

"For days and days I followed your scent;
I zigged and zagged wherever you went,
Past all exhaustion until I felt faint —
But then I detected the smell of your paint!
Across the wide forest I flew to your side;
You can run all you want, but you can't ever hide!

I'm a bird with a mission, you must understand—
To let nothing sunder our brave little band!"

Pleased with his recitation, Bumble bowed low, then fluttered his wings with excitement as he jumped up and down. Ronaldo thumped his tail on the floor in appreciation. He had to admit, for a humming-bird Bumble was quite talented. "Bravo, little poet!" he said. "Well done."

"Quite rare, I'd say," Marian added.

Then, while taking a second bow, Bumble noticed the mural. Darting from Marian's horn, he flew back and forth before the wall, pausing to study this image and that shape, humming and hawing in appreciation over the eye-catching work. "Brilliant technique," he commented in a dry voice. "Clever blend of media and materials," he added as he hovered over a streak of phosphorescent mineral. "Brush stroke and texture suggest influences of earlier masters." He paused again before a particularly intense battle scene. "A bit too representational for modern art tastes, but exceptional nonetheless." He turned toward Ronaldo. "What is it?"

Marian answered first. "History," she said. "In years to come, many will make pilgrimage to this place. They'll stand where we stand now to marvel and remember." She looked up at Ronaldo. "You truly are the *maestro*."

The Gray Dragon looked away and studied his painting again. He had to admit, for technique and impact, it was indisputably his finest work. He could scarcely believe he'd created it in only four days, but he'd worked as if in a dream, pouring the images directly onto stone with no sense of detachment at all.

With a shiver, he turned toward a structure in the center of the cavern, a solid cascade of limestone and crystal that descended out of the high ceiling and fell all the way to the floor. It stood like a broad column and looked as if it supported the weight of the world, and on the side stood a tall gray Dragon holding a paintbrush and a palette. In the firelight, its crystalline eyes seemed to shift as if studying the surrounding artwork.

A self-portrait, true in every detail.

"Did I really paint all this?" he asked quietly as he turned back to the main mural. Unconsciously, he struck the same pose as the painted version of himself on the cascade. "Or is it the talisman's work?"

The cavern echoed with the ringing of Marian's hooves as she paced across the floor and looked up at Ronaldo's portrait. Her eyes took on a fierce silver gleam. "You can't wield or control the power," she explained. "That's not your role."

"I have to go back to Stronghold, don't I?" Ronaldo said with a sigh as he set aside his palette and brush. Strange to think that with the unused paints and the unmixed ingredients they would become part of the artwork, part of the experience, for those who visited the cavern. Yet again he turned to study his creation, noting the parade of characters, the progression of the narrative. "That's where the rest of the story takes us, isn't it?"

Already halfway up the shelf that led to the outer tunnels, Marian paused beside one of the campfires. Her white hide and liquid eyes and particularly her horn seemed to take on the qualities of its dancing light, and she stood there like a creature of flame looking for a brief moment just as wild and strong and dangerous as he had painted her.

Then with a blur of wings, Bumble darted out of the shadows and perched on her forelock. As if some spell had been broken, she was just Marian again, the unicorn he knew.

"All roads lead to Stronghold," she answered as she continued up the shelf. "Or at least through it. It's become too cosmopolitan for me." Bumble piped up. "Marian prefers the rusted life."

"Rustic," Ronaldo corrected. "Stronghold it is then, but would you mind waiting for me outside?" He inclined his head toward the artwork. "I'd like just a few more moments here."

With a nod and a toss of her mane, Marian entered the dark tunnel with Bumble as her passenger. Alone once more, the Gray Dragon turned to his painting. Some familiar faces gazed back at him from the stone, but there were others he didn't recognize. Especially the human faces—they seemed so angry and so afraid.

Ronaldo spread his wings to their fullest and then wrapped himself in them as he stood on his hind legs and stretched. The campfires were beginning to die; he hadn't replenished their supply of wood for a while, but there was still enough light to bring the figures to life as he passed slowly by each one.

Yet suddenly he stopped to stare at the grandest Dragon of them all. Great Stormfire, immense and shining and golden, gazed down from the cavern wall with shimmering eyes filled with luminescent mineral and fire exploding from his throat. His long, sinuous neck and tail seemed to encompass the sprawling battles over which he flew, and in his powerful talons he clutched arrows and spears and lightning bolts. One meticulously painted wingtip touched the floor while the other stretched upward into the cavern darkness as if he were himself the link between heaven and earth. As if, like the cascade of stone in the cavern's center, he supported the weight of the world.

Ronaldo's heart hammered. There was Stormfire in all his glory, beautiful and terrible and fierce, crackling with power and magic—commander of legions! A Dragon sorcerer!

His father.

A feeling of betrayal and abandonment crept over him as he stared at the painting, and he whispered Stormfire's name. As if in response, whether by some trick of the firelight or some quality of the mineral, the great Dragon leader's gaze seemed to fall upon Ronaldo. As if entranced, Ronaldo stood still as stone himself, and he met that gaze calmly without flinching. It was a moment of confrontation that comes inevitably between all fathers and sons when they scrutinize, judge, and just as inevitably accept each other.

Ronaldo's sense of betrayal faded. He might never understand his father and might never know his motives, but he accepted him for the great leader that he was and the savior of the Dragonkin. Respect replaced the sense of abandonment, and perhaps in time love would replace that.

Craning his neck upward, Ronaldo shouted his father's name and listened to the echo. The sound filled his ears and his heart, seeming never to die, instead to grow in volume and power as if a chorus had taken it up.

A *chorus of ghosts*, he thought with a final nod to the faces and shapes in the mural. *You're the ones calling his name now—his armies and followers! Sing on!*

With a strong downbeat of his wings, Ronaldo flew up toward the shelf and the tunnel mouth. Without looking back, he landed again, and dropping to all fours to make his way through the narrow passages, he crawled toward daylight.

He emerged onto a broad white-sand beach at the bottom of a cliff and smiled at the sight of Marian skipping in the foamy surf with Bumble buzzing around her head. The sounds of wind and sea made a welcome and cheering music, and his spirits lifted as he drew a deep breath of fresh, salty air.

Marian pranced away from the water to join him. "Are you all right?" she asked.

The Gray Dragon chewed his lip as he thought about that. "I feel new," he said at last. Then he smiled. "I feel young, Marian."

Bumble circled his head and landed on the end of his snout. "It's all about you, isn't it?" He fluttered his wings and puffed out his chest. "It's always about you! Who cares how Ronaldo feels? What Bumble wants to know is when do we eat?"

Ronaldo gazed toward the sea, then winked at Marian. "I'll catch you a fat fish," he offered to the hummingbird.

"Fish?" Bumble jumped up and down, then spat in disgust. "Need bluebells! Need lousewort! Need...!"

Marian interrupted. "You need to shut your beak and get your tail feathers to the top of the cliff. It's a hummingbird supermarket up there. But be back in two minutes or we're leaving without you."

"Bumble will be back in one," he called as he shot toward the cliff. "But he'll be back with indigestion!"

Marian sighed as she turned back to Ronaldo. "Stronghold?" she said cautiously, and when he pursed his Dragon lips and nodded, she continued. "I suppose you'll want to carry me?"

"It's the only way to fly," he answered with an innocent expression. "I promise I'll be gentle."

The Last Unicorn in the World snorted and, with a flip of her tail, gazed toward the sea. When she spoke again her voice dropped almost to a whisper. "There are still things you need to know," she said.

Ronaldo thumped his tail on the beach, tossing sand into the air for the wind to catch. "I think I've figured some of it out," he confessed. "I'm the key."

Before Marian could answer, Bumble sped toward them again. He looked quite full, even bloated, as he landed on Marian's horn and danced a little jig while he sang:

"*Wyvernwood is burning down,*
burning down, burning down!

Wyvernwood is burning down!
All is ashes!"

Ronaldo looked at the little bird with a start. "What did you say?" he demanded. "What kind of a song is that?"

"Top-side!" Bumble answered, indicating the cliff. "It's all the rage up there! Everyone's singing it—even the tree frogs, and they can't carry a tune!"

Marian sniffed and turned her head to look northward. A gray veil of thin, wispy clouds hung over the horizon so far away they were barely noticeable at a casual glance. "Don't pick on the tree frogs," she muttered, suddenly tense.

Ronaldo looked northward, too. Without another word, he wrapped his paws around Marian and flew into the sky. From a higher vantage he could see more clearly, and what he saw frightened him like he'd never been frightened before.

"It's smoke," Marian reported, confirming his own conclusion. He didn't miss the tremor in her voice, nor the shiver that passed through her body.

A sharp, ticklish hum sounded in Ronaldo's right ear as Bumble took his familiar perch and settled in for the ride. "Looks like adventure time once again, mates!" he shouted. "Out of the frying pan—into the fire. So to speak!"

Neither Ronaldo, nor Marian, answered. Lost in his own dark thoughts, the Gray Dragon raced north along the shoreline, eventually turning inland when he saw hundreds of birds circling in confusion and uncertainty and heard their cacophonous cries. The appearance of a Dragon seemed to calm them somewhat, and he watched with some satisfaction as they grew quiet and settled into the trees below.

Then, from the corner of his eye, he glimpsed two more Dragons. They were far behind to the south and west of him, and flying slowly side by side. Too slowly, Ronaldo thought. Curious, he dipped his right wing and turned in a wide, gliding arc to intercept the pair.

"Ronaldo?" Marian said as she trained her own gaze on the distant Dragons. "Those are your brothers."

"I know," he answered quietly.

Uncertain of how they would receive him, but filled with a sense of urgency, he increased his speed again. Black Harrow saw him first, and the human boy riding his neck surprised Ronaldo. But the Gray Dragon's gaze fell upon Chan as he perceived something very wrong and yet very noble. Obviously sick, pale of color and trailing pieces of molting scale, Chan nevertheless flew onward, too weak to speak, yet determined.

The boy, Jake, waved and called Ronaldo's name as Harrow nodded greeting. Though Harrow didn't call out, he seemed relieved to see Ronaldo. Even grateful. And through the worry in the Black Dragon's eyes, Ronaldo thought he also glimpsed a hint of regret and apology.

With no words among any of them, he fell in alongside his brothers. *His brothers!* Wingtip to wingtip they flew, Harrow on one side of Chan and he on the other, both protective and watchful. They were flying toward trouble—maybe into danger—yet Ronaldo couldn't deny the joy he felt.

Nor the pride.

Twenty-Two

LUNA AWOKE WITH A START and stared around her cave, sure that she'd heard Ariel's voice again and something about a warning. Yet there was no sign of the little girl if she'd ever really been there at all. *Maybe I was only dreaming,* she thought to herself.

With a sigh, she snuggled more closely around her beautiful egg, sensing its increasing surface warmth and the pulsing life within. It would hatch soon, perhaps within days. Blissfully content, she gave another sigh and closed her eyes.

But the dream, or whatever it was, gnawed at her, and Ariel's voice continued to rattle in some dim corner of her brain like the faintest of echoes. Still weak, Luna crawled out of her nest and made her way to her cave's entrance.

Hundreds, perhaps, thousands of birds circled in the sky above the canyon, all eerily silent. She watched them with growing unease—larks, thrashers, waxwings, thrushes, cardinals and more, but none of the raptors. No eagles, hawks, falcons or even owls. Leaning a little farther out of her cave, she searched the sky for any sign of Skymarin.

Unexpectedly, a trio of Dragons shot across the canyon heading northward as swiftly as their wings would carry them. Paraclion and Fleer raced side by side with Starfinder right behind. The birds scattered to get out of their way, and the afternoon sun flashed on the Dragons' scales as they charged past and out of sight. Like the birds, they also flew in silence.

It's because of me, she realized, noting how, despite their numbers, they were avoiding her cave. They were trying not to disturb her. *Or my egg,* she added with a nervous glance back at her nest.

A frown creased her Dragon lips. Where was Tiamat? He should be flying close by. It was his responsibility to protect her and the egg.

She scanned the canyon rim, the Echo Rush below, and the sky to the east. Nothing, and that only increased her unease. At the very least she might have expected Diana to be near.

Luna spread her wings wide and prepared to fly, but then she hesitated and glanced at her egg again. If she left the cave who would watch over her child? She thumped her tail on the cave floor in agitation and scratched the stone with her claws. Something was going on in the village, and she didn't like being left out.

Well, I'll have to get their attention, she decided. Folding her wings back, Luna thrust her head out of the cave and blasted a stream of fire downward toward the river. Even in broad daylight it lit up the canyon. Overhead, the birds took instant notice and filled the air with a noisy chatter. A moment later, an irate Sabu rose up from the village with a roar to scold the circling avians.

Leave the little birds alone, Mother! Luna blasted a second stream of fire even more powerful than the first. Her flames bounced off the opposite canyon wall and scorched the sand below. *Your business is with me.*

Her ploy succeeded. Drawn by her insistent blasts, Sabu turned away from the chorus of birds and flew toward the cave. Yet, even as she approached, the wind changed and a stiff breeze blew down from the rim, bringing with it a faintly acrid scent.

Some lingering fragment of her dream, a whisper that sounded like Ariel, flashed through Luna's brain again. *Smoke!* it said, but there was more, too. She squeezed her eyes shut, pressed a paw to her head, and the whisper came again, clearer.

"Fire!" The word hissed through Luna's lips. Her eyes snapped open. On vast wings her mother hovered before the cave. "Why didn't you wake me?" she demanded, backing away from the entrance so Sabu could land.

"We're doing everything we can," Sabu answered as she pressed inside. Her gaze softened as it fell on the egg in the nest. "All the Dragonkin have gone north to save as many lives as they can. Only you and I remain here, me to guard the village, and you to guard your future!"

Luna's voice dropped. "Even Tiamat?"

"Even Ramoses," Sabu answered. "But that egg is your only concern, Luna, whatever happens."

"But I'm the talisman!" Luna protested as she glared at her mother. "I don't understand the power that courses inside me, yet if

Wyvernwood is in danger I might be able to do something the others can't! Our home is on fire!"

With her larger bulk, Sabu forced Luna deeper into the cave, backing her daughter right up against the nest. Dried branches cracked, and the egg shifted ever so slightly. "Don't you get it?" Sabu shouted, her eyes burning with a terrible ferocity. "If the talismans are truly found, then our time in Wyvernwood is over! They'll point the way to a new home! That's always been your father's entire damnable plan!"

Luna bristled. With an angry shove she pushed her mother away and flexed her claws in warning. "Are you mad?" she cried as fire bubbled in her throat. "Do you really think you're strong enough to fight me, Old Dragon?"

Sabu spread her wings, effectively blocking the cave entrance. "I lost an egg once," she answered, rising until her head struck the ceiling. A small shower of stone and dust fell around her shoulders as she prepared to fight. "If I have to keep you here, myself, I won't let you lose yours!"

Luna's heart pounded. Then she drew a deep breath, calming herself as she regarded Sabu. "Honor thy father and thy mother," she muttered with a forced smile, "because you never know when you'll need free child-care."

Sabu relaxed a little, but a suspicious expression lingered on her face. "What are you talking about, little rebel?" she said.

"You watch my egg for me," Luna suggested. "It's my child, but it's also your grandchild. I know you'll protect it against any threat."

Sabu's eyes widened in surprise. Then she dropped to all fours again and folded her wings. "Protect the egg?" she said, her tone suddenly gentle as she considered it. Her anger melted away. Without another word, she crawled past Luna and into the nest. With utmost care, she curled around it and began to purr.

Touched by a maternal side of Sabu that Luna hadn't seen in a long time, she studied her mother. She regretted their confrontation and the harsh words and wondered how she could ever apologize. *Perhaps I just did*, she thought as Sabu's purring grew louder.

"As quick as wings and wind allow," Luna promised, "I'll be back." Then, secure that her egg was in good care, she flew from the cave and climbed high over the village.

Chaos reigned in Stronghold. Unfamiliar faces turned up to watch her. Sad-looking Wyrms from Grendleton huddled along the rim.

Basilisks seldom seen in this part of Wyvernwood loitered in the square with trembling foxes and nervous deer. On the rooftops of homes and shops, squirrels busied themselves caring for injured birds and mice.

As Luna watched in amazement, an eagle flew screaming out of the forest with a badger clutched in its talons. A singed patch showed plainly in the badger's fur, but it seemed all right and bowed its head gratefully when the eagle set it down among the basilisks and sped back into the forest.

The regular villagers were hard at work as well. Carola and Gregor, the fomorians, moved among the newcomers with pots of salve and bandages. Fortunato, with his minotaur brothers, carried an injured bear on a stretcher into their home. Little Pear, the human girl-child, struggled valiantly with a huge pail of water from which she offered ladled drinks while her companions, Trevor and Markham, hauled more water up the narrow stone steps from the river.

Another screech sounded, and a hawk flew out of the woods to deliver a pair of rabbits to safety.

Luna marveled at the rescue effort, and although the villagers saw that she was awake, they continued to work in relative silence out of respect for her egg. In the face of such courage how could she not do her part?

The Daughter of Stormfire looked northward where smoke hung like a low gray cloud on the horizon, and her expression turned grim. With a good effort she thought she could overtake Paraclion, Fleer, and Starfinder. They would surely lead her to where she was needed most, to Tiamat and the rest of the firefighters..

Old Ramoses swept through the blazing heart of the forest fire on widespread wings. The flames couldn't hurt his tough, scaled hide, but with every breath the searing smoke clogged his nostrils, inflamed his lungs. Still he flew, coughing and searching the ground for any trapped creatures in need of aid.

While he flew search-and-rescue, the Dragon Diana labored with Maximor, Sakima, Kaos, and Snowsong. Working in concert, they strove to overturn trees in the fire's path, hoping against hope to create a firebreak and slow the inferno's swift spread. No matter how hard they worked, though, their efforts seemed in vain. The flames skipped over them, leaped around them, as the relentless wind carried sparks and burning debris into fresh tinder.

"Let us help!"

Diana spun around to stare with stinging, smoke-filled eyes as two griffins swooped down behind her. For an instant she tensed, expecting an attack, but then she recognized Morkir. "Those are the three most important words in the world!" she called over the fire's roar and crackling.

"So I've heard before," Morkir answered as he urged Diana aside.

Minhep stepped up beside Morkir and, folding his feathered wings tight against his leonine body. Then, standing on his hind legs, he placed his paws on the great trunk of a pine tree. "Personally," he said with a wink to Diana, "I'd cast my vote for *revenge is sweet*. But that could just be me."

The two griffins strained. Their shoulders bunched in muscled knots, and their backs bent. The pine gave a loud groan as roots snapped deep in the earth. Limbs shivered and cracked; dry nettles rained down. With a loud crashing and smashing, the immense tree fell.

"That's one small step for Griffinkin," Minhep said, proudly brushing dirt from his paws.

Another loud crash interrupted the griffin as, not far away, Sakima and Kaos managed a similar feat with an ash tree. Minhep stared with a frown of annoyance, but then he brightened and kicked at the roots of the fallen pine. "Ours is bigger," he boasted.

But Morkir shook his head. "Size doesn't matter," he said as he fanned his wings and turned to another tree. "We'll have to clear a wide zone between the fire and the rest of the forest, a break wide enough that the flames can't leap across it."

"So you're saying width matters?" Minhep asked as he joined his strength with Morkir's. Again the ground split open. Roots broke through the earth like twisted tentacles as the tree began to topple. "Not to sound a discouraging note," he continued as he brushed his paws again and looked around. "But we're going to need a lot more help."

"And a lot more luck," Diana agreed. She peered suspiciously at the pair of griffins. "Not to sound ungrateful, but what are you two doing here? We've heard reports that griffins helped to start this fire."

Without pausing to answer, Morkir brought his strength to bear on the trunk of a hard oak. A loud roar forced its way through his eagle's beak, an unlikely sound that rose in volume and fury as he single-handedly did battle with the ancient tree. Its limbs shook and its leaves rattled in protest as it strove to resist his assault, but inevitably it began to yield, to tilt, to fall.

"Some griffins," Morkir admitted as he shot a fierce look at the cobalt Dragon. "But not all, and not us. Do you still want our help, or should we fly on to Stronghold?"

The Dragon Diana squeezed one eye shut as she considered. Then she inclined her head toward Minhep. "As your jolly friend suggested, we need all the help we can get," she answered. "If we can't stop the fire, there are lots of creatures in need of rescue." She leaned up against a tree and began to push. "But let's see what kind of damage we can do here first."

Minhep stepped past Morkir to help her. "Do you get the same peace of mind that I do when you're causing random damage?" he asked in a cheery tone. He flicked a narrow tongue over his beak, watching Diana from the corner of his eye as he drew a breath and pushed. "Especially random, senseless, mindless damage that serves no real purpose. That's my favorite kind, you know! That's the best!"

The birds circling Stronghold gave wide berth as they saw Harrow, Chan, and Ronaldo gliding low over the trees from the south side of the canyon. Then the crowds in the Village Square also began to fall back and make room. On faltering wings, half-faint, Chan reached for familiar ground. His claws carved deep furrows as he stumbled and fell.

As Ronaldo set Marian gently down on the rim, Bumble shot from his ear and disappeared, hungry no doubt for the flowers in the forest or for Carola's window garden. The unicorn looked around, quietly grim. Ronaldo folded his weary wings and gazed up at Harrow.

"Make way!" the Black Dragon called down to the crowd, urging them farther back. "One more piece of baggage to unload here!"

"Baggage?" Jake snapped as he unfastened the knotted ropes that held him in place. "Is that how you treat one of royal blood?" He leaned close to Harrow's ear. "And if you tell anyone...!"

"You'll kick my scaly backside?" Harrow finished for the boy. "Don't worry, your secret is safe. I wouldn't brag about being a prince of Degarm, either."

Jake slapped the Dragon's neck playfully as he untied the last knot and jumped to the ground. His friends, Trevor and Markham, reached out to steady him as he landed, but after a quick round of hugs and hair tousling, Jake ran to Chan.

"What are you thinking?" Marian asked, looking up at Ronaldo as he stood silently watching.

"That the entire world is changing," he answered in a soft, thoughtful voice, "and there's nothing we can do to stop it."

Marian tossed her mane, then rubbed up against the Gray Dragon. "Not trying to stop it," she whispered, "is the beginning of wisdom."

A shout carried to them from the square. "*Sumapai!*"

Chan's sides bellowed as he fought for breath, and his wings twitched. But he opened one eye and flicked his huge wet tongue over Jake, knocking the boy down. "*Chokahai,*" he answered with a weak grin. "Gotcha!"

Through ever-thickening coils of smoke, Luna fought along with Dragonkin and Griffinkin to create the firebreak needed to save Wyvernwood. Tiamat worked at her side with the same feverish determination, and in their desperation they both found strength no Dragons had known before.

All down the line it was the same with the other Dragons. The twins, Kaos and Sakima worked side by side, toppling one tree after another. Maximor and Paraclion made another team, and Fleer and Diana yet another. Wherever greater strength was needed, Morkir and Minhep stepped up to lend a paw.

Ramoses, Snowsong, and Starfinder also joined in when needed, but their tasks were different: to scour the forest and make sure all creatures found safety, that the devouring flames trapped none. In this work an army of raptors helped them.

When Minhep suddenly collapsed, Luna saw from the corner of her eye and cried out. All work stopped for a brief time as everyone turned to stare in weary fear. Bending low, Morkir nuzzled and nudged his griffin companion, then folding his wings, he curled up beside him.

Minhep's tail thumped the ground once. He turned his head toward Morkir. When he spoke his voice was almost too weak to hear, but as his strained heart gave out, he whispered, "Have I redeemed myself, my prince? Have I done well?"

Morkir gave a soft purr as he laid his head against Minhep's. "All honor and more is yours again," he answered. "Now and forever. You've done very well."

Minhep smiled at Morkir with weak gratitude, then turned his smoke-filled gaze up to the sky. "Let me laugh one more time," he whispered. "Tell me a joke."

Morkir hesitated. "Why did the griffin cross the road?"

Minhep chuckled and, closing his eyes, sighed his last breath.

The griffin prince stopped purring. Struggling to stand, fighting emotion, he looked around until his gaze finally locked on Luna. His eyes widened. Then, blinded by rage, he attacked the nearest tree, toppling it with an astonishing display of raw power. The next one fell as easily, and the one after that exploded into kindling and splinters under his fisted paws.

"Stop!" Luna cried in despair. "Morkir, stop it!"

Tears flooded her eyes as she stared at Minhep's still form and suddenly recognized the futility of their task. The heat of the flames made shimmering waves on her scales, and the veils of smoke choked her. Even for a Dragon the fire was too intense, and the forest was far too vast.

She clenched her Dragon fists in bitter frustration. *What good is it, this drop of magic inside me*, she screamed silently, *if I can't use it to save my friends and my home?* Stretching her neck, she stared toward the smoke-filled sky. If only it would rain!

"I'm the Heart of All Dragons!" she shouted at the sky. "I command it to rain!"

But the magic remained quiescent. Luna heard no music in her head and felt no surge of power. With a cry of anguish, pushing Tiamat aside as he reached out to her, she spread her wings and rose up over the trees and higher still until, through the clouds of smoke, she saw the soaring flames and stared in numbing horror.

The fire was even closer than she had thought.

Something tingled on the back of Luna's neck, some sense of awareness, some strange knowledge. With a gasp, she twisted her neck to look around. *I'm not alone up here*, she thought as her heart pounded. *Who are you? Where are you?*

A wisp of a voice spoke inside her head. *You came to us. Now to you we have come. For days upon days searched for you we have. Some to the*

east; some to the west; some to north and south. *Heart of All Dragons—
we are Qin.*

"Why?" Luna demanded, flexing her claws in warning. "What do
you want from me that you'd come so far?"

Another voice spoke, different from the first, but just as serene. *The
Qin want nothing, because there is nothing to want. Yet even in
contemplative solitude, for others like us we are lonely.*

Like us you are, the first voice affirmed. *Different, and yet the same.
The Qin embrace difference.*

"Cousins," Luna answered. They had said the same before. Fighting
despair, she stared down into the sweeping fire below. "Can you help?"

Through veils and curtains of smoke the Qin appeared, ten in number, undulating with sinuous grace through the air as they rode the
searing breezes. They were strange, yet beautiful, and Luna felt
ashamed to remember how she had recoiled from them at their first
meeting. Now her heart rejoiced as the Qin spread out around her.

A gentle rain began to fall upon her scales, and Luna turned her
face up to wash the smoke from her eyes. "How are you doing that?"
she cried. "Is this magic?"

Not magic, one of the Qin answered. *As you make fire, rain and wind
we make. We are two sides of the same Great Wheel.*

"Qin," Luna said in thoughtful response as she flew along the crackling edge of the flames, "and Dragonkin."

To extinguish such a fire is beyond us, as it is beyond you, said another
voice in her head. *However, together we may slow its progress, and
perhaps the real rains will come.*

With new hope in her heart and new allies, the Daughter of Stormfire bowed her head to the Qin and, dipping one wing, returned to
seek her friends.

Days passed, and though small patches of fire continued to burn
and great clouds of smoke hung over Wyvernwood, the worst danger
passed. Rain blowing in from the sea fell in torrents, and the bloated
grayness in the east promised still more.

In calm morning stillness with the sun creeping up the eastern end
of Stronghold Canyon, the Children of Stormfire gathered on the village square. A great crowd larger than any that had ever assembled in

Stronghold before made a circle around them. Lined up on the stone rim, the other Dragons patiently watched. Morkir stood with them. but he fixed his gaze overhead on the Qin, their new friends, who swam gracefully through the sky, aloof and curious.

Only Sabu was absent; she remained in Luna's cave, content to watch the egg and await the hatching of her grandchild. Nothing meant more to her.

The crowd parted as Jake approached from the home of Gregor and Carola with the Last Unicorn in the World at his side. With ceremonial care he carried the Glass Dragon. The talisman caught and fractured the sunlight into its various spectra, filling his hands with color as he walked toward Chan. Still weak and frail, his *Sumapai* extended one paw, and Jake put the talisman upon it.

Marian gazed at all the faces in the crowd as she went to stand before Ronaldo. For her, this was a proud and much anticipated day. Her mane and tail had been washed and combed, her horn and hooves polished to a fine gleam. Her eyes shifted from one slow color to another. "Where's Bumble?" she whispered.

Ronaldo tapped the side of his head. "Snoring in my left ear."

Hearing his name, the little hummingbird darted into the air and straight for Marian. "Is it showtime?" he asked in a sleepy voice.

Ramoses, the oldest of the Dragonkin, spoke from the rim. In his paws he clutched one of Stormfire's books to his heart, and his moist eyes shone as he retold the tale of how their Dragon leader had brought them across the Imagination Mountains to a Great Refuge, to Wyvernwood. Everyone listened with rapt attention, and when his old voice suddenly broke with emotion, his daughter touched his shoulder and took up the tale.

"But Wyvernwood is not our final home," she reminded the crowd. With a voice as strong and reverent as her father's, proving that she had learned the stories well from him, she told of the prophecies, of Stormfire's triplet children from which would come a new leader, and of the talismans that would point the way to a new home for all the Dragonkin and any who chose to follow them. "We have suffered so much these past days and lost many friends," she said with a glance at Morkir. "Surely the time is now."

Marian's heart hammered as Ramoses and Diana spoke. Though they were stories to the others, to her they were memories, and she knew things not written in Stormfire's books, secrets she had kept for far too long. She watched the crowd, hoping Diana was right, but as she glanced around her gaze fell on Harrow. The Black Dragon stood quietly with downcast eyes, and his paws were empty.

As Diana finished, an expectant silence fell over the assembly. Ramoses spoke again. "The talismans have been found," he said, "but one has been lost again on the very square where we stand together. We hope it will return to us."

Again a hush settled over the village. Then one of the satyrs gave a low chuckle and muttered, "Talisman, talisman, who's got the talisman...."

Another satyr elbowed his brother and snickered. "Maybe if you described it," he called.

Harrow raised his head and glared sharply. "I'm to blame!" he admitted, and the embarrassed satyrs hung their heads.

Then, on the opposite side of the square, someone gave a short gasp. Heads turned, and again from the direction of Carola's home, the crowd parted. Hand in hand, Ariel and little Pear walked forth. A broad smile lit up Pear's face, but the older girl looked calmly serene in the strange light that danced around her.

Light from the Diamond Dragon.

Unnoticed by the others, Marian closed her eyes and wept. *Surely the time is now*, she thought, recalling Diana's words and grasping at them. Lifting her head, she stared at Ramoses and their gazes met. Like her, he was weeping silent tears.

"I knew you were alive!" Jake shouted.

Ariel laughed lightly. "Less than alive and more than alive," she answered in a sing-song voice, "and what is life, anyway, but a mystery in a puzzle in a riddle?" She winked at Luna. "I am what I am!"

A wind rose up out of nowhere and whispered through her hair, stirring strands and tossing them like slender snakes around her face. She turned to Ronaldo and held out the lost talisman. "I believe you dropped this," she said.

Marian shot a look at Ronaldo, and her heart beat faster. She wanted to say something, but she couldn't speak! The show belonged to this strange little girl whose scent was an impossible combination of fresh breezes and the dust of ages.

The Gray Dragon shook his head. "It doesn't belong to me," he answered.

Ariel hesitated and seemed to listen to something nobody else could hear. She smiled at Ronaldo, then said cryptically. "It's glad that you understand."

Turning to Harrow, Luna offered the talisman again. "It wasn't sure about you," she said sternly, "at first." Then she smiled again and sang:

"To claim the power prophesied
you had to set aside
your anger and your pride
and in your heart be satisfied
to let the talisman decide."

The *Diamond Dragon* appeared to fly off her palm toward the Black Dragon. Startled, he raised his paws reflexively to catch it. In the moment that his paws closed around it, his eyes widened in amazement. "I hear it!" he whispered. "Voices and music! I hear it!"

"So do I!" Chan said, seeming suddenly to grow stronger, less frail. "I thought I did before, but I wasn't sure!"

"And I hear it, also!" Luna said. "As I did before, but differently!"

Leading Pear by the hand, Ariel went to Luna. "Before, you were with child, and the magic let your child play with it as it would a bright toy."

Crooking a finger, she beckoned Luna closer so she could whisper in her ear. Marian strained to listen, but even she couldn't hear what passed between the two. Bumble's wings hummed, and he landed on her horn again. She hadn't even noticed that he'd left her. The little hummingbird looked dazed.

When Luna looked up, she wore a strange grin, and her eyes sparkled. "But why did the magic work with me at all," she asked. "Why did it take me to all those places?"

Ariel drew Pear closer and guided the smaller girl's hand to stroke Luna's cheek. "To teach you the true meaning of *home*," Ariel explained. "Because even before you found your talisman you were the Heart of All Dragons, and *home* for you will always be where the heart is." She winked.

Luna squeezed her eyes shut as she leaned into Pear's gentle touch and began to purr softly. "I don't understand," she said.

Ariel backed away a few steps, leaving Pear at the Ivory Dragon's side. Strangely, she turned toward Marian and gave a knowing wink. "You never understand magic," she answered. "You just embrace it."

Marian's eyes shot wide and she tossed her mane, inadvertently flipping Bumble into the air. She stared at the child, sensing things she shouldn't sense, hearing things she shouldn't see and seeing things she couldn't possibly hear. For a brief moment, the world became a synthetic jumble. "Who are you?" she whispered.

Ariel's lips barely moved, and her answer came like a honeysuckle's scent on a breeze, like the rustle of a single leaf.

"Wyvernwood."

Without saying more, Ariel performed a swift series of handsprings and backflips that took her into the crowd and toward the edge of the forest. Gasps of surprise and laughter followed her, and whether she ran into the woods then or simply vanished into air, no one could say, but Trevor chased after her with Markham on his heels.

When the excitement settled down, Chan held up the Glass Dragon and gazed into it for a long moment. "Well, what now?" he wondered aloud. "If these aren't just fancy music boxes there must be something more."

Still staring after the odd girl, Marian tried to shake off the disconcerting sensory experience and regain control of herself. "The entire story," she heard herself saying, "isn't yet written in the Great Book."

The crowd fell quiet again, and every eye turned her way. Marian licked her lips. "The Dragon Wars began when magic got out of control. Sorcerers and wizards...." The words froze in her throat. She fought to get them out. "...of all species, possessed of powers now forgotten, grew jealous of each other." She hung her head suddenly, and her newly washed mane dragged over dirt and grass. Looking up, she met Ramoses' gaze, and his nod gave her courage. "I was one of those. Stormfire was another. And there were humans—they were the most jealous of all. Our battles brought devastation and waste to Undersky, and still we fought until we exhausted ourselves and all our resources."

"Until we exhausted the most precious and wonderful resource of all—magic, itself," Ramoses added in a heavy voice.

Marian seized the story back. "But Stormfire captured the last drops of magic left in the world and sealed those drops into vessels—the Glass Dragon, the Diamond Dragon, and the Heart of All Dragons." She looked to each of the triplets as she spoke, "and he scattered them in different places known only to him.

"But as he forged these talismans he had a vision. The talismans would be found someday by his own children—triplet offspring made special by the very nature of their birth, because Dragon's don't have triplets."

Marian paused. Her throat dry, she looked to each of Stormfire's children again and to Ronaldo last of all. "But one hard lesson we all had learned, and this is it: power corrupts. Even a little power corrupts a little bit." She swallowed hard and looked to Ramoses with a heart full of pain and regret. "This part even you don't know, old Dragon, and it's my confession."

Drawing a deep breath, the Last Unicorn in the World spoke her deepest secret. "I warped Stormfire's spell of forging." With a certain defiance that lingered in her still after so many years, she lifted her head and tossed her mane. "I feared that someday the triplets he fore-saw would claim their father's power and ultimately misuse it as he—as all of us—had. So with just a splinter of one of the last drops of magic, I fashioned a key and cast it into the only vessel close enough that could contain it—the egg that Sabu already carried inside her." She looked to Ronaldo again. "Your egg."

"Only the key could unlock their full power," Ronaldo said, his eyes closed as he spoke. "And I'm the key. This is what I saw in my visions. I just didn't understand it."

Ramoses roared in anger and threw his book at the unicorn. "You did that to an egg?" he shouted. "To Stormfire's first-born hatchling? You could have told me the truth!"

Marian dodged the book as she spun to answer him. "I told Storm-fire!" she cried in answer. "And he agreed. There had to be a safe-guard! Some check and balance! If any of his children had turned out differently, all of Undersky would have trembled. You know as well as anyone, Ramoses, that even the last drop of magic is a potent weapon when there's no defense against it!"

Chan interrupted. "I thought the talismans were just supposed to point the way to a new home for us," he said in a calmer voice.

Marian drew a deep breath and sighed. "They'll do that," she answered, "and more."

Raising his paw, Harrow gazed deeply into the glimmering facets of the *Diamond Dragon*, his face inscrutable and distant. "Let's find out," he said as he turned to Ronaldo "Brother, I guess it's for you to judge our hearts."

Marian watched carefully as the Gray Dragon hesitated. Ronaldo might have forgiven her for what she'd done, but she wasn't sure she could forgive herself. In all her years of secretly watching, she'd grown to love him. Now everything came down to this moment.

Bumble circled Ronaldo's right ear. "What's it gonna be, boy?" He darted to the left ear and circled it. "Yes or no? What's it gonna be, boy? Do you see paradise?"

"Bumble-bird?" Ronaldo said.

Bumble perched between Ronaldo's ears and put on an innocent look. "I didn't say nothing!" he protested.

Ronaldo looked down at Marian, and their gazes locked. In his great gray eyes, so like round mirrors, the last unicorn saw herself as he had painted her in the cavern: wild and terrible and dangerous. "Who am I to judge my brothers and sister?" he said simply. He looked to the triplets. "Stormfire made the talismans for you. If all it takes to unlock them is my permission, then use them well and find the homeland our father foresaw."

In her head, Marian heard a key turn. Next came a whisper of music, a suggestion of song so sweet and powerful, and yet muted. Worse than muted. Too soon, it faded away and was gone.

The triplets vanished.

"Asgalun," Chan said quietly as he looked over the gray wasteland. He turned his empty paws up. The talisman's crystal shell was gone, but he felt its power coursing through him as Luna's coursed through her, and as Harrow's also did.

Luna nodded. "It makes sense," she said as she stared at the unlikely grouping of mountains called the Drake. "Our new home is our old home. Our original home."

Harrow scratched his flank with a hind paw. "The Haunted Lands?"

Chan nodded. Indeed it all made sense to him as well. He heard the music singing in his head, and the dead land beneath his feet reverberated with the notes, seemed to stir as if it was straining to awaken. Following Luna's gaze, he also looked toward the Drake. In a cave high atop that formation he had found the Glass Dragon.

"Follow me," Luna said, spreading her wings. "I want to show you something."

Harrow shrugged. "I'm just along for the ride."

"I don't think so," Chan answered thoughtfully as he followed his siblings.

Together they flew over the ashen landscape. In daylight it looked even worse than at night. It lacked the moon's frosty sparkle, the sense of mystery that darkness brought. It lacked the stark shadows.

"There," Luna cried as she dipped a wing and swooped low again. She pointed with a paw at structures half-hidden in the drifted dust, at broken columns and long-dry fountains, at shattered walls and cornices and empty doorways.

Harrow stared in wonderment as they landed. "It looks like a city!" he remarked. "A city for humans!

Luna scraped a bit of wall with the tip of a claw. "A city," she agreed, "or a temple or a university. Who can tell? But the Drake holds some special significance for them, as it does for us. No matter where you stand here you can see it." She pointed again. "I think they're telling us that humans and Dragons can live together in harmony."

"They?" Chan turned slowly, imagining those who must have stood here before him. "You sound as if we're not alone, Sister."

Luna smiled. "Do you believe in ghosts, brother? Harrow coughed and waved a paw to scatter the dust and ash that blew before his face. "There are no trees, no woods or forest," he grumbled. "No rivers or lakes. No sea. How can this become our home? How can we live here?"

Chan pursed his Dragon lips as he looked around at the ruins and up at the mountains. The deep dust felt soft and welcoming beneath his paws. He looked at his sister. She was having similar thoughts. "Jake said something to me once," he told his siblings. "He said that we had a lot to teach the world if we ever stopped hiding from it." He touched one of the stone columns and felt the music vibrating within it. "This place could be a university."

Luna shifted her gaze and stared up one of the mountain slopes. "It can be anything we want it to be," she said in a soft tone. "I made a rose grow up there." She turned suddenly. "I think that's why we're here, Chan! Harrow, I think that's why the magic brought us here!"

Chan nodded as the music grew louder in his head. "Yes," he agreed. "It's not just the Dragonkin coming home—the magic wants to come home!"

At first Harrow resisted, but Chan held out one paw to him. Brother touched brother, and they both held out paws to Luna. Standing together, they began to laugh. "We don't need it, and we can't misuse it if we give it back to the land!" Chan shouted. "Close your eyes! Let it go! Imagine it the way it was and the way it can be again!"

The air began to swirl around them, and the wind rose howling and singing. Near Luna's rear paw a single rose pushed up through the dust, then an entire rosebush. Then a garden. The gray dust shifted and blew away, exposing fresh green grass. Behind Harrow a willow tree grew in time-lapse perfection.

With the triplets at its center, the magic spread outward like a wave, turning death into life, barren wasteland into verdant valleys, deserts of dust into forests. The thirsty land drank up the magic like a sponge and gave back more. Snow fell on the mountains. Rain filled the ancient riverbeds and lakes

Music filled their hearts, their heads and souls. Luna cried out in ecstasy. "I understand!" she shouted. "I finally understand the words! The voices!"

"I hear it, too!" Tears streamed freely down Harrow's face, spilled over his cheeks to nourish the soil. "It's the song of Asgalun crying out to be born!"

Chan nodded, calm and serene in the eye of a storm. "A child should be born in music, and Asgalun is a child. I wish Ronaldo was here!"

"He's played his part," Luna said, beaming with joy. "Now we have to play ours!"

They clung to each other, bound by the magic as it continued to flow, drawn closer to each other than they had ever been, knowing each other's hearts and minds. For a time, it seemed as if they were one being, rising up renewed, more phoenix than Dragon, with vast and all-encompassing wings.

Then slowly, the music softened and faded until only a lullaby remained.

The Children of Stormfire gazed out over their handiwork. "Can we cook, or can we cook?" Harrow murmured. "Did that little hummingbird say something about seeing Paradise?"

Luna was quiet as she leaned against Chan. "The last time I was here I saw ghosts," she said as she looked around. "Do you think they're pleased?"

Chan smiled. The magic had worked its way with him just as it had with the land. All poison driven from his system, he felt stronger than ever. "I think they're at rest," he answered.

"I'd like to go home now," Luna said. "My egg will hatch soon."

Home. There was something about the way his sister said it that troubled Chan. When the magic had drawn them together, made them one, he'd seen her thoughts and her hopes. When the Dragonkin came to Asgalun, he knew that she would stay with her egg in Wyvernwood. For her, the forest would always be home.

With one paw Chan described an arc through the air. He'd saved just a little magic to make the passage easier, and he used it to twist space, to open a gateway between Stronghold and Asgalun. He didn't know how long he could maintain it.

Luna wasted no time. Her work done, she spread her wings and glided back to her beloved forest, to her mate and her nest, and to her future. But as Harrow spread his wings to follow, Chan stopped him. Drawing him close, he entwined his neck with his brother's and held him.

"Take another look," Chan urged as he ended the embrace. "It really is a paradise. But you can make it more. Make it a place of learning, of peace, of tolerance. Our Age is passing, Brother. It has passed. But we have much to pass on."

Harrow stepped back with a strange expression. "You sound as if you're not staying."

Chan closed his eyes as he smiled. "I'm not," he answered. "There's much of Undersky to see, and Jake and I are explorers at heart. Luna will stay in Wyvernwood." He trembled as he spoke, happier than he'd ever been to finally know what he wanted. "You will lead the Dragonkin, Harrow, as you were always meant to. You are Stormfire's true heir."

Harrow shook his head. "No."

"Yes," Chan answered. "And you'll be even greater than father, because you won't make his mistakes." He hugged his brother again. "Now follow me—but give me a moment to announce you properly."

"No," Harrow said again. With the last of his own magic, he widened the gate Chan had created. "We fly side by side as brothers."

Twenty-Three

RONALDO SIGHED AS HE LOOKED UP through the leafy canopy to the patches of blue sky and the soft white clouds beyond. The pleasant sun warmed his heart as it warmed his face. Turning his head from side to side, he admired the wild nasturtiums and the monkey flowers that grew among the old tree trunks, and he laughed silently at the antics of the swallowtails and painted ladies that played around the blossoms.

It was a beautiful day for a walk in the woods.

He called over his shoulder to Marian, who walked behind him. "So basically," he said, "when Stormfire wasn't looking you poached my egg."

Marian flipped her tail at a big green horsefly. "What can I say?" she answered. "It was a different time, and my priorities were scrambled."

The Gray Dragon ducked low beneath a stout limb and nodded to a friendly serpent draping itself among the branches. "I don't know," he continued with an easy shrug. "You sound a bit hard-boiled about it."

"I'm sorry, my scaly friend," she replied with a note of mock-distress. "I guess my brain was just, well, fried."

On rapid wings, Bumble zoomed out of the forest and hovered between them. Petunia nectar bloated his tiny belly, and his breath smelled of honeysuckle. "What do you call a thousand hummingbird eggs?" he cried.

Ronaldo and Marian answered in unison. "Not enough to eat!"

The little hummingbird turned his beak up in indignation as he perched on Ronaldo's nose. "Hmmmph!" he said. "Well, I thought it was an egg-cellent joke!"

Crossing his eyes, Ronaldo stared down the length of his snout. "Didn't see that one coming," he admitted to his green, feathered companion.

Bumble preened. "I got a million of 'em!" he said. Then his high-pitched voice softened. "It will be good to see home again, to snuggle up in the cave, to see Beatrice and Ranock and even egg-centric Granny Scylla...."

"He's on a roll now," Marian muttered. "An egg roll."

"Indeed," Ronaldo agreed. "Stronghold is a nice place to visit, but I miss the common yolk."

Marian groaned, and Bumble dealt Ronaldo a gentle kick. "That was rotten!" the little bird declared. And Marian concurred. "Egg-scrutiating!"

A short time later, walking in blissful silence, they came upon a thick patch of bluebells, and Bumble dived in. Ronaldo and Marian waited patiently, content in each other's company. But while Bumble feasted, Ronaldo turned his gaze upward again. There were fewer birds, he noticed, and fewer creatures along the path. Already the woods seemed quieter and emptier.

Marian seemed to read his thoughts. She had an uncanny knack for that. "Are you sure you want to stay?" she asked. "There's no telling how long the gate will remain open."

Bending down, the Gray Dragon carefully picked a flower with his claws and tickled the unicorn's nose with it. "If I ever go to Asgalun," he answered, "I'll take the scenic route." He lifted his head a little and gazed toward the distant peaks in the west. "Over the mountains and through the woods to grandma's house...."

He stopped suddenly and smiled as he twisted his neck to look eastward. "But Thursis appeals to me a lot more. The sand and sea, the quiet nights and quiet stars—I guess I'm just an island kind of Dragon."

"You be a lay-about, mon!" Bumble said as he landed on the tip of Marian's horn. "Smoke de music! Sun City! Be happy—don't worry!"

Ronaldo only half-listened. The forest colors had never seemed so vibrant, nor the air so fresh. He wiggled his clawed toes in the spongy earth, savoring the ticklish sensation and the earthy smell. What was sand compared to this? He wondered if he could ever really leave Wyvernwood.

Would Wyvernwood ever really let him leave? His purpose here was done; the key was turned. Yet he still felt some hold upon him as if he had more to do.

"Am I free, Marian?" he whispered as a wave of uncertainty swept over him. "Am I my own Dragon?"

Marian fixed him with a hard gaze, and her golden eyes shifted to blue, then green, then silver. "You're the first-born son of Stormfire," she said fiercely, "and despite everything you've heard or learned, that means something. You can be anything and everything you want to be."

He thought about that for a long moment as he watched a grasshopper drooling black juice on a blade of grass. "I want to be a joker," he said as he grinned at the silly creature. "I want to be a clown!"

Bumble jumped up and down as he caught Ronaldo's excitement. "A high ambition!" he cried approvingly. "Low-brow humor!"

"We'll all come see you!" Marian laughed, joining in, "and say *we knew you when!*"

In the middle of the forest, with the grasshopper giving them perplexed looks, they laughed together. Bumble danced a jig on Ronaldo's nose, and Marian rubbed her cheek against his gray-scaled shoulder.

But then Ronaldo stopped. "No," he said, holding up a paw and inviting Bumble to take a new perch. "No, we won't do that." He looked at his dearest friends, and they looked back at him expectantly. "I think we'll just go home and be exactly who we are. That's more than enough—a gray Dragon, the Last Unicorn in the World, and a crazy hummingbird."

The breeze picked up and the leaves rustled as the three friends resumed their walk southward toward the Whispering Hills. There was a lot of distance to cover, but they weren't in a hurry. When they were almost out of sight, their voices still came back through the trees.

"Oh the sky is wide and far,
But the way is lit by moon and star . . ."

"It's daylight, Bumble-bird!"
"Would you prefer more egg jokes?"
"You know, I love the way you've come out of your shell."

The grasshopper watched them go and then spat a black stream. He'd have a story to tell his buddies later.

Epilogue

FOR A LONG TIME AFTER PUCK FINISHED HIS STORY, the villagers sat quietly. The children sank back in their parents' arms, and the parents cradled them tightly and rocked them and no one spoke. The only sounds were the crackling and popping of the fire and the gentle rustle of the wind through the leaves and, in the distance, the howling of a lone wolf as it hunted.

Puck stared into the fire with watery eyes, but finally he glanced around, nervous and uncertain, at his audience. Marina's heart filled with love as she watched her son, and she smiled secretly. She knew his thoughts. Had he told it well? Had he done the story justice? His gaze turned to Marina last of all, and his eyes asked for her approval. Pursing her lips, she nodded.

With an easy sigh, Marina bid everyone good night, then turned away and started back up the hill toward her cave on the other side. The sulfurs had gone home with the coming of full darkness, but ever faithful, the fireflies rose up from their resting places in the grass to accompany her. In the late hour, they sparkled like jewels.

No, like talismans, Marina thought, still lost in the story and grateful for their company. *Like tiny sparks of real magic.* With their gentle beauty such creatures made the world a better place.

Halfway up the hill, she paused to look back. The families were rising, scattering and heading away with their children in their arms, leaving the firelight behind and walking into the darkness. But the darkness didn't matter—they knew where their homes were.

At the summit of the hill, Marina paused again. Only Puck remained beside the slowly dying fire. A couple of the older minotaur boys lingered with him. Tilting their heads back and shielding their eyes from the flames' dull glow, they seemed to study the sky under the young Dragon's guidance.

Marina looked up, too. Rono hung low in the west, but red Burbur shone directly overhead with Oculo and Brakkar in line close by. She followed the line eastward to the Piper constellation, and the Piper's belt pointed the way to Rodan, another constellation. She knew all the stars by their names, and on cool late nights when she couldn't sleep the constellations were her friends.

As she descended her side of the hill, tall trees rose to block out the starry vista, and a deeper darkness enveloped her. The fireflies twinkled more brightly without the firelight or the stars for competition. With a sigh of contentment she watched them, the nearer ones and the ones farther away in the black recesses of the forest where they drifted and darted among the older trees.

Not ready to retire, she passed her door and walked to the edge of the woods where a chorus of tree frogs singing harmonies in their ratchety voices greeted her. Marina laughed softly in response as she listened to their gossip. "You don't say!" she said. Feigning shock, she pressed a paw to her heart. "Why, I never!" The tree frogs assured her: *All true! All true! All true!*

Then a different sound touched Marina's ear—a snapping twig perhaps, or the swish of a limb as it was pushed back and suddenly released. Tensing, she held up a paw for silence, and the tree frogs grew still.

"Marian?" Marina whispered hopefully as she stared deep into the dark woods. She waited, then called again. "Is that you, Ariel?"

When no answer came, Marina's shoulders slumped. Probably it was only a club-footed moose or some bear walking in its sleep. She tried to put aside her disappointment.

Puck had told the story well, but she wished he'd told a different one. The Fall of Navigator—that would have been good. Or one of Finback's adventures—those always made her laugh.

Then again, the woods were too full of ghosts tonight for laughter. Maybe that snapping sound was Minhep prowling around or one of Agriope's sisters. On full-moon nights their spirits sometimes wandered.

"I'm too melancholy," Marina told the tree frogs. "But then, I often am when a good story ends."

Too true, the tree frogs agreed. *Too true. Too true!*

Another sound made her turn. Puck stood right behind her with his paws crossed on his chest and his wings folded. He grinned a Dragon grin as Marina caught her breath. "Why, you sneaky...! You scared the scales right off me!"

"There are no endings," he reminded her. "Only new beginnings. You taught me that yourself." Leaning closer, he coiled his neck around hers.

"You haven't embraced me like that in a long time!" Marina said in pleased surprise. "I thought you were too grown up for it!"

Puck shrugged as he stared past her into the forest depths. "I've decided that growing up is overrated," he said. "Tonight, I want to be a child again. I'm going to drink hot cocoa and sleep in your bed like I used to."

Marina snorted. "Then in the morning you can sweep the floor and weed the garden like you used to."

They both laughed and, leaning against each other, stared into Wyvernwood for a long time before they went back up the hill to Marina's cave. But at the threshold, Puck stopped, turned again and gazed back toward the woods with a frown on his Dragon lips as if he'd heard or seen something in the dark.

"Do they ever talk to you?" he asked quietly. "The ghosts?"

Turning, she followed his gaze to the bottom of the hill where the woods were thickest. The wind blew, and something moved down there. A flash of white. A trick of moonlight on a trembling leaf, maybe. Or on a snowy mane. "You hear them, too?" she said.

Puck nodded. Then after a moment he opened the door and went inside. "I'll make the cocoa," he called back, "but then I'll have to go home. So much to do tomorrow."

The breeze gusted suddenly. The old trees bent and the leaves shivered, and the bit of whiteness disappeared, if it was ever really there at all.

"You know, I realized something tonight," Puck called again as he rattled cups and pans, "You've never told me what it was that Ariel whispered in Luna's ear."

Marina smiled to herself as she went inside and closed the door. That was a story for another time.

THE END

About the Author

ROBIN WAYNE BAILEY is the author of numerous novels and short stories, including the *Brothers of the Dragon* series, the critically acclaimed *Shadowdance*, and *Swords Against the Shadowland*, which was named one of the seven best novels of 1998 by *Science Fiction Chronicle*. He was also a regular contributor to the best-selling anthology series, *Thieves World*. In addition to his own writing projects, recent ventures include editing *Through My Glasses Darkly*, a collection of stories by Frank M. Robinson, and *Architects of Dreams: The SFWA Author Emeritus Anthology*. He is preently the President of the SFWA and lives in Kansas City, Missouri.